EVIL for EVIL

EVIL for EVIL

A Billy Boyle World War II Mystery

James R. Benn

Published by
Soho Press, Inc.
853 Broadway
New York, NY 10003

Library of Congress Cataloging-in-Publication Data

Benn, James R.
Evil for evil / James R. Benn.
p. cm.
ISBN 978-1-56947-593-5 (hardcover)
1. Americans—Northern Ireland—Fiction. 2. Irish Republican Army—Fiction.
3. World War, 1939–1945—Military intelligence—Fiction.
4. World War, 1939–1945—Collaborationists—Northern Ireland—Fiction.
I. Title.

PS3602.E6644E85 2009
813'.6—dc22
2009011127

10 9 8 7 6 5 4 3 2 1

Dedicated to those men and women
who suffer violence
so that we may live free and peaceful lives.

Recompense to no man evil for evil.
Romans 12:17

CHAPTER ▪ ONE

King David Hotel
Jerusalem, British Mandate
November 1943

THIS WAS THE Holy Land, and I had never felt so far from home. From the narrow balcony outside Diana's room, I watched traffic flow along a side street, beyond the impossibly green gardens gracing the grounds of the King David Hotel. An old Arab pulling a donkey hustled it to the side of the road as a British Army staff car sped by, the sound of its insistent horn echoing off the stone buildings. The donkey raised its head, braying as the dust settled and the staff car vanished. The old man put his arms around the donkey's neck and spoke to it, nodding, and scratched the animal behind its ears. The donkey flicked its tail and followed him back into the street, where they both resumed their slow, deliberate gaits.

I wondered what the old man had said. I wondered what I would say when I returned to the room. I doubted it would be anything as persuasive.

"Billy," Diana said from inside, "are you coming in?"

"Yes," I said as I brushed back the thin curtains fluttering in the slight breeze. "I am."

Everything had been just right. We were on leave, traveling with the general, staying at ritzy joints from Cairo to Jerusalem, the kinds of hotels the British built so the Victorians would feel at home while seeing the sights. Hotels with thick walls between the guests and the funny dark-skinned locals. But I hadn't even thought about that. I'd been content to enjoy this time with Diana, until I found out the secret she had kept hidden from me.

Diana sat on the edge of the bed, holding a glass of water pressed to her chest. Her khaki blouse was unbuttoned. Water beaded on the glass and dripped onto her flushed skin. The overhead fan turned lazily, moving the heat in circles. I poured myself a glass of water and drank half of it as I sat in the brocade-covered armchair near the open balcony door. The fabric was hot and itchy but I liked my chances better in it. I might feel a breeze and I might be able to resist the sight of Diana's moist skin and the curving rivulets of sweat as they disappeared beneath the damp folds of her FANY uniform.

"Are you angry with me?" She asked the question casually, as if she had no idea.

"When were you going to tell me?" I replied.

She looked away as she raised the glass to her forehead, rolling it above her closed eyes. Little beads of water fell onto her cheeks. Or were those tears she was trying to hide? Or worse yet, were there no tears, only English sweat and Egyptian water?

"It's too hot, Billy. Please."

"You used me. Then you played me for a sap."

"No. No, I didn't."

Maybe that was true. Sort of. I had been used so often in this war that maybe I expected everyone to take a turn.

"OK," I said. "You didn't use me. But you have been stringing me along, making believe everything was fine."

"Everything is fine. Or was, until you started behaving so poorly."

"I wish we could go back to how it was."

"We worked quite well together, didn't we?" Her voice was wistful.

We had indeed. Diana Seaton and I were both on General Eisenhower's staff. I was in something called the Office of Special Investigations. Not many people had heard of it, which was the point. The general didn't want anything that warranted a special investigation to get a lot of attention. That might hurt the war effort. But he did want things taken care of—quietly, if possible. That was my job.

Diana Seaton had joined the First Aid Nursing Yeomanry at the start of the war. Then she'd volunteered for the Special Operations Executive, the British outfit that sent spies and saboteurs behind enemy lines. She'd barely survived a mission in Algiers a year ago. After her recuperation, General Eisenhower had taken her on as a liaison officer at Allied Forces HQ in Tunisia. Maybe he did that because he needed another liaison officer or maybe because I was his courtesy nephew. It was hard to tell with Uncle Ike.

"We were great together," I said. "They didn't stand a chance against the two of us." I had to smile when I said it.

We'd been sent with an advance party to Cairo, to prepare for a visit by President Roosevelt, Prime Minister Churchill, and a boatload of bigwigs who were going to stop off on their way to Tehran to chew the fat with Stalin. As part of her liaison duties, Diana had checked with various British intelligence services, including the SOE HQ for the Mediterranean Theater. They'd gotten wind of a German agent in contact with a group of Egyptian Army officers who weren't too happy about the Brits running their country. As I was of Irish extraction myself, I could see their point. The English had a way of mistaking other people's countries for their own backyard, and the people who lived there for servants or slaves. It was one of the things that made Diana and me such an odd pair. Her father had been knighted at some point, and she was definitely upper crust. Me, I was from the South End. Boston Irish. We were a bad mix.

Diana stood behind me and began rubbing my neck.

"It was exciting," she said.

"And dangerous," I said. I tried to sound adamant but it was hard with Diana's hands working on the tense muscles in my shoulders.

"I didn't want to spoil this trip," she said, finally answering my question. "I was going to tell you before we left. How did you find out?"

"Kay mentioned it. She seemed to think I already knew."

"I'm sorry, Billy."

"I don't want you to go."

"I am going."

"Why?" I shook off her hands and stood to face her. "Why you? Why volunteer?"

"Because I can make a difference. Because I can't bear to sit at a desk and have people think I'm here only because of you."

"Would that be so bad?"

"Yes! I can't sit idly by while others risk their lives. While you risk yours. I was trained by the SOE, Billy. There's a job for me to do, and I can't do it sitting around headquarters!"

"But you almost were killed—"

"Yes. I was raped, beaten, drugged, and I almost killed myself because of it," she said, rattling off the physical and emotional wounds she'd suffered as if they were items on a shopping list. She faced me. "It was a nightmare, and you rescued me, Billy. In many, many ways. But now I'm better. It's behind me, and it's time I moved on."

"But—"

"But nothing, Billy. I'm going back on active duty with the SOE. I've proved to myself that I'm ready."

"You needed me, you know."

"You bastard," Diana said.

It was true. Diana had done her part, putting the pieces together, but when it came time to hunt down the German and his renegade Egyptian pals, it was my job. Diana had begged to come along. To observe, she had said. There were four of us, all well armed, so I had agreed. It was an adventure, I'd told myself. I hadn't understood that Diana needed to test herself, to see if she could stand up once again to danger and death. She'd passed the test, and ended up saving my life to boot. But that didn't change the fact that she'd used me, no matter how she dressed it up. And that to get me to allow her to tag along, she'd used all her wiles. Succumbing had been a bad move on my part, except for the bit when she'd stopped that Kraut from killing me.

I wanted to scare her, to make her think twice about parachuting into France or Greece or wherever the SOE needed a female agent. I wanted her with me and—I had to admit—I wanted her waiting for me when I got back from wherever Uncle Ike sent me next. I hated the thought of worrying about her once more, of not knowing if she was alive or dead. Or worse.

"If you do this, I won't be there to back you up, Diana. You'll be all alone."

"I'm all alone right now," she said. She buttoned her blouse and put her shoes on. "I'm going for a walk. Please be gone by the time I get back."

"Don't go, Diana, please," I said. I took her by the arms and held her, breathed in her scent, felt the heat rising from her skin. "I love you."

"No, you don't," she said. "You want to possess me. I've been waiting for you to learn the difference."

She twisted out of my embrace and left, slamming the door behind her. I stood there, unsure of what to do next, the *tick tick tick* of the ceiling fan in the empty room marking the beats of my heart.

CHAPTER ▪ TWO

I FOUND KAY in the hotel bar. Then I saw a waiter and ordered two Irish whiskeys. Doubles. I asked Kay if she wanted anything.

"I'm fine, Billy. But what sorrows are you drowning?"

She raised her glass and drank, her gaze fixed on me over the rim. Kay Summersby was a knockout, with dark, wide eyes set above prominent cheekbones. Her smile was infectious, and I had a hard time staying miserable around her. But I was working at it as hard as I could.

"Diana and I had a fight."

"Billy, you shouldn't waste time quarreling. Not the two of you, not in the middle of a war. Life's too short, believe me." Her smile vanished, and she reached for a cigarette.

I lit it for her, but she avoided looking straight at me. Her fiancé had been killed in combat several months ago but I didn't think she was still broken up. She had the look of having suffered a more recent wound.

"It's about her going back to the SOE," I said. "I don't want her to."

"But she is anyway," said Kay. It wasn't a question.

"Yes, and she didn't even tell me! She should at least have talked it over with me."

"Oh dear," Kay said. "I didn't realize I'd spilled the beans. I thought you knew."

"I was probably the last to find out," I said, taking a gulp of one of the drinks that had been set in front of me.

"Tell me, Billy. Why is it that men always look at every decision a woman makes as if it revolves around them? You're moping about here instead of going out on the town with Diana and toasting her success, all because she did something without consulting you. As if she needed to. Your feelings are hurt, that's all."

"But she could get killed. Look what happened to her in Algiers—"

"Look what happened to you in Sicily."

"What about it? I'm OK now."

"Exactly."

Kay raised a slender hand and nodded to her empty glass as a waiter passed. He skidded to a halt and took it, assuring her he'd be right back with a fresh drink. Kay could always count on attracting attention, mostly the admiring type, from men, and occasionally the jealous sort from women, especially if they were attached to those admiring men. She'd been a model before joining up with the Mechanised Transport Corps, and it showed in her graceful movements, calm assurance, and killer good looks. But she was no debutante dressed up in khaki. She'd driven an ambulance in the East End of London during the Blitz, digging out the living and the dead from bombed and burning buildings, before she'd been assigned as Uncle Ike's driver. When Kay was sent to North Africa, her transport had been torpedoed, and she'd spent a night bobbing in a lifeboat on cold ocean waves as destroyers depthcharged the waters around the survivors. And she'd endured her own loss in this war, so I had to admit she might know what she was talking about.

"OK, I get your point. It's just that where I come from women don't go off and jump out of airplanes behind enemy lines."

"Where I come from, Billy, women don't go off to drive generals about England and North Africa. Yet, here I am." She bestowed a smile on the waiter as he placed her gin and tonic on the table and disappeared behind a potted palm tree. The bar was filling up as the cocktail hour approached. Civilians in white linen suits mingled with British officers in lightweight khaki. Except for the heat and the tropical clothing, we could have been in London.

"Where do you come from, Kay?"

"The same place as your family came from, Billy. Ireland. Country Cork, to be exact. My father was a colonel in the Royal Munster Fusiliers, and my mother was British. I'm a rare example of Anglo-Irish accord."

"It's a bit odd, isn't it? Helping the British to hang on to their empire?"

"Only half odd to me, Billy. But yes, I know what you mean. The Black and Tans burned the center of Cork in 1920, so I'm familiar with the heavy hand of the British Empire."

"I know," I said. "My uncle Dan told me that afterward the Black and Tans tied pieces of burnt cork to their revolvers, as a message to anyone who resisted them: If they burned Cork, they could burn out any town or village they wanted to." I could recall the stories Uncle Dan had told of the Irish Civil War, when the British recruited veterans of the World War to bolster the ranks of the Royal Irish Constabulary. They were issued a mixture of surplus military uniforms and police uniforms. The army uniforms were khaki, the police uniforms darker. The colors gave them their name, a name that in my family stood for brutal repression and arbitrary killings.

"Well, we're a long way from Ireland, and the Nazis make the Black and Tans look like naughty schoolboys, so I think we're on the right side."

I wasn't so sure about the comparison. The Black and Tans had been a law unto themselves, foreign soldiers putting down a rebellion in my homeland. But I didn't want to argue with Kay. I started on my second drink instead and made small talk.

"Are you enjoying the trip?" I asked. After the Cairo conference, Uncle Ike's boss, General George C. Marshall, had ordered him to take a brief vacation. Uncle Ike decided to play tourist, and took a bunch of us along to see the pyramids in Egypt, and then on a short flight to Jerusalem to see the Holy Land. Kay and a couple of other secretaries from headquarters had come along, as had Uncle Ike's aide, Colonel Tex Lee, and Sergeant Mickey McKeogh, his orderly. Diana and I rounded out the party.

"Yes, and Ike needed a break. I'm so glad General Marshall ordered him to take one. He hasn't had a day off for months. Neither have the rest of us."

"I never thought I'd see the Garden of Gethsemane."

"It was so very sad," Kay said, her eyelids flickering as she looked away from me, her hand playing around her mouth. I thought she might cry.

Uncle Ike had taken us to the Mount of Olives, where the thick, gnarled olive trees reminded me of Sicily. The Garden of Gethsemane is on the western slope, next to a church built over a rock where the Franciscan monks told us Jesus prayed the night before his arrest, while his disciples drifted off to sleep. I thought about how easy it always has been to get men to do unimaginable things. Roman soldiers nailing men to crosses, Black and Tans burning homes and shooting Irishmen, Nazis committing mass murder. Indeed it was all so very sad, but I didn't think that's what gave Kay her faraway look.

"What's wrong, Kay?"

"Don't mind me, Billy," she said, shaking her head as if coming out of a dream. "Diana is who you should be thinking of. Don't let your pride kill what the two of you have together."

"If she has her way, we won't be together."

"Don't be a fool!" Kay slammed her glass down, drawing brief stares and raised eyebrows. She grabbed her uniform jacket from the back of her chair and pulled it on, thrusting her arms in angrily. As she did, a packet of postcards fell from an inside pocket. I recognized them as the ones Uncle Ike had bought outside the church and handed out to all of us. I knelt to pick them up and Kay hurriedly pushed me away.

"Leave them," she said, her voice shaky. Our hands collided and she dropped a postcard onto the table. It fell facedown, revealing a familiar scrawl across the back.

Good night. There are lots of things I could say—you know them. Good night.

He hadn't signed it but he didn't need to. I knew Uncle Ike's handwriting well enough. Kay's eyes met mine as she scooped the card to her breast.

"Don't be a fool, Billy," she said.

Then she was gone. I was glad there was whiskey left in my glass.

Good night.

What were the things she knew, things Uncle Ike could have said, but didn't?

Good night.

What did it mean? With that question, I laughed at myself. What else could it mean? I didn't want to think about it. Outside of my dad and Uncle Dan, there wasn't a man in the world I respected more. We were some kind of distant cousins, on my mom's side. She was related to Aunt Mamie, so the general and I weren't exactly blood relations but he was family. Problem was, so was Aunt Mamie. Jerusalem was a world away from Boston and Abilene but even so I didn't think it right. I felt a bit like a prude but I couldn't help it, maybe because I looked up to Uncle Ike so much. He always seemed to know the right thing to do. He was the one I looked to when I couldn't tell right from wrong, the one who taught me the terrible mathematics of war. Some will die today so that more will live tomorrow. He bore the weight of that equation silently, and you had to look closely to see how it burdened him.

I didn't want him writing love notes to Kay. I didn't want her lecturing me on how to work things out with Diana, and I didn't want Diana going off and getting herself killed. I wanted everything to be exactly as it was before we came to Jerusalem.

"Billy? I thought I'd find you here," said Mickey McKeogh, appearing from behind palm leaves. "The boss wants you, pronto."

"OK, Mickey," I said, draining my glass. "We going back to the war?"

"Dunno, Billy. Be a shame to leave this place. Almost as nice as the Plaza."

Mickey was a fellow Irishman who had been a doorman at the Plaza Hotel in New York City before the war. He knew his hotels. Since nothing was as nice as the Plaza, this was high praise for the King David. I followed him through the lobby, hoping that whatever came next would take my mind off Diana, Kay, and Uncle Ike.

I couldn't get that postcard out of my mind. A picture of the Garden of Gethsemane on one side, Uncle Ike's unsigned declaration on the other. I thought about that slab of rock in the church, the one the monks said Jesus prayed and wept on. And then I remembered another thing from my Sunday School lessons about the Garden of Gethsemane.

It was where Judas Iscariot betrayed Jesus. With a kiss.

CHAPTER ∎ THREE

MICKEY GAVE TWO short raps on the hotel-room door, opened it, and gestured to me to enter. I wondered what he knew about nighttime whispers and things left unsaid. What he knew would never pass his lips; he was as loyal as they came. He patted me on the back and shut the door behind me, leaving me in a narrow hallway, face to face with Uncle Ike. I felt as if an accusation was written across my face.

"William," he said, his face lighting up with his trademark grin as he put a hand on my shoulder. "Come in, come in. Are you all right? You looked flushed. Too much sun today?"

"No, no, sir," I said. "I'm fine. Really." He stared at me oddly for a second, searching for some hint of trouble. I put on my cop face and the look vanished.

"Good. I'm glad you were able to come along with me on this trip. I haven't felt so relaxed since we came over from the States. I slept ten hours last night; can you believe it?"

"Yes, sir, I can. You look good."

He did. The bags under his eyes didn't look as dark as they had back in Algiers, where he had been running a war while organizing a visit by a president and a prime minister. I craned my neck to find out who was in the room but couldn't see around the corner. I never called him Uncle Ike in front of anyone else, and I didn't think we were alone now, so I held back. He seemed to read my thoughts as he lowered his voice.

"Thanks, William. You deserve more rest yourself, but something's come up." He dug a cigarette out of the pack in his pocket and lit up, glancing toward the room as he did so. "I'm afraid you're going to have to cut this trip short. Do you remember Major Cosgrove?"

I remembered. Major Charles Cosgrove, supposedly a representative of the British Imperial General Staff. In reality, he worked for MI-5, their counterintelligence and security division. We'd met when I first came to England, and he tried to use me in his intelligence games. I hadn't liked him then, and he didn't take to me. I doubted he'd changed much. I had—plenty—but it only served to make me more suspicious of him than I had been before.

"Sure, General. Swell guy."

"I know you two didn't get along during that affair with the Norwegians, William. But this time he's come to ask you for a favor, and it might be one you won't mind doing."

"It sounds like I'm going to be working for him, General."

"William, don't make it sound like a prison sentence. Remember, we're all on the same side, even though at times it may seem more trouble than it's worth."

He smiled, letting me know he understood and that he had his own English cross to bear. General Bernard Law Montgomery had been a constant source of irritation to Uncle Ike—and most Americans, for that matter—with his condescending remarks about U.S. troops and his overblown opinion of his own military genius. But Uncle Ike never said a single negative thing about him, in public anyway, for the sake of Allied unity. He rested his hand on my arm, raised his eyebrows, and waited for me to let him know I had gotten the message.

"I understand, sir. I'll be on my best behavior, I promise."

"Good, William. I knew I could count on you. Have you written to your mother lately?"

Uncle Ike walked me down the corridor, lecturing me on the virtues of writing to loved ones at home. I thought of Aunt Mamie looking forward to his letters, and of the brief but passionate postcard he'd written Kay. Did Mamie know all the things he could say but didn't? I tried to shake off the thought before I blurted out anything stupid, assuring Uncle Ike I would write soon.

"My young American friend! Good of you to drop in for a chat," Major Charles Cosgrove said. Sinking his cane into the carpet like a bayonet, he lifted his well-tailored bulk up out of a comfortable chair, teetered a bit as he got his balance, huffed as he took a few steps over to me, and shook my hand. "You're looking well, young Billy."

"You too, Major," I said, hoping the lie wasn't too apparent. There was more gray in the thinning hair than there had been, and in his waxed mustache too. He was still elegant, if you didn't count the sweat beading his brow or his immense girth held together by a spit-shined Sam Browne belt. Somebody else's spit, not his.

"Lieutenant Boyle, I'd like you to meet Subaltern O'Brien," Cosgrove said, stepping to one side as he took me by the arm. I hadn't been able to see anyone behind him as he stood but when he moved, a woman rose from another chair and held out her hand. A young woman. A young, pretty woman. And, judging by the sprinkling of freckles decorating her nose, as well as her name, a young, pretty Irish woman.

"Subaltern Sláine O'Brien, Lieutenant Boyle. Pleased to meet you." She was a bit on the short side, her eyes angling up to meet mine. They were green, her skin white, and her hair the color of honey, a mass of curls pulled back in a vain attempt to contain them.

"Same here," I said, enjoying the lilt in her voice. She both looked and sounded Irish, so her being with Major Cosgrove, wearing a British uniform, seemed damn odd to me.

"I'll leave you together to talk about this investigation," Uncle Ike said. "William understands the situation and will give you his full cooperation."

"Excellent, General Eisenhower, thank you so much for lending us the lieutenant," Cosgrove said, lifting his mustache in a broad smile.

"It was an honor to meet you, sir," O'Brien said, folding her hands like a schoolgirl as she faced the general.

"How do you spell your first name, Subaltern? I'm afraid that bit of Gaelic confused my midwestern ear," Uncle Ike said, all smiles for her after a sharp glance at Cosgrove, who seemed to be dismissing him.

"Slah-nah," she said slowly, the accent on the first syllable, "is spelled S-l-á-i-n-e."

"Sláine," Uncle Ike repeated, doing his best. He smiled, obviously enjoying her beauty, and then snapped out of it. He slapped me on the shoulder and assured me it wouldn't be long before I was back. I didn't even know where the hell I was going.

The three of us settled down into chairs grouped around a small table, where a carafe of water sweated, surrounded by cut-crystal glasses. I poured and gulped down the cool liquid, watching O'Brien and Cosgrove exchanging glances. I wondered which one was going to break the bad news. I decided to get to know this Irish lass a bit before letting them sentence me to whatever scheme they didn't want to waste an Englishman on.

"What exactly is a subaltern, Miss O'Brien? It is Miss O'Brien, isn't it?"

"It's Subaltern O'Brien," she said, stiffening. "Subaltern is an Auxiliary Territorial Service rank, equivalent to lieutenant. That's a step up from second lieutenant, by the way."

"Thanks for the reminder, sir."

"Ma'am," she said.

"What?"

"'Thanks for the reminder, *ma'am*,'" she said. "That is the proper way to address an officer in the ATS. A superior officer."

I wished Uncle Ike would return. She'd seemed nice when he was around. Now she was acting like an officer, a real officer, even though she was ATS, which was an auxiliary organization the British had put together to allow women to make their contribution to the war effort. Kay had come from the ATS, and I knew they worked as antiaircraft gunners, military police, and everything else short of carrying a rifle at the front.

Subaltern O'Brien's tropical-weight khaki uniform was neat and pressed, a remarkable feat in the heat and dust of the Holy Land. Her ATS insignia, those three letters enclosed by a laurel with a crown at the top, was shiny and bright, the brass gleaming above her breast pocket. Her buttons were polished, their golden color jumping out at me.

She caught my eye wandering over her and turned to Cosgrove, with a brief expression of disdain. I wanted to say I was only admiring her buttons but had the good sense to take another drink of water instead. I smoothed out the wrinkles in my uniform as I tried to remember the last time I'd polished my own buttons. I'd paid some kid in Algiers to do it a while ago, but he'd gotten more Brasso on the jacket than on the buttons.

"Would you like to start the briefing, Major Cosgrove?" She was all business.

"Certainly. Now, Boyle, how much do you know about the Irish Republican Army?"

"I've heard of it," I said, suspicious as any good Irish boy would be of an Englishman asking such a question. I stared at O'Brien again, overlooking her buttons this time but still wondering why she wore a British uniform.

"Yes, I'm sure," Cosgrove said. "You know the IRA came out of the Irish Volunteers and other groups involved in the rebellion and the subsequent Anglo-Irish War—"

"You mean the Irish War of Independence," I said.

"As you wish. All water under the dam now, Boyle. The treaty between Great Britain and Ireland was signed in 1921—"

"Leaving Northern Ireland in the hands of the British."

"Precisely. The Irish Republican Army split, those who supported the treaty forming the new Irish National Army and those who opposed it fighting on, against the Irish government, Great Britain, and often each other."

"What's the point of the history lesson?" I asked, steamed at having to listen to Cosgrove's version of recent Irish struggles.

"To be certain you understand the importance of what we are about to tell you. I assume you've been raised on tales of valiant IRA lads fighting against English tyranny. With your American distance from the actual events, I daresay you have a rather romantic notion of this conflict, one that has little basis in reality."

I didn't like how this was going. I got up and walked away from Cosgrove, cramming my hands in my pockets to keep from making a fist.

I stared out a window in the direction of the Golden Gate, the gate through which the Jews believed the Messiah would enter Jerusalem. A few hundred years ago, the Turks had sealed it up, and it was still sealed up tight this morning with the English running the place. That was how empires worked, no matter if it was the Turks or the Brits. Grind the dreams of the people into nothing. Brick up the wall. Sneer at the stuff of legends.

"Are you still with us, Lieutenant Boyle?" O'Brien asked.

"I am," I said with an effort.

"Now, as I was saying," Cosgrove huffed, "the IRA has continued its operations, even though it was declared illegal by the Dublin government in 1936. It has been able to do so in large part due to contributions from America. Were you aware of that?"

I shrugged.

"You lived and worked in Boston, Massachusetts," O'Brien said, her green eyes scanning the contents of a folder. "You, your father, and his brother all serve on the Boston police force. With a lot of other Irish-Americans."

"And no Englishmen," I said, answering what sounded like an accusation with another.

"Exactly, my dear boy," Cosgrove said. "Why, you have probably tossed some coins into a can at whatever pub you frequent in Boston. Irish relief, or something like that."

"Taverns," I said. "We call them taverns, or bars."

"I don't care what you call them, Boyle, all I want to do is be sure you understand the larger picture. You're no stranger to the IRA and Clan na Gael, surely!"

Clan na Gael. The Family of the Gaels, the fund-raising organization in the States for the cause of a free Ireland. It had been around since the last century, and when the Dublin government approved the treaty, some members agreed. Others didn't, and they kept up the flow of money and guns to the IRA. Dad and Uncle Dan were on the anti-treaty side. Nothing less than a free and united Ireland was how the cause was defined around our kitchen table.

"I don't know what you're talking about," I said, thinking about the Irish Hospitals' Sweepstake tickets my dad used to bring home from Clan na Gael meetings. He'd tell me it would be worth $150,000 if one of them won, and we'd treat them as if they were gold. I always believed each one he brought home was a winner; it meant a week of dreams.

"You must not have been much of a police officer," O'Brien said. "I suspect Clan na Gael was all over the Irish neighborhoods in Boston. I'd also guess that within the Boston Police Department, there would be an IRA group. A secret group, to the extent the IRA can keep a secret."

"You sound as if you're a cop yourself," I said. "What exactly do you do in the ATS?"

"Subaltern O'Brien is MI-5's country desk officer for Ireland," Cosgrove said. "Quite an achievement for a woman. Wartime contingencies and all that to be sure, but still remarkable."

"So you admit you're MI-5?" I asked Cosgrove.

"Of course. We have no secrets from our American cousins."

"Anymore, that is. You lied the last time we met."

"That was then, my boy. Now we have a bigger job to do."

"OK, spill."

"Pardon me?"

"Tell me everything. Pretend I never heard of the IRA and lay it all out."

Cosgrove nodded to O'Brien, who gave him a cold response. I wondered if she was miffed at his qualified endorsement of her accomplishment. And I wondered even more what an O'Brien, man or woman, was doing working for MI-5 on Irish counterintelligence. It wasn't an Anglo-Irish name or one to be found among Ulster Protestants, those residents of the northern counties who had fought to maintain union with Great Britain. She looked and sounded Irish, which to me meant the Republic of Ireland, the entire island, united. That it meant Catholic was understood. I have plenty of Protestant friends back in Boston and in the army, so don't misunderstand. There's not anything wrong with being a Protestant. It's the pro-British, Catholic-hating Ulstermen I don't like, and they just happen to be Protestants.

"There have been a number of contacts between the IRA and the Abwehr, the German intelligence service, that commenced well before the war," she said, her hands clasped together above her knees, which were aligned perfectly. Had the nuns taught her to sit like that, ladylike and demure, all the sinful parts protected?

"Tom Barry, the IRA's director of intelligence, visited Germany and met with the Abwehr in 1936, after the IRA was declared an illegal organization," she went on. "This was followed by a visit in 1939 by Jim O'Donovan, their director of chemical warfare."

"Chief bomb maker," Cosgrove interpreted.

"Yes. O'Donovan developed the IRA S-Plan, S meaning sabotage. With funds from Germany, he put together a bombing campaign against England early in the war. There were over three hundred explosions, some of them quite small and most ineffectual. They hit railroad stations, cinemas, post offices, that sort of thing. Seven people were killed. The attacks ended in 1940."

"Pathetic, really," Cosgrove said. "But it alerted us to increase security in sensitive military areas."

"So what are you worried about?" I asked.

"The IRA is more effective closer to home," O'Brien said. "During the S-Plan operations, they broke into Magazine Fort, the regular Irish Army ammunition storage depot in Dublin."

"The Christmas Raid," I said. I remembered a long night of celebrating and toasting the IRA at Kirby's, my dad and Uncle Dan slapping each other on the back while singing the old songs. It had sounded like Robin Hood and his merry men had pulled off a marvelous heist.

"December 1939," O'Brien acknowledged. "They broke in, disarmed the guards, and took over a million rounds of ammunition. No one killed or even hurt. It was a grand coup, except they hadn't planned for success. They took away so much, there was no place to hide it all. And the Irish Army was so red faced they tore the countryside apart looking for it. Most was quickly recovered."

I hadn't heard about *that*. Or if I had, there'd been no celebrating to help me remember.

"What worries us, Boyle," Cosgrove said, leaning forward as if to whisper a secret, "is that one of these IRA schemes might actually work. They've no shortage of imagination, I'll grant you. But we've been lucky so far that they have as much talent for mucking things up as they do for concocting grand schemes."

"Have you heard of Sean Russell?" O'Brien asked.

"Sure," I said, not seeing any reason to hide the fact. The former IRA chief of staff was a famous guy in certain parts of South Boston.

"In 1939 he toured America, speaking to Clan na Gael gatherings, raising funds for the bombing campaign. From there he went on to Italy, and then secretly to Germany. He met with the German foreign minister about recruiting Irish nationals captured fighting for the British Army into an Irish Brigade, to fight against the British in Northern Ireland. He underwent demolition training with the Abwehr, and after three months was outfitted with a radio, funds, and explosives, and sent off on a U-boat that would land him back in Ireland."

"But he died," I said, vaguely remembering reports of his death.

"Yes, on the U-boat. We believe from a burst gastric ulcer. The mission was scrapped."

"You're lucky he mucked that one up by dying," I said to Cosgrove.

"Indeed. But it gave us cause to watch the IRA even more closely. Both sides have tried to draw neutral Ireland into the war. Or all three sides, I should say." He counted them off on his fingers. "First, Churchill offered Dublin all of Ulster if the Republic of Ireland entered the war allied with England. Prime Minister de Valera turned him down. Second, the IRA sent an emissary to Berlin in 1940 with Plan Kathleen, their military plan for a German invasion of Ireland. If the German invasion succeeded, the IRA would assume control of the entire island and enter the war as an Axis partner."

I focused on item number one, unsure I'd heard correctly. "Churchill would've given up Northern Ireland?"

"Absolutely. He offered exactly what the Irish Republican movement had always wanted: a united Ireland, free of British control. But apparently there was little enthusiasm among the Irish for another war, and Eamon de Valera missed his chance."

"So what about the third side, the Germans?"

"We have come into possession of their plans for Operation Green, the invasion of Ireland, rumored to have been at the invitation of the Dublin government. Quite detailed. But I daresay the time has passed for its implementation. We are no longer spread so thin now that you Yanks have joined us."

"OK, so what's the problem? The IRA hasn't given the English a free pass because you're fighting a war. But except for Sean Russell, none of them have been able to exploit the situation. And he's dead. What do you need me for?"

O'Brien said, "Six weeks ago we intercepted a message from Tom Barry, the IRA intelligence director, to Joe McGarrity in America, head of Clan na Gael. Do you know of him?"

"I've heard the name." I didn't mention that I'd heard the name when Uncle Dan introduced me to him. Joe McGarrity had had Sunday supper at our home when he was in Boston a few years ago, along with an IRA man named Seamus Rafferty. Raising money for the Cause. I wanted to find out what this was about but I didn't think they'd keep me in their confidence if they knew the Boyle household was a regular gathering place for the Irish Republican movement. To us, Republican didn't mean Wendell Willkie, it meant a united Ireland. Free of the English. I did my best to make my replies neutral, free of politics, to keep them talking. At least listening to Subaltern O'Brien's voice was pleasant.

"The message was 'Ask Clan na Gael to rush supplies.'"

"Supplies for what?"

"Five days ago, a U.S. Army arms depot at Ballykinler in Northern Ireland was raided. They got away with fifty of the latest models of the Browning Automatic Rifle and over two hundred thousand rounds of ammunition. What do you think it's for, Lieutenant Boyle?"

"Are you certain it was the IRA? Not German saboteurs?"

"About four miles from the main gate, we found the body of Eddie Mahoney, a known IRA man. Shot twice in the back of the head and left with a pound note folded in the palm of his hand."

"The mark of the informer," I said automatically.

"You do seem to know something of the ways of the IRA, Boyle," Cosgrove said. "Do you have Republican leanings yourself?"

"It wouldn't matter if I did. General Eisenhower told me to cooperate, and that's what I plan to do."

"Excellent. We take this matter very seriously, especially given the involvement of this Tom Barry chap. He proposed an invasion of Northern Ireland by the IRA about ten years ago. He was overruled by IRA general staff then but he could be trying again. Money from America, arms from the U.S. Army, and perhaps involvement by the Abwehr. We will work on the German angle, and we want you to investigate the arms theft in Ireland."

"In Northern Ireland?"

"Of course. Ulster."

"Of course."

I had always wondered if I'd make it to the old sod someday. Now I would but it wasn't County Roscommon I'd be seeing. It was the northern counties, home of the Orangemen and the Red Hand of Ulster, where the Protestants still celebrated their victory over the Catholics at the Battle of the Boyne more than two hundred and fifty years ago. It had always seemed a dark, brutal, and bitter land of long, unforgiving memories. My childhood fear of the Orangeman welled up within me and I shivered. In my house, it wasn't the bogeyman who would come get you if you were bad, it was the Orangeman. My grandfather used to tell us about their parades every July celebrating the Battle of the Boyne, how they'd march through Catholic neighborhoods with their English flags and orange banners, thrashing any Catholic boys they found on the street.

It felt like I was being sent to hell itself.

It was a shock when Cosgrove informed me that I had to leave in fifteen minutes.

"Pack up your kit, Boyle. There will be a car out front waiting to drive you to the aerodrome at Lydda. Subaltern O'Brien will accompany you and provide further instructions. General Eisenhower will inform your Major Harding about this assignment but you are to discuss it with no one. You can expect spies and informers everywhere in Palestine with all the Arabs and Jews about. No time to waste, my boy. The RAF operates on a tight schedule."

With that, he shook my hand and heaved himself down the stairs to the main lobby. It was typical of the British to express dismay at so many of the local population in their occupied territories. It seemed to me the Brits never met a foreigner they liked or a foreign land they didn't.

CHAPTER ■ FOUR

I HAD FIFTEEN minutes to find Diana and tell her I was leaving. It wasn't the best timing, in view of the fight we'd had. A few minutes was not going to be long enough to convince her to give up the SOE while I went off on a mission, but I had to think of a way to get through to her. I went over what Kay had said as I hurried to Diana's room. *Don't let your pride kill what the two of you have. Don't be a fool.* But who was the fool here? Me, trying to keep Diana from death and torture? Or Kay, driving Uncle Ike around and clasping his secret scribbles to her breast? Or maybe it was Diana, risking death again after all she had been through and all she had lost.

Diana had gone with the British Expeditionary Force to France in 1940 as a member of the FANY, working at headquarters as a switchboard operator. But the German Blitzkrieg had turned rear areas into front lines, and soon she was part of the retreat to Dunkirk and found herself caring for wounded soldiers crammed onto the deck of a British destroyer. When the Stukas came, dive-bombing and strafing the ship, she'd watched the stretcher cases slide into the cold channel waters as the destroyer capsized. Everywhere around her, men died, the waves cresting with corpses, while she survived, unhurt. She'd been rescued and made it back to England, visions of death haunting her dreams, driving the guilt deep inside her.

Then she lost her sister, Daphne. Daphne had befriended me when I first showed up at U.S. Army headquarters in London, and had been killed when she'd gotten too close to the murderer of a Norwegian official. After that, Diana was determined to go to war as an SOE agent, telling everyone she had to do her duty. But I knew there was more to it; she had to tempt death, and find out if she truly deserved to live. When she was finally sent on a mission, it was betrayed before it began, and she was picked up in Algiers by the Vichy French police. Fascist police. It hadn't been pretty. She'd been drugged, beaten, and raped. It wasn't the clean confrontation with death that she had sought. It was dirty, sordid, horrible, painful, and demeaning. I couldn't let her go through that again. *I* couldn't go through it again.

I knocked on her door. No answer. I called to her, rattled the door handle. Silence. I looked at my watch. Ten minutes. I ran to my room down the hall and threw my kit together, shaving gear, soap, and comb wrapped into a hotel towel and stuffed in my field bag with one good spare shirt and a few other articles of clothing. There was just enough room for a bottle of Bushmills Irish whiskey, half empty, and a paperback book I'd been reading, also about half done. *The Big Sleep* by Raymond Chandler. It was a murder mystery about a detective working for a general. Seemed right up my alley.

I buckled on my web belt with the .45 automatic snug in its holster. I patted the pouches for the extra clips and did a quick check around the room. I had my razor, toothbrush, clean shirt, booze, book, automatic, and ammo. Everything I needed for a long trip to Belfast. Five minutes to go.

I began to write Diana a note, then realized I didn't know what to say. I wasn't sure about anything. Not her, myself, or where the war might take us. After seeing Kay's note from Uncle Ike, I wasn't sure whom I could trust or if trust even mattered anymore. Maybe I *was* a fool. I thought about saying I was sorry but I wasn't. I looked at my watch. Five minutes. I wrote fast.

Diana—
I've been called away. Ask the general for details. I can't say anything. May be gone for a while. Let's start over when I get back. Stay safe.
Billy

I'm no Raymond Chandler, that's for sure. I thought "stay safe" was good, though. It might mean stay safe at headquarters or it could mean be safe on your SOE mission. I slipped it under her door, and then wished I'd signed it *Love, Billy.* I was a fool. Too late for love—that summed up the day so far. I stood in the hallway, waiting for a sound to come from within the room. It was quiet, so at least she wasn't inside, ignoring me.

Two minutes. I had to go. Where had all my fine Irish words gone when I needed them? No wonder they called it the gift of gab; mine had deserted me. I could blather the whole day and into the night but when it came to putting a few words on paper for the woman I loved, I was lost, tongue-tied, reduced to a few trite lines.

I cursed myself as I ran through the lobby and out through the pink sandstone arches. Cypress trees shaded the walkway, lending swatches of green to the dusty pinks, beiges, and browns covering the landscape. I glanced back at the hotel, wondering if Diana had opened her door and found my note. Perhaps she was looking out a window and watching me leave, pack slung over my back. Part of me was glad to be going, I was ashamed to admit. It was a way out of my troubles. Not the best way but there was no denying it: I was off to another part of the world, and whatever was going to happen would happen without me. It might be the best thing for Diana and me, I told myself. Like I'd said in the note, when I got back, we could start over. And what if she wasn't around when I got back? Well, I had a long plane ride to figure that one out. I felt the same about Uncle Ike and Kay. Now that I knew something was going on between them, I was secretly relieved that Major Cosgrove had showed up to rescue me from these crosscurrents of passion and deception.

I didn't like the way things had turned out on this little side trip to the Holy Land. It was supposed to have been fun, a break from the routine of war: the paperwork, the waiting, the moments of terror, the lousy food, and more sudden terror. Instead, the people I loved were acting in ways I didn't understand, moving away from me, shifting and changing the few precious things I had counted on. Damned if it didn't feel good to leave that hotel behind me.

A British Army corporal gave me one of their backhanded salutes that always made me think they were slapping their foreheads. I gave him a snappy one in return and tossed him my pack. He opened the door of the staff car and I got in back, next to Subaltern O'Brien. She was fanning herself with a file folder marked SECRET in bold red letters.

"Am I in that file?" I asked.

"Not this one, Lieutenant Boyle," she said as the driver sped off, scattering pedestrians and the odd donkey with an utter disregard for civilians. As we turned onto the main road, I caught a last glimpse of the old walled city, the New Gate with its narrow archway into the Christian Quarter fading from view as we picked up speed.

"What are you doing here anyway?" I asked her.

"Finishing your briefing," she said as she thumbed through the papers in the file.

"No, I mean serving with the British. You're Irish."

"So are you," she said.

"It's not the same. My country is at war, yours isn't. And you're part of MI-5, the same people who go after the IRA in Northern Ireland."

"Which is exactly what you have been assigned to do, courtesy of General Eisenhower."

"You know what I mean," I said. "I don't think anyone ordered you to join the ATS, much less become part of MI-5." At that, she shrugged, silently granting the point, as she finally looked up from her file.

"Are you one of those Irish-Americans who romanticize the brave lads of the IRA, raising pints to them in your Boston bars and crying great rivers of tears when 'Danny Boy' plays? Do the pipes call to you, Billy Boyle, from glen to glen and down the mountainside? I think they must, even in Boston. But you never answer them, do you? You send your money and your guns, you sons of Eire, but not yourselves, so you never see the agony you cause as you keep open the great wounds of our nation. Well, now the pipes have called and you must answer. You must."

"It's not like that," I said, after I had recovered from the quiet force of her words. "It sounds like you don't like Irish-Americans very much."

"I'm sure there are some fine ones. One, I even admire very much. Now here's what we know about the theft—"

"Wait, who is it you admire?"

"Never mind, it's nothing to do with this. Now listen."

She went through the file, reviewing the details. The U.S. Army base at Ballykinler regularly received supplies from local farmers and shops. On the night of the raid, a truck loaded with cabbages and ruta-bagas had been admitted at the gate. Two men, the driver and a helper, had carried the food to the kitchen and then made an unscheduled stop at the arms depot. Fifty Browning Automatic Rifles, newly delivered, and more than two hundred thousand rounds were loaded onto the truck and driven out the main gate. The two men had not been escort-ed, and there was no search of the truck. Based on the time the truck was signed in and out and the estimated time it took for the food delivery, they broke into the arms depot and loaded up in under ten minutes. Eddie Mahoney's body was found at the side of the road less than half a mile from the base, hands bound behind his back.

"It must have been an inside job," she concluded. "Except for Mahoney."

"Was he an informer?" I asked when she closed the file.

"No. Our information tells us he was trusted by the IRA General Staff in Dublin."

"Would you tell me if he was an informer?"

"Yes," she said. "If it would help you, I would. There is one other IRA operative from Dublin you may run across. A man named Jack Taggart. He's called Red Jack because of his leftist political leanings. We know he lived in Dublin and that the IRA General Staff sent him north two years ago to help build up the IRA Northern Command. He fought in Spain against Franco with the Irish Brigade. He's experienced and very secretive. We lost track of him when he crossed the border. It's likely he moved his wife and children north also, since they're nowhere to be found in the Republic. They're probably living under assumed identities."

"Do you have any evidence this Red Jack character is involved?"

"No, simply a warning to watch out for him. If you do encounter him, you're to inform me and take no action."

"How do I do that—inform you, I mean?"

"I'll be in Belfast soon enough," she said. "I'd be more than impressed if you found Red Jack Taggart in your first few days. I've been hunting him for three years."

"But how will I get in touch with you then?"

"Don't worry, I'll find you."

I didn't like her attitude. I didn't like being told I was predictable, and not to worry. I didn't like her calling the shots. I wasn't used to being given orders by a woman, and the recent blowup with Diana was too fresh in my mind to allow me to take them with grace from this woman.

"What can you tell me about the truck?" I asked, changing the topic. I liked to ask the questions.

"It was found abandoned outside of Dundalk, in the Republic."

"When?"

"At exactly 6:10 a.m.," she said, consulting a sheet of paper in her file. "By a milkman, near Omeath in County Louth, perhaps twelve or so miles from Dundalk."

"So they drove the arms across the border?"

"All we can say is that the truck crossed over. It could have been empty, left there to throw us off the scent."

"OK, maybe. Whose was it? You said the food delivery was expected at the base."

"Yes, the truck belonged to a wholesaler who does business with the army. It had been stolen earlier that night, and he had reported it to the police. His story checked out."

"Any chance he knows more than he's telling?"

"Yes, its very likely, but he's not hiding anything about the truck. His name is Andrew Jenkins, and he is a major force in the Unionist ranks. We think he's behind the Red Hand Society, a Protestant secret militia."

"What do they do?"

"Kill Catholics. Sometimes suspected members of the IRA. Sometimes IRA sympathizers. When they want a reprisal killing, any Catholic will do."

"Reprisals for what?"

"Practically anything the IRA does. They started the very day Great Britain went to war. The IRA shot a British soldier, to show the war made no difference to them. Then the Red Hand killed several Catholics unlucky enough to be in Protestant neighborhoods. None had any connection to the original shooting that we know of. At some point, the killings take on a life of their own, if you'll excuse the expression."

"How so?"

"So many blood debts build up that it's impossible to keep track of what is a reprisal for what. The Red Hand is a reaction to the IRA actions around Belfast. Most of those are supported from the south, by Clan na Gael funds sent from America. If it wasn't for that support, the IRA might wither and die but instead it gets enough money to keep the fanatics on both sides busy."

I avoided looking at her, not wanting to react to her statement about America. We drove through an intersection with shops and three-story buildings made from the same pink stone as the King David. More cypress trees rose up along the side of the road, creating spindles of shade that fell across the dwellings. An Arab village dotted a hillside, small gray stone buildings with graceful curved openings set among shrubs and trees. It reminded me of my Sunday school lessons.

But it wasn't Bible stories I had on my mind. It was the Browning Automatic Rifle. The BAR M1918A2, is capable of firing three hundred to six hundred and fifty rounds per minute, effective up to six hundred yards. Nearly a third of a mile. Fully loaded, it weighed twenty-one pounds. Not something you'd want to run around with, but a fine weapon to fire from ambush, a specialty of the IRA. This I knew from Uncle Dan, who used to tell me stories of his cousins who fought the British and then the Dublin government in the Irish Civil War. In our family, the heroes always were the antitreaty IRA boys, not the Irish police or army. We grieved for Michael Collins, for all he had been, but agreed it had been best that he'd been killed in ambush on that road in County Cork, by those who could not bear the thought of the northern counties of Ulster ruled by Britain, the Irish nation split in two.

"Do you think the Arabs and Jews will ever live together in peace if the English leave Palestine?" Her question brought me back from thoughts of BARs sending armor-piercing M2 slugs into columns of vehicles as they turned a corner on a narrow country lane. American, British, or Irish—which would be the first target?

"I wouldn't know," I said. "I'm not Arab, Jewish, or British."

"I think they'll slaughter each other," she said in a soft voice as she looked out at the buildings on the hillside, their rock houses blending into the land as if they were natural formations.

"The Red Hand is already slaughtering Catholics," I reminded her.

"Only a few. It would be more if the Royal Ulster Constabulary and the British Army weren't containing them. Can you imagine Northern Ireland if the English gave it up? There would be a bloodbath."

"Churchill did offer to give it up, you said."

"Aye, but he knew de Valera would never accept. The Irish don't want another war so soon after the last ones. Thousands fought in the Great War then lived through the Anglo-Irish War and the Civil War. It was enough."

"But not for you. You're in uniform."

"I have my reasons," she said, leafing through the folder again.

"Where are you from? How did you end up in England?"

"That's not important. You need to focus on where you're going. When you land, someone will meet you and take you to the 5th

Division headquarters in Newcastle. The Ballykinler depot is in their area. They will have been alerted to your arrival and will provide whatever logistical support you need. It's all in your paperwork."

With that, it was all business for the rest of the thirty miles to the RAF air base. She gave me my travel orders, joint ones from U.S. and British commands authorizing my investigation, instructions allowing me to draw supplies and transport, just the sort of paperwork any commanding officer hates to be presented with by a mere lieutenant. I wasn't going to Northern Ireland to make friends.

"Here are copies of reports on the theft from the police and military investigations," she said as she handed me a thick envelope of paperwork when the staff car stopped near a hangar. "The name of the RUC detective you'll be working with is in one of them. You should see him as soon as possible."

"I have to work with an Orangeman?"

"Of course. His name is Hugh Carrick. He's a district inspector in the Royal Ulster Constabulary."

"What do I do if and when I—I mean this Orangeman and I—find the weapons?"

"Don't worry. Major Cosgrove and I will be joining you in a few days. We can organize enough troops to take them back."

"What if they're in the Republic?"

"The Republic of Ireland doesn't want the IRA on the loose with fifty BARs any more than we do."

I took the paperwork, grabbed my pack, and got out of the car. Then I leaned in and tried one more time.

"Sláine, you're asking me to risk my life and possibly betray my countrymen, no matter how misguided they may be. Don't you think you owe it to me to tell me how you came to work for MI-5? Most Irish I know, no matter which side of the fence they're on, would call you a traitor." I waited for the word to take hold, to light a fire hot enough to explode into a reaction. She turned her face to me. It was flushed a bit, but she was a fair-skinned Irish lass in a burning hot climate, so it could have been from the heat.

"And what will they call you, Billy Boyle, when all is said and done?"

CHAPTER ▪ FIVE

I LOST TRACK of the hours, even the day. I had started off in a Bristol Beaufighter, cramped in the single seat behind the pilot, for a short hop to Alexandria, where I switched to an RAF Sunderland Flying Boat to Malta, where it refueled, made another stop at Gibraltar, then began the long flight over the Atlantic, arcing out as far as possible from the German fighter bases along the coast of France.

The Sunderland was like a flying house. It had a wardroom, a small stove, bunks, and even a washroom. I drank, I read, I slept, but mostly I wondered. What was Diana doing now? Had she come to her senses and given up on the SOE mission? Or was she on a ship or a plane somewhere, launched with doubtful chances of survival?

I held an empty mug cupped in my hand, the sweet tea warming my stomach, as I watched the sun rise over the North Atlantic. Gray clouds brightened and I looked for the first sight of land. The sea below was dark and choppy, and I realized this was the stretch of water my grandfather must have steamed across on his way to America, heading west with Ireland at his young back. He'd come to America alone at the age of eleven, the last survivor in his family of the Great Hunger. His uncle, also alone after the death of his entire family, had saved enough to send Granddad Liam off in steerage with a loaf of bread, a few coins in his pocket, and a note pinned to the inside of his jacket.

Did he regret anything he left behind? Did he worry as he watched the waves beneath him, unable to fathom what America might be like? I felt the pull of the familiar as I waited for the unknown to reveal itself. And I missed Diana. It was a pure longing, separate from the fight we'd had, but tangled up in it nonetheless. What I felt was desire for her and an unselfish wish for everything good for her. What I thought, instead of felt, stirred up angry notions of how she'd ruined everything. Did Granddad weep or feel joy, I wondered, as Ireland fell away and the unknown land drew closer?

"Watch off to starboard, Lieutenant," the navigator said as he opened the wardroom door. "We'll make the cliffs of Donegal in a few minutes."

"Thanks," I said, pressing my face against the window as streaks of moisture raced across it. We were descending, beneath the clouds now, where the sunlight shone brightly on the crests of rolling waves. I wondered how my grandfather, crammed into the hold of an old wooden ship, had endured the voyage in steerage, and how many times he'd read that note.

I knew it by heart. When he was alive, he would take it out and read it on his birthday. My dad kept up the tradition, with all the family gathered around. He would remove the paper from the family Bible, where he kept it folded in the book of Exodus. He handled it carefully, afraid that smoothing it out too much would brush away the lines traced by a pencil stub in the middle of the last century. Then he would clear his throat, take a sip of whiskey, and read.

Never forget your name is Liam O'Baoighill, and you were born in County Roscommon. Your father, my dear brother, was named Patrick, your mother Cliona. Never forget the English took our farms and let your parents, brothers, and sisters starve. I know this. I earned your passage working at the Galway docks, loading freighters with sacks of grain, firkins of butter, barrels of barley, sacks of lard, ham, and bacon. British soldiers guarded the ships until they set sail. Such are the men who rule our land. Grow strong in America. You or your sons, or their sons, must one day return to smite them. God indeed gave us the potato blight, but the English gave us this famine.

His accusation and admonition had struck deep in our hearts, and as a child I learned to hate the red-coated British soldiers I conjured up in my mind, bayonets at the ready, guarding food being shipped to England while poor Cliona and her children starved to death.

By the time my father and his two brothers, Frank and Daniel, went off to fight in France in 1917, Granddad was dead. And a good thing too, Uncle Dan always said, that he did not have to suffer the sight of his three boys going off to fight for the English, and only two of them returning, with poor Frank, the oldest, left in a grave on the outskirts of a village called Chateau-Thierry.

Dad and Uncle Dan came home to a hero's welcome, but they never thought it fitting. While they were mustered out, the IRA was fighting the English for a free Ireland, and they felt no elation in having helped England keep its empire. They joined Clan na Gael, raising money for the cause, and taking in IRA men on the run. Some of them, according to the stories, were from the Squad, Michael Collins's assassins who targeted British intelligence officers throughout Ireland.

Uncle Dan's involvement went deeper. When raising money through Clan na Gael wasn't enough for him, he secretly became an IRA man. But it seemed to me that with the IRA, secrets were meant to be bragged about to those you trusted. Uncle Dan came to the house after he'd been sworn in as a member of the North American IRA, and told us all about it. Mom was worried, and said maybe he joined because he didn't have a wife and kids to keep him from storing guns in the cellar and inviting hard men with cloth caps pulled down over their faces to sleep on his couch whenever they pleased. Dad listened, and stayed with Clan na Gael. They both rose in the ranks of the Boston PD, they and their buddies doing what they could for the Cause, turning a blind eye when they needed to. Sláine O'Brien thought this was keeping a wound from healing but in my family, a wrong still demanded righting, a silent hand from the past reminding us of it every year.

For the first time since Granddad's uncle had charged him and his descendants with the duty of smiting the English for their crimes, a Boyle was returning to Ireland. On a British aircraft, working for the British, against the IRA. I hoped Granddad Liam wasn't watching and weeping for what had become of his clan. What would he make of Sláine O'Brien, working for British counterintelligence? What did I make of her? What secrets, if any, drove her to wear the British uniform?

I felt the Sunderland descend and saw the tall, sharp cliffs of Donegal, the sea raging against them. We went lower, and the green fields of Ireland appeared, distant patchworks of foggy emerald that gave me no joy at all. Sunlight danced on lakes, and as we flew over the largest, Lough

Neagh, I saw Belfast to the north, a sprawl of smokestacks and industry fronting the Irish Sea. The plane banked south, headed for a landing in Dundrum Bay, an inlet close to Newcastle, where I was to report to 5th Division headquarters. I shivered as the damp chill seemed to rise from the ground and penetrate the metal skin of the flying boat, and I made a mental note to ditch my tropical khakis for a good thick woolen uniform.

The Sunderland slowed as Dundrum Bay came closer, rushing up at the last second, and finally it *thumped* once, then twice, before settling into the water and easing up on the props until it chugged along, almost quietly, to a long dock built out into the bay. As soon as the engines shut down, a small boat motored out and pulled up to the main hatchway up front. As I got in, an old gray-bearded fellow revved the small engine and headed for the dock.

"Welcome to Ireland," he said. "There's some who are in a hurry for your company."

"I'm a popular guy," I said as I extended my hand. "Billy Boyle."

"Grady O'Brick I am," he said. We shook, and I couldn't help but notice the old man had no fingernails to speak of. The tips of his fingers were thin, with rutted scar tissue where the nails had once been.

"You're Catholic then, by the sound of your name."

"Aye, as are you. You have the look of the altar boy about you. Mind how you go here, lad."

"Where?"

He only nodded toward the dock as he eased up on the motor and gently brought the boat alongside as he leaned close and spoke softly. "If you find yourself in Clough, at the head of the bay, stop in the Lug o' the Tub Pub. Most nights you'll find old Grady there."

I started to climb onto the dock. "Lieutenant Boyle?" The question came from a GI as he offered me a hand.

"That's me," I said. I took his hand and hoisted myself up. The old man was busy tying up his lines and paid me no mind.

The GI was an MP sergeant dressed in a wool overcoat with a white helmet, white leggings, and a white web belt, all bright and gleaming. It wasn't hard to figure out why GIs called MPs snowdrops.

"Sergeant Patterson, sir. I'm here to take you to the Newcastle area."

"OK, Sergeant," I said as we walked off the narrow dock to his jeep. "After I present myself at division HQ, I'll need to find your quartermaster."

"I'm not supposed to take you to headquarters, Lieutenant. The provost marshal himself gave me orders to bring you to him." He took my pack and threw it in the back of the jeep. I pulled my light jacket tight as I climbed in. The canvas cover didn't do much to keep out the chill, which seemed to match my greeting.

"And where is he?"

"Near Newcastle. We're set up in an old factory building. Gives us space for prisoners."

"This provost marshal, is he your CO?"

"No, that's Lieutenant Burnham, he's the CO of the MP Platoon, 5th Division. Captain Heck is the provost marshal in charge of all military police in Ireland."

"Northern Ireland," I said.

"Huh?"

"Patterson, are you Irish?"

"I'm American, Lieutenant. I don't bother much with all that old country stuff."

"OK, but just remember this is Northern Ireland, which belongs to Great Britain. The Republic of Ireland is a free country."

"England's a free country too, ain't it, Lieutenant? Ain't that what we're fighting for?"

"Forget it. Tell me why Captain Heck wants to see me. And what the heck kind of name is that anyway?" I had to laugh at my own joke. Patterson didn't.

"Look, sir, Captain Heck don't like jokes. About anything. And about his name even less."

"What's his first name?"

"Hiram. Hiram Heck." He couldn't keep a straight face. "Beats the heck outta me why he wants to see you." He laughed at his joke, and I was polite enough to join in.

"I can see why he doesn't like to be kidded about his name. Do you know why I'm here, Sergeant?"

"To get your ass chewed out by Captain Heck, Lieutenant. Other than that, no one told me anything."

We drove along a coast road with a beach to our left. A stiff breeze came off it and Patterson pulled on a pair of woolen gloves. I stuck my hands in my armpits and tried not to shiver. Ahead of us mountains loomed in the distance, their peaks hidden by mist and fog. Tucked beneath them, along the curving shore, was a town. The larger buildings featured black slate roofs and orange brickwork, while the smaller homes and shops were painted pastel shades of blue, green, and yellow. Sheep grazed on the fields to our right, each holding enclosed by a gray stone wall. The sea and the land were beautiful, blues and greens as vibrant as the cold sunlight could make them. But it was the mountains that held my eyes. These, I knew from the map of Ireland I'd had pinned to my bedroom wall growing up, were the Mountains of Mourne, the place from which, according to the legends, Saint Patrick had banished snakes from Ireland.

Patterson pulled a hard right and the peaceful scenery gave way to rows of tightly packed houses, some rundown shops, and a junkyard. A few hundred yards beyond them, he turned onto a side road and parked the jeep in front of a cinderblock building with a corrugated tin roof and loading dock off to the side. It looked like the kind of place in which a Boston mobster could take his time fitting a pair of cement overshoes onto an unlucky guest.

"Here we are, Lieutenant. Let's not keep Holy Heck waiting."

IT WAS A big room, and cold. Cold like any concrete-and-cinderblock building in a damp, wet climate, the chill climbing through the soles of your feet while your teeth were performing an echoing chatter. I was tired and grimy, still wearing the same lightweight uniform I'd put on in Jerusalem, and I didn't like being rousted like some criminal and pulled in for questioning. Grady O'Brick's warning played in my mind. Was a guy who had lost his fingernails somewhere along the line worth taking advice from?

Patterson pointed me to the far end of the room, where a small stove gave off a glow. Two officers who stared at me didn't. The guy on the right had to be Captain Hiram Heck. He was hogging the warmth and wore a jeep coat, a warm, wool-lined waterproof garment that was in high demand for cold nights at the front but always seemed to be in short supply until you saw rear-area officers looking important and warm in them. Heck was tall, rail thin but not weak, muscle and bone, not much else. His beak nose traced an arc from his eyebrows to his upper lip. He stood with his hands behind his back, rocking on his heels, his feet encased in highly polished, dark brown paratrooper boots. Behind him stood a lieutenant, a less elegantly dressed straightleg. Burnham, I thought, the MP Platoon leader. Two desks were arranged on either side of the stove, close to the heat. A filing cabinet and a pinup of Veronica Lake completed the furnishings.

"Lieutenant William Boyle reporting, sir," I said as soon as I was close enough to smell his aftershave. I saluted crisply, a proper junior officer. It made Heck respond to me, and I could see it threw him off. He liked that pose of his. He knew his height worked for him, so I got close to show I took no notice.

Heck reluctantly unclasped his hands and tossed off a salute. "At ease, Boyle," he said in a voice that sounded like a rasp on metal. "You look like a bum. What the hell are you dressed for?"

"My apologies, sir. I just traveled from the Mediterranean and haven't drawn supplies yet. I know I look disgraceful, especially to a paratrooper."

Burnham's eyes were ready to pop out. He shook his head in a friendly warning, but I decided it would be more fun *not* to mind how I went.

"What on God's green earth are you talking about, Boyle?"

"You, sir. You must be a paratrooper. Those are jump boots, right? And your trousers are bloused. That's the sign of a paratrooper. At the front, no one except the real McCoy would ever dress like that. Where'd you get your wings, Captain Heck?"

"You get this straight, you pipsqueak," he said, a bony finger prodding my chest. "You shut up about paratroopers and answer my questions, or so help me I'll throw you in the stockade so damn fast your ass will land in there while your shoes are still on the floor. You read me?"

Now I could smell his breath as well as his aftershave.

"Yes, sir. I'm glad to answer any questions. First, though, allow me to extend the thanks of General Eisenhower and the British chief of staff for the assistance you will render me while I am here."

"Eisenhower is in North Africa," Heck snarled. "This is Northern Ireland. I'm the law here."

"As far as drunken GIs and traffic jams go, you are. But, as you say, this is Northern Ireland, British territory. Which is why my orders are also from the British chief of staff." Figuring that Uncle Ike's true location was a military secret, I refrained from informing Heck that Palestine was not part of Africa. Or that my orders, signed by Major

Cosgrove as a representative of General Alan Brooke, chief of the Imperial General Staff, were really from MI-5, and probably worthless if anyone ever checked. I'd been in Ireland about an hour and already I was indulging in evasions and keeping secrets.

"GIs and traffic jams! Jesus Christ, Boyle, who do you think you're talking to? I'm the provost marshal, I run the Criminal Investigation Division. Do you really think you can waltz in here and take over this investigation?"

"What investigation, sir? Pilfering of supplies? Theft of jump boots?" I was surprised Heck knew why I was here. I wouldn't have been surprised if a Brit officer had known, but I doubted that MI-5 informed American MPs or CID agents of their plans. I thought if I could get him to blow his top he might scream before he thought.

"Lieutenant Burnham! Arrest this man," Heck said. He poked his finger at me again, above the sternum, where it hurt. He smiled as he did it.

"What charges, Captain?"

"Disrespect directed against a superior officer. Provoking speech. Put him in a cold cell now." Heck hooked a thumb toward a door, still smiling.

"Sir," Patterson said, "those charges aren't going to make it to court-martial. There are no grounds."

"You may be right, Sergeant. We'll know in two or three months." His grin widened.

"Those jump boots are a violation of Article 83," I said as calmly as I could. "Or 84, I can never remember. Which is it?"

"Both, actually, since those are only issued to paratroop units," Burnham said, his eyes flicking between Heck and me. "If you were a stickler for those things, that is. Wrongful disposition of any military property belonging to the United States: Any soldier who wrongfully disposes of any horse, arms, ammunition, accoutrements, equipment, clothing, or other property issued for use in military service is in violation of the Articles of War."

"I don't have a fucking horse," Heck said, turning on Burnham. "What are you, some jailhouse lawyer?"

I could see Burnham hold back an answer, bite his lip, and straighten up.

"I'm just saying that if Lieutenant Boyle presses the point, we'd be obliged to look into it. Just as we'd have to look into any disrespect charges if you press the point. Sir."

"You want us to hold him, Captain?" Patterson asked, offering him a way to change his mind. I could tell that Heck and these fellows weren't in cahoots. They looked practiced at calming the captain down and keeping him from being his own worst enemy. Much as I appreciated their efforts, I didn't need a calm Heck. I needed Holy Heck so he would spill the beans.

"You want provoking speech, Captain? How about this: I'll bet you don't have a single lead yet. I bet you don't have the contacts around here to know what goes on outside your base. I bet you don't know squat."

"Contacts? How do you think I knew you were landing in Dundrum Bay today? How many people on this island even know you're here, Boyle? Four people, and you're looking at three of them."

"Don't forget Grady O'Brick."

"That crazy old coot? He doesn't even know what day it is, and half of what he says is gibberish. Him and a general out in the desert—that's not much backup, Boyle. You better watch yourself. The IRA or the Red Hand boys might put a bullet in your head." I tried to ignore the heavy-handed threat, and wondered what kind of local contacts Heck might really have.

"So who's the fourth guy?" Silence settled into the space between us as Heck took in two deep breaths, his eyes boring into mine as his frustration rose. He was used to threats and bullying working to his advantage. When they didn't, or when a guy like me was too dumb to be scared by them, he didn't know what to do.

"Get out of my way," Heck said, shoving me as he strode for the door. He opened it and rain slashed at him, drenching his face. The sky beyond him was dark, heavy with clouds, and he looked pleased. "You two remain here. Do not leave your post, do not call for transport for this man. That is an order."

The door slammed behind him. Petty, vindictive orders from a superior officer are a lot easier to take when you've talked your way out of an arrest and a cold cell.

"Looks like I won't be court-martialed," I said, approaching the stove and rubbing my hands to warm up.

"Yet," amended Burnham.

"One or two years of law school?"

"One and a half," he said. "It shows?"

Patterson laughed. "I think he's memorized half of the Articles of War. Have a seat, Lieutenant." We sat around the fire, the cold ebbing as we drew closer, the tension faded from the room.

"You guys not fans of Captain Heck?" I offered.

"He's OK," Burnham said. "Doesn't get in our way too much. This is the 5th Division MP Platoon, not one of his headquarters MP companies. We don't cross paths too often."

"My dad didn't like MPs much in the last war. Always told me they were too damn busy keeping the doughboys from a drink and some fun with the ladies. But then he'd add, every time he said it, that his division MPs were different. They went into the trenches like everyone else, and when a divisional MP spoke, they listened."

"Wise man, your daddy," Patterson said. "Question is, did he raise a wise son?"

"Sometimes I do wonder," I said.

"You made an enemy out of Heck," Burnham said. "You could have let him chew you out and been done with it."

"He already was an enemy," I said. "Otherwise he wouldn't have brought me here. Someone from your division HQ was supposed to meet me, not you guys. I'd bet Heck has someone at headquarters, maybe in the communications section, and they intercepted the message. The real question is, why does Heck give a heck about me?"

"He doesn't tell us his business, Lieutenant Boyle," said Patterson. "We were just detailed to bring you in and stand by."

"Call me Billy. I'm not much for the formalities."

"OK, Billy, I'm Jack, and the law student is Sam Burnham. Now tell us, did Eisenhower really send you all the way up here to look into the BAR heist?"

"I was invited by some British pals of his, and he agreed. They want to be sure the IRA doesn't stir up too much trouble."

"Why you? Are you CID?"

"No. I used to be a cop back in Boston. And I'm Irish. I think a certain British major enjoyed the irony."

"Can't say I've heard much about the IRA around here but we're pretty cut off from the locals. Except for leave and passes off the base, which usually lead straight to a pub, we don't mix much. Not a lot to do around here but drink warm beer," Jack said.

"We know some workers," Sam said. "Carpenters and other trades. Plus manual laborers like Grady. He's a jack-of-all-trades; everyone knows him. Friendly guy, more apt to stop and talk with you than most. But he is a bit off."

"What about the local cops, the Royal Ulster Constabulary?"

"I know the village constable up in Clough. Adrian Simms. Young guy, but the locals like him. We've talked a few fellows out of fights, had some drinks together. That's about it."

"At the Lug o' the Tub Pub?"

"Yeah," said Sam. "You must really be a detective. No wonder Ike sent you."

"Never underestimate an Irishman's ability to find a pub. Have you or Constable Simms heard anything about the BARs? Or the guy who was shot? Mahoney?"

"I heard he was an informer," said Jack.

"Simms told me the pound note in his hand was a sign from the IRA. Death to informers," added Sam.

"Was he from around here?"

"I don't think so," Sam said. "Simms did say he wasn't local. But that could mean he was from Belfast or points south."

"Other than picking me up, has Heck brought your platoon into the investigation?"

"Not at all. Simms asked me the same thing. He was surprised we weren't out searching the countryside the day after it happened."

"What about Heck's CID investigators?"

"They don't do much other than background checks on the locals we hire to work in sensitive security areas."

"Like arms depots."

"Yeah," said Jack. "Maybe one of Heck's boys let an IRA man slip through, and he wants to cover it up."

"Maybe. So who's in charge of the investigation?"

"Major Thomas Thornton, 5th Division executive officer. I've waited for orders, but so far he's been handling it himself, along with some RUC inspector."

"Hugh Carrick?"

"That's him," Jack said. "I met him at HQ a couple of days ago. I asked if we could be of any help, and he said we could, possibly, if we stayed out of his way."

"Sounds like he and I will get along like the Katzenjammer Kids and the Inspector. Now how can I get to 5th Division HQ?"

"What were those orders Heck gave us?" Jack asked.

"Not to leave our post, and not to call for transport," Sam answered.

"We could let you steal a jeep," Jack said, "or you could wait about twenty minutes for the chow wagon to show up. The cooks bring dinner for us and our guests back in the cells. They'll give you a ride into Newcastle. Be a lot less trouble for us."

"Plus, you can grab some Spam and beans before you go," said Sam. "Washed down with our local product, Bushmills Irish whiskey." He pulled open a desk drawer and drew out a three-quarters full bottle.

"God bless the U.S. Army and the Irish," was all I could say.

CHAPTER ▪ SIX

THORNTON HADN'T BEEN on duty when I'd reached 5th Division HQ. Which was just as well, given how much the Spam and beans had needed to be washed down. The cooks had gladly given me a lift, after they'd helped us finish off the bottle. Patterson and Burnham seemed all right. They hadn't tried to pump me for information, and, as they said, they were divisional MPs, with no rear-area investigative duties. I filed them away as possible friends, not because I was certain but because I had so few yet in Ireland.

Headquarters was on the other side of Newcastle, through the seaside town and up a wooded slope beneath Slieve Donard, the highest of the Mourne Mountains. The main building was a long two-story house with a dark gray thatched roof and a covered stone entryway. On either side were rows of Quonset huts, leaving the house a quaint but odd stranger among the invading steel-ribbed prefab huts.

I'd presented my orders to a bored corporal who wasn't at all impressed by the high-ranking names and British military jargon. He had taken one look at me, sniffed, and sensibly told me where I could find the showers, draw new gear, and locate my quarters. I'd managed all three, in the right order, and had even lit a fire in the small stove in my section of the hut. I had gone from lightweight khakis and a small pack to a duffel bag's worth of heavy wool, all courtesy of the division quartermaster who had taken pity on me as I stood shivering at his supply counter, my low ankle-length service shoes drenched and muddy. He had snarled at me when he first saw me, standing there dirtying up his wood floor, but when we both started talking, the Boston accents smoothed things out. He was from Everett, across the Mystic River, not Boston proper, but this far from home, it was like meeting an old neighbor. He'd loaded me down with a tanker jacket, trench coat, plenty of woolen trousers and shirts, mess kit, even a pair of long johns, all the while cursing the constant Irish rain and the major he worked for, saying they were both cold and miserable when they hit the ground in the morning, and that neither was bound to change.

I could vouch for the rain. It came down as a heavy mist, and I was glad of my new boots and thick wool socks as I hunched my shoulders and trotted to the mess tent the next morning. It was crowded with all the usual personnel attached to a headquarters unit. Clerks and typists stood in line with bandsmen and engineers, along with a group of wet and muddy GIs who looked like they'd been out on maneuvers all night. Cooks hustled pots of hot food in from the stoves outside the tent, protected from the rain by smaller open-sided tents.

Lots of guys complain about army food, and when you're eating rations in the field, there's plenty reasons to gripe. But I had to hand it to these cooks, preparing meals for hundreds, sometimes thousands, every day, in the heat or freezing cold. Dozens of loaves of freshly baked bread were set out, trays of hash and scrambled eggs, urns of coffee, all the smells mingling with the damp green earth and lingering scent of cut pine. I saw one of the guys who had brought the chow out last night and waved. We weren't exactly buddies but it felt good to have a few faces to recognize in a strange place.

I loaded my mess plate up with hash and eggs on top of white bread, sugared my black coffee, and found an empty spot on a bench at a table of soaked GIs.

"Night maneuvers?" I asked as I blew on my coffee. Most of them ignored me after a quick glance determined I was a stranger, clean and shaved, and a mere lieutenant to boot. They returned to the hot chow and talk of showers, girls, and beer.

"Up Slieve Donard and down the other side," the guy across from me said, his own lieutenant's bars barely visible through the drying mud on his collar. "Bob Masters, I have the I&R Platoon. You a new transfer?"

"No, just here to see Major Thornton. Billy Boyle's the name."

"Welcome to Donard Wood or at least what's left of it, Billy."

"Thanks," I said, raising my cup in salute. "Intelligence and

Reconnaissance Platoon? What kind of intelligence are you gathering in the Mountains of Mourne?"

"How not to fall off," one joker said, and laughter rippled along the table.

"It *is* a narrow path," Masters said, grinning to let me know it was he who took the tumble. "Mostly it's to build endurance and sharpen night infiltration skills. Recognizing each other in the dark, locating the enemy, that sort of thing."

"Who's the enemy up there?"

"We see the occasional shepherd and other locals. There's not much cover so I usually send a couple of the boys to follow anyone we spot and see how long they can track them."

"How do they do?"

"Damn good. Last week, Searles and Blakefield tracked a guy leading four sheep down the mountain through the Donard Bog, then to a farmhouse in a forest along the Annalong River. A few days later we met a sheepherder who accused us of rustling some of his flock. We told him about the guy and the farmhouse, and last night he thanked us and said he got his sheep back."

"Making the world safe for lamb chops," the wise guy at the end of the table said.

"When we finally get into action, you guys will thank me," Masters said, wagging his fork at them.

"I heard someone lifted a load of BARs from one of your depots. What's the scuttlebutt on that?"

"German agents, the IRA, black marketeers, the Red Hand, you name it, I've heard it. I don't think anyone has a clue. All I know is we were supposed to get one of those BARs."

"Are you short one?"

"No," Masters said. "Thornton had worked the supply system to get an additional complement of Brownings. He wanted the heavy weapons companies to have more firepower. There were a few extra, and one was for us."

"How is Thornton as an exec?"

"Chomping at the bit for a promotion. His only problem is he's too good at staff work."

"Is he investigating the theft?"

"Thornton? I guess so. Why are you so interested? Are you one of Heck's boys?" The air had been full of chatter, friendly ribbing and cursing, but at the mention of Heck's name the sounds faded as all eyes narrowed and turned on me.

"No, I'm not. As a matter of fact, he tried to throw me in jail yesterday." Laughter rose along the benches, and the GI next to me clapped me on the back, saying I must be all right, even for an officer, if Heck couldn't arrest me.

"Heck doesn't have a lot of friends around here," Masters said. "Probably not anywhere, for that matter."

"Why is that, do you think?"

"He wants to get ahead in the army. The only way he knows how is to kiss up to anyone above him and kick down."

"Glad Thornton isn't one of those. I couldn't stand two in a row."

"If you're not with Heck, why are you asking questions about the BARs?"

"I see not much escapes the I&R Platoon."

"Intelligence is our first name," Masters said, tapping his head.

"I am here to look into the theft. At the request of a command higher than Heck. The Brits are nervous about the IRA working with the Germans."

"No wonder Heck tried to toss you in the slammer. You might make him look bad."

"What did you say your name was, Lieutenant?" asked the GI next to me.

"Boyle."

"Mine's Callahan. Funny you didn't say anything about the Brits being nervous about the Red Hand. With a name like Boyle, I mean."

"The thought has occurred to me, Callahan. But the Red Hand isn't likely to be in league with the Germans."

"No, they don't need the Nazis. They have the English."

"OK, Callahan, can it," Masters said. "Remember the lecture. We're guests in this country. Guests don't discuss religion or politics."

"Kinda leaves us speechless around these parts, Lieutenant."

"*Erin go bragh*," I stage-whispered to Callahan as I got up.

"Go get our BARs, Billy," Masters said. "Good luck."

"I'll do my best," I said as I waved to the group and left to clean out my mess kit.

I liked Masters and his easy way with his men, and how he pushed them beyond regular training to prepare them. An I&R platoon was likely to be sticking its neck out far into enemy territory, and I could see how even one more BAR could make a difference in giving covering fire when they needed to skedaddle. What I didn't like was Callahan reminding me of everything I thought was wrong with this assignment. I wondered if I would still be sitting in a Jerusalem hotel arguing with Diana if it had been clear that it was the Red Hand who had stolen the Brownings. Would MI-5 be as worried if those weapons were aimed at the Catholic minority in Northern Ireland? Especially if they might be used against the IRA active in Ulster?

Erin go bragh, I thought as I wiped down my kit. Ireland forever. Except it wasn't true. How could it be, with six of the Ulster counties still ruled by England? What would it be like if the English had held on to New England at the end of the Revolutionary War? Would we have accepted that, said it was enough, and abandoned six states to be ruled by our former masters?

Liam O'Baoighill had left this island with a note pinned to his coat, charging his descendents with revenge upon the English for what they had done to his family. O'Baoighill was the Gaelic spelling of O'Boyle. We'd dropped the *O* along the way and become Boyles, making our way in the new world while forgetting the worst of the old and remembering the best as if it were everything that had ever happened. Now I was back.

It was a helluva war.

CHAPTER ▪ SEVEN

"AT EASE, BOYLE."

Major Thomas Thornton had been at a desk too long. He had soft, pudgy cheeks and red-rimmed eyes with dark bags beneath them. He wore a mustache, which suited him, and had his black hair slicked back with too much Brylcreem, which didn't. His ashtray was already half full of ground-out butts, and he shifted uncomfortably in his chair as he read through my orders, spitting a bit of stray tobacco onto his desk, where it landed, a tiny brown speck lost amid a pile of requisitions, files, manuals, and all the tools of a division's executive officer. In the corner behind him, three cases of Jameson Irish whiskey were neatly stacked. Liquor was also a tool of the trade, bartering and smoothing the way for whatever your commanding officer needed.

"Ike and the British chief of staff? Jesus Christ, Boyle, you move in exalted circles. Are you any good? Can you find my BARs?"

"I don't exactly move in those circles, Major. I just go where they tell me."

"Sit down, sit down," Thornton said, as if that was something I should have taken for granted. He waved his hand toward a chair and I pulled it up to his desk. "I want my goddamn BARs back, Boyle."

"Yes, sir. Can you fill me in on what you've come up with? I have the police report from the RUC and an initial report from the provost marshal but nothing from this command."

"Listen, Boyle, do you have any idea what kind of workload an XO has? I don't have time for reports in triplicate. I'm spending every waking moment getting this division ready for combat. It doesn't take a genius to figure out we're positioned for the invasion, whenever and wherever that comes."

"Probably right, sir. All the divisions that were here in '42 ended up in Operation Torch."

"Goddamn right. While they were invading North Africa we were pulling occupation duty in Iceland. Iceland, Boyle! You know why they call it Iceland?"

"Because it's cold?"

"Cold and dark, and too much damned ice. Except in the summer, when it's light twenty-four hours a day so you can't sleep. I was sent there in 1941 with the first units of this division. I've been pushing paper and freezing my ass for two years, and I don't intend to keep it up for the rest of the war. Iceland makes Ireland look like Miami Beach."

"The BARs, sir?"

"OK, OK. Sorry to unload on you. The project to build up our weapons companies was all mine, and now these fucking Irish have gone and screwed it up. Goddamn it!" He threw down his pencil like a knife; the lead broke and left a piece stuck in a stack of papers. His face was red and a vein pulsed in his forehead.

"You know, sir, I saw plenty of division staff in North Africa. They were all pretty close to the front. It won't be like you're missing out on anything if you stay in this job," I said, trying to ease Thornton's frustration. He seemed to be banking on his ideas about added firepower to get him out from behind his desk.

"Thanks, Boyle." He brushed the piece of lead from the papers and then neatened up the stack, glanced at it, and put it away in a desk drawer. He seemed to lose track of the conversation and looked at me quizzically.

"The investigation?"

"OK, OK. Between butting heads with Heck and everything else I have to do, I haven't had much time for playing detective. You know about Jenkins, right?"

"Andrew Jenkins, head of the local Red Hands, and he supplies the base with produce, right?"

"Right. He buys stuff from all the farmers in the area and sells it to the army. Potatoes, whatever the hell they grow around here. Whiskey, ham, fresh eggs, all sorts of stuff for the officers' messes."

"Besides his truck being used, do you have any evidence of his involvement?"

"Evidence? No. Except that I know he'd do anything to hit the IRA. I wouldn't put it past him."

"Why do you say that?"

"I can tell," Thornton said, as he tapped the broken pencil on his desk. "I can tell when a man wants something, something larger than himself. Something grand. Do you know what I mean?"

"Yes, I do. I've seen it," I said, knowing what he meant. Combat, glory, promotion. "It's not grand at all. But you won't believe me until you've seen it yourself."

"Why?" For the first time in our conversation, Thornton seemed to relax and actually listen, genuinely curious about what I had to say.

"Because I wouldn't have."

"Yeah, that's the hell of it, isn't it?"

"Sure is."

Thornton looked at the broken pencil for a while, then sighed and tossed it into the wastepaper basket. He drummed his fingers on his desk, his frustrated energy keeping his body moving even while seated. I sat, the visions of that thing, the unknowable, the unimaginable, flowing through my mind. It wasn't grand at all, I had told the truth about that. It was gruesome and dirty, painful and demeaning, but at times—especially when you realized you were alive and had cheated death—there was something grand *about* it, something around the edges, in the light of explosions in the distance, the loud thuds of artillery, the rush of adrenaline, the eerie calm in the midst of a fight when time slowed and everything crackled with crystal clarity. There was grandness in the confusion I felt then, the feeling of wishing I could erase it all from my mind while knowing that it was the most significant, important, otherworldly thing I'd ever experienced. Sometimes I wondered if there was something holy in it all, as if I could almost see the best of creation in the midst of the worst of it.

"There's one more thing," he said. "Mahoney—the dead guy with the money in his hand? Well, I'd seen him before. He looked a bit different then, with his brains all inside his skull, but I saw him drinking in a pub in Annalong, a little south of here."

"When was this?"

"The Sunday before the theft. I had to get out of here for a while, so I drove down the coast road and ended up in Annalong. There's a place, the Harbor Bar, right on the water, where I stopped and got something to eat and had a few pints. I noticed him because he was arguing with someone—quietly, but you could tell it was heated by the way they strained to keep their voices down."

"Would you know the other man if you saw him?"

"No, his back was to me, and he had a cap on. But as soon as I saw the red hair on the corpse, I recognized him. Bright orange, like a carrot. That was Mahoney."

"OK, that's something."

"I told Heck and Inspector Carrick about it, you can check with them."

"Yeah, I will. Anything else you remember?"

"Nope. Now tell me what you need to find my BARs."

"Transport. I'll need a jeep. And if I need some muscle, can I call on your MPs? I met Burnham and Patterson yesterday. They seem pretty capable."

"They're good men. I'll let them know you may be in touch. But go through me. I need to be kept up to date. Check in with me every day." He scribbled out an order for a jeep and a pass to all 5th Division installations and handed them to me. "Motor pool is out and to the left. Follow the lane through the trees, about a quarter mile. Need a ride?"

"No, sir. But one more thing. Can you tell me who received the radio dispatch about my arrival?"

"I never saw one. Northern Ireland Command told me to expect you any day now but I never heard when or how you were coming."

"Then I'd like to start at your Signals Company, talk to whoever was on duty yesterday."

"Is there a problem?"

"No, strictly routine."

He eyed me for a few seconds, then lifted his telephone and made a call.

Ten minutes later I was in a Quonset hut crammed with radios and noisy with the static and tinny crackling sounds of communications gear. A technical sergeant named Lasner leafed through clipboards of dispatch sheets, all the documentation for signals sent and received. Below his sergeant's stripes were two service stripes, meaning he'd been in more than six years. A regular, and it showed in everything from the shine on his boots to the gleaming brass Signal Corps emblem on his tunic's lapels. There were six clipboards, all neatly arranged on a table with wire baskets where the forms were deposited when received.

"Nothing here with your name on it, Lieutenant Boyle," he said as he finished with the last clipboard.

"It wasn't for me, Sarge."

"I understand that, Lieutenant. I mean there are no messages here that include your name. Anywhere."

"Got it. Looks like you run a tight ship."

"Yes, sir. Anything else, Lieutenant?" I could tell he was eager to get rid of me but then again most noncoms would be eager to get a second louie out of their hair, especially if he was from another outfit and was making extra work for them.

"Are all these receipts for messages received? If a message came into Northern Ireland Command HQ to be passed on to you, would they have the same kind of documents?"

"They ought to. And sent, as well. But if I don't have a record of it coming in, they didn't send it."

"I can believe it, Sarge. Everything looks fine on your end."

"Is there a problem, if you don't mind me asking?"

"You know Captain Heck, the provost marshal?"

"Know of him," Lasner said, his tone carefully neutral.

"I think he intercepted a message meant for Major Thornton about my arrival here. Sound likely to you?"

"From what I hear, he'd be careful to cover his tracks. Not that I'm accusing the provost marshal of anything."

"That would mean he had someone working for him at HQ."

"Let's just say I've heard Heck will do you a favor if you find yourself at the wrong end of an MP's nightstick. Only problem is, once he's got you over a barrel, the favors have to keep coming."

"So he'll withhold charges for a price?"

"He doesn't take money, if that's what you mean. He's always looking for an angle, so he'd rather have information. He's smart, Lieutenant. Watch yourself around him."

"You're not the first to warn me. If that's his game, and he's so slick, how can you be certain it wasn't one of your men here who killed the message to Thornton and gave it to Heck?"

"I know my men. I trained them all, and they know what would happen if they pulled something like that." There was a hard look in his eyes, a combination of resentment that I'd asked the question and fury at the thought of such betrayal.

"How about your captain?"

"I couldn't imagine it. Besides, he doesn't spend a lot of time here."

"He lets you run the show?"

"The captain wisely delegates responsibility. I think he's been in Belfast for the last few days."

"Doing what?"

"Whatever it is that officers do while the work gets done, Lieutenant."

"Understood, Sarge. One more question, though. You know anything about the BARs stolen from the depot at Ballykinler?"

"Only that Major Thornton is mightily pissed off about it. Heck has been nosing around asking a lot of questions too, looking through stacks of shipping receipts, bills of lading, making himself a real pain. Every time he shows up, it takes us a day to put the place back together. You investigating that?"

"Yeah. And I'm not working for Heck, to answer your next question. Any rumors about who was in on the heist?"

"A million of them, but I won't waste your time. Hang on, there is something here." He flipped back through the message receipts until he found what he was looking for. "I guess it's OK to give you this, since Major Thornton said I should help you out. Or did he already tell you?"

"Tell me what?"

"Here. This message came in yesterday morning from some inspector from the Royal Ulster Constabulary. Local flatfoots investigating the heist. Inspector Carrick asked the major for service records for Sergeant Peter Brennan." He handed me a copy of the message form.

"Who's that?"

"Pete's a buck sergeant at the Ballykinler Depot."

"You know him? What kind of guy is he?"

"We're not pals but he seems OK. He's been with us about six months now."

"Thanks, Sarge, you've been a big help. Can I have this?"

"Sure. I've got another, we do them in triplicate."

"God bless army paperwork."

"So who do you work for, Lieutenant, if you're not part of the provost marshal's office?"

"I'm here at the request of the British."

"Well, you know what they say. It takes a thief."

"What do you mean by that?"

"That the English are pretty savvy, sending an Irishman. Boyle—that's Irish, right?"

"We're not all thieves, Sergeant," I said in my best stern disciplinarian officer's voice.

"Sorry, sir. No offense intended. It's just a saying."

It takes a thief to catch a thief. I never believed that saying. In my book, it took a cop to catch a thief, and that's what I was. A cop on loan, courtesy of my Uncle Ike, who even now might be writing love notes to the beautiful Kay Summersby. Another Irish thief, this one out to steal a general's heart. Or was it an inside job?

CHAPTER ▪ EIGHT

I THOUGHT ABOUT asking Thornton why he hadn't mentioned the request for Brennan's files. If Brennan was a suspect in the eyes of the Royal Ulster Constabulary, I shouldn't waste a minute before I talked to him. I could always find Thornton later, but if an Ulster cop was interested in a guy named Brennan, then I figured I had better get to him first.

I drove the jeep out of the headquarters camp, splashing through water in muddy potholes as shafts of sunlight split the gray clouds drifting out over the Irish Sea. Thick, green grass grew along the sides of the boreen on the wooded hillside, which descended to the main road running along the coastline. The wet ground smelled fertile, the warmth drawing out odors of loam, pine, and sheep dung as a breeze from the sea salted the air. Gray stone cottages dotted emerald fields encompassed by stone walls, every rock the same uniform color and size, as if they came out of the ground ready-made for building fences and thick cottage walls. I squinted my eyes against the welcome sun as I caught the smell of smoke from a house close to the narrow road. It wasn't wood smoke, I was sure. It was more of a musty, green leaf smell, and I realized it must be peat. There wasn't a tree thicker than my arm in sight, and except for the small pine forest I'd left, there had hardly been any trees anywhere I'd passed. Another reminder that even though this country looked and felt familiar, far more familiar than North Africa or Sicily, it was still a foreign land, a land of strange habits and ancient hatreds, a place my ancestors had come from and of which I knew little but fables and stories.

Brennan was an Irish name, a Catholic name. Not that there weren't Irish Protestants, and a few who weren't pro-British—the IRA even had some Protestant members—but historically, the Irish were Catholic, and religion had been a weapon used against them for hundreds of years. The only reason any Protestant was in Ireland now was because the English had sent them here generations ago, to rule the land by taking it away from the natives, who all happened to be Catholic. The British had called them papists, and passed laws eliminating all rights to land and life. Those laws were now gone but the memory of them hung in the air that every Protestant and Catholic on this island breathed, reminding them of the wars, wrongs, and oppressions their people had borne. So a Brennan suspected by a Carrick of any crime here could expect little sympathy and less justice. The RUC wouldn't have jurisdiction on a U.S. Army base, but if Brennan was a suspect and went into town for a drink at the wrong local pub, he could disappear out the back door faster than you could say Red Hand.

The road to Ballykinler took me back through the town of Newcastle, past the railroad station at the edge of town, as its brick clock tower chimed eleven. I turned inland, skirting the bay where I'd landed in the seaplane, then headed through the small village of Clough, where I saw the Lug o' the Tub Pub, the joint where Grady O'Brick spent most evenings, and where I hoped to have a chat with the old man tonight. From Clough, the land rose up, a small plateau with views of the Mourne Mountains across the bay to the south and the Irish Sea to the east. The U.S. Army depot was at the highest point, a flat, windswept stretch of land enclosed in barbed wire. Thornton's pass got me in without a question, and I followed signs for the Ordnance Depot, navigating through muddy lanes between rows of long barracks buildings. GIs were everywhere, doing calisthenics and close order drill, whitewashing rocks to serve as path markers, all the usual chickenshit routine of army life.

The Ordnance Depot was at the center of the camp, surrounded by its own barbed wire fence. Two guards stood at this gate; they scrutinized my papers much more carefully than the guards at the main gate had. I looked at the fence; the wood posts were new, fresh cut. The earth was still turned over where the postholes had been dug. Somebody had learned something from all this.

"Go on in, sir," a corporal said after he checked my ID against my face. "The lieutenant is expecting you."

"Is he?" I said, and drove to a small parking area at the end of a long wooden building. It was sturdier than the others, built on a stone foundation, and twice as wide. At the far end was a loading dock and room for trucks to back up. Easy access, or at least it had been.

"Lieutenant Boyle?" The voice came from the doorway, where a tall, thin fellow wearing the silver bars of a first lieutenant stood, slightly stooped to fit within the door frame.

"That's me," I said as I got out of the jeep. "I heard you were expecting me."

"Major Thornton is eager to have this mess cleared up," he said as he held the door open for me.

"I know. He wants his BARs back, Lieutenant . . . ?"

"Jacobson, Saul Jacobson. Come on in."

I followed him into his office through a room of small desks, big filing cabinets, and four clerks running between them, beating on typewriters and stacking forms. He shut the door behind me, not that the plywood divider would do much for privacy. His desk was a table stacked with papers, bearing in and out baskets and two telephones. Half a dozen clipboards, marked with dates, hung on the wall behind him.

"How long have you been in charge here, Lieutenant Jacobson?"

"Call me Saul, OK? We're just a couple of lieutenants here, aren't we?"

"Sure. I'm Billy. You're a first lieutenant, though. I didn't know if you were a stickler for the formalities of rank." He didn't seem to be. His face was friendly and open, his dark eyes darting at the documents on his desk, then to me, giving me his attention while still drawn to his tasks.

"Hardly. These are brand-new," he said, tapping his silver bars with his long fingers. "Got promoted when Thornton transferred me here. I was a lowly second louie like you, personnel officer for the regiment. Then they lifted the BARs, and suddenly there was an opening here."

"Where's the previous officer in charge?"

"Beats me. Busted to private, shipped out. Italy, some say. Others say back to the States. Hard to say which is worse."

"It is? Why?" I asked.

"Stan Hayes was a good man. *Is* a good man, I should say. It would break his heart to have come this far and not get into the fight."

"It might do worse to his heart if he's in it. Italy is pretty rough."

"You know for a fact?"

"I've been there," I said, and let the silence fill in the gap between us. Personally, I hoped Private Stan Hayes was peeling potatoes state-side somewhere, where he could grow to be an old man reminiscing about how he'd missed the big show. But I knew it was probably eating at him, and he'd be thinking his life was over, when in fact it had likely been saved.

"In any case," Saul said, glancing through the papers on his desk, "he's gone." He picked up a folder, then put it down. His hands were smooth and clean, his nails filed evenly. He might have been a year or two younger than me but he'd probably look a lot older real quick after dodging bullets and shrapnel.

"Yeah, just what I like to find when I'm investigating a week-old crime. One of the key people whisked out of the country."

"No one thought he had anything to do with it," Saul said.

"Maybe not, but that doesn't mean he didn't know something or that he hadn't noticed something odd before the theft, something he might not even have realized. Now I'll have to go back to Italy or state-side to find him. One is undesirable, the other impossible."

"All I can tell you is that he thought he was being made the scape-goat, being blamed for lax security. You and I know that responsibility goes higher than a lieutenant's rank."

"It doesn't reach too high either, from my experience. I'm sure everyone from the rank of major on up was glad to see him gone."

"You mean Major Thornton?"

"You tell me," I said.

"No, I don't see it that way. Thornton's not that kind of guy."

"You said it was Thornton who transferred you here."

"And promoted me, yeah, but that's not why I said that."

"OK, OK," I said. "No offense meant, just asking questions."

"I guess that's your job. It is, isn't it? Thornton said you were sent by the Allied High Command." Saul sounded impressed, which was good, since I wanted his cooperation.

"Yes. The British especially are nervous about the IRA working with the Germans. This arms theft could mean something is in the works."

"Let me know what I can do to help."

"First tell me if you've heard or seen anything outside the ordinary. Any rumors about who was involved, scuttlebutt of any kind?"

"Of every kind," he said. "That the people who took the BARs were German agents, for one. That two GIs were found shot in

Downpatrick and .30 caliber shell casings were found nearby. That an RUC car was shot up in Banbridge, that a farmer outside of Clough was seen shooting rabbits with a BAR, that a German sub came into the bay and landed commandos. You want more?"

"No. I suppose there's nothing to any of those rumors?"

"Well, I can't say for certain it wasn't German agents who broke in here. As for the rest, I'm pretty sure not."

"OK. Show me around, then I'd like to talk to Sergeant Brennan. I assume he's still here?"

"Pete? Yeah. He's one of our best ordnance guys. He's hasn't been here long, but he's a hard worker. Doesn't mix with the other men much. He does his job and spends a lot of time down on the beach, staring at the waves."

"The base goes all the way to the coast?"

"Yeah. The locals call the beach Tyrella. Nice stretch of sand. Our fences go down to the water but the beach is open to personnel."

"Is that where the German sub was sighted?"

"No, that was in Newcastle Harbor, after a few pints, I think. Come on, I'll show you around and we'll see if we can find Brennan."

"Why is he such a loner, do you suppose?" I asked as I followed Saul out of his office.

"Couldn't say. He does his job, so I don't see any reason to force him to be chummy with the guys."

"Is he fresh from the States or another unit here in Ireland?"

"Neither. He was wounded in Italy, at Salerno. After he recovered, they sent him here."

I followed Saul out of the building, wondering what had happened to Brennan at Salerno, but knowing that the details didn't matter. Salerno had happened. In his fresh-faced world, through no real fault of his own, Saul couldn't make the connection. God bless him for it then. His time would come.

"This was all one big parking area," he said, gesturing at the fence in front of the building. "Any vehicle could drive right up to the depot."

"Was the fence your idea?"

"Yes, and the guards as well. We also locked a side door. Now the only way in is through the office, which is in clear sight of the guards. And we have one guard on the loading dock at all times."

"What about before, when Stan was in charge?" I asked as I followed Saul to the other end of the building, about thirty yards.

"Hey, it wasn't Stan's fault! No one gave it a second thought; the depot is right in the middle of a military base, for crying out loud. We have most of the 11th Regiment here, we're surrounded by GIs."

"OK, I get the point. Just tell me what the procedures were."

"No fence, no guards. Pretty much anyone could enter the building, although any locals would have been stopped. To draw any supplies, you'd need a signed requisition. We have men on duty around the clock, in the arms storage areas and ordnance repair shop."

We entered through the loading dock, which opened into a wide area for temporary storage of items coming in and out of the building. Behind it, through a narrow hallway, was the ordnance repair shop. Workbenches ran along each wall, and every type of small arms imaginable was stacked everywhere, in various stages of disassembly. Rifles, machine guns, and mortars, along with pistols hung from their trigger guards from hooks on the wall. Two GIs in oil-stained coveralls greeted the lieutenant and went back to their work.

"Brennan around?" he asked.

"Said he was goin' to the beach coupla hours ago," one of them said. "He got that MG42 workin' 'fore he took off."

"Why do you have a German machine gun?" I asked.

"Familiarization," Saul answered. "Another one of Thornton's ideas. We have some British weapons as well, and we run everyone through a familiarization course, so they can recognize the sound of each weapon, and understand basic operation."

"Believe me, you don't need a course to recognize one of these," I said, laying my hand on the smooth black metal, so dark it almost absorbed the light around it. It felt cold, as cold as a corpse. "It fires so fast you can't even hear the individual shots. It sounds like ripping cloth, one long, long piece of fabric being torn. Or a chain saw, some people say. The Germans call it the Bonesaw, with good reason."

I closed my eyes and heard it, and jerked my hand away as if the gun barrel were smoking hot. I saw Saul and the two GIs staring at me, and I couldn't escape the sensation of a spray of blood against my face. I knew it wasn't happening. But it had happened, the last time I heard the Bonesaw at work.

"Come on," I said to Saul, sorry that they'd caught a glimpse of things to come, and desperately trying not to rub the blood from my face. I took some deep breaths and walked away from the MG42.

Saul led me into the cellar. Boxes of ammunition were stacked chest-high around us, and crates of M1 carbines stood along the walls. A bright red sign proclaimed No SMOKING next to a poster cautioning that careless talk costs lives. Or BARs. Another, more faded poster looked like a leftover from the last war. John Bull, his big belly tucked into a union jack vest, standing in front of a line of British soldiers, asking, WHO'S ABSENT, IS IT YOU?

"They came down these steps, right to where the BARs were," Saul said.

"How do you know that?" I asked.

"It had been raining all day. Stan told me there were muddy boot prints from the loading dock, straight to the cellar and right to the crated BARs. Besides the ammo, they didn't take anything else."

"It must have been tempting but they had to get out fast and hide the stuff," I said, half to myself. "How long do you think it took them?"

"Assuming no more than two or three guys, I'd say twenty minutes. Half hour tops."

"Who was on duty?"

"Sergeant Brennan. He was in the office, said he never heard a thing."

"Is that likely? He wouldn't notice a truck pulling up?"

"Probably not. Remember, there was no fence, no gate around the place, and it was dark. They must have come in from the opposite direction, backed up to the loading dock, and broken in."

"How'd they do it? I assume the door was locked."

"It was. They popped the hinges. It wasn't hard; this building wasn't designed as a bank."

"And Brennan heard nothing?"

"It was raining to beat the band, Billy. It was windy too. I can believe it. And night duty didn't mean anything other than being ready if a call came in for something. No one ever thought we needed guards in the middle of the camp."

"Do you know if anyone checked the boot prints?"

"For what?"

"Never mind." Maybe Carrick had. Saul didn't have a suspicious nature, that much was clear. The first thing I would have done was see if any of the boot prints had a GI tread.

I scanned the room in back of the stairway. Another faded, yellowing poster was nailed to the side of a shelf. BRITISHERS, ENLIST TODAY!

"Obviously this was an English base in the last war," I said.

"Yeah, I think a lot of the local units went through here. They have some sort of militia or something."

"The Ulster Volunteer Force," I said, remembering Uncle Dan talking about the Covenant, the document many Protestants signed in their own blood, vowing to resist Home Rule for Ireland if it was granted. The UVF was formed to be ready to fight to keep Ulster British, but they didn't have to. UVF units signed up to fight in France, and this would have been where they would have been trained and turned into real soldiers.

"Something like that. I think Inspector Carrick said he'd been in the first war. Maybe he'd been through Ballykinler back then."

"Maybe," I said. "Maybe he knows the place very well." Had he signed the Covenant in his own blood? For the first time I thought about the assumption that the IRA had been behind the theft. It was fair enough, since an IRA man had been found dead nearby, but that raised the issue of who had killed him. The IRA, because he was an informer? Or the Red Hand, to confuse things?

"I'm going to the beach," I said, hoping the salt air would clear my head of the swirling suspicions and mistrust that seemed to spring from the soil of Northern Ireland.

CHAPTER ▪ NINE

TUFTS OF GRASS bent away from the sea as the breeze freshened and blew gray sand against my boots. I pulled my garrison cap down tighter and trudged across the wide dunes, watching the clouds that covered the peaks of the Mountains of Mourne in the distance. A single aircraft droned out over the Irish Sea, but other than that faint noise and the rhythmic crashing of waves, it was quiet. I moved out of the dunes and onto the beach, looking both ways for a sign of Brennan. In the distance, to my right, I saw a figure seated on a driftwood log and figured that had to be him. As I walked in his direction, I noticed how peaceful this place was, how far from the camp filled with marching men, how calming the water was with the sound of smooth stones being pulled back in the surf, and realized that I hadn't thought of beaches that way in a long time. They had become beachheads, bristling with machine guns, blood-soaked obstacles to be overcome, no longer places for solitary meditation. What did Brennan think about out here? The Germans at Salerno? The next beach the 5th Division would hit, maybe the big invasion everyone was talking about? Or did he think about where those BARs had gone to?

As I drew close, I started to call out, but stopped when I heard him speak. He was holding something in his hand, and it seemed like he was talking to it. There was no one else around. I took a few more quiet steps, and stopped.

"Now, Pig, you know that the one who gets me gets you. So you do your part, and I'll do mine. OK, Pig? That last one wasn't for either of us, and the next one won't be either. OK?" He held a small carved wooden pig in one hand and rubbed its belly with the thumb of the other. He stared at it, as if waiting for an answer.

"That sounds like one lucky pig, Sergeant Brennan."

He rolled off the log, falling behind it and reaching for a .45 automatic in a shoulder holster. His eyes were wide in panic.

"Hold on, hold on!" I hollered, my hands outstretched. I had my own .45 by my side and I didn't want him getting the wrong idea. He grunted, an exasperated, somewhat embarrassed look on his face.

"Jesus Christ, why'd you go and sneak up on me like that?" Brennan said. He let out a breath and gulped air into his lungs. His hand moved away from the pistol as he glanced at my lieutenant's bars. "Sir."

"I didn't sneak, I walked up. And you were deep in conversation."

"It's not a conversation. Pig doesn't talk back to me, I'm not crazy." He got back up on the log, and I joined him. He unclenched his fist, and there sat Pig, his belly smooth where Brennan had been rubbing it.

"Pig?"

"I got him onboard a troop transport from a gob who carved all sorts of animals. We have pigs at home and I like them, so I bought him."

"How'd he get so lucky?"

"You pulling my leg, sir?"

"No, I'm not. I've seen plenty of guys with good luck charms. Once you find one, you keep it. I knew a guy who had a book of matches in his pocket when the truck he was in hit a mine. He was the only one in the truck who lived, and he was convinced those matches did it. He never went anywhere without them after that. He even gave up cigarettes so he wouldn't be tempted to use them."

"Where was this guy?"

"North Africa."

"You been in combat, Lieutenant?"

"Some. How about you?" He didn't answer right away. He blew sand from a few spots where it had stuck to Pig, rubbed the animal some more, and put it in his shirt pocket, over his heart. We watched the waves curl and crash onto the shore as he pulled a pack of Luckies from his jacket. He offered me one and I declined. He flicked a battered Zippo and shielded the flame with his hand. When he lit up, he cupped the cigarette in his hand, like you would at night, in your foxhole.

"They said it was going to be easy," he began. "The Italians had just surrendered. Our officers said the beaches didn't need a preliminary bombardment, that we'd just stroll ashore. So all those big naval guns sat quiet. It was going to be easy."

"It wasn't," I said.

"No, it wasn't. Mortars and machine guns hit us as soon as the landing craft dropped its ramp and took out half the guys, everyone up front. We had to step over the bodies to get out. Then the machine guns really started up. I was the only guy to get to shore alive. Just me and Pig. There was no one else to talk to, no one else close by that I even recognized. I was scared, so I started telling Pig that nothing was going to happen to us there, more to convince myself than anything else. There was so much machine-gun fire, their tracer rounds hit my pack and it started to burn. You couldn't even lift your head up off the ground. But they didn't kill me. So I kept on talking to Pig every day. I'd tell him to watch out, to do his part, because if I went, so did he."

"It worked?"

"For ten days. We got hit hard by them Germans. They were on the high ground all around us. Seemed like the only way we had to attack was up. They had lots of tanks, too goddamn many tanks. They counterattacked one morning and them Panzer Grenadiers infiltrated our rear area. Tanks out front, Jerries behind us, mortars everywhere. I couldn't even talk to Pig, it was so loud with those 88s slamming into us. Next thing I knew, there was an explosion, some kind of fireball. My back was filled with shrapnel, they told me. I ended up in a hospital in England. When I recovered, they transferred me here. Didn't matter much to me, my buddies are all dead."

"So you came to Ireland with Pig."

"Yeah, I managed to hang on to him. I haven't missed a day since. I figure if he makes it, I make it. Sound nuts to you, Lieutenant?"

"It might, in polite society. But that's not where we are, is it?"

"Hardly. Say, how did you know my name, Lieutenant? Why are you here?"

"The name's Billy Boyle. I came here to look into that arms theft last week. I have a few questions for you."

"Are you with Captain Heck?"

"Everybody asks me that, in a sort of worried tone. Why is that?"

"I dunno, cops make people nervous, don't they?"

"Well, that depends. Some people like cops; they feel more secure with them around."

"Military police? Belfast police? You said your name was Boyle, didn't you?"

"That I did," I said, letting a bit of the brogue roll into my voice. "Is that why you're going around armed? Not many people wear a piece around here when they're off duty."

"Makes me feel safe. Sort of like having my own personal cop around. You're a cop, aren't you?"

"Was, back in Boston. Which is why they asked me to look into this. And I don't work for Heck."

"Didn't think so. He's put me through the wringer, him and that Carrick guy."

"If you're not in the stockade they must think you weren't involved."

"There's barbed wire all around this place if you haven't noticed. What questions do you have?"

"Was Lieutenant Hayes lax on security?"

"Hell no, he was a good ordnance man. He knew his stuff. I was glad when I got transferred to the Ordnance Depot. I spent my first two weeks here working in the mess hall, and let me tell you, I was glad to get off that detail."

"I bet," I said. "How does Lieutenant Jacobson compare to Hayes?"

"Saul is all right, he runs the place OK, but he doesn't know weapons like Stan did. They needed a scapegoat, and Stan was their choice. Protected everyone else. There hadn't been any security orders for the arms depot. Just like there aren't any for the motor pool. We're inside an army base, for Christ's sake."

"Makes sense. What about that night? You had no idea what was going on?"

"None. I was at the opposite end of the building. It was raining sideways, and with all that noise and wind it would have been impossible to hear anything. I did notice the truck driving away, though. It switched on its headlights, which I thought was odd. That's when I went in the back and saw the door had been forced open."

"I suppose you called Lieutenant Hayes?"

"First I tried to call the main gate, to stop the truck. But they'd cut the telephone wires. I couldn't get anyone. By the time I roused Stan, they were long gone."

"What time was this?"

"Close to midnight."

"Any idea who was behind it? Any rumors floating around?"

"None that make any sense. Everyone seems convinced it was the IRA."

"You're not?"

"Well, they used Jenkins's truck, right? And he's big with the Red Hand boys around here. Now that would be a slap in the face to the Protestants, wouldn't it?"

"Yeah, if that's why they did it. But he had access to the post, he made regular deliveries here, so it makes sense to grab one of his vehicles."

"No, you don't understand. Do you know your Irish history, Lieutenant?"

"It's a fairly big deal in my family."

"Mine too. So think about this. The IRA steals a vehicle from the leader of the Red Hand and uses it to steal automatic weapons, adding insult to injury. What would Jenkins's first reaction be?"

"Retribution," I said, as I began to see what Brennan meant.

"You are a cop! And as an Irish cop, you'd know that any Catholic would do, IRA member or not."

"Have there been any reprisals? Retaliation of any kind?"

"Not against Catholics by Protestant militia. The IRA shot a Belfast cop a couple days ago. With a pistol. That's it. At least that's all that's been in the newspapers."

"Could've happened that way. Or maybe with everyone looking for the BARs, the Red Hand decided to lie low for a while."

"Lieutenant Boyle, if you know anything about recent history here, you'll know that lying low isn't something either side does." He drew Pig out of his pocket and began to rub the creature absentmindedly as he gazed out over the sea.

"I just got here. To Ireland, I mean. What's it like for someone with a sense of Irish history to be here in the north?"

"Helping the British garrison their part of Ireland, you mean? I don't like it much, but we probably won't be here long anyway. It is strange, though. Most of the IRA activity these days goes on up here or along the border. After hearing so many stories, it's odd to see it really happening. I mean, back home, who cares if you're Catholic or Protestant? Here it could get you killed if the other fellow has his blood up."

"Tell me, has anyone from the IRA ever approached you? Appealing to you as a patriotic Irishman?"

"I'm not sure. There was one time—it was in a pub in Ardglass—a guy asked me what church I attended. I thought it was a strange way to strike up a conversation, but it turned out to be common around here. Lets you know right away if you're drinking with the right kind or not. He said he went to Saint Mary's, which meant he was Catholic. Once I told him I went to Saint Brigid's back home, he started talking about how we all have to stick together, even those who'd left Ireland for America. It could've been nothing but talk except that he asked a lot of questions about what type of guns we had, almost as if he knew I was assigned to the arms depot."

"Did you ever see him again?"

"Once, over in Clough. It's a lot closer than Ardglass, and I wondered if he was looking for me. I waved and he nodded back but that was it. He was deep in conversation with another guy, some GI, and I didn't want to butt in."

"What did he look like?"

"Pretty average looking, except for his red hair. Bright red, like a carrot. The other fellow was tall, forty or so, balding."

"Do you remember his name, the guy you'd talked to before?"

"Yeah, it was Eamonn, he said. A Gaelic name. He talked about how it used to be illegal for an Irishman to even say his name in Gaelic. Can you believe that?"

"Yes, I can." "Eamonn" was "Edward" in English. Eddie Mahoney had bright red hair, and this was the second time he'd come up. Or the third, if you counted the time someone had shot him in the head.

CHAPTER ▪ TEN

I SAT ALONE in the mess hall, drinking coffee and trying to figure out what do next. So far, all I knew was that Eddie Mahoney had been sighted in two area pubs, once arguing with someone, and once chatting with a GI. Not evidence of anything, not even a clue. I knew that Major Thornton hadn't bothered to tell me Inspector Carrick had asked for Brennan's file. Again, nothing really suspicious; worth asking about but I doubted it meant anything. Brennan was in the know about the IRA, and sympathetic, but so was I, and likely hundreds of other GIs in Northern Ireland. I needed to check out Andrew Jenkins to see if he was brazen enough to have used his own delivery truck in the heist. Something about Mahoney and how he was found bothered me. It seemed as if there was a missing piece to this puzzle but I couldn't see it.

Also, I had been warned by old Grady O'Brick as soon as I landed, warned to watch my step. He'd nodded in the direction of the MP waiting for me but was that what he'd meant? Or was he gesturing toward the land itself? I didn't know, which pretty much summed up where I was in this investigation. No answers.

I watched the men in the mess hall, eating chow, laughing and talking, doing everyday things, as much as that was possible in the army. Some of these guys had been on garrison duty in Iceland; others were fresh from the States. A few, like Brennan, were transfers from outfits that had been in combat. Maybe the army wanted to add experienced men to the unit but it never made much sense to me. Until men went through combat and saw for themselves, veterans like Brennan would be viewed as oddballs, paranoid and superstitious, strangers in their midst. Brennan himself, his pals all dead, stood apart, doing his job, but unwilling or unable to form the bonds of friendship with men who might get chopped up beside him on the next invasion beach. Instead, his only buddy was a carved pig.

Matches, bottle caps, pocket knives, Saint Christopher medals, coins, and the ace of spades. I'd seen them all grasped in sweaty palms, tucked in pockets and continually patted down to make sure they were safe. There were rituals too—prayers, curses, songs, finger tapping, the sign of the cross, all those charms and amulets each GI was certain he couldn't do without when the lead started flying. They knew that without it, they'd be dead. With it, their chances might be slightly better than average, but nothing was guaranteed. Finally, after enough time up on the line, they realized luck had nothing to do with it. Skill and alertness—those things could give you an edge, at least until exhaustion set in, but luck was meaningless. Sooner or later, unless they pulled you off the line, you were going to get it.

I stirred my cold coffee and stared at the dark liquid swirling like a whirlpool.

"Lieutenant Boyle?"

I jumped, startled. I looked up and saw a man in a dark green uniform staring at me. He had a square jaw and a thin-lipped mouth set beneath dark eyes. Crow's-feet showed at their corners, and I judged him to be in his midforties. The uniform had a high collar with the Irish harp on each collar tab. His black leather belt and holster were gleaming, the butt of his revolver high and forward, ready for action.

"You must be Hugh Carrick," I said, rising from my seat. I didn't offer my hand.

"District Inspector Carrick, if it's all the same to you," he said as he sat down across from me. He gestured with his hand for me to be seated, as if I had just walked into his office.

"It is," I said. "Do district inspectors in Ulster have to wear Class As all the time?"

"Pardon me?"

"The fancy dress uniform. Back in the States detectives dress in suits except for special occasions."

"I just came from a funeral in Dromara. A constable, murdered by the so-called Irish Republican Army. Shot four times in the back, twenty yards from his home. His wife and two wee girls reached him first."

As he spoke, his tone didn't vary. No emotion crept into his voice, and his eyes stayed focused on me as he sat there, hands folded in his lap.

"I'm sorry, Inspector—"

"District Inspector."

"I am sorry, District Inspector. I'm a policeman myself, or was. In Boston, before the war. The death of a brother officer is a serious matter."

"Serious? To a Catholic from Boston? I understand the IRA murder squads enjoy a great deal of support from the Irish settled in Boston."

"How do you know I'm Catholic? Maybe I'm an atheist."

"Do not joke with me, Lieutenant Boyle. Your name tells me what I need to know, and your city tells me the rest. It's in the blood with you from across the border, whether you've gone to America or come north with a pistol to shoot a good man in the back." His words spilled out with the Irish accent I was used to, but with a harder, clipped edge. The only part of him that moved was his lips.

"Perhaps we should talk another time, District Inspector. I'm sure passions are running high after the funeral."

"Passions, Lieutenant Boyle? We have no time for passions. We have murderers to apprehend. We have a war to fight. Perhaps you allow yourself to wallow in passions but personally I find them distracting."

"Passion is what usually leads to murder, DI Carrick."

"But not what solves them, in my experience. Now I am told that I must cooperate with you, and I am sure you have been instructed to cooperate with me."

"I have been. I've only been here one full day. I don't have much information yet." I tried to keep my response neutral, to match his tone and his approach to me. It was an interrogation technique my dad had taught me. When a suspect was giving you a hard time, watch how he sits and how he speaks. Copy his stance and tone, and give it back to him. Sometimes it can defuse a touchy situation.

"Very well. What information do you have?"

"I know that Edward Mahoney was seen in the area in two different pubs, by Major Thornton and then by Sergeant Brennan. That you've questioned Brennan and requested his file. I know that Provost Marshal Heck was not pleased with my arrival. And now I know that you also are less than pleased. The only person glad to see me has been Major Thornton, who seems certain I can find his BARs for him, which will guarantee his command of a combat outfit."

"Major Thornton has not yet seen the elephant, or he wouldn't be so eager. Do you think you can find the weapons, or that your IRA friends will hand them over if you ask?"

"I just explained that I don't have any friends in Ireland. How about being a pal anyway and telling me what you know? Some of that promised cooperation would be nice."

"I can tell you I have my suspicions about Sergeant Brennan although his record is exemplary. Stood up well at Salerno after your generals sent good men ashore to be slaughtered."

"Suspicions?" I asked, resisting the urge to take a swipe at him or at least respond to his barbs. But that was what he was looking for, so he'd have a good excuse to write me off as an inexperienced pro-IRA Yank.

"He spends all of his free time in the villages around here, alone. He never goes anywhere with his mates."

"His mates are all dead, and he doesn't seem to want any new ones."

"Nevertheless, that could be how he made contact with the IRA. The Catholic pubs are sure to be full of them or their sympathizers. And of course who better to let them know when and how to strike?"

"That's good circumstantial stuff. But I have a question for you. If the IRA pulled this off by stealing one of Andrew Jenkins's trucks, that would leave him looking the fool. Why hasn't he retaliated? Have there been any IRA men or innocent Catholics gunned down?"

"No. I've told Jenkins to sit this out and let us handle it."

"You give orders to the Red Hand Society? And they obey them?"

"I'm not part of that rabble, Lieutenant Boyle. The Ulster Volunteer Force are all good men, good Protestant Unionists who will fight for our right to be part of Great Britain. The Red Hand are criminals and bullies, acting under the guise of patriotism. Most would sell out their own mothers if there was a quid in it for them. Andrew Jenkins isn't the worst of the lot; he does listen to reason on occasion."

The missing piece came to me when Carrick mentioned selling out.

"Eddie Mahoney was found with a pound note in his hand, the sign of the informer," I said.

"Aye, he was."

"Well, whom did he inform on? Whom did he inform to?" I asked.

"What do you mean?"

"It's simple. If he was correctly marked as an informer, he must have been informing to someone. Was he one of yours?"

"No, he wasn't. But they could have made a mistake. On the run, suspicious of everyone, any one of those IRA men could have turned on him."

"Not really. The IRA has its court-martial process. It might not be pretty but one man couldn't shoot another like that without approval."

"How close are you to the IRA in America, Lieutenant Boyle?"

I leaned in on my elbows, as close I could get, and looked him in the eye.

"Close enough. Close enough to know something stinks here. Tell me, are you in on the cover-up, or are you not high up enough to know who was running Mahoney?"

I watched his face for a sign of rage and kept half an eye on those folded hands, in case one came up a fist to slam me. It didn't.

"It wasn't us, and it wasn't the British Army," he said, his face relaxing slightly. He rested one arm on the tabletop, the most casual pose he had yet taken. "You're right about that—it doesn't add up, unless the IRA got it all wrong."

"Or it wasn't the IRA."

"I doubt that. The Red Hand would have an easier time stealing British arms, don't you think? More sympathizers among the British troops, just as the IRA has its sympathizers among the Americans."

"That makes some sense, although if the opportunity presented itself—"

"Jenkins would surely take it, yes."

"But if it was the IRA, then either they were wrong about Mahoney or there's something going on you don't know about."

"Doubtful."

"What if they were right about an informer but wrong about who it was?"

"Wouldn't surprise me at all. They can be incredibly stupid at times, very clever at others. And no, you will not be allowed to review information about our current informants."

"But you will."

"It may be worth the time. I'll let you know if I find anything," he said, sounding as if the possibility was remote. Still, he had taken to the idea. "Tell me, are there any other Americans investigating this case? A civilian perhaps?"

"Not that I know of, no. Why?"

"We've had reports of an American, always in civilian clothes, asking questions about certain IRA associates in this area. No name, and not much of a description. About my age. Wears a fedora hat and a trench coat. Nothing else to go on."

"Sorry, it's news to me. Is there anything else about the case you can tell me, DI Carrick?" I asked that with the most sincerity and humility I could muster.

"We've just had a name come up in connection with this case. Jack Taggart."

"Red Jack?" The man Subaltern O'Brien was after.

"So you've heard of him? He had a falling-out with his comrades after he came home from fighting against Franco in Spain with his tail between his legs. Seeing Bolsheviks up close seems to have cured most of their romantic notions. But they still call him Red Jack."

"Is he senior in the IRA?"

"We think so. He seems to have operated as their channel for funds from Germany and America. He had something to do with the bombing campaign in England—the S-Plan, as they called it. Not directly, mind you, but most of the money to support it came from him. Lately there've been sightings of him in Northern Ireland. He may have been here for some time."

"So you think he's part of this plot?"

"It would be the kind of thing he would be part of. Not just the theft but what they intend to do with the arms. It's the German connection that worries us. He worked with Seamus Rafferty—I'm sure you've heard of him—smuggling arms and agents in from Nazi Germany."

"Yes, I've heard of Rafferty. He was in the States before the war." I didn't mention the dinner at my parents' house, when he was the guest of honor along with Joe McGarrity, head of Clan na Gael.

"Right. That's when they raised most of the money for the S-Plan. Perhaps some of the funds used to kill innocent civilians came from your hometown, Lieutenant Boyle."

"Perhaps. A lot of people die in wars, DI Carrick. Perhaps there are a few innocent Catholics who would be alive today if you did your job and put those Red Hand boys behind bars. How many of them have you arrested?"

"You must know it's impossible to get evidence against them," Carrick said through gritted teeth. "They close ranks and swear on a stack of Bibles they were all having tea with their mothers. And their mothers lie and serve you stale biscuits while telling you what God-fearing lads their boys are."

His eyes were wide and he was panting. With that tight, high collar choking him, I thought he might burst a blood vessel. He was steaming mad but not at me. It was those mothers, pouring tea and covering up their sons' gruesome murders. Maybe he was a real cop after all.

"Do you have a picture of Taggart?"

"I'll give you one," he said, rubbing his forehead with one hand. "There are some at the RUC station at Killough, about five miles from the gate. You've a vehicle?"

I told him I did.

"Follow me if you're done here. Some of the local constables are gathering at Killough to toast the dead tonight. It will be a chance for them to lay eyes on you, take your measure."

"Have you?"

"You're no fool, which is saying a lot for a papist Yank. You may be of some help if you don't get yourself killed first," he said without an apparent trace of regret at the thought. He drummed his fingers on the table, staring at me as the rhythmic sound increased in speed, then stopped. "I hate them all, you know."

"Who?"

"The Red Hand, the bloody IRA. Fools like you who sleep with them and then get up in the morning and wash your hands clean. All of you." He rose, brushing off his uniform as if it were dirty. He tucked his cap under his arm.

"His wife and his wee girls found him. Did I tell you?"

He didn't wait for an answer as I followed him out.

I thought I'd better give Major Thornton a call before going off with Carrick. He'd told me to check in every day so I decided to get that over with now, before toasts to the dead constable got too far along. I called from the Ordnance Depot office while Carrick and Jacobson chatted. I reached a clerk at 5th Division HQ who said Thornton was out on the rifle range. I left word that I'd met up with Carrick, that we were going to the RUC station at Killough, and that I'd picked up a lead. I figured I'd give the major something positive. I had no idea how the name of Red Jack Taggart would help me find the BARs, but it was something. At least I'd have a picture to show around, like a real policeman. And I had a few places to show it: the pubs in Annalong and Ardglass, where Mahoney had been sighted, as well as the Lug o' the Tub Pub in Clough. I was heartened that the suspects so far were all drinkers, rather than operagoers or bird-watchers.

As we left the office, Sergeant Brennan approached, stopping short when he saw Carrick. His mouth opened for a second then he clammed up. He saluted and I returned it, watching his face as he mumbled a greeting and hurried past us.

"No need to worry, son," Carrick called after him. "I'm not here to take you away."

The unspoken word *yet* hung in the air. Brennan had his hand on the doorknob but didn't open it. He turned to face us, his body rigid.

"One of you will, soon enough," he said. "I don't expect justice from the army or the British."

"I am an Irishman too, young man," Carrick said. "I was born here, unlike you or your lieutenant here."

"He's not my lieutenant," Brennan said. "I just heard from my CO that Major Thornton is bringing me up on court-martial charges. Unlawful disposition of military property in wartime. Is that what you're here for, Lieutenant Boyle? To build a case against me?"

He didn't wait for an answer. The door slammed and Carrick and I looked at each other in surprise.

"Perhaps Major Thornton has some new evidence," he said.

"Perhaps he wants someone else to take the rap before some colonel starts eyeing him. Brennan is a sitting duck, an enlisted sitting duck at that. Thornton busts a lieutenant to buck private and ships him out then gets a noncom thrown in the slammer. The heat's off him and the brass are happy. If he gets me to find the BARs he'll come out smelling like a rose."

"It's natural you'd defend Brennan," Carrick said.

"Because we're both papists?" I asked, with an edge of anger I couldn't keep out of my voice.

"To some extent. But no, that is not what I meant. I mean since you have both seen the elephant, and Thornton has not yet been in combat. I've found that's a greater divide than the one between the Church of Rome and the Church of Ireland. Wouldn't you agree, Lieutenant Boyle?"

Once again, he didn't wait for an answer.

■ ■ ■

I FOLLOWED HIM along the coast road, the wind sending white fluffy clouds over our heads and out to the Irish Sea. As we neared the village of Killough, houses appeared, their whitewashed fronts close up to the road. Driving on the left, I could have stopped and knocked on a door without getting out of the jeep. To our right, gray pebble beaches curved into the distance. The seawall running along the edge of the road was crumbling, with weeds and moss growing in the cracks. A church steeple rose in the distance, the only structure that seemed solid and lasting. Carrick turned and I followed him down the main street, which was lined with stately sycamore trees that looked in better shape than the two-story homes and shops that bordered it. He turned again and parked behind a row of cars in front of a white building with a sign marking it as an RUC station.

"It looks like someone's home," I said after I'd parked the jeep and joined Carrick.

"It is. In villages of this size, the RUC has built station houses for married personnel. Mostly sergeants. In the smaller villages, like Clough, the constables make do out of their homes. Here, we'll go around back," he said as he opened a gate that led into a small backyard. Late-season flowers still bloomed in a garden next to cauliflowers and onions. The yard was surrounded by hedges, and at its center was a table in a small grassy area. It looked like a pleasant place to spend a warm afternoon, which this wasn't.

We entered a long kitchen, a stove at one end radiating heat. About a dozen men in the dark green RUC uniform turned and greeted the district inspector, and a woman of about forty, dark haired with pearl white skin, leaned forward and gave him a kiss. I could have been back home. A gathering of cops after a funeral of one of their own. Telling stories, drinking, feeling glad and guilty it wasn't them, and working hard at not giving away a thing.

"Lieutenant Boyle, this is Mrs. Chambers, wife of Constable Robert Chambers, that tall fellow over there."

"Pleased to meet you, Mrs. Chambers," I said as I nodded to her husband, who made his way over to us.

"Always glad to have a Yank as a guest. Call me Mildred," she said. "Bob, look, we've another American."

"Bob Chambers," her husband said as he walked up and we shook hands. "Boyle, is it?"

"Yes, Billy Boyle." I expected a comment about my Catholic Irish name, but it appeared that Chambers simply wasn't sure if he'd heard correctly. He nodded and offered me a whiskey. I took it gladly and looked to Mrs. Chambers, who had waited for her husband to finish his introduction.

"Bob, I was just starting to tell Lieutenant Boyle about the other Yank, the military policeman. Adrian's friend, what was his name?"

"Burnham," he said. "Samuel Burnham. He's in the parlor with some of the lads. Do you know him, Boyle?"

"We've met. He helped me out of a difficulty when I first arrived—"

"You mean your trouble with Heck?"

"Word travels fast," I said.

"That man's away in the head, and I'll tell him so to his face," Bob said.

"Not with that uniform on you won't," Carrick leaned in to say, clapping Bob on his shoulder.

"Right enough, sir, right enough."

"What is he?" I asked, not understanding what he'd said.

"Sorry, Boyle. Well, he's an eejit of the worst kind."

"You don't have eejits in America?" Mildred asked.

"Idiots?" I hazarded as a guess. "We have them."

"Aye, eejits, like I said. Heck is a prime example. Always getting in the way, he is. Not like the local MPs, like Burnham in there. Heck has to be in on everything, to the point he plain wastes our time."

"Your Captain Heck is preparing for a new army regulation, as I understand it," Carrick said. "Apparently your military police have limited powers. They do very basic police functions but any investigative matters are handled by the area commander."

"Right," I said. "Like this investigation is in the hands of 5th Division."

"Heck is awaiting a directive from the provost marshal general, assigning the Criminal Investigation Division which he is in charge of the primary responsibility for investigating all criminal activities."

"That explains a lot," I said. "Heck doesn't want anyone else to solve the case. As soon as this directive goes into effect, he can take over and grab the glory."

"Or be saddled with a dead-end investigation."

"No, I don't think so. He must be holding something back. Otherwise, why would he want to hinder me?"

"Aye, that's why we weren't surprised when he wanted to arrest you," Bob said. He finished off his whiskey with a smack of the lips.

"How did you know?" I asked.

"It's our business to know everything that goes on in these parts. Right, sir?"

"Right you are, Constable. Introduce Boyle around, will you? He needs to know who his friends are while he's among us."

Bob filled my glass and his, and brought me around to quiet knots of men while his wife put out plates of cheese, pickles, soda bread, and potato bread. I met constables from Lowtown, Seaforde, Maghera, and Kilcoo. They all had Protestant names, I was fairly sure, but no one called me a papist—at least not to my face. They felt familiar, the way they loosened the collars of their uniforms, the way they stood with each other, hands draped over shoulders in easy intimacy, the relaxed laugh when away from the scrutiny of civilians. It could have been my kitchen and it could have been Dad taking around a cop from out of town, making him feel at ease. It felt comforting and wrong at the same time. The RUC probably had some fine cops, and Carrick seemed like the real thing, but they also had their fair share of Catholic-hating thugs. Some of these fine boys could be with the Red Hand. Any of them could have been in on the arms heist. I wanted to flee, I wanted to stay. They were my enemy; they were my brothers.

I let Bob take me into the parlor, trying to understand what all this meant. Who was who. Who was an Irishman and who wasn't. These Northern Irish weren't British but they were undoubtedly Loyalists, which meant they'd prefer all of Ireland still to be ruled from London. Failing that, it was their mission in life to keep Ulster part of Great Britain forever. The blood oath. Who were these boys but my mirror image? On our side, the side of the antitreaty IRA, we hadn't signed in blood as literally as the Orangemen had, but we shared the same sort of fixation: Ireland ruled our way, all of it, but from Dublin. Change capitals, change color, change church, and Bob's your uncle, as the English say. I laughed out loud and realized I needed to watch how fast I drank my host's whiskey.

"Billy," Sam Burnham said, surprise registering on his face. He was dressed in his pinks and greens, shoes shined and brass buttons gleaming. "I didn't know you'd be here."

"Neither did I until I ran into DI Carrick, and he invited me along to meet the local cops. Did you go to the funeral?" I felt a bit outclassed in my tanker jacket and boots. At least I had a tie on—or field scarf, as the army insisted on calling it—which helped.

"Yes. I thought we ought to have someone there after Adrian told me it was today. Like he said, we're all brother officers."

"He's right. Back home cops will travel pretty far for a funeral, especially when an officer has been killed in the line of duty."

"Yeah, I hadn't thought of myself as a real cop, like you, but I guess it was good to have somebody there in uniform. I'm glad Adrian told me it was a dress uniform occasion. I hadn't worn my Class As over here before now."

"Any other Americans attend the—"

"Billy," Sam interrupted, "this is Constable Adrian Simms from Clough." He reached out to a young constable as he passed by. "Adrian, Lieutenant Billy Boyle. He's the detective from Boston I told you about."

"Pleased to meet you, so I am," said Adrian. He looked to be the youngest of the constables here, maybe twenty-five or so, and on the short side. He had light sandy hair and a fair complexion, with freckles on his cheeks. His smile was quick and genuine. "Sam tells me you were sent here by General Eisenhower himself."

"He's definitely interested in what happened here," I said, trying not to sound too full of myself.

"As am I. That's my turf, you know, even though it happened on the base. An arms theft and a murder on my patch—don't like it a bit, I don't."

"Some folks might not worry too much about an IRA man being executed by his own," I said.

"Aye, true enough. But I say if we let the IRA or the Red Hand go about dispensin' their own justice, then we've given up any chance of havin' any justice of our own, Catholic or Protestant alike. Know what I mean?"

"I do, Adrian. Justice should be blind."

"Well, I don't know about that. I'd like the lady to keep at least one eye open to mind the store, don't you think?" He winked and raised his glass.

"See why we get along so well, Billy?" Sam said. "Adrian and I have done our fair share of keeping the peace around here, especially between civilians and GIs."

"Aye, when they see the two of us standin' side by side, neither of us favorin' one or the other, they tend to patch things up quick like."

"Have you come up with anything on Mahoney's murder? Any leads at all?"

"No, but I've got my eye out for Red Jack. You've heard about him?"

"Yes, Carrick told me. I also just found out about this new regulation that will give Heck jurisdiction over all criminal investigations. Did you know about that, Sam?"

"They've been talking about that for months. Sounds like it's finally going to happen."

"You think that's why Heck wanted me in jail? So he could bide his time and then solve the crimes after the new regs come out?"

"I hadn't thought about it that way. That would mean he's got something up his sleeve, otherwise he'd only get handed a pig in a poke."

"That's what I think. This also explains why Thornton is so fired up to get the BARs back. The sooner it happens, the sooner he gets the credit instead of Heck. That's his ticket to a combat command."

"Combat? Thornton?" Sam asked.

"Yeah, he told me he wanted one of the heavy weapons companies, that he had this plan to add more firepower, which is why he had all those BARs."

"Then he must've had a change of heart. Last I heard, he'd put in for a transfer to Corps HQ, to the Ordnance Battalion. That's a good safe distance from the front."

"Then that's two lies he's told me," I said, taking in what Sam was saying now.

"The other one?" Adrian asked.

"I asked if he'd told me everything he knew, and he said he had. But he left out that Carrick had just requested Sergeant Brennan's file. That would make Brennan a suspect, so why would Thornton not tell me about it?"

"Maybe he's just trying to sound gung ho to impress General Eisenhower's investigator. And maybe the Brennan thing slipped his mind," Sam said. "Did you ask Carrick what he was going to do about Brennan?"

"No, I didn't get a chance. He was pretty prickly at first."

"That's the DI, it is," said Adrian. "He's not broad-minded on certain matters touching religion and the Crown. He's a fair man, though, at the end of the day. I doubt a Catholic has ever stepped foot in his home or ever will, but he works the law as fair as can be."

"How fair is that?" I asked.

"Well, the poor lady is blindfolded and holding those heavy scales. We can't expect miracles from her, can we? You need your drink freshened?"

"Good idea," I said, and followed Adrian and Sam to a table where bottles were lined up. I knew that I couldn't press Adrian any further.

"*Guid forder*," Adrian said, raising his glass. "That's good luck the way Ulster Scots say it. I think we'll be needin' a wee bit of luck before this is done."

We clinked glasses and drank, the warmth of the whiskey filling me as I tried to sort out what this new information meant. I was sure Adrian was right about the luck.

"Adrian," I said. "Your accent is a bit different from the others. Are you from around here?"

"Not originally. I was brought up by my aunt in Dublin. I think bein' in the minority down there made me a bit more tolerant of the minority up here. Live and let live, I say, and each man to his own church, neighborhood, and pub."

"Not a bad philosophy. You must have friends on both sides."

"Aye, and enemies too, even within my own family. There's no easy way these days. Now excuse me while I visit with some of the lads. We don't all get together but for funerals or retirements."

"He seems like a good guy," I said to Sam as Adrian left us.

"He is. Treats everyone fair and square. Say, Billy, will you give me a lift back to camp? I drove up with Adrian but it will save him a detour if you're going that way," Sam said. "He'll probably want to stay a while too."

"Sure thing."

Sam moved to a window that faced the backyard. The living quarters were all at the back of the house, separated from the station house by a long hallway.

"It'll be dark soon," he said, pulling the curtains to look at the sky. Clouds showed their pink undersides, and the blue sky was starting to turn a deeper, darker shade. I moved to set my unfinished drink down, figuring that if I finished it I'd be in no shape to drive in the dark on the wrong side of the road.

Sharp, loud cracks of rapid-fire gunshots exploded in the air, over-riding the sound of shattered windowpanes. Sam clutched a white curtain as he fell. It settled on top of him, soaked in crimson red as it lay across the two holes in his chest. I dove for the floor as more bullets sprayed the house. In the parlor, bottles burst and stuffing from chairs floated in the air.

I crawled to Sam. His eyes were open, but there had been only bad luck for him.

CHAPTER ▪ ELEVEN

IT HAD BEEN a BAR, there was no mistaking the sound. And it had been a full twenty-round clip. The first two rounds had hit Sam dead center but the rest were sprayed wildly at the house, a warning to stay put. He was gone; there was nothing to do for him. The only sound registering after the deafening rounds was the tinkling of glass as loose shards fell to the floor. There was one chance, and I took it. I covered my face with one arm and dove through the window, the last bits of glass and wood giving way easily. I hit the soft grass and rolled, pulling my .45 from its holster and flipping off the safety.

If the shooter was still behind the hedge and reloading, I was dead. A BAR clip can be changed in seconds. But I doubted that he'd hang around a station full of armed constables.

Shouts and cries came from the house, but no gunfire from behind the hedge. I sprinted across the yard and vaulted the gate, crouching as I turned with a view down the back of the shrubbery. A path led along the rear of the houses beside a small stream. Birch trees grew on the opposite bank. I ran to the end of the hedge. Shell casings lay scattered on the ground from where the gunman had fired.

It was slow going. Each backyard had a toolshed or section of fencing that could be a hiding place. I had a clear view of the stream for a good distance. Had he crossed the water into the birch grove? Would he have had enough time? I cursed as I dashed by the next backyard, trusting to speed and surprise.

No, I decided, he wouldn't have, especially not lugging a BAR around. The damn things weighed around twenty pounds loaded. And he couldn't take a chance on being seen. There had to be a getaway car, close enough to reach quickly but far enough away not to be seen from the station. Time to take another chance. Maybe I'd gotten all the *guid forder* Adrian had offered up.

I jumped a fence into a small garden. It took up most of the rear yard, except for a stone patio that connected to the house. A woman in an apron standing in the kitchen door held her hand to her mouth. Her eyebrows rose halfway up her forehead in shock as I trampled her chrysanthemums. She shook her head, removing her hand to hold it out, cautioning me to stop. I did. Ahead of me, a bed of pansies spread purple and white, perfect except for two footprints crushed into them. She pointed to the side of the house, to my right, then shut the door and disappeared.

If he was planning to ambush me, he'd probably be at the back, waiting to catch me as I came around either side; if a car was there, he might already be in it. Damn. I ran as lightly and quietly as I could along the left side of the house. I peeked around the corner, watching for the steel barrel of a BAR. It wasn't the best weapon for close quarters like this. He'd have to expose himself to fire it at me. I edged along the house, my back to it and my .45 in my right hand ready to fire.

I heard a car engine turn over. That had to be him. Maybe he'd cut across the neighbor's yard. I moved to the corner of the house and took a stance aiming down the side. Nothing. I ran out into the street in time to see a car pull out from the other side of the road. Parked on the left side, ready for a getaway in the opposite direction from the station. A perfect spot, I had to admit.

As the car pulled out, a truck rumbled down the road toward it. The road was narrow, and the driver of the car had to hit the brakes and wait for the truck to pass by. I sprinted out into the street and made for it, a small gray Austin saloon, the driver up front, one guy in back, probably cradling a BAR. The Austin wasn't that large, and it would be damn hard to maneuver the BAR out of the window.

"Stop!" I yelled, at both the car and the truck. If the truck stopped, the Austin would be hemmed in. But the truck didn't stop. Instead he leaned on his horn and increased speed, probably wondering what the crazy Yank was going on about.

"Halt!" I was close to the Austin now, close enough to take out the driver if I had to. As it continued to pull out of its parking spot, the man in the backseat leaned out, a revolver in his hand. Two shots cracked in the air as his sparse hair flew around his head. I dove flat onto the pavement and squeezed off a single shot, going for a tire. I don't know what I hit, but with houses all around I couldn't take any chances. I watched the Austin disappear, my only reward a glimpse of the shooter's face. A round, balding head, dark brown hair, a sharp chin, and eyes that darted up at the sides, like an imp. I thought I heard him laugh as he fired.

I got up on one knee, winded, as footsteps pounded the pavement and a whirl of dark green surrounded me.

"Did you see him?" Adrian gasped.

"Yes, I got a look at him. Car was an Austin, gray, four-door, license plate began with FZG, but I couldn't get anything else."

"You're certain it was the fellow who fired at us?" Carrick asked, less out of breath than Adrian.

"One man in the backseat, and he fired at me twice."

"I heard pistol shots. Was the last one yours?"

"Yes," I said as I got to my feet and holstered my automatic. "I went for a tire but I don't think I hit anything."

"That was quick thinking, Boyle, and brave, going through that window. I doubt he thought anyone would give chase so quickly. Well done," Carrick said.

"It's terrible about Sam, terrible it is," said Adrian, looking at his feet as he rubbed a sleeve across his eyes. "He was standing right next to me."

"Anyone else hurt?" I asked.

"Luckily, no," Carrick said. "Let's get back and call out a description of the car. Probably pinched it around here, and they've switched by now, but still . . ."

But still, it was best to go through the motions, to do something that helped reduce the chaos unleashed by one man with an automatic weapon and the will to kill. There was glass to be swept up, windows to be replaced, bullet holes to be filled, and an All Points to be put out. Activity to help us return to normalcy what violence had shattered. None of it meant anything to a dead man.

THEY PUT OUT the call, and we waited for the base to send an ambulance to take Sam's body away. He was laid out on a table in the backyard, wrapped in a sheet stained a rusty brown. Two constables stood by him, tunics buttoned and caps on. They nodded as I walked past, grim gestures of acceptance, shared anger, and grief.

Mildred was sweeping the kitchen while Bob pulled pieces of glass from the windowpanes. Another constable came in and put a tin can on the table.

"Twenty shell casings, sir," he said to Carrick. "Haven't touched a one."

"We'll check for fingerprints," Carrick said, "although I doubt there will be any. A good deal of the ammunition stolen was already loaded in clips, if that was a Browning."

"It was," I said. "Very distinctive sound."

"Yes, it didn't sound like a Thompson, which the IRA favors. I think using it may have been a message."

We sat, and a glass of whiskey appeared at my elbow. It was odd how gunfire and death sobered you up. I took a gulp and let myself feel it settle into my gut.

"What kind of message?"

"Leave it alone," Carrick said.

"The hell I will."

"*I* wasn't suggesting you should. I certainly won't, not when one of my stations is attacked and a guest murdered. But there's something you should think about, Boyle."

"What?"

"Who was the real target? For the past hour or so, constables were passing by windows. If they wanted to kill just anyone, they could have done so at any time. But the person they hit first was in an American uniform. Now I ask myself, was that random or planned? And if it was planned, who did they think they were killing?"

"Me?" I took another drink.

"Simms, did Lieutenant Burnham say if anyone knew he was coming to the funeral?"

"Not exactly, sir, but he gave me the impression he decided to come on his own, to pay his respects."

"So it's likely no one knew officially that he went to the funeral at Dromara. But even if they did, they couldn't have known he was coming here. We decided only at the last minute."

"But I called Thornton," I said, seeing where he was going. "I left a message for him that I was headed here."

"Yes, from the arms depot, where any number of people heard you, including Jacobson, who certainly would have told Brennan if he inquired. Not to mention anyone at the Newcastle base who handled your message."

"And they would have expected to find only one American here, so they didn't even need to know what I looked like. Jesus. If Sam hadn't looked out that window . . ."

"He might be alive, and you'd be dead," Adrian said, a touch of bitterness catching in his throat.

"Aye, and if you'd been standing close to Billy when he next went to the window, you could be lying outside under my best sheet as well," Mildred said. "You catch yourself on, Adrian Simms!"

"Sorry," mumbled Simms, his face reddening.

"Good lad," Mildred said, and returned to putting the kitchen back together. Bob taped cardboard over the windows, darkening the room. He pulled the curtains before he turned the light on.

"No sense giving them a target, just in case," he said.

"This does give you one advantage, Boyle," Carrick said. "But it won't last long."

"What's that?"

"If I'm right, whoever intercepted your message will think you're dead, until he hears there was another American present who gave chase."

"You're right."

I stood, anxious to get to Ballykinler and say hello to Brennan and Jacobson to see their faces. I needed to get there before the ambulance transporting Sam's body showed up. Word was bound to travel fast once it got on base.

"Do you want a constable to go with you?"

"No, no thanks. But that picture of Taggart, can I have that now?"

Carrick asked Bob to fetch one from the station office. Mildred pressed a cheese sandwich wrapped in wax paper on me, and set down a small cup of tea.

"You drink a wee bit of that now, Billy. And be sure to eat something, dear."

"Thanks, Mildred." I put the tea to my lips and blew on the steam. Bob came in and tossed a mug shot onto the table.

"That's Taggart, about two years ago," he said, tapping his finger on the picture. "We brought him in on suspicion of IRA activity but couldn't prove anything. Had to let him go. Apparently, he'd just come north and we had no idea he was such a big fish."

I set the tea down and studied the picture. Thinning brown hair, a chin that jutted out, and those eyes, with that amused expression. A roguish charmer, perhaps.

"That's the man in the car, the man who shot at me. The man with the BAR."

"Red Jack Taggart, here?" Adrian said, as if it seemed impossible.

"Aye, it was a message all right," Carrick said. "And one he may well deliver again. Watch how you go, Boyle."

That was exactly what Grady O'Brick had said to me, less than two days ago, and already someone was dead, someone at a window who might have been me.

"No. Red Jack needs to watch how *he* goes."

CHAPTER ▪ TWELVE

IT HAD STARTED to rain but I drove the jeep fast, my .45 on the seat next to me, safety off, round in the chamber. I didn't know whom I could trust, with the strange exception of just about any Ulster Loyalist. Someone was feeding the IRA information, and it sure as hell wouldn't be one of them. It could be someone wearing khaki but not someone wearing the RUC dark green.

I sped down narrow country lanes as whitewashed thatched cottages stood out in the darkening evening light. Each was a threat, and I scanned windows for the snout of a BAR. I downshifted too late as I took one curve, and the jeep slid on the slick roadway. The tires kicked up loose gravel as I gunned it out of a ditch and regained the road. That slowed me down. No sense getting myself killed—one dead lieutenant today was more than enough.

Names swirled through my head. Brennan, Jacobson, Thornton. Maybe Lasner, the sergeant at the communications section? Heck? Maybe even him, if he'd been at headquarters when my message came through. Parties unknown? Sure were plenty of them around here. Could it have been pure chance that Sam was killed? Wrong window, wrong time, wrong bullet?

No, I didn't think so. If I was an IRA man, I'd wait instead of shooting an unknown Yank, in case he might be a sympathetic Irish-American. But those first two shots were right on target, to the chest, and then everything else had been to keep people flat on the floor while Red Jack made his getaway. The only American he thought would be there was me, a sympathetic Irish-American if ever there was one.

Either my reputation as a Boston detective preceded me, or I had stumbled onto something, something that pointed to him. What?

I had no idea, I admitted to myself as I stopped at the main gate to Ballykinler. The GI on duty glanced at the automatic on the seat next to me. I told him there were bandits on the back roads, and he nodded as if it were common knowledge as he opened the gate. I went through the second gate, to the Ordnance Depot, with my .45 holstered, remembering that these guards were sharper than the others.

A few minutes later I opened the door to the office. A clerk was on the telephone, going down a checklist. Jacobson was on the phone in his office, standing with his back to me, waving one arm in the air. I walked closer to him.

"How was I supposed to know . . . yeah, yeah . . . I'll call you." He hung up.

"Hi, Saul," I said. "Is Sergeant Brennan around?"

"Jeez, Boyle, knock or something, why don't you?" He did look surprised but maybe that was because he didn't expect to find me standing right behind him. "Why is everybody looking for Brennan? Is it about the BARs?"

"Who else is looking?"

"Thornton. He's sending MPs over to pick him up."

"Was that him just now on the phone?"

"No, that was Joe Patterson, he's a sergeant in charge of the MP detail. I told him I'd given Pete an evening pass. He has to be back by midnight."

"Any special reason for the pass?"

"When he gets jittery he likes to get out, have a few drinks with the locals. I think it calms him down to be away from the army for a while."

"Him and a million other guys. Any idea where he went?"

"He said he'd probably go in to Clough. He likes the Lug o' the Tub, know it?"

"I know where it is. Anything unusual going on? With Brennan, I mean?"

"He was OK after he talked to you. We were out on the loading dock after a shipment of bazookas came in. One of Jenkins's trucks went by on its way to the mess hall. He clammed up. Came back an hour later and asked for the pass. Why, what's going on?"

"An MP was shot a while ago," I said. "Sam Burnham, know him?"

"Lieutenant, right? Yeah, I know who he is. What happened?"

"Long story. Listen, any idea why seeing Jenkins's truck would make Brennan nervous?"

"I have no idea, Boyle. Maybe Pete is mixed up in all this, I don't know. I have enough problems as it is. I got bazookas without rockets, 81mm mortars with no ammo, 60mm mortar shells but no mortars—you want me to go on?"

"No need, I'll leave you to your troubles," I said, thinking that Brennan must not have mentioned anything to Saul about the MPs coming for him. "Thanks."

"Find those BARs, that'll solve one of my problems at least," Saul said as I left. Everyone wanted me to find the BARs but I was more worried about them finding me first.

Saul had acted completely normal after his initial shock when he turned around and saw me. Did Brennan's departure have anything to do with the attack on the station? I didn't see how it could. Maybe the sight of the truck had made him jumpy, or maybe he'd started a fight in the wrong pub over politics or religion, and he was worried about the Red Hand. But why leave the base? Did Saul know the MPs were coming for Brennan, and if he did, why would he give Brennan a pass?

I drove out of the Ballykinler base, turning left on the road to Clough. The last thing I wanted was another drink, but I had to check on Brennan. Besides, by now it was likely that word had gotten back to Thornton about Sam being shot. As soon as they sent the ambulance for his body, the XO would get a report. Executive officers got reports all day and all night, from every formation under their command. Which probably meant that Thornton had known Sam was going to the funeral. He was probably the only person who knew there would be *two* American officers there. Not that I could come up with a reason to suspect him, other than having caught him in a couple of lies, but it did make me wonder. Was Sam the intended target after all? If he was, why? What could he have known that was worth his life? I needed to talk to his sergeant, Patterson, to see if there was anything I was missing. Adrian too, since he seemed to be a pal of Sam's.

The Lug o' the Tub sat near the edge of the road, its whitewashed stone walls gleaming in the moonlight. The overhanging thatched roof loomed darkly, and the smell of peat smoke floated in the night air.

There wasn't much room to park, so I edged the jeep off the road as best I could. Bicycles leaned against the building and one old sedan was parked beside it. No other jeep was in sight.

I opened the door and stepped into a haze of yellow lamplight, cigarette smoke, and murmured conversations. The bar was set along the wall to my left, and necks craned as they do in neighborhood bars all over the world, checking out the newcomer. I had *new Yank* written all over me, and the locals, in their white shirts and vests, or shabby old suit coats that had once been their Sunday best but now wore the shine of decades, turned away as one, grinding out cigarettes and sipping their Guinnesses. The barman nodded, ever so slightly, keeping his eyes on me as I scanned the room. Tables were set along the walls, and small groups huddled over their drinks. Four GIs sat at one, grimly drinking warm beer and probably thinking of bars back home that had actual women in them. Clough was not much for nightlife, and the clientele was decidedly male, and on the grayer side of that sex. In the farthest corner, with his back to the wall, sat Grady O'Brick. He raised his glass to me and as he did, his drinking partner turned around. Pete Brennan grinned when he saw me, a cigarette at the corner of his mouth drifting smoke across his squinting eyes.

"Come join us, Billy Boyle from America," Grady called out to me. I saw they were near the bottom of their glasses, so I nodded and went to the bar.

"What are they drinking?" I asked the barman, hooking my thumb back in Grady's direction.

"Tonight it's Caffrey's Ale," he said. "They brew it up in Antrim, a good Ulster ale."

"Make it three of those. They drink together often?"

"You new around here, Yank?" He raised an eyebrow as he began the slow pour from the tap, expertly wiping foam from the glass and starting another. His shirtsleeves were rolled up and his forearms were strongly muscled, as the rest of him looked to be. His weight was starting to settle, though, and from the flecks of gray in his dark hair I figured him to be close to fifty, and not a man to speak out of turn.

"Yes, I am."

"I can tell by your color. You've been in the sun, and we don't get near enough for that shade of yours."

"You should be a detective," I said.

"If I were, I wouldn't walk into a pub in any part of Ireland and start asking questions about regular patrons. Apt to be bad for business. Know what I mean?"

"Listen, I didn't mean anything by it. Grady asked me to stop by, and I didn't know they knew each other, that's all. The name's Billy Boyle," I said. "My family came from Donegal, in the Republic."

The barman set aside the first glass, topped off with an inch or so of foam. He wiped his hands on his bar rag and offered me one for a shake. "Tom McCarthy. You must be that officer Grady rowed in from the flying boat."

"Like I said, you should be a detective." He grinned, and it seemed that I'd fallen on his good side with my name, family history, and maybe the connection with Grady O'Brick. "Do you know Pete Brennan as well?"

"Oh, Pete, he comes in when he can. Likes to sit by himself most nights, but he and Grady have struck up a friendship, as you can see." He finished with the second glass and began to work on the third, tilting it and letting the amber liquid slide down the side, stopping for the foam to settle down. "Young Pete has seen the elephant, he has."

"You can tell?"

"I served with the Dublin Fusiliers in the last war," Tom said. "Saw a fair bit. I survived Gallipoli. Not many men standing today who can say that." He brushed the foam from the top of the last glass and set it down.

"You can tell then."

"Aye, and Pete has seen more of the old rogue than any man's a right to. It weighs on him, the idea of going back to all that. They sent us from Gallipoli to the trenches in France, and I can tell you, these things do weigh on a man."

"Has Pete told you any of this?"

"Not in so many words. Grady passed some on, the rest is in his eyes. I can see you've come from the war but it hasn't torn you up complete yet."

"Doesn't mean I want to go back either," I said as I counted out the price of three ales.

"Aye, but you will."

There was nothing I could say to that. I left the money on the bar, grasped the three glasses, and headed for the table.

"Saint Billy it is, come to the rescue of some thirsty gents," said Grady, laughing at his own wit.

"Thanks, Lieutenant," said Brennan as I sat down next to him.

"Name's Billy, Pete, at least while we're drinking together."

"OK, Billy, then here's to you," Pete said as he raised his glass.

"*Fad saol agat*," Grady offered, raising his glass and smacking his lips.

"Long life to you," I translated for Pete.

"Ah, a Yank who knows the old tongue!"

"*Fad saol agat, gob fliuch, agus bás in Eirinn*," I said, giving out the full version of the toast. "Long life to you, a wet mouth, and death in Ireland."

"I'll take two out of three," Brennan said.

"Well, it is the first time I said that one here in Ireland. It sounds a lot more nostalgic back home in Boston."

"It's a fine thing to hear you have visions of the old sod in America, Billy Boyle. Do you know your name in Gaelic, boy?"

"I know the family name used to be O'Baoighill. My grandfather came to America with that name on a note pinned to his coat."

"It's good you know that, boy. But it's a thing for certain that he never spoke it aloud in Ireland. Them peelers would beat you to a pulp. Ó Bruic, that's my name in Gaelic, but I still speak it quiet like—force of the habit, you know."

"So, Grady Ó Bruic, tell me, why did you warn me to watch myself the day you picked me up in that boat?"

"I knew the American police were fallin' over each other to find the lads who took those guns. Are they good guns, boy? Anyway, it seemed to me that with a Yank copper waitin' for you, and you lookin' a good Irish boyo, that they'd be bringin' you in to do the dirty work as it were. Get in with the locals, you know, and worm the truth from them. If you put the finger on the IRA, your life wouldn't be worth an empty glass of Tom's good ale. And if you didn't, then all the blame would fall on you like spring rain comin' off the Mournes. Just my way of thinkin', mind you."

"I'm in no position to disagree. Someone emptied a BAR into the Killough RUC station this evening while I was there. They missed me, but killed one of our guys, Lieutenant Sam Burnham."

"Jesus Christ," Brennan whispered.

"Only him?" Grady said. "Why, for heaven's sake? Why shoot an American and leave all those RUC coppers alive?"

"Jesus Christ," Brennan said again, staring into his glass, as if there were answers floating in the foam.

"Easy, Pete, easy, boy," Grady said, his voice low and soothing.

"He was a decent man," Brennan said through gritted teeth. "They always seem to go first. Then the brave ones, then the guys who keep their heads down, and finally the cowards and goldbricks. It got so I'd watch the replacements come ashore and I could tell right away which they were, how long they'd last. I hated them, with their quick, nervous laughs, always wondering what to do to stay alive when they were already dead."

"This isn't Salerno," I said, trying to match Grady's tone. Brennan's eyes stayed glued to his glass.

"The place doesn't matter, don't you know that? It didn't matter to Sam, and it doesn't matter to those guys over there," Brennan said, his head nodding in the direction of the GIs drinking at the other table. "Italy, France, it doesn't matter. Do you want to know what matters, Billy?"

"What?"

"Geometry. Intersecting lines. They're everywhere, you just can't see them. Right now, this very minute, there's a bullet in a case of ammo somewhere, maybe in a factory in Germany, maybe stockpiled in Rome. It's moving, slow or fast, but it's moving, and so are you. Sometimes you both sit for a while, but sooner or later, you move. They send us to some beachhead, and the Germans order more ammo. Think about it," Brennan said, drawing lines in the air. "You can't stop it. A German truck brings up ammo, including your bullet, close to the front. Another truck brings you up to the line. Now you're in your foxhole, maybe a quarter mile away. You and that bullet have traveled hundreds of miles, from different parts of the world, and now you're close. A Kraut sergeant brings a case of cartridges up to his platoon, hands them around. Another Kraut loads his rifle, all the while you're moving, just like that bullet, on a path to an unknown place."

"Intersecting lines."

"Yep. And that's the only place that matters. Where the lines intersect. Don't matter what country, because once they do, once you and that bullet finally meet up, you're nowhere." Pig was in Brennan's left hand, his belly being rubbed smooth.

"Maybe they won't intersect," I said. Brennan looked up from his glass for the first time, and drew on his cigarette. He tilted his head and exhaled, then turned to look at me, his eyelids halfway shut against the smoky haze.

"I had you figured for a smart guy, Billy."

I took a drink. It was my turn to stare into the foam. The GIs at the other table all laughed quick, nervous laughs. I'd seen it too, the eager-to-please grin, the darting eyes, the intense desire to learn the secret of staying alive, as if we were magicians who had learned a special trick.

"Pete," I said. "Thornton wants to bring you in. He has the MPs out looking for you."

"Why?"

"Couldn't tell you. Why do you think?"

"I haven't done anything."

"Do you know Andrew Jenkins?"

"That bastard," Grady said, setting down his glass with a thump. "That Unionist coward Jenkins? Why would a good lad like Pete know the likes of him?"

"I don't know that he does, Grady. I do know that one of Jenkins's trucks was used in the theft, and that he delivers foodstuffs to the base regularly. As he did this afternoon, right, Pete?"

"How would I know?"

"Because you saw him, or his truck, at least. Made you a little jumpy, according to Lieutenant Jacobson. Why would that be?"

He put Pig back into his pocket. "Jumpy? He's wrong."

I put the picture of Red Jack Taggart on the table. "Is this the man you saw with Eamonn, the red-haired guy?"

"Yeah, that's him. Beady little eyes."

"Old Red Jack himself," Grady said. "I didn't know he was up north."

"Yeah, it's him. Pete saw him in here with Eddie Mahoney."

"Hey, I just had a drink with Eamonn once, that's it."

"Pete, if you have anything to be worried about, now would be a good time to let me know."

"I got plenty of worries, but they're all named Fritz or Hans. Now excuse me."

I slid off the bench and let him by. He was heeled, as I was. Except for MPs, Brennan and I were the only two I'd seen walking around wearing sidearms on and off duty.

"Where's your jeep?" I asked.

"Around back."

"I didn't see it anywhere, and I looked. Where?"

"Down a lane, behind a hedge. What do you care? Sir?"

"Well, Sergeant, it seems to me you're hiding from someone. I have to wonder who."

"Good night, Grady," Brennan said. He ignored me and walked out with that rigid straight-legged walk of someone who knows he's had too much to drink and is doing his damnedest not to show it.

CHAPTER ▪ THIRTEEN

"THE CURSE OF the livin' among the dead, that's what the lad's sufferin' from," declared Grady. "He believes everyone but him has a date with a bullet. It's comical like, if you know what I mean. All a soldier wants to do is go on livin', and there's one who can't stop, and it eats him up inside. Almost comical but it fails the test," Grady said.

"What test?"

"No one's laughing, boy." With that he let out a wheezy string of air, more sigh than laugh. Grady O'Brick's hair was gray and his face lined and pale. His shirt was worn at the collar and elbows. A ragged scarf hung around his neck against the chill. His glass was empty and the look in his eyes said he was too proud to admit he was broke.

"This is good ale," I said. "Will you have another with me?"

"That's kind of you, boy, I will. They teach good manners in America."

"My folks tried their best," I said, and brought the empty glasses over to Tom. I wasn't thirsty, I was tired, but I knew Grady would be more talkative with a fresh pint to lubricate his tongue. While Tom pulled our pints, I watched the four GIs trying to figure out the British coins. Farthings, pence, and shillings were spread out on the table as they ran their fingers over them, arguing about their worth. It made me feel like an old hand, and as I confidently thumbed out shillings to pay for my ales, I realized I was older than these guys. They looked nineteen or twenty tops. When I was their age I was still wearing blue, and now here we were in khaki and brown, the only difference between us an easy familiarity with English coins and killing men.

That depressed me. I'd been shot at, either directly or indirectly, and I was far away from anyone who cared about me, if Diana still did. I was in the country of my ancestors, but on the wrong side of the border. One of the few people who had treated me decently was dead, and the closest I'd gotten to finding the BARs was the business end of one. I shuffled back to the table and slid onto the bench. Cool foaming bubbles spilled onto my hands as I set down the glasses.

"*Sláinte*," I said, toasting Grady.

"And to your health too, Billy," Grady said. "Best you look to keep it."

"Couldn't agree with you more," I said. "Tell me, Grady, do you think Pete is hiding from Jenkins?"

"There's plenty good folk who fear to speak to the man. Any Catholic who wanders lost into his neighborhood in Armagh is not likely to leave alive. Those streets and alleys belong to the Red Hand. Jenkins is a devil, a man filled with hate, the worst of a bad lot."

"I'd bet there are some Catholic neighborhoods a Protestant should be afraid to walk in."

"Maybe, maybe. But here in the north there's no justice for a Catholic. The RUC are as likely to kill us as arrest us, and they turn a blind eye to Jenkins and his crew. Some say the Red Hand gets their arms directly from the RUC and the British army. It's a bad business all round."

Grady shook his head and took a drink. I did too, and the fresh, sharp taste of the ale cut through my weariness.

"You didn't really answer my question."

"Pete's a good lad who's been through a lot. Why not leave him be?"

I wasn't getting anywhere with my questions, so I thought I'd circle around and come at them from another direction. "You've been through a lot too," I said, glancing at his hands.

"Aye, but that was long ago."

"What happened?"

"I was a young man, that's what happened," Grady said, offering a sad smile that faded as quickly as it came. "I had ideals, and I was ready to die for a free Ireland. After the Easter Rising, I joined the IRA. They had us training out in the hills, climbing Slieve Donard, showing us how to set up ambushes, that sort of thing. A lot of foolishness, we all thought. We wanted guns, and we wanted to fight the British and the Loyalists too."

"Did you get them?" I asked, as Grady wet his whistle.

"Oh, aye, we got them. We'd been broken down into cells, as they called them. Ten lads in my cell, and the only person who knew anything was the man in charge, to best keep plans secret, you know. Everyone in the IRA swore to keep secrets, and everyone told their pals and mothers everything. But Mick the Master, he took it all serious."

"Mick the Master?"

"Aye. Mick O'Flaherty. He was foreman on a Protestant farm, and that's what everyone called him. And it fit, let me tell you."

The door opened, and a couple of local fellows came in. Grady's eyes darted over them, to Tom the barkeep, and then back to me. He leaned in, his voice lower.

"We did get our guns. Mick the Master got an Enfield rifle; the rest of us got pistols or old shotguns. They weren't much, but we put them to good use. We raided police stations, ambushed Black and Tans, and built up our own arsenal. Mick the Master knew his job well, and he made sure we followed all the rules. Never say nuthin' is what he told us. Not a word to anyone outside the cell, not even to brag you were in the IRA. We went about our work like there was no war at all. Some of the boys didn't like the idea of folks thinkin' them cowards for not joining up but Mick didn't care. When we've won, he'd say, then everyone will know. One lad, he couldn't wait. He told a girl, and she told her da, and he told Mick."

"What happened?"

"Mick took him out into the hills and came back alone."

"He killed him?"

"Executed him. Difference bein' it was war, and the poor lad had to die so's none of us would do the same, and get everyone killed. To be fair to Mick, it worked, in a way."

"But someone talked?"

"I'll get to that, but I think I'll be needin' a whiskey to tell that tale. It's not something I speak out loud more than once a decade."

I got a double whiskey from Tom. The GIs had left, and the pub was quiet. Soft clinks of glass on glass, the strike of a match, and an occasional word from Tom to the two men seated by the door were the only sounds in the room. I set the glass in front of Grady and waited. He wrapped his ruined fingers around it, watching the amber liquid swirl and settle.

"Mick the Master told us we'd become famous among the IRA chiefs.

The Black and Tans hunted for us but no one could tell them a thing. That was bad for those the bastards questioned, since they didn't stop until they got what they wanted. If you had nothin' to give, then too bad for you. But that's not the point. Do you know what a Lewis gun is?"

"Sure. British machine gun."

"Aye. Lightweight, easy to move and set up. Perfect for an ambush. Spray the lead vehicle and it stops dead, with the others bunched up behind. We wanted one, and the IRA command gave it us. They also sent crates of Enfields for us to hide, since we kept our secrets so well. We had our own arms dump, hidden in the ruins of a burned-out house in the hills. It was there we hid the Lewis gun, its ammunition, and the rifles. We took the Lewis gun out often, and let me tell you, it was a frightful thing to see so many men killed so quick. I was nearly ashamed of myself at how I enjoyed seeing them Black and Tans go down. I cheered, I have to say. That Lewis gun, it made all the difference. It was my job to keep it clean and well oiled. I knew it better than anyone."

Grady stopped, raised the glass to his lips, frowned, and put it down. He shook his head, his eyes narrowing. I thought he might weep. He rubbed his thin fingertips over his eyes, sighing as he did.

"The peat, you know. It's a lovely aroma, but it stings the eyes, it does. I shouldn't complain, though, it keeps me warm and I make some money with it when there's no other work."

"You dig peat?"

"Aye, in the bog back of my place. Dig it, cut it, dry it, haul it to my croft, stack it in ricks high as a man, and sell it to folks all around here. My peat is glorious, black as coal, the best in County Down."

"Sounds like hard work," I said. He nodded in agreement as he took a drink, smacked his lips, and set the glass down.

"Now where was I? The Lewis gun, aye. One night, we set up outside the RUC station in Downpatrick. We were waiting for a patrol to come back. Didn't have the Lewis gun on that job, it was to be a quick volley with the rifles, and then disappear. It was a good plan but we had no luck that night. The police came on as we thought they would, and we cut them down. What we didn't know was that a column of Black and Tans were on the road behind us, makin' for the station themselves. They heard the gunshots and came on at a run. I took a bullet in the leg. Two other boys were shot dead, the rest got away. I was draggin' myself after them when the bastards got me."

"Last call," Tom said from the bar. I waved him off, and waited for Grady to go on.

"They beat me somethin' fierce, which I can understand. They brought a doctor in for my leg, and then I knew I was in deep trouble. They weren't going to kill me, which meant they had somethin' worse in mind. They wanted the arms dump, you know. A British officer came into my cell, and he knew more about us than I thought he would. He knew of the Lewis gun, of course, but he also knew of the arms dump. He didn't know Mick the Master so he must've got that from someone higher up than him. It was the arms dump they wanted."

"They did that to your hands?"

"That British officer weren't no toff, I'll tell you. He didn't mind some work with pliers. He had me tied to a chair, my hands bound to the arms. Then he pulled the first nail before he even asked a question, just to show me he meant business, so he said."

He stopped for another drink. The two men left the pub, a cold wind blowing into the room as they opened the door.

"Then he asked me where the arms dump was. I didn't answer, so he went to work on the next finger." Grady looked at his left hand, and winced at the memory. "He told me he was doin' me a favor, starting on this hand, so I could save my right hand if I wanted to. I told him the joke was on him, I'm left-handed. We actually laughed, can you believe it? He said I should tell them everything right then, that no one lasted through ten fingers anyway."

"But you did."

"Oh, Billy Boyle, it was terrible, I tell you. But there was the Lewis gun, and I couldn't give it up. The rifles, yes, on the second finger I would've taken them there myself. If not for the Lewis gun, I would've told them all. It was hard work on the officer, and as he moved to the other hand, he grew angry. I was screaming bloody murder, and that got him all worked up too. Finally, there was only one thumb left untouched, and the pain was unbearable. He took to smashing each finger after the nail was pulled, and that hurt like the devil and wouldn't stop either. I couldn't help myself. I told them, I gave up the Lewis gun."

Grady took a drink, one swallow, then another.

"I gave up the Lewis gun. That officer was so mad I hadn't done it sooner that he took the last nail just for spite. To teach me a lesson, he said."

"I'm sorry," I said. I didn't know what else to say.

"Well, that weren't the worst of it. The next day they put me in a truck and gathered up some prisoners from other stations, to take us all to some prison or other they had set up. The convoy was ambushed, and the sound of a Lewis gun broke my heart. But I got away in the confusion. I hid out and made contact with one of my cell. But Mick the Master would have none of me. He knew I'd talked, since the Black and Tans had cleared out the arms dump and killed three lads who happened to be there. He drummed me out of the IRA and told me I was lucky he didn't put a bullet in my head."

"You went through all that, and he kicked you out?"

"That he did. And after the treaty was signed he let it be known what I'd done. I was persona non grata, as they say."

"He sounds like a son of a bitch."

"A hard man, aye. Those were hard times, as are these."

"You don't sound angry," I said, wishing I'd ordered my own whiskey at last call.

"I was, for a long time. Now I find myself thinking about the Lewis gun most of all. As if maybe it was recompense, for everything I'd done with it, all the lives I took, even though they were Black and Tans for the most part. If I hadn't hung on to it, this wouldn't have happened to my hands. To Mick the Master, ten fingernails or one, it made no difference."

"What happened to him?"

"He was protreaty, so he joined the new Free Irish State police. The antitreaty IRA ambushed and shot him. It was a bad end for all."

"You weren't involved in the Civil War?"

"No, it took me a while to recuperate. When I did, I tried to find the antitreaty boys, since I thought all of our own country is what we deserved. But around here, no one wanted me. Mick the Master had poisoned the well, and even his new enemies remembered I'd been the one to give up the Lewis gun. To this very day, there's folks here who won't speak to me."

"Why didn't you move south, to the Republic?"

"Strange as it may sound, this is home, I couldn't leave. Even with all the bad memories and too damn many Loyalists about. It's not so bad if I keep to myself and do what work comes my way. Ah, but if not for the Lewis gun . . ."

We sat together for a long time and said nothing else as the echo of Grady's last sentence, uttered with a sigh and a glance at his terrible fingertips, slowly died between us.

CHAPTER ▪ FOURTEEN

"I'LL SEE GRADY home," Tom said. "In this state, he'll never make it alone."

"He hasn't said a word, this half hour," I said, looking at my watch.

"He told you about the Lewis gun, did he?"

"Yes. Is it true?"

"Too true, lad. It ruined him. And what little spirit it left, Mick the Master finished off. They call him a patriot, but he was a right bastard, I'll tell you. And that comes from one who fought at his side. Grady doesn't tell his story often, but when he does, it leaves the black dog hanging over him."

"Did you fight against the British or the antitreaty IRA?"

"I fought the English, after fighting with them against the Turks. But after that I couldn't bring myself to shoot down my mates in the IRA. When they partitioned the north, I put my rifle down and settled for life as I found it. Grady never could. Couldn't leave, and most folks here wouldn't forgive. The three boys the Black and Tans killed were all local, all well liked."

"It's easy to judge a man, isn't it? Makes people feel so good." I rubbed my eyes, the weariness of the day, or the smoky peat, almost forcing me to weep.

"Aye. Come, Billy, my new friend. One for the road, on the house," Tom said, placing a plain bottle on the bar, along with two glasses. "Local brew this is—poteen, we call it. Whiskey with the taste of the land in it. Blood and rain is what I call it."

"Blood and rain," I said, as we clinked our glasses. The whiskey smelled like damp earth and oak leaves, a little musty and sharp tasting on my tongue. It burned my throat and warmed my stomach.

"What do you think?" Tom asked, corking the bottle.

"I think it's the best thing I ever tasted, and Ireland is nothing like I ever imagined."

"Aye. I imagine I'd feel the same if I went to America. I'd expect gangsters, cowboys, and Indians on every corner. Now I've got to close this place. Help me get Grady into the cart, while I hitch up me horse."

Grady went with us like an obedient child, and I helped him onto the small two-wheeled cart as Tom put a sturdy bog pony into the harness, leading him from a lean-to shelter. When he was done, Tom climbed onto the cart and gathered up the reins, nodding good night to me. Grady stirred a bit, as if suddenly awakened.

"Mind how you go now," he said, and then his chin slumped to his chest. I slapped the pony on its rump, and the cart clattered off, the sound of hooves and wooden wheels on hardpack filling the damp night air. Soon they were gone, and I was alone in a strange land of blood and rain, where fairy tales and fratricide were as common as green grass. I kicked a stone and walked to my jeep, an aching tiredness reaching up from my boots to my skull.

I drove in the moonlight, a thin slit of yellow from the taped headlights dancing over the roadway. The wind felt fresh on my face, and it reminded me of a piece of poetry my dad used to recite about the Wild Geese, the Irish exiles who for centuries fought against the English in European armies far from their homes.

The whole night long we dream of you, and waking think we're there,
Vain dream, and foolish waking, we never shall see Clare.
The wind is wild to-night, there's battle in the air;
The wind is from the west, and it seems to blow from Clare.

Dad was big on poetry and reading. He'd recite the poems he liked the best, storing them up, and letting loose down at the tavern once the crowd had thinned out. He had plenty of them, but the vain dreams and foolish wakings of the boys from Clare always made me sad. Now my home was far away in the west, and I wondered if I'd dream of it tonight. Or Diana. Perhaps in some dark and dangerous place, alone and scared, she was feeling the wind from home. I missed her, more than I'd allowed myself to know.

I AWOKE IN my quarters shivering. It was dark and cold in the Quonset hut. My head hurt, and my eyes were gritty from the effects of smoke and shame for my countrymen. I lit a fire, blowing on the flames in the small stove until the wood scraps caught and flickering yellow light filled the room. I drank long gulps from a canteen, the water cold and metallic on my tongue.

What was I missing? The question kept playing over and over in my tired, aching head. How could I get close to the IRA when anyone who mentioned them could expect to earn a pound the hard way? There had to be another approach, something I hadn't thought of. Carrick didn't seem to have anything solid to go on either. Was he holding back? But why? To protect someone? Not the IRA, or any Catholic, for that matter. Jenkins? The Red Hand? Maybe. But I had no way of knowing if Carrick actually had any information I didn't. He didn't seem to be a friend of any extremists. But he had promised to check out his informants and those run by the British. It would be interesting to find out why Mahoney had been executed. If he wasn't a traitor to the IRA, then why had he been killed?

Thornton? I'd have to ask him in the morning why he'd held back about Carrick requesting Brennan's files, and try to figure out if he was on the level about getting a combat command or if he was trying to position himself farther to the rear when the shooting started. But so what if he was? No law against saving your own skin.

Heck? He was a wild card. He obviously wanted to step up the command ladder but again, no law against looking out for number one. I wasn't sure he'd done any more actual investigating than Thornton. Yet Lasner had told me Heck went through paperwork in the communications center. That was something at least. Maybe I should ask him what he found. Maybe he'd tell me if I asked nicely. Or arrest me.

Wait a minute. I tried to think back to exactly what Lasner had said Heck was looking for. He hadn't said anything specific, just that Heck had been looking through receipts and bills of lading. But what did that have to do with BARs? There would have been one bill of lading when the freight shipment of weapons came in and that was it. So what was Heck looking for? Lasner had made it sound like he was pawing through *stacks* of paper.

I drank some more water and tried to think it through. Nothing made sense. What could Heck be looking for here that had anything to do with the BAR theft at Ballykinler or Sam Burnham being murdered at Killough? And had Sam been the real target at Killough? Or had it been me?

I climbed back into my sleeping bag and tried to keep the wooden supports on the canvas cot from digging into my ribs. Tomorrow, I thought, tomorrow talk to Lasner about those papers. Go see Jenkins about the truck. And Thornton, something about Thornton twitched at the back of my mind as a steady rain drummed on the curved corrugated steel, lulling me to sleep, images of shattered windows and blood red curtains filling my dreams.

DEW HUNG HEAVY on the grass and clung to my boots as I walked from the mess tent to the communications center. White clouds to the east were parted by the sun, which cast the shadows of fir trees over the camp. The air was rich with a damp, green aroma and I breathed it in deeply. The cool air cleared my head.

There was something wrong with the paperwork, there had to be. Only thing was, I was fairly certain it didn't have anything to do with the weapons theft. There wasn't any reason to sift through stacks of receipts, shipping orders, and bills of lading to solve that crime. The other thing I was certain of, since I had asked one of the cooks who had given me a ride the other night, was that this mess facility didn't use any local produce. All grub was courtesy of Uncle Sam. But Ballykinler was a much bigger base. This was only a headquarters camp, and there was no place to store fresh foodstuffs. That might be important if my hunch was right.

"Good morning, Lieutenant," Sergeant Lasner said as I entered his communications center. "I heard about your close call yesterday. It's too bad about Sam Burnham."

"Real bad," I said. "News travels fast."

"This is the communications center," Lasner said, "sir." He looked offended that anyone would doubt he was well informed.

"When was Major Thornton told?"

"I told him myself last night, as soon as the message came in from Ballykinler about the ambulance going for his body."

"What did he say?"

"I don't recall exactly, Lieutenant. Something about it being horrible. Why?"

"Did he ask about me?"

"Not a word. What exactly is this about?"

"Nothing, Sarge, nothing at all. Listen, can you show me the files Heck was looking through, the ones you told me about?"

"No, I can't."

"Why?"

"They're gone. I had them all boxed up too. It took one of the clerks all day to sort things out after Heck pulled papers from every file cabinet we have. It was a mess. But we straightened it out and put everything back in the right order. Then Major Thornton came by asking what Heck had been looking for. I showed him the box and he took it."

"Why?" I asked. It seemed to be the only question I could come up with.

"Because he's a major, and I'm a noncom."

There was nothing to say to that.

I walked to the main building, heading for Thornton's office. GIs in fatigues and packs stood around outside, waiting for someone to order them to march somewhere for no discernible reason. Clerks clutching files and flimsies scuttled in and out, moving the paperwork that kept a division in red tape. So much paper, so many forms and orders, it was paperwork that kept the wheels turning, and if you knew how to work it, you could get just about anything you wanted, especially if it could be painted green.

But you could get other things too, and if you were part of a unit bivouacked in one place temporarily, then you could count on paperwork getting lost or tossed as nonessential, when your next destination was an invasion beach. I was taking a gamble, but I was ready to give odds that Thornton and Brennan, along with Jenkins, were tangled up in something that had nothing to do with BARs or the IRA. I'd been righter than I thought when I goaded Heck about not having a single lead. He didn't; he wasn't even trying to find who took the BARs. He probably knew he was out of his depth there. But his interest in bills of lading and the like told me he was onto something, something that was more in his line.

I was steamed at being sidetracked but that didn't mean I couldn't make time to deal with the source of my anger. I was nearing Thornton's office, my mind racing with ideas on how best to take this major down, when out strolled Sergeant Pete Brennan, whistling a tune, his hands in his pockets as if he didn't have a care in the world.

"Hi, Lieutenant, how are you doing?"

"What do you mean, how am I doing? Aren't you going to be court-martialed?"

"No, no," Brennan said, waving his hand back and forth. "That was all a little misunderstanding. The major and I are copacetic. I gotta get back now."

"Wait a minute," I said, grabbing him by the arm. "I know what's going on here. Between you, Thornton, and Jenkins." I wasn't as sure as I sounded, but sounding sure was a good technique for rattling suspects. "Tell me, Pete, what do you have on Thornton?"

"I don't know what you're talking about," he said, his voice lowered to a whisper. "Now let me go."

"You're playing a dangerous game," I said. "Not with Thornton but with Jenkins. If he's involved, you could be in big trouble."

"What do you mean *if*, Lieutenant? A second ago you said you knew what was going on. Leave me alone, please." With that, he pulled his arm from my grip and walked out the main door, glancing left and right as he headed for a jeep. I took a deep breath, shaking my head at Brennan's foolishness. Hoping I was wrong for his sake, I walked into Thornton's office and pushed the door hard, so it slammed against the wall.

"What the—I'll call you back, I have to go," said Thornton, slamming down the receiver. "Boyle, are you drunk?"

"I was last night, Major. You know what would have tasted really good for breakfast? Ham and eggs. Not powdered eggs and Spam, but the real thing. Know what I mean?" I sat myself down on the corner of his desk and stared at him.

"Any problem, Major?" A corporal leaned into the office from the hallway, glanced at me and back to Thornton.

"No, nothing wrong," Thornton said. "Wind took the door. Shut it, will you?"

The door clicked shut and we were alone. Thornton didn't say anything. He didn't ask me why I was blabbing on about ham and eggs, like any innocent guy would've. Instead, he gulped as sweat broke out on his forehead.

"I have a few questions," I said.

"Have you found the BARs yet?" Thornton was putting a brave face on things, trying to put me on the defensive. It might have worked with some lieutenants but not this one.

"Gee, Major, no. You see, things have been kind of confusing, trying to figure out who's involved in a dangerous arms theft and who's involved in penny-ante bribery and skimming of army funds."

"What are you talking about?" He tried to put some indignation into it, but it came out as desperation.

"First, where did the whiskey come from?"

"Huh?" I knew I was right. Any honest senior officer would have called the MPs by now. Instead, Thornton sat looking up at me, his mouth hanging open.

"That's one of my questions. Where did the whiskey come from?" I pointed to the corner of the room, where three cases of Irish whiskey had been the last time I was there. This morning, only one remained.

"You know how it is, Boyle. . . ."

"OK, let's try this one. How did Brennan find out?"

"Find out what?" The last word had a long, drawn-out sound, as if he were about to start crying.

"That's OK, Major, I have more. Like what did you do with the paperwork you took from the communications center?"

"It's around here somewhere, I may have misplaced it. I wanted to look into it myself, I thought maybe I, I . . . I don't know," Thornton said, exhausting himself with lies.

"What's in that drawer?"

"Which drawer?" Thornton asked, his eyes darting for a second to a desk drawer.

"That one," I said, pointing to the middle drawer on his right. "The one you stuffed some papers into when I was here. It's locked I bet. Right?"

"No, look, it's empty," he said with pathetic eagerness. He pulled the drawer open, revealing a paper clip and dust.

"Your other drawers empty too?"

"No, they aren't. Why?"

"Because, you stupid oaf, why should that drawer be empty unless you got rid of everything in it?"

"Boyle, you can't talk to me like that, really."

"OK, call your CO. Tell him. Tell him there's a second louie in your office saying real bad things about you."

"Hold on, hold on. We can work this out."

"Maybe," I said. "Let's start by me telling you a few things, and you tell me if I've gotten anything wrong." I raised my eyebrows, waiting for him to answer.

"Huh? Oh, OK, sure." He shook a cigarette from a pack and lit up. He didn't offer me one.

"You and Jenkins cooked up some sort of scheme. My guess is that he started with a few personal gifts to you. Whiskey to start, then some nice cuts of meat, pork, and lamb, just for you. You liked it, and then one day he suggested an arrangement. Basically he bills the army for more than he delivers and gives you a kickback. Who's to know? It's all food to be consumed, and you're in charge of the paperwork. Once you leave, it will all disappear anyway. Why not make some dough while you can? Hell, you know the division is headed for trouble, might as well make some hay while the sun shines, right?"

"He's a very nasty man."

"I'm sure he forced the arrangement on you. But then Brennan comes along, assigned to kitchen detail. I don't know how, but he sees that things don't add up. Maybe he compares a bill of lading from a delivery with the invoice or the receipt, it really doesn't matter. I bet he went straight to you."

"I told Jenkins it had to stop. I did!"

"But he said no. He told you he'd take care of Brennan."

"I didn't want that to happen."

"No, it would draw too much attention. So you move Brennan out of the kitchen, which suited him just fine. I'm sure you said you'd implicate him if he said anything. Then you started pulling paperwork, getting rid of any evidence. That's what was on your desk the other day. That's why you were so upset."

"How did you know?"

"Heck has been pawing through Lasner's communications, you knew that. It didn't make any sense that it was part of his investigation into the BAR theft. He had to be looking into something more long-term. I knew Brennan had been nervous about seeing Jenkins's delivery trucks on the base, and then I remembered he'd been working in the kitchens when he first got here. I figured Jenkins had threatened him, and that you and Brennan were each holding the threat of talking over each other's heads. Then, when the BAR raid came along, you figured it was the perfect opportunity to take Brennan down for a crime he had no part of."

"But I'm not arresting him; there isn't going to be a court-martial."

"Right. Because he's got something on you. Something he probably showed you this morning." I leaned to look into the wastepaper basket by his desk. A thin layer of ash lay at the bottom. "Which you burned. What are they? A stack of invoices and receipts that don't match?"

"Yes," said Thornton, as he held his head in his hands. His voice cracked with emotion. "He had receipts from the deliveries at the mess hall, matched up with invoices I signed off on. It's enough to put me away."

"What does Brennan want?"

"That's just the thing," he said, looking up to me as if I might have the answer. "He said all he wants is to be left alone. But Jenkins won't leave him alone as long as he has that evidence. I tried to reason with him, to give him money, but he won't listen."

"Why was he so cheery when he left here?"

"I told him I'd work on a transfer for him, back to his old outfit."

"In Italy?"

"Yes. They're still on the line, attacking along the Volturno River, someplace I never heard of. Can you believe it? He wants to go back to that."

"Yeah, hard to believe a guy would want to go back into combat rather than associate himself with you."

"Hey, if Brennan had just kept his mouth shut, everything would have been fine. But no, he had to go and screw things up. If Jenkins does anything to him, it won't be on my head, I'll tell you that."

"Where's the money?" I asked.

"What money?"

"Don't even try—"

"Listen, Boyle, if you've got some evidence against me, go ahead and take it to Heck. Come to think of it, why isn't he here? If you've broken this big case, why aren't the MPs taking me away in irons?"

Thornton was finally adding it up. He was right. All I had was a story. If he'd gotten rid of all the evidence, except for what Brennan had squirreled away, then I'd have a hard time making it stick.

"How come you lied to me about wanting a combat command?"

"I do."

"Ordnance officer at Corps HQ is not exactly in the line of fire."

"Get the hell out, Boyle."

"OK," I said, thinking over my options. I should just walk away, forget about Thornton, and get on with the investigation. "Mind if I take this?" I pointed to the whiskey.

"If it gets you out of here, then with my compliments. No reason you can't share in the wealth. Maybe you're not as dumb as you look after all."

"Could be," I said, lifting the case. "We'll see."

CHAPTER FIFTEEN

I STOPPED AT the communications center, gave Lasner a bottle of Bushmills, and said I needed to use a telephone in private. He put the bottle in his desk drawer, me in a small office down the hall, and shut the door without asking a question. I put in a call to Captain Hiram Heck, and held the receiver away from my ear until he calmed down enough to listen. I managed to get a few words in, got a grunt in return that I interpreted as agreement, and winced as he slammed the phone down, his way of saying goodbye.

It was about sixty miles to Brownlow House in Lurgan, according to the directions Lasner gave me. I could tell I'd gone up a notch in his estimation of me as a rookie second lieutenant when he took the time to walk me out to the jeep, going over the route he'd marked on a map to lead me to Corps Headquarters.

"In the center of Newcastle you'll see a sign for Castlewellan Road. Take that; it goes to a town of the same name. You'll cross the Dublin Road in Castlewellan, then take the Ballyward Road to the village of Ballyward," he said, pointing out the towns. The next one was Katesbridge.

"Let me guess. Then I take the Katesbridge Road?"

"Yeah, but you have to watch out. They also name the roads from the other direction, so this same roadway becomes the Castlewellan Road again, once you get to Banbridge. Then you're almost there. After Banbridge, take the Lurgan Road."

"To Lurgan."

"Right. In the town center there are signs for Corps HQ. Brownlow

House is a huge place, a manor house, I'd guess you call it. Hard to miss anyway; it's the biggest thing in town."

"OK, thanks, Sarge," I said as I took down the canvas top to the jeep. I saw him glance in the back at the case of whiskey.

"You have a whole case of Bushmills," he said, a slight petulant tone creeping into his voice. I guess one bottle seemed like a lot when he thought that was all I had to give.

"Less one, Sarge. Sorry, I need these. I'm not even keeping any for myself."

"Well, OK, Lieutenant, if you say so. I haven't seen that much quality hooch in one place since I've been here. Good liquor doesn't seem to make its way down the chain of command."

"Ain't that the way of the world?" I waved as I drove off, glad that Lasner seemed cheered by the thought that he had one more bottle than I'd end up with. He was right about all the good stuff going to the higher ranks, and I was too low on the rank scale to disagree with him. Lieutenants were a dime a dozen and didn't get much of a cut; the valuables went up to captains, majors, colonels, and generals. Stuff like scotch, whiskey, fleece-lined leather coats meant for bomber crews, penicillin, these things all flowed in a supply line from the States to bases all over the world on their way to the front. At each stop, the freight got lighter and guys like Heck sported jump boots and other gear they needed to make themselves feel like they were real soldiers.

Booze was one thing, especially here when we were practically in the backyard of the Bushmills distillery. But cold-weather gear, ciga-rettes, morphine, I'd seen it all pilfered at rear-area supply depots, and it made me sick. I had no desire to hack another foxhole out of the hardpacked Italian ground, but if I did, I'd want to be warm once I climbed into it. If I was wounded, I didn't want to run out of morphine syrettes because a quartermaster had a habit or a connection in Belfast, London, or Algiers who was offering top dollar.

Everyone's a thief, I told myself, enjoying the sun on my face as I drove through the pines, down the hill to Newcastle. From the cop on the beat who takes an apple from the greengrocer to the government that takes a cut out of your paycheck. It's simply a matter of how much harm you cause when you take what isn't yours. I didn't know where the line was, the place where the harm was serious, but I knew enough to stay on the side of it that let me sleep at night.

I found Castlewellan Road in Newcastle and quickly left the town behind, as homes and shops gave way to neatly squared-off fields, their stone walls and thin lines of trees corralling masses of sheep, all quietly eating, their heads down to the ground, intent on nothing but the green stalks in front of them. Fattening up for the hard winter, as were the GIs at Ballykinler and bases like it everywhere in Great Britain, North Africa, and Italy. Those who had been based here before them had gone ashore in North Africa when I did, and now a lot of them were dead, more wounded, some prisoners, and others, like Pete Brennan, alive by no grace they could understand. Me, I wasn't that deep a thinker. I was glad to be alive and I was as ready to thank God for the favor as a carved wooden pig. I had no idea if God played a part in deciding who was going to die on the battlefield or in the parlor of an RUC policeman's house. Not too long ago, a guy next to me on a ridgeline in Sicily had taken a bullet to the forehead. If that was how God spent his time, I'd take my chances with Pig.

I slowed as I drove through Castlewellan, sharing the wide roadway with trucks, motorbikes, and farmers' carts drawn by sturdy horses. In the town center the road was lined with large, old chestnut trees, hanging onto the last of their greenery before the harsh cold took hold and pulled it down. I passed a Celtic stone cross set in the middle of an intersection and a series of shops in whitewashed stone buildings. Henry Devlin, Spirits and Grocer. Bustard's Shoes and Boots. Shilliday Hardware. For the first time since I'd landed, I felt as if I was in Ireland. Not the Republic but the island of Ireland, away from the war, the British, and the IRA. The names, the streets, shops, and people all felt comfortable to me, like a pair of old boots I might have bought years ago at Bustard's.

I resisted the urge to find a pub and have an early lunch and chat with the regulars. I felt that if I did, I might not ever leave. Strange that in this alien place of my childhood nightmares, where Orangemen lurked to lop off the heads of young Catholic boys, I should feel as if I were driving home, maybe from a Sunday outing to Weymouth, coming back through Dorchester and seeing the familiar shops and stores drift past my window, as Dad waved to the town cop directing traffic, his white gloves moving in gleaming arcs toward Southie.

The ground rose west of Castlewellan, the rock-enclosed patches of land tilting themselves upward on either side of the road, a damp chill blowing around me as I pulled my cap down tight. The sun was bright but not warm, the November air cooling the rays that cast shadows at my back, as if the sunlight itself were a lie.

This wasn't the hot warmth of Jerusalem, it was the shining light of my ancestors' homeland, and I shivered in it, thinking of Diana, wondering if sweat was still running in rivulets between her breasts, or if she too had been sent to serve under a different sun, and if she was warmed or chilled under it. Too soon, I told myself. It's too soon. She'd have to be briefed and made ready. Outfitted with the right clothes, all with European labels, that sort of thing. They can't produce that stuff overnight, can they? I ached to have those moments in Jerusalem back, to say the right things to her. I didn't know what they might be, but I knew I hadn't said them. I couldn't have; I was only thinking of myself, how her choices affected me. I felt like a bum.

Thinking about Diana started me worrying about her, and that made me drive faster. I took a curve too quickly and had to brake hard to keep from drifting off the road. I downshifted and took a deep breath. OK, relax, I told myself. Think about something else. BARs. Think about BARs.

Before I could, I had to brake again, this time for a slow-moving wagon coming my way, pulled by two thick-hoofed horses clip-clopping along, their load of manure destined for some farmer's field. Lucky him. I tried not to breathe as we passed on the narrow road. Except for that stretch through Castlewellan, I hadn't seen a wide road anywhere since I'd gotten here. The roads of Northern Ireland—and I expect those of the Republic as well—had not been built for the volume of army traffic they were seeing these days.

That's right. It was slow going around here. And on a rainy night, like the night the BARs were stolen, how far could you drive? I reminded myself to check out a map and estimate the maximum distance, and compare that with where the truck was found. If it was at the outside distance, then they transferred the BARs right there. If not, they could have done it elsewhere and then dumped the truck. But why? Close to someone's home? Or did they have another car nearby? It was worth looking into.

I drove into Lurgan, which was a sizable town with cramped, sooty brick buildings hooded by gray slate roofs. It looked like it needed a good rain to wash the grime away. Past the town center, the buildings thinned out and I followed a sign for U.S. Army Corps HQ, taking a right and driving along a road with a tall, black wrought-iron fence pacing me on the left. I slowed and turned at a gate in the fence, which was decorated with all sorts of curlicues. The monstrosity in front of me had to be Brownlow House. The sun bathed the brown stone with yellow light, turning it almost golden. It was topped by a single large turret, something out of *Aladdin and the Magic Lamp.* Surrounding the turret was a forest of chimneys, set at every height the house had to offer. It looked like every room had one, which meant they were probably the only source of heat.

I pulled the jeep over behind a line of others, grabbed my case of whiskey, and walked up to one of the snowdrops guarding the main entrance.

"Hey, pal," I said, "Where's the G-1's office?"

"Whaddya got there, Lieutenant?" The MP asked. Apparently the word BUSHMILLS, printed in three-inch letters, white on black, didn't mean anything to him.

"You a teetotaler?" I asked him. His buddy snorted a quick laugh, and then looked away.

"No, I ain't," he said, fast and loud enough to tell me he'd rather be pegged as illiterate than as a nondrinker. "I just can't let you walk in here without checking, that's all." He opened the case as I held it. "You're missing one," he said as he closed it back up.

"Thanks. Must be a crime wave. So where's the G-1 and what's his name?"

"That'd be Colonel Warrenton. Go up the main stairs and ask at the duty desk. This place is a maze."

He was right. At the top of a staircase wide enough for a squad to march abreast, a duty officer guided me down two hallways and pointed to a door. As I walked up to it, I glanced into the office across the hall. The door was open, and the chair at the desk was empty. A tall, wiry officer in a jeep coat stood with his back to me, smoking as he stared out an open window. I turned away and knocked on the closed door with G-1 stenciled on it.

"Come," an abrupt voice sounded out.

"Colonel Warrenton?" I asked as I shut the door with my foot.

"Who the hell are you?" Warrenton sat with his back to the window, a broad green lawn stretching out into the distance. My first thought was that I'd turn the desk around and look at that instead of a wooden door. "Come on, man, I don't have all day," he snapped.

"Lieutenant Boyle, sir. Major Thornton told me drop by and give you this, with his compliments." As I looked for a place to set the case down I realized why Warrenton hadn't turned the desk around. Every square inch of it as well as the table beside it were filled with stacks of files, forms, and carbon copies of what were probably the same forms. I doubted he'd ever have a chance to look at the door, never mind the lawn.

"Major who?" he said, eyeing me as he spoke. He had a sallow, square face, his jowls starting to drape, probably from bending his head over a desk full of papers all day and half the night. His eyes darted back and forth, looking at anything but me. He was a lousy liar.

"Colonel, there's nothing to hide. Don't worry, this is only a gift. I'll put it down here," I said, placing the case at the side of his desk. "Major Thornton hopes that you can bring me along with him, if his transfer works out."

"Sit down, Lieutenant, and tell me what you're talking about," Warrenton said. As I did, he leaned over and flipped open the case. "There's one missing," he said as his head came up.

"One what?" I asked in mock ignorance. I waited while silence filled the space between us. Finally, he laughed.

"Very good, Lieutenant—what was it?"

"Boyle, sir. William Boyle."

He wrote the name on a piece of paper, folded it, and opened a drawer, carefully placing it in an envelope. "How long have you worked for Major Thornton?"

"Not long. I got transferred from North Africa. Too hot for my taste."

"Things might get hot for you again in a few months. Scuttlebutt says the division is training for the big invasion. You have any ordnance experience?" He'd gone from "Major who?" to acknowledging he knew Thornton and the assignment he wanted, in less time than it would have taken to open one of those bottles.

"None, Colonel. I'm what you might call a supply specialist. You need a supply of something, I make a special effort to get it. Like this whiskey."

"You said it was from Thornton."

"Well, in a way it was. It was his. Now it's yours. You see, every-thing that he's been organizing for you, well that was me doing all the work. I figured he probably didn't mention that, so I thought I'd bring you the last case by myself."

"He said there wasn't any more."

"Well, goes to show, know what I mean?"

"Lieutenant Boyle, I think we can use someone with your initiative at corps, I really do. Thanks for stopping by for a visit."

"Don't mention it, sir."

"Don't you mention it, Boyle. To anyone—understood?"

"Not even the major?"

"Major who?"

Now it was my turn to laugh. Before I was on my feet, his head was buried in his papers again, rearranging folders, assigning personnel to wherever his whim dictated or wherever the payoffs led. Like a councilman back home, he had the power to grant favors, but his were of the life-or-death variety. You, to a rifle squad. You, with the whiskey and hams, over to HQ. Maybe he thought that since people were going to die anyway, he ought to get fat off it. Or rich. I shut the door behind me and walked into the office opposite.

"Well?" Heck asked as he flicked a cigarette out the window. His Adam's apple bobbed in that scrawny throat.

"I was right. Thornton's paying him off for a transfer to corps. Probably others too; he seemed like a smooth operator. Check the second drawer to his left, he put my name in an envelope there."

"OK, Boyle, I can break him. I'll tell him we just picked up you and Thornton, and that the only way he can save his hide is to tell all. Good work." He placed a thick envelope in my hand and brushed past me, into Warrenton's office. I shut the door behind him, sat down at the empty desk, and opened it. Out spilled his side of the bargain.

I'd made a deal with Heck. I'd promised him it would make him look good, and that I'd stay out of the limelight. I figured he'd been on the trail of whoever was shorting supplies being delivered to the division—why else would he be looking through all those shipping invoices and bills of lading? He might have been trying to make a connection between the weapons theft and the supply pilferage, but I doubted he'd gotten anywhere with that.

The key was to find someone who would turn on Thornton. I didn't think Brennan would, for a lot of reasons. He'd gotten what he'd wanted from Thornton, and anyway I didn't want to interfere with whatever he felt he had to do. It had to be someone else, preferably a higher-ranking someone else, who'd be happy to let all the shit roll downhill in Thornton's direction. The gamble I took was that Thornton was trying to bribe the corps G-1, the personnel officer who could approve his transfer to the corps ordnance unit, which would be about as far to the rear as you could get and still claim to be in the shooting war. It all fit, though, with the lies about Brennan and the story about wanting to get a combat command with the heavy weapons company. I'd figured the worst thing that could happen was that Heck would get even madder at me, which hardly seemed possible, and that an innocent G-1 would get a free case of Irish whiskey.

In return, Heck agreed to hand over his file on the BAR case and give me free rein, plus any manpower I needed. All I had to do was share the glory with him if I found anything. Glory was the last thing I wanted. All that did was create the notion that I was the guy to call on when things were really tough, like Cosgrove had for this job. I preferred to stay with Uncle Ike, farther away from the shooting than Thornton ever dreamed of. So glory, that would be all Heck's, yet I bargained hard to give up my share of it. He had to think it was as important to me as it was to him. That's what bought me the promise of help if I needed it.

I dumped the contents of the envelope Heck had handed me onto the desk. Photos of the crime scene showed empty shelves where the BARs had been stored. The broken lock on the storeroom door. Tire impressions left in the mud. All the usual stuff, nothing helpful, since we had already identified the truck.

There were several photos of Eddie Mahoney with the back of his head missing. He lay in a ditch by the side of a road, facedown. The rain had soaked his clothing and he'd sunk into the mud, as if he'd been half buried in a shallow grave. There was a shot of his hand, with the edges of a pound note visible within his grasp. Another of his face, after they'd turned him over. It was hard to tell what he'd looked like in life; the violence of the gunshots to his head combined with the mud caked around his face to make him look misshapen and grotesque. Another shot showed the surrounding area, including the road. Mahoney's feet stuck out from the edge of the ditch, as if he'd been standing by the side of the road when he was shot. Another photo showed him from the opposite direction. There was one photo of Mahoney alive on a city street. Could have been a surveillance shot. I put that one in my pocket.

I squinted my eyes to make out a building visible at the side of the road, maybe twenty yards or so from where Mahoney lay. It looked familiar, with its white walls and thatched roof. It was the Lug o' the Tub Pub, and this was the road I'd watched Tom McCarthy drive Grady O'Brick down last night.

Eddie Mahoney had been shot yards from the pub where Grady drank most every night! Had Grady walked by the body, not noticing it in the darkness? Or had Mahoney's killer shot him on the return trip from the base, after closing hours? Why not? It would be smart to keep him alive to help with the loading, and wait until after the theft to dispose of him. But that depended on why he was shot. If he was an informer, Carrick probably would have known. But neither he nor Sláine O'Brien had owned up to running him. Was he a danger to his companions? Dangerous enough to kill during the course of such a bold theft? It didn't make sense, but then, that was my job, wasn't it? To make sense out of a mass of unrelated facts.

I glanced at the RUC report, which was a copy of the one Sláine had given me. There was one new page, a note saying no fingerprints had been found on Jenkins's truck; it had apparently been wiped clean. There was a longer provost marshal's report. Nothing new about the theft or the murder but Heck had assigned one of his men to tail Jenkins the day after. The surveillance report covered three days. On the first, Jenkins drove to Newry, near the border, and went to the RUC station to make arrangements to get his truck back. The second day after the theft, he went to a pub in Portadown and met a girl. All work and no play, as they say.

A photo was attached. A man I assumed was Jenkins held open the door of Bennett's Pub for a young woman. Although it was a grainy black-and-white photo, I knew her hair was red. It was a mass of curls, pulled back to reveal her face, which was turned back to the street, as if she was checking whether anyone had seen her. Sláine O'Brien, entering a Portadown pub with Andrew Jenkins, leader of the Red Hand.

I sat with the photo in my hand, trying to understand what it meant. Two days after the theft and the killing of an IRA man, Sláine O'Brien meets with Andrew Jenkins. Three days later, she's sitting in a Jerusalem hotel room, telling me he's some sort of big wheel with the Protestant secret militia, engaged in reprisal killings. Was this a setup? No, I couldn't see how that would work. If she were working with

Jenkins, taking down IRA men, why travel to the Middle East and bring me in? Unless it was the other way around, and Jenkins was working for her. Was the head of the Red Hand part of MI-5? They were practically hand in glove with the Brits already, so what good would that do?

Plenty, I realized. Although wartime powers gave MI-5 enough muscle to do whatever they wanted, sometimes there was no substitute for cold-blooded killing. British forces could kill all the Germans they wanted by whatever means. But if someone from a neutral country, like Ireland, or a British subject from Northern Ireland, needed to be put in the ground, then who better for the job than one of Andrew Jenkins's Red Hand boys?

I moved on to day three of the surveillance, which ended abruptly when Heck's man was spotted following Jenkins on his way to work in Armagh. One hour later, with Jenkins at work in his office, an alibi confirmed by half a dozen employees, persons unknown assaulted Heck's man and put him in traction. End of surveillance.

The report detailed the follow-up to Thornton's reported sighting of Eddie Mahoney at the pub in Annalong. I realized I hadn't told Carrick about Pete Brennan's possible meeting with Mahoney in Ardglass. Redheaded Irishmen weren't exactly in short supply but it was something to go on. The barman at the Harbor Bar in Annalong remembered Mahoney, who had called himself Eamonn. That, combined with his red top, made him memorable during the week or so he frequented the place. The barman hadn't recalled who Eamonn had been with, he said, until an American, a civilian, had come around with a picture, asking if the man in it had been in the pub recently. The American matched the description Carrick had given me: about forty or so, wearing a trench coat and fedora hat. The barman had remembered the man who'd been with Eamonn: He'd had receding dark brown hair and a sharp chin. That fit Red Jack Taggart to a T.

But that was not a surprise. I knew Mahoney had been in on the theft, and obviously so had Red Jack, since I'd seen his handiwork with the BAR. The report noted that no other investigator from the provost marshal's office had been detailed to investigate the matter. So who was the Yank with the picture of Red Jack, and how did this mystery man know he'd recently been in Annalong?

Heck had included a copy of a memorandum sent to various other commands, inquiring if anyone had initiated an investigation in the Annalong area, without mentioning any names. He'd come up empty.

I was beginning to wish I hadn't thought up this deal. Now I knew I couldn't trust Sláine O'Brien, and that an unknown person was tracking Red Jack Taggart, for an unknown reason. Great.

There was a knock at the door, two tentative, light raps.

"Yeah?" I said, rubbing my eyes and wishing I was someplace else.

"Uh, can I have my office back, if it's convenient, I mean?" The door opened an inch or two and the guy on the other side barely spoke above a whisper.

"Yeah, come on in. What's going on across the hall?"

"Captain Heck took Colonel Warrenton away," said a chubby captain, wearing glasses and clutching a pile of papers. "What's going on anyway? Who are you? No, never mind, I don't want to know." He stood against the door, holding his papers even closer to his chest as if they might protect him.

"Captain," I said as I gathered up my files, "that's about the smartest thing I've heard anybody say in the past few days. You can have your office back now, and thanks. Is there a mess hall in this joint where I can get a cup of joe?"

"Ask at the duty desk. I still get lost in this place." With that, he dumped the paperwork onto the desk and sat down as soon as I got out of his way. As I walked out, I noticed the sign on his door. G-2. Intelligence. Sometimes all you can do is laugh.

IT WAS THE fanciest damn mess hall I'd ever been in. Two huge fireplaces opposite each other, big enough to stand in. Four long tables that could seat fifty each, with portraits high up on the walls, stiff-necked men all looking down on us colonials. I ate my cheese sandwich and drank good strong coffee with sugar. I wondered how much sugar went for on the black market, and how much of the stuff Thornton had pinched. I'd heard there were regular smuggling routes over the border into the Republic, where butter and sugar weren't rationed. I wondered how hard the RUC or the Garda Síochána, the Republic's police force, worked to stop smuggling. I added a touch more sugar to my coffee and stirred it in, thankful at least that the army had first dibs on the stuff.

"Billy, right?" a voice said from behind me. "Mind if I sit with you?"

"No, have a seat," I said, trying to place the lieutenant setting down a tray of food.

"You probably don't recognize me all cleaned up. Bob Masters. I&R Platoon."

"Sorry, Bob, you look different without all the mud. How are you doing? Still running your men up and down the mountain?"

"Up, down, and around. What brings you here?"

"Paperwork," I said. "How about you?"

"Briefing on infiltration tactics. I'll be glad to get out of here; this place gives me the willies."

"What do you mean?"

"You don't know about Brownlow House? And you, one of the true Irish rebels?" He smiled as he gobbled down some sort of stew.

"Except that it's ugly as all get-out? No."

"Billy, this building is the headquarters of the Royal Black Knights of the British Commonwealth. That's a very exclusive Protestant society."

"Never heard of them."

"Exactly. They're more orange than the Orange Society. And twice as secretive."

"You're kidding, right?"

"Nope. I've seen their rooms in the south wing. The Ulster government took over the building for the duration, but let the Black Knights keep a section. They meet here every month. They even say there's a secret tunnel somewhere that the original Lord Brownlow had dug so he could sneak out at night without his wife knowing."

"I'm still trying to get the Black Knight thing straight, so never mind about the secret tunnel tall tales, OK?"

"It's true, one of the chaplains told me. It's more of a religious thing; they're not into politics as much as the Orange Society. More like the Masons back home maybe. Pretty hard to get admitted, the padre said."

"Why?"

"I forget. Basically you have to be Protestant every which way and never have had any family connected with the Roman Catholic Church."

"Was it a priest who told you this?"

"No, a Methodist minister. Said he was studying up on the local religious customs."

"He'll need a scorecard for that."

I LEFT BOB Masters to his stew, glad to escape the gloom of Brownlow House and visions of Black Knight rituals held within its rooms. I walked down a staircase to the third floor and along a corridor lit by tall windows along the outside wall, which I was fairly sure led to the way out. I looked into the courtyard below to make sure I was on the right side of the building. Below me, leaning against a wall that angled off to the left, was a guy in a trench coat, wearing a gray fedora. He flicked a cigarette and jammed his hands into his pockets. He was too close beneath me to get a look at his face, but he moved like an American. Too casual for a Brit. Was this the mystery Yank?

I looked for another exit, one that would put me behind him. But by the time I found a door, I wasn't sure which side of this crazy building I was on. There were so many angles and twists that I'd gotten myself turned around. I ran along the wall, peeking around each corner I came to, until I found the spot where he'd been. Nothing. He was gone, not a fedora in sight. I heard a motorcycle start up from around the corner and ran to look as the rider gunned it and drove off down the driveway. He was bareheaded but his collar was turned up and buttoned tight, so I couldn't catch a glimpse of his face. A jeep and a slow-moving truck followed him. I knew there was no hope of following that motorcycle into city traffic.

The sky was turning gray and I put my jeep's canvas top back up, for protection against a sudden November rain. I'm getting jumpy, I thought. There have to be a few thousand guys in hats and trench coats in Northern Ireland right now, and I didn't have time to sneak up on every one. I drove south in the direction of Armagh, checking my rearview mirror for a tail, but not seeing one. I stayed on the Armagh road, figuring it was time to have a little chat with Andrew Jenkins. One advantage I had was that I doubted he knew about the picture of him with Subaltern O'Brien. I wondered what his Red Hand pals would think of his date with a British intelligence officer? The Ulster Unionists were probably ninety percent in accord with the British government but they hated and feared the notion of becoming part of the

Irish Republic. So ten percent of the time they were thinking about Churchill being ready to sell them out to get Ireland into the war. That kind of thinking could lead to paranoia, and even the hint that Jenkins was working with MI-5 could get him killed. Of course, that worked both ways. Hinting at it could get me killed. I had to think of a way to approach this subtly, which I knew was not my strong point.

I navigated through the city, passing the tall twin spires of a Catholic cathedral and then the short, squat tower over the Protestant cathedral. As different as night and day, they stood in defiance of each other, even the architectural styles seeming to scream at each other, *Blasphemer, nonbeliever!*

I had to stop and ask directions for Jenkins's business a few times. It was on the outskirts, where green fields mingled with creeping industry, and train tracks crossed muddy lanes. The sign at the closed gate read JENKINS FOODS LTD. I took that to mean Andrew Jenkins was a plainspoken, literal kind of fellow.

"What about ye?" asked a skinny kid, from the other side of the gate. His stringy black hair hung over his ears, and his hands were as dirty as his boots.

"What about me?"

"What's up, is what I mean. Whaddya want here?"

"I'd like to see Mr. Jenkins," I said, leaning out of the jeep.

"And about what do ya want to see him?"

"Who are you, his secretary? Open up, kid, I'm on official U.S. Army business."

"Hold your hour now; I'll go see if he's about." The kid ran off toward two warehouses, long buildings with sheet-metal roofs and loading docks facing each other, with a cobblestone drive between them. At the end of one was a door with a sign hanging over it that looked like an office. The kid went in and I waited, trying to figure out what "hold your hour" meant. Fortunately, I didn't have to wait an hour. He came trotting out and stood at the gate, catching his breath.

"What's yer name?"

"Boyle," I said, wondering if you needed a Protestant name to get through the gate.

"OK, come on in," he said as he unlocked the gate. "He's been wonderin' what kept ya."

He held open the gate as I drove through, pointing toward the office. I parked the jeep and wondered who'd told Jenkins about me. Sláine O'Brien? Hugh Carrick? Thornton? The unknown Yank? The possibilities of betrayal were endless.

"So you're Boyle, are you?" A voice boomed out from the doorway as a sturdy middle-aged man, barrel-chested and bowlegged, emerged from the office, holding a clipboard. The wind picked up and a gust flapped the sheets against his hand. He had short brown hair with gray strands showing, and he needed a shave. If he was a Black Knight of the British Commonwealth, he didn't look the part. "Come with me, there's work I need to do. It's going to rain; is that all you've got?"

He pointed to my tanker's jacket as if I'd dressed for a blizzard in a pinafore. He was wearing an oilskin coat and shook his head. I grabbed my trench coat from the back of the jeep and pulled it on, watching Jenkins run his fingers across the sheets of paper on his clipboard. His lips moved as he studied each line. He might not be well educated but he was smart enough to gauge the weather. And to present himself as a harried businessman, kindly enough to wait while his American visitor buttoned up, instead of an ultra-Unionist killer.

"Did someone tell you I was coming, Mr. Jenkins?" I asked, hurrying to keep pace with him. He held up one finger, perhaps to tell me to hold my hour, as we turned a corner to the space between the warehouses.

"Campbell," he roared. "You got them potatoes sacked?"

"Nearly done, we are."

Inside were storage bins of potatoes, mounds of them, with two workers loading them into burlap sacks. It was the same up and down in each warehouse. Piles and mounds of cabbages, beets, cauliflower, and other vegetables still in season. Refrigerator units were stocked with hanging hams, sides of beef, and large cans of milk. In each, workers were readying orders for delivery.

"I've got to stay on top of these boys. I've got more produce coming in every day, and it's got to be sorted out, weighed, and parceled out for your army. You've brought a lot of hungry lads with you, haven't you?" He laughed before I could answer. "All right, let's get out of the way before the trucks arrive. I can feel the rain, can you?"

As if on cue, the gray clouds let loose, and Jenkins trundled his squat body forward, tucking his clipboard inside his oilskin. He pushed open the office door and stood aside, shaking the water off as if he were a big, friendly dog.

"Take off your coat, Mr. Boyle, come into my office, and rest your-self. Frances, wet the tea, will you?"

Frances took my coat without a word but gave me a hard stare up and down as if she were judging the value of this Yank she had to make tea for. She hung it on a peg near the door then went around her desk and plugged in an electric kettle. I followed Jenkins down a narrow hallway and into his office, the warmth hitting me as I entered. A small coal stove stood against the wall, and he opened it, shoveled in a bit from a bucket, and rubbed his hands together in satisfaction.

"Ah, that's better, isn't it?" He sniffed and brushed the back of his hand across his nose, sat in an armchair in front of the stove, and motioned for me to take the other one. A narrow table pushed against the opposite wall served as his desk. A newspaper, a telephone, and a few stray pieces of paper were all that were on it. Jenkins looked like he spent most of his time outside. In this room, he probably sat in front of the fire more than at that table. He was constantly in motion—fidgeting, talking, moving, and generally seeming amused at everything around him. So it was a shock to see him finally settle down, look me straight in the eye, and say, "So, what is it you want?"

There was a lot I wanted to know but it all boiled down to one thing. In that moment, I decided Andrew Jenkins was a man who hid himself behind his bluster, a cunning man who could lull people into not taking him seriously, and find an edge, an advantage, by doing so. In business, politics, and perhaps in war.

"I want to know if you stole those BARs," I said, warming my hands in front of the stove, as he had. It was a trick my dad had taught me. A con man had told him he gained people's confidence by mimick-ing their movements in small ways, things they wouldn't pick up on. He claimed it put people at ease since they'd unconsciously identify with you. I didn't know if that was true or not, but I began doing it during interrogations, and it did seem to help calm things down. I rubbed my hands together, then set them on my knees, as Jenkins had done.

"Ha! You're not one for beatin' around the bush, are you, Mr. Boyle from America?"

"I'm a lieutenant, although I'd prefer the rank of mister."

"Lieutenant is it? Well, excuse me, Mr. Lieutenant Boyle. I'm sorry you don't like the army life but that's not a care of mine. Now tell me why you think I stole them guns."

"Your truck and a dead IRA man."

"What kind of mingin' fool would use his own vehicle with his name plastered on each side to rob the very army that's payin' him good money every day for legal goods, I ask you? And I'd be a worse eejit to waste a pound on a dead Fenian, now wouldn't I?"

"A very smart mingin' fool, whatever that means. I thought you people spoke English."

"Ha!" Jenkins said, his laugh sharp and short. "That's a good one, it is. I say the very same thing sometimes, especially when you Yanks get to talkin' with that chewin' gum in your craws. There was a fellow from a place in New York the other day—Brooklyn, he said it was—and I couldn't understand half of what he was tellin' me. Ha!"

"So you didn't?"

"Didn't what?"

"Steal the guns."

"Now that's an example of a waste of good breath to ask that question. If I did, you know I'd never admit it to you, just because you asked. So I'd say, No, I didn't steal them guns, and I'm offended you asked. And if I didn't, I'd say the exact same thing, maybe with a touch more of the righteous indignation. So what can you learn from that question? Nothing. Ask me another, one that won't waste my time and the good air in your lungs."

"Are you the head of the Red Hand?"

"Ach! There you go again. Do you suppose whoever is the leader of that fearsome pack of defenders of the faith would admit to it, do you?"

"My mistake," I said. Jenkins leaned back in his chair, resting his chin on one hand. I leaned back as well, and set my chin in my hand, deep in thought. "OK. Here's one. Do you know Captain Hiriam Heck?"

"Sure, he's that stiff-necked Yank copper."

"He's no cop," I said. "Take it from me."

"Why should I? Are you a criminal yourself that you can sniff out the peelers?"

"No, I'm a cop, or was. In Boston."

"Ach, one of the Boston Irish," he said, and left it at that. "So what about Heck?"

"He'll probably be coming around here, maybe with the RUC. He's uncovered a plot to defraud the U.S. Army through phony invoices, kickbacks, that sort of thing."

"In time of war? That's a terrible thing, it is. Who's the villain?"

"You probably know him. Major Thomas Thornton."

"And I'm not surprised. He tried to extort me, the bastard. I told him I'd go straight to the police but he warned me off, said he'd swear that I offered him bribes. So I kept my mouth shut, I did. I'm glad someone finally found him out."

"Do you know a sergeant by the name of Brennan? Peter Brennan?"

"Brennan, Brennan, that sounds familiar," he said, rubbing his jaw. "Yeah, I do. Haven't seen him in a while, though. He used to be on duty at one of the kitchens at Ballykinler. I've made deliveries there myself. What's become of him?"

"He's returning to the front. Decided it was safer in Italy than around here."

"Sounds daft to me but there you have it."

"He was nervous every time he saw one of your trucks. Why would that be?"

"Who sent you here? The milk and vegetable police? I thought you were looking for Fenian killers, German agents, stolen guns, that sort of thing. Instead, you come to see me, a man you accuse of being part of the Red Hand, and ask me about cabbages and such. Is that how you protect the good citizens of Boston? Question working folk? They must love you over there. Ha!"

"No, that's not what I do," I said patiently. "What I need to know is if there's any connection between Brennan and the theft. He's been acting strange lately."

"There's a war on, they say," Jenkins said, looking away. There was more, but I could tell he needed coaxing.

"Listen," I said quietly and in a conspiratorial voice, "I don't have an argument with you about cabbages or parsnips. And I think you're smart enough not to worry about that. But I do need to know the real story about Brennan. I don't think he was involved with the weapons theft but he seems too happy for a guy headed back into combat."

"You seem on the up-and-up, boy. There might be something I could tell you but it would have to be between us. Repeat it and I'll call you a liar."

"If it doesn't have anything to do with the guns, then tell me and it goes no further."

Now it was Jenkins's turn to whisper. "Sergeant Brennan, he's one for the straight and narrow path, as long as it don't demand too much of him. So if he were to have noticed some . . . inconsistencies, let's say, with food deliveries, then he'd be one to trot off and report it. A real Boy Scout."

"Yeah, that's what he did."

"Well, if the fella he reported to was involved, then it would make sense, in terms of business, purely, to let it be known that he could have an accident or something if he squealed. Right?"

"Just business."

"Right. And that would work well enough, since Brennan would know what to keep his mouth shut about. But then your Red Jack comes along and stirs up the pot, and all of a sudden, everyone from DI Carrick to you yourself is asking about the theft. Throws everything out of balance."

"So you have him killed?"

"That'd be one way," he said, rubbing his chin and turning the thought over as if it had just occurred. "But that could cause problems too. Why not take advantage of the fact that Sergeant Brennan has taken a real dislike to our little island?"

"So Thornton gives him his transfer. What do you do?"

"Nothing, since this is conjectural, purely. But if I were to do something, it would be to speed the good sergeant on his way, with a last and good memory of Ireland."

"And how would you do that?"

"Cash, boy! Hard English currency," he said, and patted a canvas deposit bag with NORTHERN BANK, ARMAGH stenciled on it. "He has his transfer and a hundred pounds to remember us by. Or forget, I should say, since by taking the money, he becomes complicit. Something for everyone."

"Purely a business decision," I said.

"Aye, and a good investment at very low risk. There would be no reason for me to make the sergeant uneasy. He doesn't have to leave, but that's his choice."

"What about Eddie Mahoney?"

Jenkins said, leaning forward and pointing his finger at me, "That's a different matter. Mahoney came north lookin' for trouble. If he'd stayed at home and minded his own business, he'd be alive still. But he didn't, and paid the price. I don't know who killed him but you can't tell me an IRA man didn't deserve such an end."

He relaxed back into his chair. "Now, mind you, I only say these things about your sergeant as pure conjecture. How I would have approached it, if it were my problem."

"I can't argue with you about Mahoney; he knew the chances he was taking," I said. I stuck my feet out in front of me, letting the heat from the stove warm my boots. "I came here from Brownlow House. Is it true that the Royal Black Knights have their headquarters there?"

"The Royal Black Knights of the British Commonwealth," Jenkins said stiffly. "That's no secret. Yes, they do."

"Are you a member?"

"No, I never bothered with it. I'm a member of an Orange Lodge, no need for another meeting to go to. The Black Knights is more for businessmen who wear a suit and tie, if you get my meaning. Mud on your shoes doesn't set well with that bunch. The manager of my bank, he's one," he said, crooking his thumb at the canvas Northern Bank bag.

"You also have to be purer than pure, don't you?"

"Aye, no connections with the Roman church, none atallatall. What do you want with the Royal Black Knights?"

"Nothing, just curious," I said. "Do you have any ideas about who stole the weapons from Ballykinler?"

"Why the IRA, of course. Who else?"

There was a knock at the door and Frances entered with a tray that held a pot of tea and two enamel cups in which dark tea steamed. She set the tray down on a small table between us and left without a word. We both added sugar.

"Ach, that's good," Jenkins said, smacking his lips. "Now tell me, who else but the Fenians would have stolen them guns?"

"I meant names; do you know any names?"

"I'm not one to hang about with IRA sympathizers. I wouldn't know the name of any of that rabble."

"You've heard of Red Jack Taggart?"

"Old Red Jack? Sure, his name is well known, bloody Bolshevik that he is. Or was, some say. They say he saw too many comrades put up against the wall for thinkin' different than the party line. What makes you bring up his name?"

"Because I saw him the other day, firing a BAR at me. He killed another American."

"So Red Jack's come north, has he then? Well, there's a name to put to that theft and killing." He slurped his tea.

"Not that you know much about the IRA," I said with sarcasm.

"You can't help but pick up a few things here and there," Jenkins said. "I go all over Ulster making pickups and deliveries. A man hears things."

"I know what you mean. Like I heard that Heck may want to look at your books."

"Yes, exactly! Not that my books aren't all in order but I do appreciate knowing when the police may come calling, so we can put the kettle on, you know."

"Wet the tea," I said.

"Now you're learning, Mr. Lieutenant Boyle. Not bad for a papist Boston Irish Yank."

"I'll take that as a compliment."

"You should take it as a warning too, boy. A friendly warning. There's them who would not be so welcoming. You Americans from Boston forget where you came from. Those of us who have stayed have not lost our memories. Memories that go back hundreds of years."

"We're all on the same side in this war, aren't we?"

"You've a lot to learn. There's half a dozen sides to every question asked in Ulster, and don't forget it. Now drink your tea. I'm sure Frances didn't spit in your cup."

He grinned but I wasn't so sure and I held my hands around the cup for warmth and watched the dark, steaming tea for signs of Frances.

"Who told you I was coming?" I asked.

"Oh, I hear things. I heard a new Yank was nosing around looking for them guns, and his name was Boyle. That was the real news, that the Yanks sent a man with a name like Boyle. A Catholic." He pronounced it *cat-o-lick*.

"It takes a thief to catch a thief," I said, echoing what I'd already been told.

"That's a big pack of thieves you're after. You may need some help."

"If you hear anything about the weapons or Red Jack, I'd appreciate a word."

"Why would I do that?"

"Because I warned you about Heck. Because fifty BARs in the

hands of the IRA is a lot of firepower, and I doubt the stout defenders of the faith, good Protestant lads that they are, can stand up to that."

"Good reasons, them. All right, if I hear anything, I'll let you know. Just keep it quiet, where you got it from."

"You can reach me—"

"I know where to find you, Mr. Lieutenant Boyle, any time of the day or night, don't you worry." He sipped his tea and stared at me with unblinking eyes. I didn't want to match that look; I don't think I could have. I set the tea down and held my hands out to the fire, close to the heat, as I felt the weight of centuries of hate bearing down on me. The hearty, friendly businessman's facade had cracked and in those dark, hooded eyes I saw the depths of the gulf that separated us. I saw my ancient enemy whom I'd been taught to fear, fight, and hate. It brought to mind a poem recited by a nun in religious class, an Irish poem she'd read with joy, about the differences between Irish Catholics and Protestants. I only remembered one line: *The faith of Christ with the faith of Luther is like ashes in the snow.*

I was now certain Frances had spat in my tea.

CHAPTER ■ SIXTEEN

JENKINS AND I left together, he to drive to the bank to make a deposit and me to get back to Newcastle. It was slow going; the narrow roads were wet and crowded. Military convoys choked them, truckloads of GIs going to or from maneuvers, crammed shoulder to shoulder, heads bowed under their steel pots. They all looked alike in their sodden uniforms, faces hardly visible between turned-up collars and helmets canted against the rain blowing into the canvas-covered trucks.

This was how some generals saw them, squads and platoons of soldiers, a percentage certain to be casualties, all of them ready to be sacrificed for a promotion, none of them with a name or a face to remember in your dreams. Maybe that was why they made us march in step. It made it impossible for the individual to stand out. I'd seen plenty like that. General Fredendall in North Africa, who commanded II Corps and had his engineers dig underground shelters for his HQ seventy miles from the front. Uncle Ike blew his lid when he heard about that, and not long after sent George Patton to relieve him. I'd also had occasion to meet up with General Mark Clark a few times. He was the genius who decided there wouldn't be any bombardment at Salerno. Plenty of faceless GIs, including Brennan's pals, died because of it. But General Mark Clark was still there, spending as much time as ever making sure every press release 5th Army put out had his name alone on it. GIs had started to call him Markus Clarkus for his desire to take Rome, not so much from the Germans as before the British.

There were plenty of fine senior officers, men like Colonel Jim Gavin, whom I'd seen up close in Sicily, weeping over the graves of his men after the stand at Biazza Ridge. And Uncle Ike himself. I didn't know anyone who agonized more over the price in lives this war had claimed, and who shouldered a heavier burden, short of a dogface with a fully loaded combat pack under fire. So why was I so hard on him? Thousands of miles from home, under the twin pressures of politics and death, what was wrong with enjoying a little affection? Kay worshipped him, and she knew what the deal was, I hoped. I couldn't see him ever leaving his wife. Kay had to know this was just one of those things. Didn't she? Didn't he?

What about Diana? What did she think about us? Just one of those wartime romances? The wild Irish boy and the aristocrat whose lives were thrown together, experiencing the passion of life amidst death. Who would expect them to last out the peace?

Diana and I wouldn't have ever laid eyes on each other if not for the war, and if I hadn't gotten her sister involved in a murder investigation that turned more deadly than I ever could have imagined. And Diana wouldn't have gone off with the British Expeditionary Force to France, barely surviving Dunkirk, if not for the war. It was death that bound us together, it seemed. Not the fear of death at all, but the thought of living through so much of it. How could love come out of that? Need perhaps; desire certainly. But love?

So what about Diana? For that matter, what about me?

I stopped at an intersection and waited while a column of deuce-and-a-half trucks rumbled by. The rain hadn't let up. It pelted the canvas cover like sudden bursts of machine-gun fire as I turned my thoughts to Jenkins and whether or not he'd pass information on to me. I had done him one favor, warning him about Heck, as an investment. But the picture of him with Sláine O'Brien was too good to waste, a major bargaining chip. If I put that on the table, it would be in a neutral location, somewhere public, not in a Protestant neighborhood, and I'd reserve it for when I needed something big in return.

Finally, the traffic eased and I took the turnoff to Clough, to drop in on Constable Simms. I'd planned on talking to him about Sam Burnham. I remembered Simms worked out of his home, so I stopped at the Lug o' the Tub to ask directions from Tom. I found him tossing peat onto a low fire, alone except for one old-timer in his well-worn suit jacket.

"Billy," he said, "have you dropped by for an afternoon pint?"

"No, still on the job. Can you tell me where Adrian Simms lives? Have you seen him?"

"Not today. You can check with his missus, though. Go up the side road here, past the castle ruins, and you'll see a line of cottages. The constable lives in the first one. The wife's name is Julia, but I doubt you'll be on a first-name basis."

"Not the friendly type?"

"Not until she knows you attend Presbyterian services regularly."

"It'll be Mrs. Simms then. Tell me, is that anywhere near where they found Eddie Mahoney?"

"Yes, it is."

"You didn't hear any gunshots that night?"

"No, and I wouldn't have, even if they'd gone off outside my door. It was raining something fierce, the wind blowing and howling, enough to make today look like a spring shower."

"Does Grady live in one of those cottages?"

"Ach, no. There's a boreen about a hundred yards before them, it takes you to Grady's place."

"A what?"

"Oh, sorry. A boreen, you mean? It's a dirt track, a cart path at best. Grady lives in the house he was born in, dirt floor and a hearth for heat. Nothing like the line of cottages; they're proper modern houses. Indoor plumbing and all. But he keeps his roof in good repair, and there's plenty of peat for him to burn. It's no grand palace, but it's home for Grady. And not far from the pub," he added with a wink.

"Do you think Julia Simms would be impressed that I was at Brownlow House, headquarters of the Royal Black Knights?"

"Oh, don't mention those words, atallatall, Billy. Oh no," Tom said, shaking his head and laughing, "if you don't want to cause Adrian to miss his supper."

"Why?" Tom looked around and leaned in close, whispering, even though we were a good ten feet from the old fellow at the bar, who hadn't moved since I came in.

"Because Adrian applied to join them at the urging of his wife. To get ahead, you know, make the right contacts. The Royal Black Knights are Unionists through and through, but they spend their time giving money to the church, not rabble-rousing. It's for the well-to-do or those who want-to-do, if you understand."

"Sure. Like the Knights of Columbus back home."

"Well, aptly named, but I don't know them. Anyway, Adrian applies, and he gets past the first few hurdles. He's a member of the Orange Society, all fine and good. But the Black Knights are even stricter than the Orangemen about who they let in. All of a sudden, he's out, and Julia Simms, who is not too proud to boast of something that has not yet come to pass, has to hang her head at Sunday services and for the rest of the week. I think she's still not forgiven poor Adrian."

"For getting blackballed?"

"For not telling her about his background. As far as I know, Adrian met all their requirements—including being born in wedlock and of Protestant parents—all but one."

"What was that?"

"From what I understand, an applicant has to swear that his parents were never connected in any way with the Roman Catholic Church. He did but was called out on it, and that was that. No marching in the July 13 parade every year, under their black banner with the red cross, celebrating our defeat at the Battle of the Boyne. No social gatherings, in suit and tie, so he and Julia can hobnob with their betters. Oh, it was hard times in that cottage for a while, I'll say."

"What was his connection with Catholics?"

"Mrs. Simms made it clear that question was not to be asked of her, nor ever answered by Adrian. Hard times, as I said."

"Are you married, Tom?" I asked.

"Yes, I am. Nearly twenty years now."

"Worth it?"

"It is. Most days." Then he laughed, perhaps to let me know today was a good day, and slapped me on the shoulder. I left wondering how I might answer that question someday. Would I wistfully think back to that English girl and our wartime whirlwind of emotions before I'd settled on a wife, a good Catholic Boston lass? Would "most days" be good enough?

I started the jeep, drove down the road, and passed by what must have been the spot where Eddie Mahoney's body had been left. I stopped and looked back. It wasn't far but I doubted pistol shots could have been heard from inside the stone building. I did wonder why the killer had picked this spot. He wanted the body found, that was certain. The pound note was a message to any would-be informant so the corpse had to be where people passed by, to guarantee it would be discovered. It was the perfect place.

A little farther on, I saw the boreen on the left. Muddy tracks between two stone walls curved behind a small rise, and a wisp of smoke rose beyond it, probably from Grady's peat fire. I pulled in front of the first of three whitewashed cottages, all with thickly thatched roofs and black varnished doors with small windows on either side. I dashed from the jeep and knocked, holding my hat against the growing wind.

"Yes?" A thin, black-haired woman held the door open with one hand and clutched at her shawl with the other as rain blew against her. She didn't invite me to enter.

"Mrs. Simms? I'm looking for Adrian. Is he in?"

"No," she said, shaking her head. "Away on police business, he is."

"Do you know where I can find him?" I had to raise my voice to be heard over the wind.

"No, I don't know where he is or when he'll be back. Your name?"

"Billy Boyle, Mrs. Simms. Pleased to meet you," I said, trying to be friendly.

"I'll tell him you called, Mr. Boyle," she said, and the door shut.

"Lieutenant Boyle," I said to the black varnish.

I decided there wasn't much else I could do that day, other than head back to the pub and start on some afternoon pints, unless I caught up with Brennan before he left. I couldn't find it in myself to blame him for the decisions he'd made. The first was the right one, reporting the fraud he'd encountered while on kitchen duty. But then he was stymied by his own senior officer, who was in on the deal, and found himself threatened if he talked. He had been transferred to the Ordnance Depot only to end up a suspect in an arms theft. Take the money and run, Pete, is what I wanted to tell him. But I wasn't his drinking buddy, I was an investigator sent by General Eisenhower, so it would be better all around if I shook hands with him and told him to stay low.

The wind was up but the rain slackened as I drove up the slight rise leading to the Ballykinler base. Dundrum Bay to my south looked choppy, and the Mournes were invisible behind low, leaden clouds. By the time I got to the main gate, the rain had stopped, and to the west a thin slant of blue promised better weather. As I negotiated the security around the Ordnance Depot, the wind was chasing cloud cover out over the Irish Sea, and the Mournes began to reveal themselves.

Sunlight sparkled over the landscape, reflected in the dripping wetness over everything. The transformation was sudden, magical; the world had changed from sullen gray to vibrant green in seconds. Diana was still on my mind, and thinking about her was exactly like that. I could feel angry and hurt, and images of her face would be frozen in dark shadow. Then I'd remember something else, and she'd be smiling, lifting her head to the sunny sky, pulling her hair back behind her ear, her laughter like music on a summer night.

I paused before I opened the door, looking one more time at the clearing sky. Was it possible? Would the anger and disappointment between us clear away, fresh winds dispelling whatever wounds we'd inflicted on each other? I wasn't certain it was possible. I wasn't sure we'd both be alive to find out.

"Billy, what brings you here?" Saul Jacobson was in an unusually relaxed position, his feet up on his desk, his clipboards all neatly hung on the wall behind him.

"I'm looking for Sergeant Brennan," I said. "Is he back in the shop?"

"No. I thought you knew that he's got himself a transfer out of here."

"I wanted to stop by and wish him luck. Where is he?"

"I don't know. He finished up a few things here this morning and asked if he could take care of some personal business. He's shipping out tomorrow, so I figured, what's the harm?"

"What kind of personal business?"

"No idea. It seemed that giving him a free afternoon was the least I could do before he heads back to the shooting war. He isn't in any kind of trouble, is he? I thought that was all cleared up."

"He's not in trouble with me. When did he leave?"

"About 1100 hours. He signed out a jeep."

"Damn, sorry I missed him. You don't look too busy. Pretty quiet around here?"

"Every unit has been ordered to get its gear together, weapons cleaned and ready. No one's on the rifle range, and they canceled maneuvers, so there's not much for us to do. Rumor is the division might be shipping out."

"Where to, and when?"

"Some say back to Iceland, others think it's to England. Maybe Italy. Looks like something's up, though. Hey, did you hear about Thornton?"

"No, what?"

"Heck had him hauled away. The MPs handcuffed him and took him to Belfast. They say he'll be court-martialed for taking bribes."

"Well, well," I said, trying to sound surprised.

"You have anything to do with that?"

"No, I'm looking for BARs, remember?"

"If you find them, you can give them to the next guy who inherits this place," he said, gesturing with his hands to encompass the splendor of his plywood-enclosed office.

"OK, Saul. Good luck if I don't see you again. Keep your head down." We shook hands, and I left, glad to have imparted that bit of military wisdom to someone. I hadn't known how low I could stay until I'd felt the air vibrate from machine-gun bullets flying inches above my head. I could feel the *thrumming* again as I sat in the jeep, as if hornets were buzzing my neck. I watched the comings and goings, GIs on errands, marching, loafing, standing guard. How long before they felt it, and found out what the Bonesaw could do to infantry out in the open? Stay low, boys, I wanted to tell each and every one of them. They'd been told, I knew, a hundred times, but it wasn't the same as feeling it, knowing in your gut that nothing was as important as hugging the ground, digging deep, staying off the ridgeline, keeping your eyes open, not bunching up, using every fold of ground for cover. . . .

I gasped, realizing I'd forgotten to breathe. I'd felt the hot Sicilian sun on me for that moment. The ground had been brown and broken, not green and smooth. I clutched the steering wheel, relaxing my white-knuckled hands. Never mind, I told myself. They'll have to find out for themselves. In their place I wouldn't have listened to anyone else either. I hadn't, and I knew how Brennan felt, seeing all these faces and knowing so many would die, stunned at the rapid violence of combat, unfired rifles in their hands, calling out for their mothers, as they always did. Mama, *mutti, madre.*

I started the engine and gazed straight ahead, driving through the base, avoiding looking at each face I passed along the way.

CHAPTER ▪ SEVENTEEN

AT 5:00 A.M.—OR 0500, as I was informed—someone thumped at the door to my Quonset hut with a message. Too early for me. I'd stopped at the the Lug o' the Tub and stayed longer than I should have, watching GIs drink their beer while trying to sound manly and brave in the face of the unknown. I'd listened to Grady tell stories of the Anglo-Irish War without mentioning the Lewis gun. In turn I had told him about Diana but never mentioned Jerusalem. We each kept our wounds hidden.

The message had been from Hugh Carrick: Come to Clough immediately. I retraced my route of not so long ago, watching for some sign of the RUC. Clough wasn't so big that I was likely to miss anything. As the early morning mist rose from the ground, it looked like each stone wall corralled a field of fog. The top row of stones stood above the thick grayness, like grave markers all in a line. The sun came up over Dundrum Bay to the east as the sound of sheep bells echoed from hill to hill. Farmers and police, early risers both, tending their respective flocks.

I knew which way to turn even before the pub came into view. Not far down the narrow road to Grady O'Brick's dirt-floored cottage and Julia Simms's proper Presbyterian home, a gaggle of police cars and a military police jeep were parked. Not to mention a gray Austin four-door sedan, license plate FZG 129. The car Red Jack Taggart had been in, slewed to the side of the road, the front caught up in brambles along a stone wall. When I saw the Austin, I knew there would be a body inside. It had been driven off the road at the same spot where Mahoney had been left.

District Inspector Hugh Carrick stood in the middle of the roadway, dispatching constables to search the fields on either side. Adrian Simms stood, with Sergeant Jack Patterson, next to the Austin.

"Lieutenant Boyle, good morning," Carrick said. "I thought you'd want to be here."

"Who's inside?" I asked, hoping I was wrong.

"Your Sergeant Brennan. In the trunk. Local man who makes the milk deliveries saw the car and stopped by Constable Simms's home to report it. When he gave Simms the license-plate number, Simms called it in straightaway."

Pete's name hit me like a two-by-four. Why him? It made no sense. He was free and clear, set to ship out today.

"Are you sure?" I couldn't take it in. I'd been imagining Pete boarding a ship in Belfast Harbor.

Carrick beckoned me to follow him to the car. Patterson vaguely stood to attention and gave me a quick salute. I touched my hand to my forehead and froze as Simms opened the trunk. It was Pete Brennan, expert ordnanceman, veteran of Salerno, last survivor of his squad. He was on his side, his back to us, knees drawn up to his chest. Two black-and-rust-colored holes punctured the back of his skull.

"Small-caliber weapon," I offered, although I was sure that had been apparent to Carrick. No exit wounds.

"Execution," Carrick said.

"Aye," Simms said. "Typical IRA job."

"Who owns the car?" I asked in a low voice.

"A Catholic businessman in Londonderry. He reported it stolen four days ago. He appears to have no connection to this business."

"Why would the IRA kill Pete?" I said out loud, but I was speaking to myself.

"Maybe a falling-out over the BAR theft?" Simms suggested.

"He had nothing to do with that. He was shipping out today to Italy. Why kill him?"

"That is what we are going to find out, Boyle," Carrick said.

I barely heard him. I leaned into the trunk, careful not to touch anything. I studied Pete's head, ignoring the face with its contorted puffiness from the gunshots. I smelled his uniform.

"What are you doing, Boyle?" Carrick demanded.

"It rained yesterday," I said. "His hair is dry, and so is his uniform. If he'd been thrown in here wet, it would smell damp."

"There is an army trench coat in the backseat, a trifle damp to the touch," Carrick said.

"He left Ballykinler yesterday morning, probably before it started raining. He was out in it for a bit, but not enough to get himself soaked. I'd say he was shot after it stopped, which was about four o'clock. Then dumped here, after the pub shut its doors."

"Aye, Tom said the road was clear when he closed up, not long after you yourself departed," Simms said.

Was there a question left hanging? Did Simms wonder where I'd gone after I left the pub? Did he envision me firing a gun twice into Pete's skull?

"Did you see Brennan at all yesterday?" Carrick asked me.

"No, I tried to find him in the afternoon, to say goodbye, but I'd missed him. His lieutenant had let him off to take care of some personal business."

"And you're convinced there was no connection between Brennan and the BAR theft?"

"I'm convinced he wasn't involved. But there had to be a connection."

"Why?"

"Because what other reason is there for two bullets to the head? There must be something, some clue that we're missing but Pete didn't."

"Where do you suppose he went yesterday?" Carrick asked.

"No idea," I said as a very good idea formed in my mind. I had no reason to let Carrick in on it yet, since he wouldn't like it one bit.

"That's obviously where he got into trouble. Pity he didn't stay on the base," Carrick said, shaking his head sadly.

"Jack," I said, turning to the MP, "he left Ballykinler in a jeep. Has one turned up?"

"We're looking. I thought he might have gone to the pub last night, so we started checking the back roads between here and the base."

"The only thing we know for certain is that you saw Taggart in this car, and now Brennan has turned up, dead, in the trunk. The IRA connection is fairly clear," Carrick said, but he sounded less than certain. "Perhaps there was an entirely different connection, one we're not aware of, and Brennan was killed over that. Perhaps because he was being transferred, deserting the cause?" Carrick rubbed his chin, thinking as he spoke. I could tell he wanted to believe the IRA had shot Brennan. It was so neat, I could hardly blame him. It fit into his view of the world, which was a powerful reason for belief. Still, I sensed the doubt in his mind as he considered different theories.

"Have you searched the body?" I asked.

"Yes, I have, along with Sergeant Patterson. Nothing of note. Cigarettes, a lighter, a few pound notes."

"He usually went out armed."

"No evidence of a weapon, sir, but you're right. Pete always carried a .45."

"Not entirely legal for him to go out armed while off duty and outside the base, but I understand his reason," Carrick said.

"You didn't find anything else?" I asked.

"Nothing. His coat and cap were in the vehicle. Otherwise it looks clean. We will have it checked for fingerprints, but I doubt we'll find anything. It looks like all the surfaces were wiped down."

"That's odd. Why would Red Jack care about his fingerprints?"

"He has help," Carrick said. "There are a number of cells operated by the IRA Northern Command. Most of them operate in secret, and their members lead outwardly normal lives. It would be to protect them, not his own identity."

"Makes sense. Do you mind if I take a closer look at the body?"

"Be careful," Carrick said. "Don't touch any surfaces."

I nodded, holding back the question I was about to ask: So in case you find my prints on the car, you'll know I was involved? Or was Carrick merely exercising crime-scene control? It was the kind of thing my dad would have done, a natural caution against accidentally interfering with evidence. Maybe I was being overly sensitive. Maybe I was being framed. I ran over a list in my mind of any personal possessions I might have lost in the past few days, in case something showed up in the car. But I didn't possess much except for army-issue gear, which, for once, was a blessing.

I didn't bother looking in Pete's pockets. I knew DI Carrick and Patterson would have done a thorough search. I did look at his hands. His left was open, fingers splayed across his right arm in the cramped pose he'd been left in. His right hand was clenched in a fist, rigor mortis had already set hard.

"He's real stiff," I said. "He had to have been killed at least twelve hours ago."

"That would be six o'clock last night," Carrick said. "If he left an hour before noon, he could've traveled for two hours, which would leave two hours for him to return. Killed between one and four o'clock then."

"Too many factors we don't know," I said. "Who would have known he was going off base? I wonder if his execution was planned or a spur-of-the-moment thing?"

"Saul knew," Patterson said. "And anybody at the depot Pete might have told."

"But Saul told me he didn't know where Pete was going."

"An accidental encounter? But with whom?" Carrick asked. "Constable Simms, have you seen any strangers about? Anyone suspicious?"

"No, sir, it's been very quiet."

"We need to find the jeep Brennan drove," I said as I pulled at Pete's fingers, reminding myself it was only his body, that he was long gone. I managed to pull two fingers apart. I took the small wooden object and held it in my palm. It was cold.

"What's that?" Constable Simms asked. Carrick moved in to take a closer look.

"It's a carved animal of some sort," he said.

"Its name is Pig," I said.

CHAPTER ▪ EIGHTEEN

PETE BRENNAN HAD died with his good luck charm in the palm of his hand. Pig hadn't kept him alive but at least had been there at the end. Maybe Pete was a fool to go wherever he'd gone. Maybe he was wrong to volunteer to return to the front lines before he had to. Maybe he would've been killed in Italy anyway. It didn't matter. He'd been executed. Like Sam Burnham had been executed?

Despite the car I didn't think the IRA was responsible. As I stood in the road, watching the searchers in the fields and rubbing Pig's belly, I could think of only one person who would have had a reason to meet up with Pete yesterday. Jenkins had told me his part was to give Pete one hundred pounds, and Thornton's part was to authorize his transfer. I'd assumed Jenkins had already paid out the money. But he hadn't actually said so. And he'd been headed for the Northern Bank in Armagh yesterday afternoon. The timing would have worked out. Jenkins could have met Pete between one and two o'clock, perhaps near the bank, but somewhere they wouldn't be seen together. Instead of a hundred quid, Pete had ended up with two slugs. I couldn't figure how Jenkins had gotten the Austin, but the scenario was perfect in its symmetry. The IRA boosts his truck and implicates him in the arms theft; he uses their stolen car to point the finger at them for Pete's murder. I liked it. It fit into *my* view of the world, which was that Jenkins was a thieving Orangeman who'd gladly kill a Catholic rather than hand over more than four hundred dollars to him.

A U.S. Army ambulance showed up, trailed by a British Army staff car. This was turning into a full-scale international incident. I put Pig in my jacket pocket and watched them move Pete's body from the trunk of the Austin to the ambulance. It was an awkward process due to the body's rigor. Patterson helped steady it on the stretcher as they gingerly loaded it into the ambulance. Simms looked away as Carrick stood ramrod straight, eyes front. I think if he'd been in uniform, he would have saluted, no matter what religion Brennan had been baptized into. But there were no funerals today. He wore a dark woolen overcoat over a suit, the slightly askew knotted tie the only sign that he'd dressed in a rush in response to an early morning call. I watched his eyes move to the staff car, his forehead wrinkling. It looked like it was a surprise to him as well as me.

Its driver, a British Army sergeant, approached me and gave a stiff, palm-out salute. His eyes wandered to the body, then focused on me.

He was short and compact, a neatly trimmed mustache above a thin mouth. A scar ran along his jaw, a jagged white line of puckered skin. He was armed, a revolver holstered at his side. He might have been posted behind a wheel, but he looked like more than a driver. I returned the salute.

"Lieutenant Boyle?"

"Who's asking?"

"You'll be him then. Please step inside the car, sir."

"That isn't necessarily the safest thing to do around here, Sergeant," I said, nodding toward the ambulance as it pulled away.

"What's this about?" DI Carrick asked the sergeant.

"Military matter, sir. No need to involve civilians, if you don't mind."

"I do if it involves this crime."

"Military matter, sir. Now please excuse us. Lieutenant?"

I could tell we'd get no more out of this sergeant. I shrugged and followed him to the car. It was a Ford Fordor, the kind I'd seen in North Africa, a Canadian station wagon converted for military use. I'd never seen one with anything less than a full colonel in the back, but I couldn't even see inside this one, since the rear windows were opaque. The sergeant opened the rear door and held it for me. It was dark inside, and the rear seat was pushed back, so I still couldn't see who was waiting for me. I stooped and entered. The first thing I saw was a pair of crossed legs.

"Sit down, Lieutenant Boyle. I don't bite," said Sláine O'Brien. "Unless it's called for."

"I was wondering when you were going to show up," I said as I settled into the wide backseat. I'd been in smaller living rooms. "How does a subaltern rate one of these?"

"I don't have time for small talk, so let's get down to business, Lieutenant. What have you found out about the BARs?" She held a pen in one hand while flipping through a file. It looked like she was about to give me demerits.

"Well, I got shot at by one. Two Americans have been murdered since I arrived here. Oh, yeah, and a major has been arrested for bribery, but that was over black market produce, not guns."

"It sounds as if you've been busy," she said, "investigating cabbages." The pen started tapping against her knee.

"I forgot to mention. It was Red Jack Taggart who shot at me and killed at least one of the Americans. With a BAR. And do you have another Yank working this case? Older guy, wears a gray fedora hat."

"Taggart? Are you sure?" She sounded shocked that an IRA man would shoot at anyone, much less Yanks.

"Damn right I'm sure. He murdered Lieutenant Sam Burnham while we were at an RUC station after a funeral. I chased him but he got away."

"I'd say you're lucky to be alive. Taggart is not known for letting his quarry escape his clutches."

"He's the one lucky to be alive. He was *my* quarry. I think he was after Burnham for some reason. Taggart shot Burnham, as he stood at a window. Then he sprayed the house, to keep the rest of us down."

"But you didn't stay down?" She uncrossed her legs, smoothing down the green wool fabric. Her buttons were as shiny on her dress uniform as they'd been on her khakis in Jerusalem. I was distracted as I watched her shift in the seat. I always was a button man.

"No, I don't like being a stationary target."

"Neither do I, Lieutenant Boyle," she said, crossing her legs again, the smooth sound of her nylons rubbing against each other filling the silence. Or maybe filling my imagination, I'm not sure.

"You haven't answered my question about the other American, the one in civvies," I persisted.

"I'm finding that one American is quite enough, Lieutenant. Do you have any idea who he is or what he wants?"

"No, but he's mixed up in this somehow. I think he's following me."

"Why would another Yank follow you?"

"I've been wondering that myself. I thought you might have brought someone else in. Or maybe army CID. But no dice there. So who is he, and why is he here?"

"I'll have my people look into it," she said. She tapped her pen on the clipboard, impatient at the unanticipated complication. My eyes went from the pen to those buttons to her legs before settling on her eyes. All the choices, except the pen, were mesmerizing. Her eyes met mine, and I looked away, embarrassed, as if she could read my mind. She wasn't like any woman I'd ever met. I had the odd thought pop into my head that it was going to be tough to go back to Boston and settle down with a nice girl who worked in a department store or a deli.

"Who's the corpse?" Sláine said, nodding toward the automobile by the side of the road.

"Pete Brennan. GI from the base at Ballykinler."

"Is he involved in the BAR theft?"

"He was on duty the night it happened but I don't think he was killed over that."

"Coincidence?"

"I'm not sure. I think there is a connection but it has more to do with the black market than with the IRA. I need your help with that."

"What exactly do you need?"

"I need to know more about both Jenkins and Taggart."

"Such as?"

"Anything and everything you have. Background, connections, all the dope you must have in your security files on them. I'm working blind here, and I need to know more about these guys to try to get a handle on what to do next."

"Why Jenkins? Do you think he's involved in the weapons theft?"

"I don't think so but I'd rather be sure. How well do you know him?"

"I know what he's capable of."

"But do you know him personally?"

"I've questioned him, yes."

"In a Portadown pub?"

"Wherever necessary. Don't forget what you are supposed to be investigating, Lieutenant Boyle, and whom you are working for."

"Is that a threat?" I asked.

"A reminder to stay focused. Part of my job is to keep tabs on the militia groups, including the Red Hand. It's an open secret that Jenkins controls them, so of course I meet with him. He knows I'm with MI-5. One hand washes the other, as they say. I don't know how you found out about that rendezvous but it has nothing to do with this case."

"I still want to see his file. And I need to know more about Taggart. He obviously knows where the BARs are; he demonstrated that pretty clearly."

She tapped her pen against the file folder in her lap again. "Very well. I have other business here today but meet me at the Slieve Donard Hotel in Newcastle, eight o'clock tomorrow morning. I'll take you to Stormont Castle in Belfast and you can review the files. Will that do?"

"Sure. The hotel is the big brick one with the tower, right?"

"Aye, you can't miss it."

"Does your business here have anything to do with this killing? Are you keeping something from me?" I asked.

"Many things, to be sure, but nothing germane to this investigation. I'll give you what I can about Taggart and Jenkins. Is there anything else?"

"I thought perhaps I could buy you dinner, and you could tell me about the one Irish-American you admire."

"Pardon me?"

"In Jerusalem, when I asked if you didn't like Irish-Americans, you said there was one you admired very much. I'd like to know who."

"If you find the BARs, Lieutenant, there will be two. I'm quite busy now, so if you're done?"

"One question before I go. How did you get here so quickly? Who told you?"

"That's a matter of security."

"What isn't?"

"Until tomorrow morning, Lieutenant?"

She didn't look up from the open file on her lap but I saw one corner of her mouth turn up in a smile. I wasn't sure what I was doing with her. Part of me said the invitation to dinner was to interrogate her. Another part of me said it would be nice to spend time in her company. She was an Irish girl, after all. Ultimately, I was glad she'd turned me down. I got out of the car and nodded to her driver, who leaned against the front fender as he smoked. He looked past me, eyeing something down the road. It was Grady O'Brick, riding in a pony cart, the rear stacked high with black peat held in place by slats of wood bound with rope.

"What's this now?" Grady asked, fixing his gaze on me. The ambulance was gone, but the Austin still had its nose in the ditch, with DI Carrick and his constables searching it. Grady glanced at the staff car, the sergeant, then back to me. "Have you got yourself in trouble, Billy Boyle?"

"Not me, Grady. Pete Brennan," I said as I walked over and scratched the pony on its withers.

"What kind of trouble?"

"Dead. Murdered, found in the trunk of that car," I said, looking at the gray Austin. "Same car that Red Jack Taggart got away in after the shooting in Killough."

"Red Jack? Do you think he did this?" Grady sounded incredulous that Taggart would kill Pete, that I'd even consider the possibility.

"I have no idea. Same car, that's all. It could mean anything. It's no coincidence, though."

"No, you're right about that, boy. Damn!" He shook his head, gripping the reins tighter around his ruined hands. "May the devil swallow him sideways, the fellow who did this."

"Move along now," the sergeant said, waving his hand in the direction of the village.

"Move yourself, you English thief. Don't tell me to move along in my own village!"

"Take it easy," I said, holding my palm out to the sergeant, who had stiffened at the insult, his hand resting on his holster. "The soldier who was killed was a friend of ours; he doesn't mean anything by it."

The sergeant let his hand drop to his side. I looked up at Grady.

"I don't much like the sight of that uniform, as you know," said Grady, his face stern as he gazed straight ahead. His tone contained all the apology he was capable of, and the British sergeant moved away and got into the staff car.

"I know," I said.

Grady looked down at me and winked.

"The curse of his own weapons upon him," he whispered, and laughed. "What are you doing with a bastard like that anyway?"

"It's a long story."

"It'll keep. I'll be back in an hour, Billy Boyle. Meet me at my home and I'll put the kettle on. It's a cold dawning for all here."

"OK, I will."

"First turning back there," he said with a backward nod as he flicked the reins and the pony clip-clopped away. Grady turned and stared at the Austin as he passed it, and his shoulders sagged. The staff car, mysterious with darkened windows and shining grillwork, started up, its growling engine powerful and alien in the small country lane. The driver turned the car around in the road, leaving deep tire marks on the soft shoulder and spitting mud as he gained traction. He drove behind Grady slowly; the old man didn't coax the pony into a trot or move an inch from the center of the lane. Finally, the road branched near the pub, and the staff car accelerated, disappearing around the corner.

The curse of his own weapons upon him. A frightening curse, and I shivered. Even the memory of Sláine's legs and the enticing soft sound of nylon rubbing against nylon did not warm me.

"Who was that?" Adrian Simms asked. He seemed chilled too. His hands were stuffed into his pockets and his shoulders hunched.

"Military matter," I said.

"With that sleekit sergeant? Who is he driving around in that big automobile?"

"What did you call him?"

"Sleekit. What you might call a sly one, with a dab of dishonesty thrown in."

"Do you know him?" I asked.

"I've seen him around. Cyrus Lynch. He's one of the secret bunch up at Stormont. He's brought in IRA boys and Red Hand boys. Most are never seen again."

"What about the Black Knights?"

"What about them?" Simms said, his eyes darting to where Carrick stood by the car. "What do they have to do with anything?"

"Just wondering if they were ever arrested along with the Red Hands."

"I doubt it," Simms said, sounding affronted. "They're mainly businessmen, respectable citizens. They do good works for the church."

"Is DI Carrick one?"

"Ach, aye. A man in his position almost has to be."

"And you?"

"None of your damn business, Boyle. When are you going to stop wasting time and find out where Taggart is with those weapons? You know, the fellow who killed Sam Burnham?"

"Right about now," I said, but it was to his back.

CHAPTER ■ NINETEEN

THERE HAD BEEN nothing else in the car. Carrick said I should watch out for Sergeant Lynch, that the man wasn't trustworthy. Maybe because he was an Englishman who arrested Protestants as well as Catholics, which made him sleekit. We waited until a truck came to tow the Austin out of the ditch, searched the ground some more after it was pulled out, and found nothing but flattened grass stained with engine oil.

I'd asked Jack Patterson to dig up a picture of Pete. I wanted to show it around the branch of the Northern Bank in Armagh, but I didn't tell him that. He said he'd get one from Pete's personnel file. Then I asked DI Carrick for a photo of Jenkins, figuring they had to have surveillance shots of him.

"Sorry, Lieutenant Boyle," Carrick said, sounding like he actually was. "We can't do that. Jenkins's file is sealed. Orders from Stormont."

He wouldn't say more, and I got the same feeling from him that I used to get from my higher-ups in the Boston PD when the heavy-weights in city hall hushed something up. Frustration and embarrassment, mixed with a sternness fueled by anger at having to toe someone else's line. I didn't press him.

■ ■ ■

THE ROAD TO Grady O'Brick's place was more like a track, suited to a pony and narrow cart. Branches reached out low into the road, caught on the jeep's fender, and brushed against the windscreen. Washed-out ruts kept the going slow but the land was even on the shoulders, and when I had to I went up on one and plowed through the underbrush. I wasn't the first, as crushed bushes ahead showed. They were starting to pop up and send out shoots. I recognized elderberries, just like the bushes we had at home in our backyard, behind the garage. My mother loved the purplish black fruit that hung in clusters, since it attracted songbirds. Most of these berries were gone now, eaten or dropped to the ground, leaving their long, narrow leaves and reddish network of stems to brush against the jeep.

The path opened to a clearing and I parked on a flat rise, where long slabs of gray granite rose from the ground like giant steps. At the top sat Grady's cottage, the whitewashed stonework solid under the thatched roof. A single small window faced me, next to a door painted bright red. There was no sign of him or his pony, so I got out, stretching my legs in the warmth of the sun. The land sloped down behind his house, a rocky grade descending to a low, flat expanse of green and brown grasses, interspersed with standing water, soggy paths, deep trenches, and piles of sodden peat. A cart path led to a long shed, set just below the rear of the cottage. The sides were alternating slats of rough-cut wood, letting the wind through to dry the harvested peat, which was stacked higher than my head. It all smelled faintly of cut grass, rotting vegetables, and thick mud.

"If a man has water and peat on his land, 'tis all he needs for the hard times," Grady said. He'd come up so quietly, I hadn't noticed he was standing right behind me. "Let me unhitch Dora and then we'll sit."

We left Dora with fresh hay and an apple Grady produced from his pocket. He sat on a wooden bench by his front door and removed his rubber boots, thick with drying mud. He set them under the bench and sighed deeply, leaning back to rest against the rough stone, letting the early morning sun wash his brow.

"It's a hard job, the peat," he said. "But there's nothing like the death of a young man to make an old man glad of his pains."

"My father once told me the saddest sight he ever saw was the dawn the day after his brother was killed." I was surprised I had said that. It had come out without a thought, something my dad had mentioned once when we'd gotten up early to go fishing. I'd been fourteen, maybe fifteen. I still remembered that dawn, Cohasset Harbor at our backs and the red-streaked horizon to the east, my dad and Uncle Dan sharing a thermos of coffee with their pal Nuno Chagas. Nuno was a Portugee lobsterman who had smuggled rum and whiskey during Prohibition. He'd had some dealings with Dad and Uncle Dan that had resulted in cases of unmarked bottles down cellar and a more open friendship after repeal in 1933.

The light dawning over the far Atlantic horizon had turned from dark reds and blues to gold reflected off the chop. At my age then, the talk and actions of men like Nuno, Dad, and Uncle Dan were strange territory. Little was ever said but they all moved with certainty around each other, as if they knew each other's thoughts. I remember wishing I could be like them, confident in their silence and ready for whatever the day offered. I wanted strong arms like theirs too, and all those things that seemed to be forever beyond my body and mind.

Uncle Dan had taken a pint bottle from his coat and poured whiskey into their coffees. Nuno drank his, one hand on the wheel, eyes watching the water ahead. Dad and Uncle Dan touched their cups in a toast, nodded, and drank. Dad looked at me as if he'd forgotten I was there, and maybe he had.

"The night Frank was killed," he said, then stopped. I froze, waiting for him to speak again. I knew Uncle Frank, the oldest of the three brothers, had been killed in France during the war, but no one spoke about it. I can still hear the thrum of the motor, the sound of the bow hitting each wave, the *thump, thump, thump* as we moved through the water. If I breathe deep enough, I can smell the whiskey and coffee mingling with the salt air.

"The night Frank was killed," he said again, "it was raining. Hard. It was cold, and the clouds were so low the flares would get lost in them, and then burst into brightness when they came down. We brought him in from patrol and laid him out in a communications trench. We sat with him in the rain, the mud a foot thick all around us. Finally, the rain stopped and a breeze kicked up, sending those clouds back to Germany. When dawn came, it was beautiful, just like this. It was then I cried. What kind of joke was that, to follow death in the rain with golden sunlight?"

The next thing I knew, Uncle Dan had put a chipped mug in my hand, poured in a little coffee, followed by even less whiskey, and said, "To Frank." They clinked their mugs against mine, and I had the sense to drink and not make a face, being unused to both coffee and liquor. I hadn't understood what Dad was trying to say but that didn't matter. I was happy simply standing at their elbows, feeling the currents of emotion that ran beneath the surface, flowing along with them like a cod following its school, not understanding why, knowing it must.

"In the last war?" Grady asked, drawing me back to the present. It might have been the second time he said it.

"Yes. The last war for the English, as they'd say."

"The death of a brother is a terrible thing. I would not go against a word your father uttered. He had every right. But I tell you now, Billy Boyle, you look at that gorgeous sun drenching our green fields. That is for the living, it is. If each dawn were for the dead of the night before, it would be darkness forever. Now come inside and we'll have strong tea."

Grady's cottage was low ceilinged, the thick wooden beams dark with age. The floor was flat stones laid over dirt, and a peat fire burned low on an open hearth. A kettle hung over the fire, and other pots and a skillet stood to the side. Against the rear wall, a hand pump on a wooden counter was positioned over a bucket. Water to drink, peat to burn. Besides whiskey, what more does an Irishman need?

As Grady busied himself with the fire and the kettle, I sat in a worn but comfortable armchair near the hearth. The chair opposite looked like Grady's: It was leather, cracked and dry, with indentations in the seat and back that marked it as the owner's favorite. A wooden table, a bed at the far end of the room, some shelves, and a chest of drawers completed the interior.

Two pictures hung on the wall. One was religious, showing the way of the cross on the Via Dolorosa, where I had walked with Diana not too long ago. It looked like a print from a magazine, framed under glass, faded with time. Jesus with the crown of thorns, his head bloody, his body sagging under the weight of the cross. Next to it was a still life of a dead rabbit laid out alongside a copper pot, flecks of blood around its mouth under wide, dull eyes. I didn't know much about art but I knew these weren't to my taste.

"Here you go, just the thing, it is," Grady said as he pulled over a stool and set down a tray. I was surprised to see real china and a sugar bowl. "Ah, you expected a dirty mug, I can tell by the look in your eyes!"

"No, it's only—I didn't expect anything so nice—for me, I mean," I said, trying not to say anything stupid, and failing.

"Don't you worry now. These came from my mother, a wedding gift. I had sisters but they all died. Some before they were grown, the rest taken by the influenza. I never wed a wife myself, not that any offered themselves up," he said, pointedly not looking at his hands. "And I don't have much in the way of company, so it's a rare treat to use this. Take all the sugar you want, boy. It's rationed, sure, but the border isn't far, and enough makes its way here that we don't go without."

"Things always find a way, don't they?"

"What do you mean?"

"When we had Prohibition, people made their own beer, and plenty of liquor made it in from everywhere. You couldn't stop it."

"Ah, well, that was a silly thing to try, keeping folks from their drink, don't you think?"

"Well, as my dad said, we don't explain the laws, we just enforce them."

"Your father is a policeman too, like you?"

"Not like me. He's more cop than I'll ever be, a homicide detective. His brother, my uncle Dan, he's on the force too."

"All those Boyles on the police force in Boston? What a safe town it must be," he said, chuckling and blowing on his tea. "So tell me, what would your father or your uncle say about poor Pete being killed like that?"

"They always said when a murder seemed to make no sense, it had to be about love or money."

"Who loved Pete Brennan on this island, or in the whole world, for that matter?"

"He kept to himself," I said. "He didn't want to get close to anybody, he'd lost all his friends once. Pig was the closest thing he had to a friend."

"Aye. He rubbed that pig's belly 'til it shone, he did!" Grady laughed, then sighed, the small, sad sound you make as grief overwhelms a fond memory.

"So it was money. And I know who was getting ready to pay Pete off. Question is, who else knew?"

"Jenkins, you mean?" Grady said, a sly eye on me.

"How do you know?"

"Pete and I raised too many pints to have secrets. As you say, he made no friends of men he might have to watch die in battle. But he was friendly to me since I'm hard to kill, and no longer in the fight."

"Do you think Jenkins killed him?"

"Now, you know I don't have a high opinion of the man, even on his best days. But I won't say he isn't a smart fellow. Ignorant perhaps but smart, if you know what I mean. He's kept out of trouble, even though he runs the Red Hand, and that takes a bit of work up here," Grady said, tapping his head. "Would a smart man endanger all that by shooting an American soldier? That brings down a whole new set of troubles upon him, he who has everything worked out so well that the English and the IRA can't touch him. Why risk upsetting that apple-cart, I ask myself? Money? Maybe. I've never been cursed with it myself, so I can't say how it would make a man behave. More tea?"

"Sure," I said, holding out my cup. I stirred in some more contraband sugar and let the steam warm my face. What Grady said made sense. Would Jenkins endanger his position over a payoff? If he had, what did that mean?

"So what did that brute of an English sergeant want with you? Did he give you trouble?"

"No, he's just a chauffeur with a lousy attitude. I have to go up to Belfast tomorrow with him and another officer."

"Well, keep your wits about you, Billy Boyle. I did not like the looks of the man."

I nodded, drank my tea, and let the fire warm my feet. I looked at the pictures again, a dead rabbit and Jesus wearing a crown of thorns, and tried to remember what we had hanging on the walls of our house in South Boston. I was fairly certain there were no framed pictures of blood and death.

CHAPTER ▪ TWENTY

I'D ARRANGED TO meet Joe Patterson at the Lug o' the Tub at eleven o'clock. I parked my jeep next to his and knocked on the locked door. It was a few minutes before opening, but Tom let me in. Sergeant Patterson was at the bar, busy with a bowl of stew.

"Rabbit," Tom said. "You boys have had a hard day already. I can't serve drink yet, but you're welcome to a bowl. Short on rabbit, long on potatoes."

Based on how Jack was wolfing the stuff down, I accepted the offer. Jack handed me a picture of Pete Brennan, smiling into the camera, standing in front of a tent, his fore-and-aft cap set at a jaunty angle. Basic training, maybe. A lifetime ago.

Tom leaned against the bar and sighed. "How many lads have had that same photograph taken? I think I have one like it myself," he said.

"Yeah, me too," Jack said. "I took that from his personal effects. Give it back when you're done, OK?"

"Sure. Find anything else?"

"No," said Jack, scraping his spoon around the bowl to get the last of his stew. "Nothing from around here, nothing recent."

"Nothing that looked like receipts, invoices, shipping records?"

"Nope. Is this about the guns?"

"I'm pretty sure Pete didn't have anything to do with that but he did know about some shady deals between Jenkins and Thornton. Looks like he used that as leverage for a payoff and a ticket back to Italy."

"Not a smart move," Jack said.

"I think it was his only move. He lost everything at Salerno, which means he had nothing here. Maybe he was going back to the only place that meant anything to him. But he shouldn't have trusted Jenkins."

"Do you think Andrew Jenkins had a hand in this?" Tom asked. He had moved to the other end of the bar, setting out glasses, but he had a sharp ear.

"Nothing I can prove, just shoptalk. Keep it under your hat, OK?"

"Under my hat it is, Billy. Watch your step, though. Jenkins is not a man to sit idly by if an accusation of murder is made against him. He's been suspected often enough but always manages to shake loose of it."

"How? Do witnesses end up in ditches?"

"Some change their minds, to be sure. A visit from the Red Hand can be persuasive. Other times, the investigation just dries up. I knew a fellow down Dromara way who gave a statement that he saw Jenkins and two men walking toward Slieve Croob in the Mournes, and later saw only Jenkins and one man return. Two days later, the body of a Catholic was found in a small wood in that area."

"So what happened?" Jack asked.

"Nothing. The constable took his statement. Hugh Carrick was investigating, or so I heard, and then nothing."

"What happened to the witness?"

"Nothing. He told me no one ever made a threat or asked him to withdraw his statement. This was two, maybe three years ago."

"Is he still around?"

"No. Joined up, even though he had helped the IRA now and again. Last I heard, he'd been captured in Libya somewhere."

"It doesn't add up," Jack said .

"Doesn't it?" Tom asked. He set down two half pints of ale in front of us. "On the house, along with the stew. To fortify your investigation. Close enough to opening time."

"I'm not supposed to drink on duty," said Jack .

"A half pint? You call that drinking?" Tom said in amazement.

"He's got a point," I said, and raised my glass. The ale tasted cool and crisp after the hot stew. Actually, he had two good points. You couldn't call a half pint serious drinking, and it did add up. Someone was protecting Jenkins, giving him enough cover that he didn't have to bother with intimidating witnesses or worry about shooting a GI in order to save some dough. How high did you have to go to get that kind of protection? Maybe I'd find out tomorrow when Sláine O'Brien let me see the secret files at Stormont Castle. But maybe she held more secrets than her files did.

I took my time with the half pint, thinking about what my next move should be. I would drive to Armagh to ask around the Northern Bank if anyone had seen Brennan the day before. Then I thought I'd head toward the border to get the lay of the land around Omeath, where Jenkins's truck had been abandoned. I couldn't cross the border myself without risking internment but I could check out how easy a crossing might be. If the roads were jammed with traffic then maybe I could stop on the way back in Annalong and have a drink in the pub where Thornton said he had seen Eddie Mahoney arguing with an unknown man. It sounded like a lot of driving so I savored the half pint and leafed through a local weekly newspaper, the *Newcastle Times*. Rugby scores, war news, local weddings. One story about U.S. Army maneuvers ruining fields as tanks chewed up farmland and trucks clogged the roads. Next to it was a picture of a convoy making its way through Clough, with Constable Adrian Simms standing in the road, holding up local traffic, Sam Burnham in full snowdrop regalia next to him. The line of trucks stretched into the distance. It was going to be a long wait, which probably hadn't made the villagers very happy.

"That happened last week," Tom said. "Big row all around. Farmers on about their crops being ruined, traffic backed up everywhere, although I'm not complaining. Some folks waited it out in here, so it was good for business."

"Lot of damage done?"

"Not so much. It's more that folks don't appreciate being told they have to put up with it, like it or not. Human nature," he said, shrugging.

I finished up a few minutes later and waved goodbye to Tom. Outside the sun was bright and promised a clear day. From in back of the pub came the hoarse sound of a motorcycle revving up and taking off. As I got into the jeep, I thought about how much fun it would be to make this trip on two wheels, as long as it didn't rain. A piece of paper on the passenger-side floor, held down by a stone, caught my eye. I looked around to see who might have placed it there and heard the distant sound of a motorcycle fading away, maybe the same one I'd glimpsed at Brownlow House. I unfolded the paper. In large block letters, the message read WATCH OUT FOR SIMMS. It was signed YOUR YANK FRIEND.

My Yank friend warning me about Adrian Simms. The guy with the fedora. Why? Why should I worry about Simms, and why should this guy bother warning me? Whose side was he on, and how come no one seemed to know who he was? Well, a warning was a warning, no sense ignoring it. I went back into the pub, and took the page from the paper with Adrian's picture on it. Now I had pictures of Pete Brennan, Eddie Mahoney, and Adrian Simms. Plus, I could give a good description of Red Jack Taggart and Andrew Jenkins. I needed to find someone who'd seen one or more of them in the wrong place at the wrong time, someone who wasn't with the IRA or the Red Hand. But I could have used someone to watch my back, not to mention my flanks.

I missed Diana as a partner. She had a different way of viewing information, and when we talked about a case she would often ask a question or make a comment that made me think about things in a new light. I felt lonely without her, and without Kaz as well. Lieutenant—not to mention Baron—Piotr Augustus Kazimierz was assigned to Eisenhower's HQ by the Polish Army in Exile. Kaz had lost his entire family when the Nazis invaded while he was studying languages in England. I'd showed up, and then he'd lost Daphne, Diana's sister, the only person left in the world he loved. Since then, he'd worked with me, and for a short, rail-thin, bespectacled intellectual, he'd proved damned handy with a gun as well as with his razor-sharp mind. Kaz might have stood out a tad in Northern Ireland but he knew how to keep to the shadows. This mystery Yank wouldn't have been a mystery for long if I'd had Kaz on the prowl.

But I was alone so I headed down the Banbridge Road and thought about the note. The writing bothered me. The clumsy block letters might have been an attempt to disguise the handwriting of the person who wrote it, which meant I might have a chance of comparing it to some sample I had. But in Northern Ireland whose handwriting might I recognize? Kaz was good with codes and ciphers, and he might have been able to pick up on disguised handwriting.

That led me to wonder what role Adrian Simms played in all this. A friendly local cop, got along well with Yanks, and was reasonably tolerant of Catholics for an Orangeman. A guy who hadn't made the cut for the Royal Black Knights, who had a social climber for a wife, according to Tom. It could just be village gossip or could be absolutely true and have nothing to do with anything. I thought Adrian had told me he'd been brought up in Dublin, then moved north. He'd accounted for his live-and-let-live nature by acknowledging that he'd been the minority in the Republic, so he knew how it felt. But why had the Knights turned him down? And why had I been warned about him?

The only reason for the warning I could figure was money. Maybe Simms had wanted to shower his wife with cash so she'd forgive him for a Catholic in the woodpile. That was a stretch, though.

I slowed as I passed through Banbridge on the same route I'd taken the day before. As my speed decreased, my thoughts seemed to slow down too, making it easier to see a pattern. Usually the simple answer was the right one, and the simple explanation here was that Simms was more of an extremist than he let on. Perhaps he was in the Red Hand, and Jenkins had been irritated by my papist questions. Maybe I was being warned about the Protestant militia. But then why didn't the note say that? *Watch out for Simms.* That was all he'd written.

Slow or fast, nothing much made a lot of sense. I decided to let it percolate in my subconscious. *That's what it's there for,* Dad always said when he was stuck. *Let it earn its keep.* OK, I decided to give it a try. I let my mind go blank and watched the scenery drift by. Thirty minutes later, I was in Armagh, my mind still empty. I guess my subconscious was working really hard but what I was aware of was how hard the seat in the jeep had become. I drove along a narrow roadway, row houses built of light brown stone glowing in the sunlight, their brightly varnished doors in red, green, and blue flashing by as I kept the wheel turned into the curving road. In the distance, the twin spires of the Roman Catholic Saint Patrick's Cathedral reached high from the crest of a hill overlooking the city. I was driving by the other Saint Patrick's, the Protestant cathedral that stood on the ground where Saint Patrick himself had built his first stone church, four centuries after the death of Christ. They'd drummed that into us in catechism class, and it had always stuck with me, that the Protestants held the sacred ground where Patrick himself had laid the stones of the first church in Ireland. That and the fact that Patrick had voluntarily returned to Ireland after having been kidnapped from Britain and sold into slavery in Ireland, then escaping and making it back to his home across the Irish Sea. There he'd had a dream that the people of Ireland begged him to return to preach to them. I always thought it could have been a trick, and he should have stayed home. Maybe there would still be snakes on the island but it might have saved everyone a lot of trouble.

CHAPTER TWENTY ONE

I SAT IN the jeep, parked across the street from the bank, and watched. I wanted to get a feel for the pattern of movement in and out, where people came from and where they went after their banking was done. The clientele was mixed, businessmen and workers, older ladies in big hats, and a couple of guys in uniform. Respectable, like a downtown bank in Worcester or Springfield on a slow day.

I walked up and down the street. Lots of limestone had gone into this burg, the buildings all three or four stories, neat and square, the line of rooftops following the curve of the ground, chimneys dotting their procession like a connect-the-dots drawing. I heard the bells of both cathedrals chime, the high notes of the Catholic Saint Patrick's competing with the deeper tones of the Protestant Saint Patrick's. Either way, they both told the same story. Time was slipping away. It would have been helpful to have Kaz along. We could have split up, asked our questions, and be done in half the time. But there had been no chance of that. Kaz hadn't made the trip to Jerusalem. He'd been ordered back to London by the Polish Government in Exile—the folks who actually were in charge of him, if anyone was. He was listed as a liaison officer with Eisenhower's headquarters but he worked with me in Ike's secret Office of Special Investigations, dealing with low crimes in high places, the kind of thing Uncle Ike wanted taken care of quietly, so as not to hinder the war effort. With me in Northern Ireland helping the Brits, Diana with the SOE, and Kaz back in London on whatever was up with the Poles, the only guy minding the shop in Algiers was Corporal Mike Miecznikowski—Big Mike—a Detroit cop who'd joined us after

Sicily. I hoped Kaz would be back soon, and I began to think about the past few months as the good old days, the four of us working together, never thinking we'd soon be scattered all across Europe like this.

I stopped in O'Neill's pub. It looked bright and cheery, the outside painted yellow and the door sporting a fresh coat of varnish. I asked the barkeep if he'd seen any of the guys in the pictures I laid out on the bar.

"Are you not drinking?" he replied, more in amazement than confrontation.

"Too many stops to make. I'd be drunk before I was done. Recognize any of these fine fellows?"

"Who are you then?" He kept running a rag over a glass that was by now bone-dry.

"Just a Yank. Humor me, OK?"

He puffed out his cheeks and sighed at the demands I put upon him. He looked at the two old men at the bar and one older gent at a table, and probably decided this was the most interesting thing that was going to happen today. He looked at the photos of Pete Brennan, Eddie Mahoney, and Adrian Simms, picking up each one, studying it, and setting it down with careful ceremony.

"Never saw any of them," he said. "But I know that's Clough." He tapped his finger on the picture of Adrian with Sam Burnham standing near him as he directed traffic.

"Congratulations," I said. I described Red Jack Taggart and Andrew Jenkins. He said they reminded him of several fellows, all regulars. I guess bald and stocky did cover a lot of men.

"Do you do your banking over there?" I pointed with my thumb toward the Northern Bank, visible through the front windows.

"Course not, are ya daft? That's a Protestant bank. Bank of Ireland for us. For a smart lot of boys, you Yanks don't really know very much, do ya?"

"Lucky for us we're quick studies. Thanks."

I stretched my legs for a couple of blocks and turned around, crossed the street, and walked back to the bank. A few doors short of it, I stopped at a small tobacco shop and newsstand. I bought some penny candy from a barrel so I could at least hand some coins over as I asked my questions. This fellow wasn't as wary or talkative as the barkeep.

"No, no, certainly not."

"Why 'certainly not'?" I asked, noticing he had said that after looking at the picture of Adrian.

"Don't care much for the RUC. They killed my brother, they did."

"I'm sorry."

"Twelve years ago this December." He handed me my change.

"I am sorry."

"Murdered him."

"Thank you," I said, and left, wondering how these people lived within sight of each other every day.

I walked past the bank and stopped at a greengrocer's shop. A gray-haired fellow in a heavy green sweater was stacking apples out front. I picked one and he put it on a scale, hardly looking at me. I guess it wasn't a big enough sale to impress him.

"Can you tell me if you've ever seen any of these men around here? It would be a big help."

"To who then?"

"Well, to me."

"Exactly," he said, holding my change in his hand.

"Keep the change," I said. "And the apple."

He frowned but dropped the coins into the pocket of his apron and dutifully wiped his hands on it before handling the photos.

"Hmm. No. No. This fellow, yes," he said, snapping his finger against the photo of Adrian. "He liked my apples, I remember."

"How long ago?" I asked.

"Four, maybe five days. I can't be sure, son, but he stood out because of the uniform. We don't get many Yanks shopping for apples here."

"Yanks? What do you mean?"

"This fellow you showed me, right here." He pointed to Sam, standing beside Adrian.

"The American, not the constable?"

"Aye, that's what I'm telling you. He liked my apples, he did. They come from an orchard not two miles away. Do you want to buy some for him?"

"He's dead." As if that explained everything.

"Terrible, this war. Anything else, lad?"

"Was he alone?"

"Let me think. I was stacking cabbages, I believe. He stopped by and asked, real polite, if he could buy just one apple. I said sure, and he went off, biting into it. After that, I didn't pay him any more mind. He may have stopped in front of the bank and chatted with some fellows, now that I think back, but I'm not sure. Maybe a half hour later, he came back and bought another apple. Said they were sweet and crisp, and they got no such fresh fruit on his base. And now you say he's dead."

"Where do you buy your fruits and vegetables? From Andrew Jenkins?"

"Well, aren't you full of the odd questions! Some, yes. Most from the local farmers, right outside of town. The rest from Andrew. A good man, he is."

"Thanks," I said, walking down the sidewalk, trying to figure out what this meant. What had Sam been doing here? Sightseeing? Was he meeting someone here? Who, and why? Was it a coincidence or did it have something to do with why Sam had been targeted by Red Jack? Good questions, all. Problem was, I didn't have answers, good or bad.

I took a deep breath, inhaling the city air, hints of chalky limestone, coal smoke, piss, and buried anger floating on the wind. It had grown colder, and heavy gray clouds hung in the eastern sky, promising rain before the day was out. Irish weather fit the mood of the island, bathing you in warm sunshine one minute, then pelting you with cold rain the next. It made me homesick for the constant heat of North Africa or the clammy fog of London, and I wondered how I would ever describe my feelings to Dad and Uncle Dan. Or if I would try.

I decided to transact some business, to get the wind off my back. Pushing on the brightly shined brass handle on the main door, I entered the bank. The floor gleamed as well, black and white tiles spread out in a geometric pattern. Tellers' cages ran along the wall to my left, and a series of desks, out in the open, were on my right. Straight ahead, a secretary sat at a small wooden desk near a door of pebbled opaque glass. A custodian in a dark blue workman's coverall worked a cloth around the brass doorknob with gusto.

"Is the bank manager in?" I asked, giving the secretary a smile before I added, "Miss...?" I could see she was married, but my policy with secretaries and doorkeepers of all stripes was to butter them up with the Boyle charm.

"Whom shall I say is asking?" The *whom* came out like the foghorn on Little Brewster Island. She fixed her eyes on me as she tapped a very sharp pencil on the nameplate at the edge of her desk. It left no doubt, she was Mrs. Turkington.

"Lieutenant William Boyle," I said. "U.S. Army."

"Quite. Mr. McBurney is unavailable." She sat with her hands folded on the desktop blotter, waiting for me to leave. She was on the distant shore of forty, lines beginning to creep in at the edges of her eyes, double chin starting to show. Her eyes, hazel with flecks of green, had zeroed in on me.

"Well, it's official business, Mrs. Turkington. He's expecting me."

"I doubt that, young man."

"I doubt that he'd reveal confidential information to you. It might be dangerous." I leaned closer to her and lowered my voice. "I'm on the trail of a German spy."

Her only response was to button the top button of her blouse.

"Pardon, sir," the custodian said. "You're in me way." I stood aside as he knocked, then opened the door to the office and stood in the doorway, applying polish to the knob on the other side.

"Bailey, really!" Mrs. Turkington said.

"Mr. McBurney, he'd have me head if I left one knob unpolished, right, Mr. McBurney? Today being polishing day, that is."

"Right you are, Bailey," came a distracted voice from inside. I leaned forward and saw a balding man at a desk, jet black hair circling his crown, nothing on top. His five o'clock shadow was getting a jump start on the afternoon. He glanced up and met my eye.

"Someone to see me, Mrs. Turkington?"

"A Mr. Boyle," she said, laying heavy emphasis on the Catholic last name. She probably imagined I had had a roasted Protestant baby for breakfast.

"Oh, well," McBurney said as he squinted and took in my uniform. "An American, is it? An officer? Show him in then."

"All done here," Bailey said, giving the knob a final polish and holding the door for me. As I passed between him and Mrs. Turkington, he winked.

"What can I do for you, Lieutenant Boyle?" After checking my bars, McBurney stood and extended his hand, then gestured to the chair next to his desk. Either he was more liberal in his religious views than the Turkington outside his door or he might have hoped I was bringing the army payroll to deposit. Or maybe being American and an officer, no matter how lowly, made a Boyle acceptable here. It was clear to me that Bailey, by his name and his accent, was closer to the Boyles than the McBurneys or Turkingtons.

"I'm conducting an investigation, Mr. McBurney. Sorry, but I can't reveal the details—"

"An investigation of what? I assure you, this bank—"

"The branch is not involved, Mr. McBurney, in any way that would discredit you or the Northern Bank. But you may have been used."

"Used?" He said it as if he didn't understand the meaning of the word. Tiny beads of sweat popped out on his shiny forehead.

"By enemy agents," I whispered, leaning in over his desk.

"I can't believe it," he said indignantly.

"Exactly," I said, as if he'd proved my point. "They're very clever."

"Do you have any idea who the agents are?"

"That's what I'm working on. All I want you to do is look at some pictures and tell me if you recognize anyone. They aren't necessarily enemy agents, I just need to know if you know them or have seen them in the bank. OK?"

"Very well," he said, straightening up in his chair for the task ahead. I almost expected him to add *For king and country*.

I laid out the pictures, Adrian and Sam first, then Pete, then Eddie Mahoney. He stared at all of them, his eyes flitting from one to the other. He licked his lips. Nervous or hungry, who knew?

"No, I don't think so," he said.

"Look again, take your time," I said. "Give your subconscious a chance."

"I don't go in for all that Jewish claptrap," he said, shaking his head. "Freud, indeed."

"My father's not Jewish, and he sets a lot of stock in the subconscious," I said. "I didn't know the Jews invented it. You learn something new every day."

I stood and walked around his office, leaving him to study the photos. He had a grand view of the back of another building and a gravel parking lot. Lots of pictures on the walls, most including Mr. McBurney himself, shaking hands with various dignitaries a local fellow might have been impressed with. In one, he was standing with a bunch of other dark suits, all of them wearing bowler hats with red sashes around their chests. It was a parade, and they all carried flags or banners. British flags, black flags with red crosses and a crown, one with a skull and crossbones set beneath a red cross.

"No, I'm certain. I haven't seen any of these men."

"Andrew Jenkins does his banking here, doesn't he?"

"I don't intend to reveal any details about our customers, Lieutenant."

"But he is a customer?"

"It would stand to reason. He's a prosperous local businessman, and we are the leading bank in the area."

"For Protestants."

"I'm sorry, Lieutenant. Your people don't make the effort to better themselves, so most don't have funds to save. The bank would be happy to take their deposits if they did."

"My people?"

"Don't take offense; you've obviously done well for yourself in America. Unfortunately, those papists who remained here were the least able to care for themselves and their families. That is the source of many of our troubles."

I resisted the urge to snap off a quick left hook and break his nose.

"If no offense was intended, then I won't be offended. You're a Royal Black Knight, I see."

"Yes. It's a local lodge. Like the Freemasons. I believe you have them in America."

"Yeah, we do, along with the Knights of Columbus, and they all march in the same parades. You must be a head honcho, leading the parade here," I said, tapping my finger on the framed picture.

"Worshipful District Master is my title. That was taken at our annual Last Saturday in August parade," he said, huffing himself up.

"Impressive. You must be involved with checking new applicants, to see if they're good Protestants through and through."

"I don't see what this has to do with anything. I've a mind to call the police."

"Me too. Let's get District Inspector Hugh Carrick down here. He's a Royal Black Knight too. And some U.S. Army military police, a whole bunch of them. Some of them might be Catholics and Jews, but I'm sure they'll behave themselves. And I heard there was a detachment of Negro MPs due in soon."

"What is it you want?" I couldn't tell if the Jews or the Negroes had pushed him over the edge, but his voice was strained.

"I want to know why you're lying about Adrian Simms, Worshipful

District Master. The constable who was blackballed and kept from joining your lodge. I want to know why you felt you had to lie. You must have recognized him."

"Not on bank business," he said, grasping on to that distinction as if it were a life preserver. "I didn't think it necessary to mention him, since it wasn't bank business. You see?"

"No. My people, we're known to be slow. Explain it to me."

"I did recognize Mr. Simms, I did. But it hadn't anything to do with the bank so I didn't think it necessary to mention." He held a fountain pen in his hand, nervously twirling it between his fingers.

"Mr. McBurney," I said, "I told you this investigation has to do with enemy agents, and you decide to withhold information. Do you know what British security would think about that?"

"I assure you—"

"Don't assure me," I said, standing over him with my hands on his desk. "Tell me the truth, it's so much more helpful."

"Mr. Simms did apply for membership in the Royal Black Knights, and I recognized him. I can't say I actually know him, as a friend or even an acquaintance."

"And? What happened?"

"Well, everything seemed to be in order. He's a member of one of the Orange Societies. But membership in the Royal Black Knights is on another level entirely, since it is the most senior of all the lodges and societies. One has to prove one's lineage in the Reformed Faith."

"There was a problem?"

"Must you know? I don't see why it matters."

"Mr. McBurney, please let me decide that. I'm certain there are details in the banking business that seem unimportant to the average person but that are critical to you. It's that way in an investigation. Discovering little things often brings you to the larger truth. If it turns out to be a dead end, then it's forgotten, along with who passed on the information."

"And if it does turn out to be important?" He had stopped fiddling with the fountain pen and folded his hands on his belly.

"Then the person who provided the clue becomes quite important. Perhaps a hero, Mr. McBurney."

"Very well," he said, leaning forward and glancing behind me, making sure the door was shut. "The membership rules are very strict, as I said. The applicant must swear that he was born in wedlock, and neither parent was ever, in any way, connected with the Roman Catholic religion. No exceptions."

"Did Simms?"

"Yes, he did. But given that he came from Dublin, and no one locally could vouch for the veracity of his statements, we checked with our sources in that city. His mother had married a *Catholic*."

"Did that make Adrian Simms a Catholic?" I tried to keep my tone neutral. I wanted the information to keep coming, and I didn't want my distaste for this pasty-faced little man to show.

"No, no, he is not a Catholic," McBurney said, leaving the *God forbid* hanging in the air. "And neither were his parents. His mother's first husband died, and she remarried, this time to a Protestant, who was the young man's father."

"So the problem was the first husband, who died?"

"Not just that. It could have been overlooked, perhaps, though the rule is very strict. But there was a son from that first marriage, so Mr. Simms has a half brother. A half brother baptized in the Roman Catholic faith! That was that."

"I understand Mrs. Simms was none too happy with your decision."

"No, she was not," he said, one corner of his mouth rising in a sneering smirk. "Not what she expected, I'd say."

"Women," I said. "Who can figure 'em, right?" I hoped the common bond of men perplexed by the fair sex would trump my being a papist.

"The trick is," he said, leaning closer across his desk, "to figure out the one you marry, before you take the vow. That's what I always say."

"Adrian Simms didn't?"

"I'd say not." He drew his chair closer to his desk, lowering his head, his eyes darting about as if eavesdroppers were hiding somewhere. "She wants more than young Simms can give, in terms of social status. She was more upset over his application being denied than he was. Came right in here, and called me a liar. Demanded he be given another chance. It was quite a scene."

"What did you do?"

"I showed her the material our people in Dublin sent up. Copies of birth certificates, baptismal records, the whole lot. She didn't like it much, but it quieted her down."

"Sounds like a thorough background check. I'm surprised they haven't asked you to join the security services," I said.

"Oh, well, it was nothing really. Child's play compared to your job, I'm sure, Lieutenant Boyle. Is there anything else I can do to help?"

"Do you still have the file on Adrian Simms?"

"No, no reason to keep it. Mrs. Simms asked for it, and I gave it to her."

"OK. One more thing. I don't have a picture, but another man I'm looking for is about your age, a bit taller, balding, with dark brown hair. Sharp, prominent chin. Very lively eyes, always on the lookout."

"Do you have a name?" McBurney asked as he sat up straight, his eyes narrowing. I could tell he recognized the description.

"Yes, but I doubt it means anything. Does the description fit anyone you know?"

"A few chaps, certainly. All customers of the bank, and I can't divulge information concerning them."

"I could arrange for the government to insist."

"I doubt that even your connections at Stormont Castle would produce any results, Lieutenant Boyle. There are Royal Black Knights everywhere, you know."

He smiled when he said it but it wasn't a nice smile. We weren't talking about women anymore, so our bond was broken, and I had been warned.

CHAPTER TWENTY TWO

I STOOD ON the sidewalk outside the bank, zipping up my jacket against the chill. I still had a long drive ahead of me, down to Newry along the border, to see where the delivery truck used in the BAR theft had crossed over. I hunched up my shoulders and turned my face into the wind, wondering who my description of Red Jack Taggart had reminded McBurney of. I doubted a renegade ex-Bolshevik IRA fighter would ever have stepped foot in that bank without a Thompson and an empty sack.

I felt someone walking close behind me, to my right. I turned and saw Bailey from the bank. He nodded a greeting and subtly motioned me to follow him. He quickstepped ahead of me, looking more nimble than he had in the bank, where he'd moved from one brass doodad to the other at a snail's pace. We passed an RUC station, a solid three-story stone building that dominated the street. I followed him as he turned on Barrack Street, leading me past another imposing gray granite three-story structure, this one set back from the street in a small square. ARMAGH GAOL, the sign said. There were black iron bars on the windows and a high fence surrounded the place. Finally, he turned into a more pleasant street, leading to a long stretch of green grass and wide paths. A bunch of guys in white were playing cricket. They all yelled at one point though it didn't look like anything had happened. I trudged along in Bailey's wake until he came to a bench, out of sight of the street and the cricket players.

"Let's set ourselves," he said. He puffed out his cheeks and sighed. "I never like walking past the gaol, but it was the quickest way here, and this is a nice, quiet spot, away from prying eyes. Micheál Bailey is my name." He said it in the Gaelic fashion, *mee-hawl*.

"Billy Boyle," I said as we shook hands. "Pleased to meet you. Gives me a chance to thank you for getting that door open."

"As soon as I heard your name, I knew you had no chance of getting by Mrs. Turkington. She doesn't take kindly to Catholics, unless they're cleaning something, and then she's never happy with the result."

"But why did you help me, Micheál? What if you'd gotten in trouble?"

"I'll tell you, Billy. There are two reasons. The first is the month I spent in that gaol, for saying my name in Gaelic. It was right before the War of Independence, and soon enough they needed room for prisoners who done more than speak out of turn, so I was out on the street. Thin as a rail and black and blue from the beatings. So naturally I'd help a fellow like you out."

"What's the other reason?"

"I reckon you're asking about the American lad they took away."

"Who took away?"

"It was yesterday, about this time. I was leaving work, since I start my day at dawn, and I was on my way to O'Neill's for a pint. A Yank was walking toward me, whistling a tune. He looked happy, not a care in the world. Then a copper stepped out from a store and put his hand to my chest, and told me to stay put. A car pulled over and I could see someone beckon to the Yank. Quick as a flash the door opened and someone pushed the Yank in. The car drove off, and the copper told me to keep my mouth shut if I knew what was good for me. There was another, about twenty yards down the sidewalk. It was a trap, laid out by the RUC, which is nothing that should surprise me, except that they took a Yank! Well, that's a new one."

"You didn't report it to anyone?"

"Are ye daft, boy? I'm telling *you*, aren't I? Who else should I go to? The British Army? It'll be more than a month in gaol if anyone finds out what I've told you, so mind what you say about it."

"Is this the American they took?" I handed him the photo of Peter Brennan.

"Aye, that's him. You've been looking for him then?"

"Found him this morning. Dead. What kind of car was it?"

"An Austin—gray, I think. That's a pity about the Yank, it is."

"More than a pity, Micheál, a crime. Did you recognize either of the men who took him?"

"Aye, I know one by sight, but I won't even say his name. If he heard I talked, my home would be burnt with the missus and me inside."

"Andrew Jenkins."

"I didn't speak that name."

"OK. Recognize anybody else here?" I showed him the pictures of Adrian with Sam, and Eddie Mahoney.

"That's the other fellow, right here."

"Which one?"

"The constable. Only he wasn't in uniform yesterday."

"He's the one in the car?"

"No, he was the one who pushed your Yank in, and got in after him."

"Adrian Simms."

"If that's his name, then that's him."

Adrian Simms. Blackballed out of the Royal Black Knights. Working with Andrew Jenkins. Kidnapping and maybe murdering Pete Brennan. But why? How had he gotten hold of the Austin used by Red Jack? Who had pulled the trigger on Pete?

"Anything odd going on at the bank lately?"

"How do you mean, odd?"

"I don't know. Out of the ordinary. Large deposits, strangers visiting McBurney, anything unusual."

"No, it's the same boring business every day. Wait! About two weeks ago McBurney did give me a few hours off. Told me to go home early. That's unusual."

"Was anybody else told to go home?"

"Now that you mention it, one of the newest tellers. He told her she was looking peaked, and she should leave at noon. That was strange. He's not one to worry about anyone's health but his own."

"Is she Catholic?"

"Oh no, boy, that wouldn't do, not in a Protestant bank. It's one thing to have a papist clean the floors, it's another to have one count out your pound notes. Oh no!" He got a chuckle out of that. "But she was new, hadn't even been with us a couple of months."

I gave him my description of Red Jack Taggart, and asked if it sounded like anyone he'd seen.

"Now that's a strange thing to be asking, if you don't mind my saying."

"What do you mean?"

"What you said about the eyes. It does bring someone to mind. But you're asking an awful lot of dangerous questions here. Have you any idea?"

"Some," I said. "Have you seen this man at the bank?"

"If I did, I'd keep it to meself. Which is what I'm doing right now. I'd be a fool to betray an IRA man, now wouldn't I?"

"Did you think he was planning a bank heist?"

"The only thing I'll say is that I caught a glimpse of a fellow who looks much like this one, less than a week ago, sitting as pretty as you please in McBurney's office. I made it my business to mind my own business after that. But I did catch a glimpse of Mrs. Turkington's calendar the next morning, before she came in. The appointment the day before was listed as Mr. Lawson. He was also on the schedule the afternoon McBurney had given us off."

"Did you see who else was with him?"

"I'll say no more. I've said too much already." He held up his hand, as if turning back my question.

"OK," I said. "Subject closed. But tell me this, was there any other reason they threw you in that gaol? Maybe you were one of the Volunteers?"

"No, not then I wasn't. And afterward, when I was, they never caught me!" He jabbed his elbow in my side and laughed. "You're a smart one, Billy. But smart or not, I don't know you well enough to trust you with all my secrets. I'm retired from everything but bank cleaning now. When the war ended and Ulster stayed with the English, I decided that like it or not, it was my home. So I've made the best of things. It might not have been the best decision but here I am. I can rest easy knowing I did my part and that once most of Ireland was free, I suffered no more blood to be spilt. It's a terrible thing, Billy, terrible. You look as if you may know. The spilt blood doesn't fade with the years, I'll tell you."

"No," I said, thinking of the dead I'd seen at my feet. "It doesn't. What about Red Jack, have you seen him since?"

"I can't say for certain it was him I saw, or some fellow named Lawson who looks like him. And if I'd seen him this morning, I wouldn't tell you. If I say more, both sides would be looking to kill me. I'll just tell you the description you gave matches the man named Lawson, and leave it at that. He wasn't there when the Yank was taken so I don't know that it matters much."

"OK, I understand."

"Well," he said, standing. "I'll be off now. Time for my pint. Will you join me?"

"Can't, Micheál, I've got a long drive ahead of me. And don't worry, I won't say where I heard any of this."

"Good. I'm glad we met. It's good to have told someone what happened. Come, walk with me. I saw your vehicle back near O'Neill's."

This time he took me along Abbey Street, skirting the Armagh Gaol and RUC station.

The wind had died down and the sun shone for a few minutes before being engulfed by clouds again.

"Micheál, do you happen to know Grady O'Brick? From back during the war?"

"He's from Downpatrick, right?"

"Clough, a little village nearby."

"Aye, I haven't heard that name in a while. Them boys was famous for not being famous, if you follow me."

"I know the story. Mick the Master was their leader."

"Oh? Perhaps. It's not how I heard the story but facts change with the telling and the years."

"What did you hear?"

"Billy, you've got to get it into that Yank head of yours. This is not ancient history, as it may seem to you folk in America. This is all still happening here. You can't go about asking questions like that. Someone may take offense, on either side. If it's the Red Hand, you're most likely to disappear. If it's the IRA," he said, lowering his voice to a whisper, "then two in the brain is what you'll get, and your body dumped out in the open, so others will see. That's how each side likes it. So you mind your step here."

"But what did you hear?"

"Never mind. Drink with me or go, but stop asking questions that will only cause trouble." We were nearing the bank, and his eyes searched the street for anyone watching.

"Sorry, Micheál. Thanks, and don't worry."

"Someone should worry about *you*, Yank. I hope there's one who does."

CHAPTER ∎ TWENTY THREE

Sᴏ ᴅᴏ I, I thought as I drove out of Armagh, leaving the red brick and limestone buildings behind, the countryside opening up in brilliant greens once more as the sun filtered through gray clouds. Was Diana worrying about me now, or was she too busy being outfitted in French clothes, learning a new identity, being tested over and over again? Shouldn't I worry more about her, as she might be about to parachute into occupied Europe? It would be a waste of time, I told myself. I might not ever see her again, and if I did, we'd have a rocky time of it. It was all so far away—Jerusalem, the SOE, Uncle Ike—that it felt as if I could put it aside and forget about it for a while. The cool air, the emerald green landscape, it was so different from the life we'd shared the past few months. Had that life been real? Had we turned to each other to see a living face, someone who was not dead, drowned, or dying? Or was ours a fantasy of wartime, to fool ourselves into thinking we had a future?

Part of me said that was wrong. The memories of Diana were too vivid, her draw too strong. I'd come to understand that exposure to so much death made life more valuable. Love could be an antidote, a surety against being swallowed up by the war and left for dead, unmourned, far from home. What kind of life could Diana and I expect if we found ourselves alive in peacetime? Would there be an embarrassed silence as we tried to make small talk? No more dinners with generals, secret missions, shared agonies, or thrilling news from the front to form the substance of our days. Who would we be? A Boston cop and a cop's wife? An English lady and her American husband, on her father's country estate? I couldn't imagine either life.

I put it out of my mind as I drove through small villages, southeast toward Newry and the coast. First Markethill, with its neat white-painted brick buildings facing each other across the road, a pub anchoring one end of the village and a church the other. I waited outside of town for a parade of cows to cross the road, as men brought them in from a field into enclosures, where an auction was going on. The automobiles and trucks were old and well used, maybe because of the shortage of new vehicles for civilians, or perhaps because these were thrifty folk. Either way, business had to be good with the U.S. Army paying to feed thousands. Food was rationed for the civilians here as it was in England, and it must be tempting to take advantage of the black market and the food being smuggled in from the Republic, where there was no rationing.

Animal and vehicle traffic lightened as I drove. Through Whitecross, with one pub, a blacksmith's, and a few shops, all gone before I had a chance to slow down. Then to Forkill, a little village with an odd-sounding name stuck between two large hilltops. Beyond was the border. I parked the jeep near the town center and stretched my legs, checking my watch. It was late afternoon, and the sun was at my back, casting a long shadow on the road. I unfolded my map and laid it open on the hood, holding it down. A cool breeze flapped at the corners.

I was trying to figure out how long it would have taken the BAR thieves to get the truck over the border, unload it, and leave it outside Omeath. There was only one way to get to that stretch of border from Ballykinler, and that was along the coast. The Mournes blocked any other route. So they would've driven out of the base, through Clough, where they stopped to kill Eddie Mahoney and dump his body, then on through Newcastle, south along the coast, passing through Annalong and Kilkeel, then west to drive along Carlingford Lough, a bay about fifteen miles long that formed part of the border with the Republic of Ireland. Then a few more miles, north into Newry, where they'd cross the river, drive south for a while, and cross the border just east of where I was standing. Omeath was the first town across the border. So that's where they would have unloaded the BARs and ditched Jenkins's truck. It would have been time to get rid of it, since Jenkins would have reported it stolen.

"You lost, Yank?" a voice from behind me asked. I turned to see an RUC constable and an older fellow looking over my shoulder. The constable was young, reminding me of my kid brother Danny. He still had freckles across the bridge of his nose, and his skin was fair. The older guy was short, with a weather-beaten face that spoke of long, hard hours outdoors. He wore the usual collarless, once-white shirt, vest, and shabby jacket.

"I just wanted to make sure I didn't cross over the border by accident," I said. "Don't want to spend the rest of the war in an internment camp." Actually, the thought was kind of appealing but I knew it wasn't in the cards.

"Well, you be careful then," the constable said. "You take the right turn there and it's only a hop and a skip to the crossing. They wouldn't let you in, though, not with that uniform on."

"It's guarded?"

"Aye, by the customs officers on our side, and the Garda on theirs. There's some smuggling of foodstuffs and other rationed items, so it's well manned."

"Aye, some," said the older fellow with a wink.

"There's probably places where you could cross over without going through all that paperwork. If you knew the back roads and all," I ventured.

"Sure," said the constable, "but that's what they pay me for, isn't it? To keep an eye on things like that."

"You've only got two eyes, John," the older man said. "There's a dozen places a man could cross where no one would see."

"Aye, that's true."

"What about a truck? A big delivery truck?"

"Ach, that's different now," the old fellow said. "A truck of any size would have to keep to the roads. It's all farmland or grazing pastures here. Each field is bounded by rocks and trees; there'd be no way for a truck to get through. A man on a horse or pulling a donkey, now that's more like it. But a truck, no."

"I'd take Kieran's word for it," said the constable. "He seems to have a good supply of butter on hand." They both chuckled, and I got the idea that a little free trade over the border was not high on the list of crimes to be tracked down. I explained why I was asking questions without going into detail. I gave them both a description of Jenkins's truck and the date of the heist. Neither had seen a truck matching my description.

"They left it empty outside of Omeath, so it probably came through here."

"Why do you say that?" asked Kieran.

"Aye, why wouldn't they take the ferry, coming from Newcastle direction?" John added. They both looked at me as if I were daft.

"The ferry?"

"Aye," said John. "Look here, on your map. There's a ferry that runs from Warrenpoint to Omeath, direct across the lough. There'd be no need to make a big loop all around Newry."

He was right. It would shorten the trip and keep them out of a big city, where the RUC was more likely to have heard about the theft.

"The ferry has to be guarded as well, right?"

"Aye, same as here. Customs on our side, Garda on theirs. What was in the truck anyway?"

"Fifty automatic weapons."

Kieran whistled.

"I don't think our customs lads would miss that. Or the Garda. If that truck went over on the ferry or down our road, it was empty," John said with certainty.

"Then where are the guns?" I asked, not expecting an answer.

"Well, I'd say somewhere between where they were taken and the ferry," Kieran said, rubbing his chin for all he was worth. "Wouldn't you, John?"

"Unless the driver knew of an unguarded crossing to our west, down Crossmaglen way. Or the weapons might have been transferred to pack animals and brought over."

"Fifty Browning Automatic Rifles and over two hundred thousand rounds of ammunition," I said. "That would require a sizable herd."

"Aye, I'm not saying it's likely now. Odd though," John said. "Why would they send an empty stolen truck across the border?"

"Not on a whim," I said. "For a purpose."

"Still," Kieran said, "it could be done. Drive the truck to a farm, transfer the guns and all to a tractor maybe. Then across the fields to another farm in the Republic and onto another truck. Or else buried all nice and tidy."

"Not that you would know of such things," John said.

"There was a time I did," Kieran said. "But I'll speak no more of those days. All the best, Yank." With a wave of the hand, he left us.

"Sounds like he knows a few secrets," I said.

"My father—he was in the RUC too—says Kieran was one of the local IRA boys, and that he was sure they traded shots during the war. A decent man, though, law-abiding once the fight was over."

"Except for the butter."

"Well, there's laws and then there's plain common sense, now isn't there?"

"You'd get no argument from me or my father either."

"Are you a policeman in America?"

"Yes. Family business for me, too."

"So you know how it is then. Sometimes you save a lot of trouble by looking the other way, when the only law that's broken is one preventing a man from putting food on his family's table."

"Must help keep the peace to think that."

"It's like letting pressure off a steam valve," John said. "Keep things all bottled up and sooner or later it will blow up in your face. If I let the boys run around the hills and get themselves all tuckered out bringing butter and sugar home to the missus, then they don't have time for other mischief."

"Too bad you don't work up near Ballykinler. Too damn much mischief up there."

He gave me directions to Newry, told me to follow the Newry Canal south, and keep on the road to Warrenpoint, where the ferry docked along Carlingford Lough. As I drove out of town on a narrow country road I thought about John's theory of law enforcement. It sounded smart, especially along the border where the population was more heavily Catholic, and the IRA could slip across and back with ease. How many men would it take to haul all those arms and all that ammo on their backs or slung over ponies? A lot, especially since there had been no trace of the crates found. Boxes of ammunition and crates of BARs were heavy, and a big group of men and animals were bound to attract attention. Maybe at the ferry, someone would remember something. Maybe.

I FOLLOWED THE canal, and as it widened into Carlingford Lough, I was looking a few hundred yards into the Republic of Ireland. Free of the British, land of my ancestors, brought forth in blood. I felt my heart should stir, that I might see ghosts of the martyrs floating above the sacred ground of free Eire. But I didn't. Instead, I felt cold and tired, the fairy tales of my youth dispelled forever. I remembered the day I'd decided there were no leprechauns. I'd long before figured out Santa Claus but made believe I hadn't so I wouldn't tip off my kid brother. But leprechauns had remained real and vivid in my imagination, the distance only increasing the mystery of their hidden world, until that day when my childish imagination gave way to hard logic. The same thing was happening now with those other fairy tales, the Robin Hood stories of dashing IRA boys outwitting the clumsy and heavy-handed Brits by night. I'd discovered that they didn't always fool the English, and if they were caught, the consequences were terrible. And when they did elude the enemy, their antagonisms festered, and one day a little girl would see her father gunned down, or a bomb would explode in a movie house, killing and maiming happy couples. Because a man turned in on himself, nursing secret hates on the mother's milk of religion and revenge. Maybe women too. Sláine O'Brien had to have her reasons for wearing the uniform of the British Empire at the Irish Desk of MI-5.

I felt guilty, wishing God hadn't given me the sense to see two sides of a thing. It had been so easy before, daydreaming of my return to Ireland, to wreak the vengeance Granddad Liam had ordained. I was certain he had every right to do so. But did he have the right to hand it down? Would I?

I shook off those thoughts, as certain of damnation for thinking them as I was for having impure notions in church. Which, now that I thought about it, I'd often been unable to stop for a minute when I was younger, no matter how hard I had tried to conjure up visions of red pitchforks and rivers of molten lava. Maybe merely thinking wasn't really a sin. If it was, it pretty much didn't matter by this point.

The road along the river curved to reveal Warrenpoint, a cluster of buildings around a single church steeple huddled along the waterfront. The setting sun lit the gray, heavy clouds drifting across the darkening blue sky, the last, sideways light of the day reflecting off the white buildings' gables and turrets. Fields and hills rose emerald green beyond, ascending slowly up the distant Mountains of Mourne. It took away my breath—the beauty of the land, the sun-washed cluster of homes and shops, the ebbing tide— like something I'd known all my life but never opened my eyes to. Brits and borders be damned. I had come home, home to Ireland.

I drove slowly, not wanting to miss a thing. A few pedestrians walked along a promenade, and the occasional automobile drove by in the other lane. It was quiet, the lazy kind of quiet that comes at low tide when the day's work is done and the boats are all tied up, waiting for the next tide to lift them. Small sailboats and fishing boats were moored along the quay, and ahead I saw a boat launch, a concrete roadway leading into the muck and rocks where the water had receded. A flat-bottomed boat, big enough for a large truck, sat at the end, tied to a mooring and canted at an odd angle, waiting for the tide to set her straight.

I parked the jeep next to McCabe's Market, where two Union Jacks fluttered defiantly in the quickening breeze. Mr. McCabe was evidently a proud Unionist, defining his territory at this outpost of the Ulster border. I walked across the street to the broad sidewalk that paralleled the quay. A couple of kids played along the water's edge, squawking each time their feet slid on a slippery stone and dipped into the cold water. A few people strolled by, in no great hurry. The view across the lough to Omeath was stunning, and even at low tide the water glistened with colors, greens from the fields and blue from the sky rippling across waves and currents. It was beautiful all right but I wasn't here for the view. I watched the ferry for a minute, saw no movement, and headed back to the jeep, thinking I should look for the local RUC station.

I heard the sound of boots on pavement as a column of British soldiers marched out of a side street and headed my way. The few folks out on the sidewalk didn't pay any attention but the two kids scampered up from the waterline, hooting and whistling at the twenty or so young men who trooped by, led by a gray-haired sergeant who held his head high and his back straight. They were unarmed and seemed sheepish as they worked to keep in step and not look at their young tormentors.

"Home Guard," said a voice from behind me. It came from a small, wiry man, standing in the open doorway of McCabe's Market. He wore a white apron and a pencil stub stuck out from one ear, half hidden by curly hair going gray. His sleeves were rolled up above the elbow, and from the muscles in his forearms it looked like he was used to hoisting sides of beef or sacks of flour all day. "They like wearing a uniform without the likelihood of getting it all filled with holes."

"That sounds good to me," I said.

"Sounds good to any soldier who stands a chance of facing the enemy. Like I did in the last war, and like you may in this one, Yank.

But those fellas? Most of them joined up after America came into the war, when any real danger of Jerry landing here was long gone."

"Are you the owner?" I asked, pointing to the sign above his head.

"Aye. Malcolm McCabe. And you are?"

"Lieutenant Billy Boyle, Mr. McCabe." I stuck out my hand and waited to see if he'd take it. With the English flag flying from his store and a name that sounded Scots-Irish, I wondered if he'd take the hand of a Boyle.

"Pleased to meet you," he said with no hesitation. His grip was strong. "That's the rank I ended with, back in the days of the Ulster Division. Went in a private, made sergeant before we shipped out, and then once we lost most of our officers, I found myself leading a platoon in time for the Battle of the Somme. Imagine if I'd stayed home and joined the Home Guard? Wouldn't be able to live with myself."

"There's no draft in Northern Ireland, right?"

"That's right, we almost had riots in Belfast when they talked of conscription. Too many of your lot, if you don't mind me sayin' so, declared they wouldn't fight for England. And too many of my lot, and I don't mind sayin' it, didn't care to see Catholics trained and armed. Might give 'em ideas once they were done with the war, that's what they thought."

"What do you think?"

"You been in the war yet, Lieutenant?"

"I have."

"Well, I'll tell you then. There's nothing like a healthy dose of carnage to reduce your appetite for more. For any sane man, that is. I say they should have raised a few divisions of Catholics and Protestants together, never mind if they're Nationalist or Unionist, IRA or Red Hand. Put 'em together so their lives depended one upon the other. Given 'em a common enemy, let 'em kill Germans until they'd had their fill of it. Know what I mean?"

"Best plan I've heard yet."

"Ah, well, no one listens to an old shopkeeper," McCabe said, lighting a pipe and pulling on it until he was satisfied with the glow in the bowl. "What brings you here, Lieutenant? Seeing the sights?"

"I'm investigating an arms theft from the army base at Ballykinler."

"And how does that lead you to Warrenpoint?"

"That ferry," I said, pointing to the boat at the end of the ramp. "I think the truck that was used took that ferry across to the Republic."

"Sure, that could be. The MacDonald brothers run it. They can fit a good-sized lorry on it. But the RUC on our side and the customs or the Garda across the lough, they'd check the load. How many guns were taken?"

"Fifty Browning Automatic Rifles, lots of ammo."

"Well, Lieutenant Boyle, there's no way a truck loaded with that much armament went over unnoticed. They search the produce when they bring some over for my shop."

I told him the date of the theft, described Jenkins's truck, and asked him if he'd noticed anything that next morning.

"Jenkins, you say? Sure, I remember that truck. It sat parked in back all that night."

"What? Are you sure? Who drove it here?"

"Course I'm sure. Had the man's name painted along the side. Andrew Jenkins, it was. My nephew, he works for me, and he drove it onto the ferry the next morning like the fellow paid him to do."

"What fellow? What was in it?"

"Can't say. His name, that is. But I know what was in it."

"What?"

"Nothing. It was empty. This fellow had come by a few days before, saying he had to get this truck delivered to a mate over in Omeath and that he knew he'd miss the last ferry so could he leave it here and would someone just drive it onto the ferry the following morning. Said it would be worth a crown to save him staying overnight. I let Samuel have the job; he's used to driving tractors. We live above the shop so he kept an eye on it during the night."

"When did this man bring the truck?"

"Oh, I'd say maybe three o'clock in the morning. We'd arranged that he'd knock on the back door and give the key to Samuel. I heard the knock but paid it no mind. I did hear the clock strike three before I went back to sleep."

"Did he give you his name?"

"No, that was a bit odd. Said he didn't want it getting back to his boss—Jenkins, I took that to be—that he'd left the truck unattended. Said it would be better if we didn't know his name so we could truth-fully say we didn't know who'd left it."

"Did you ask why anyone might come around asking?"

"Well, when you put it like that, perhaps I should have. But I saw no harm. That lorry was examined on our side and then again across the water. Clean as a whistle, it was. He even paid my boy to wipe down the dashboard, told him not to leave any smudges anywhere."

"Can you describe him?" I said, realizing that was why no fingerprints were found.

"Sure. Going bald, dark brown hair, worn a trifle long. Had a quick laugh about him, you know the kind of fellow? Puts you at your ease."

"Yeah. The kind of guy who enjoys life."

"There you go! That's him. Made me trust him straightaway. Has he done something wrong?"

"Murder. Two that I know of, not to mention stealing fifty automatic weapons for the IRA."

"Jesus! And Samuel took his money and did his bidding. He fooled me. Thanks for telling me about this, Lieutenant Boyle. That other Yank just showed me a picture."

"What other Yank?"

"The one not in uniform. I didn't get his name either. Older than you, came in on a motorcycle."

"Did you get a good look at him?"

"He came right into my shop. Bought some food, asked some questions, then showed that picture. I'd say he was a tad taller than you, bit heavier, but in good shape, maybe about forty or so. Blue eyes, I think, now that I see yours. Anyway, I said yes, I'd seen the man. I thought it had something to do with his leaving the truck, and I didn't want to get him in trouble. I'm sorry I let him make a fool of me."

"There's no way you could've known. And he might have harmed your nephew and you if you'd asked too many questions."

"Think you'll find him?"

"I intend to."

"That's what the other Yank said."

CHAPTER · TWENTY FOUR

WHAT THE OTHER Yank said. I sat in the jeep, trying to figure out who the other Yank was, and what he was after. I thought he'd
been following me but now it seemed he was one step ahead of me. He
could be someone Pete Brennan had brought into his scheme with
Jenkins. Or maybe he was a deserter.

What I did know now was that the timing didn't add up. Pete had
told me the truck left the base at about midnight. If it arrived in
Warrenpoint only three hours later, and empty, that meant . . . what? It
meant that it had to have been a trick to throw us off the scent. Finding
it empty the next day, over the border in the Republic, was a ruse to
make us think the weapons were out of our reach. But if Jenkins's truck
had showed up here empty, then the weapons had been stashed somewhere between Ballykinler and Warrenpoint. A lot of ground to cover,
to be sure, but it narrowed it down. A modest deduction but it made
me feel I was making progress.

I was alone on the street. Mr. McCabe had gone in to close up
shop. The two boys who had been playing down by the water were running along the sidewalk, laughing as they raced each other along the
seawall, their voices high and shrill, echoing against the stone. I closed
my eyes and felt a remnant of childhood still within me, the thrill of
play with dusk closing in, the rush to a warm house where supper was
being put on the table as hunger drove me home, the daily routine that
seemed it would always be, my child's view of time stretching no farther
than the next holiday, or perhaps summer, if not too far off. I wished I
had someplace to go where I'd find a friendly face, home-cooked food,

and no dead bodies. I started the jeep, feeling adrift in a world of divided loyalties.

I left Warrenpoint behind, taking the coast road to Annalong, almost full circle to Newcastle, where I'd started the day with news of Pete Brennan's death. The wind came in hard from the Irish Sea, and rain soon began to lash the jeep, drumming on the canvas top like Max Roach.

I parked in front of the Harbor Bar, the pub where Major Thornton had told me he'd seen Eddie Mahoney quietly arguing with another man. I was hungry so it seemed like a good place to do some investigating. The rain came at me sideways as I ran to the door, holding my cap down with one hand. Fishing boats rocked at their moorings to one side, and on the other the gray granite buildings seemed to disappear in the foggy darkness. I pulled the door shut behind me and shook water off like a stray dog in a thunderstorm. I hung up my trench coat next to a line of fishermen's foul-weather gear and stood by a peat fire that glowed in the wide fireplace, rubbing my hands. I heard the murmur of conversation rise after the quiet as the locals eyed me for a long moment before returning to their pints and talk. There were booths along each wall, with the bar between them. Chairs and a bench surrounded the fireplace, but they were all empty. Eight or nine men, mostly fishermen, to judge by their clothes, were scattered about, smoking and drinking.

"A pint," I said to the barman as I took a seat. He nodded and began the slow pour. A chalkboard on the wall announced the food choices were fish and chips, Irish stew, and boxty.

"What's boxty?" I asked.

"That's a pancake made from potatoes. My wife fries 'em up nice and crisp, she does. You can have 'em alone or with sausages. Or with the stew, it's all good."

"With sausages," I said, the smells from the small kitchen behind the bar whipping up my hunger. A few minutes later I was sipping my Guinness while listening to the sizzle of a fry pan coming from the next room, and it almost did feel like home.

"Not many Americans stop by here," the barman said as he busied himself with pulling another pint. It was good bartender talk; if I wanted to chat, I could expand on the subject. If not, the answer could be short and sweet without being rude.

"Too bad," I said. "It looks like a nice spot, from what I could see of it."

"It is indeed. Rough weather today, though; brought most of the boys back in."

"Tough to fish when it's raining this hard?"

"Raining? It wasn't raining," a voice boomed out behind me. "It was lashing and pissing, spitting, pelting, pouring, bucketing, and we came in stinking, dirty, soaked, drenched, saturated with seawater, cloud water, and fish guts. But it wasn't raining. Rain is that nice stuff what comes down straight and keeps your vegetables growing. This blow is more than raindrops from Saint Peter. Another pint, Colin."

"Sure you're not too wet already, Emmet?"

"Oh, now he's a funny one, he is! Right, Yank?"

"I make it a rule never to take sides against the man working the bar," I said, pointing to Colin.

"A fine answer, that, Yank. Emmet Kennedy's my name."

"Billy Boyle," I said as we shook.

"Colin there took the wise course a few years back. He sold his boat and bought this place. Stays dry most nights, and keeps us in the black stuff. The Guinness, if you don't get my meaning."

"I got it. Sounds like you don't see many Americans down this way."

"Every now and then," Colin said. "But not enough to help pay the bills. I hear up in Belfast they run out of ale some nights, there's so many coming through."

"I'm based up in Newcastle, and there are GIs all over the place. Why don't they come down this way?"

"Well, I've seen them on maneuvers, running around the Mournes, and some along the coast," Emmet said. "But I'd guess once they have a chance to get out, they go into Downpatrick or Newry. They're cities, this is a sleepy coastal village. This here is the evening's entertainment, as good as it gets!"

"True enough," Colin said, as he worked on Emmet's pint.

"I came on the recommendation of a Major Thornton. Know him?"

"No, but I'm glad he spoke well of the place."

"He said he saw this guy in here," I said, laying a picture of Eddie Mahoney on the bar. Colin and Emmet leaned in to study it.

"What's this fellow mean to you?" Emmet said, his manner not quite so jovial as before.

"Nothing much anymore. He's dead. Name was Eddie Mahoney."

"Christ," Colin said, looking at Emmet.

"You know him?" I asked both of them.

"How sure are you he's dead?" Colin asked.

"As sure as two bullets to the back of the head."

They looked at each other a while. "You a copper?" Colin asked.

"Not exactly. But I have been asked to look into it. By the U.S. Army, not the RUC. I mean, if there were any local laws broken here or there, it wouldn't matter to me." They seemed afraid, and I wanted them to know I wasn't after them.

"That's not the problem," Colin said, tapping his finger on the photograph. "He's the problem. Bastard stayed here a week; we've two rooms upstairs. Started having visitors, and one night he has an argument with one, right there." He pointed to a corner booth.

"Was there a fight?"

"Aye, I saw it," Emmet said. "That one, the redheaded fellow, he and the other man came to blows but they stopped as soon as one of them dropped his pistol. Everyone saw it. Around here, that only means one thing. Or two, actually. IRA or Red Hand. But seeing as this is mainly a Catholic pub, it wasn't hard to figure."

"We haven't had much trouble here," Colin said. "Most folks are friendly enough but keep to their own. On the main street, we have Protestant shops on one side, Catholic on the other. The Protestants have their pub up the road. So nobody wants the Irish Republican Army stirring things up."

"What happened?" I asked.

"The other fellow left straightaway. This fellow—he called himself Davies, though I doubt it was his real name—he comes up to Emmet and me, standing here as we are now, and says he'll have us killed if ever anything is said. A hard look he had in his eyes too, and I believed him."

"You can thank the one who shot him for me," Emmet said, taking a long swallow from his fresh pint.

"I'd like to meet up with him and do just that. What did the other fellow look like?"

"He wasn't here long; I don't really remember. On the tall side. Losing his hair but letting what he had go long."

"Aye," Colin said. "Dark brown it was."

"That was Red Jack Taggart," I said. "Ever hear of him?"

"Christ Almighty," Colin said. "Who hasn't? Himself?"

"In the flesh," I said. "You're not ignorant of the IRA then?"

"There's them who did what needed doing in the war against the British and came to know such names," Emmet said. "And some thought it best, finding themselves north of the border, to quietly return to the life they led before. I say this, hearing your name is Boyle, since I think you'll know what I mean."

"I do, and I understand. I'd appreciate anything you can tell me, and it won't go any further."

"Nothing much to tell, is there, Colin?"

"No. Last I'd heard of Red Jack, he'd got himself a nice cushy job in Dublin, with the Irish Hospitals' Sweepstake."

"The Irish Sweepstake?" I said. "Doesn't sound like the kind of job an IRA man would have."

"Oh, don't be so fast, Billy," Emmet said. "A lot of those tickets make it to America, don't they?"

"Sure. My dad always bought them."

"And the money has to come back to Ireland. I hear that it was a regular practice to send the IRA money through the same channels so it could be hidden from the American authorities and the Dublin crowd that swallowed the treaty."

"You're well versed in the ways of finance," I said.

"A man who knows how to handle his boat in rough waters ends up learning a lot of things, and no more will I say on the matter. Understand, though, that Red Jack was well regarded by those on the IRA General Staff. You'd do well to watch your back if you're after him."

"Do I need to watch my back when I leave this room?" I asked, feeling the tension flow from Emmet as he leaned in close to me.

"No, no," Emmet said, shaking his head as if waking from a dream. "You've no worries from us, right, Colin?"

"None at all. That's all behind us now. It's come down to the likes of this redheaded fellow threatening us, who have served the same cause. It's a miserable business now, I say."

"Thanks. I'm trying to stop things before they go too far, that's all."

"What has Red Jack done exactly?" Emmet asked.

"Stole fifty automatic weapons from the U.S. Army."

"That sounds like him, it does! Oh, what a grand scoundrel our

Red Jack is, and no offense to you, Billy," Emmet said, slapping me on the back. "Reminds me of the old days, or at least the best of them."

"It pays to forget the worst of them," Colin said.

"Aye. Or to try," said Emmet, his eyes searching the floor.

"Can I buy you both a whiskey?" I asked.

"Well, sure you can, and we'll have a toast," Colin said, setting up three glasses and pouring the Bushmills. "To what?"

It was Emmet who spoke. "To those who lived and those who died, whether they be right bastards, thieves, fishermen, bartenders, or Americans. All were brothers once." We touched glasses and drank.

A voice called to Colin that my food was ready, and we locked eyes for a second, unwilling to return to the common world.

"Eat hearty, Billy," he said, putting down the plate of sausages and boxty, which looked and smelled delicious, the meat crisp and glistening from the fry pan, the potato pancake thick and steamy.

"If you come upon any next of kin of Mr. Mahoney, you tell them I have his things all packed up nice and proper."

"What?" I said, dropping my fork.

CHAPTER ▪ TWENTY FIVE

COLIN WAS AN honest man. Eddie Mahoney had left his wallet behind with four twenty-pound notes inside. A driver's license in another name—John Davies—and a few odds and ends made it look like he was a guy named Davies and not a feared IRA killer. He'd left all traces of identity behind when he went out on the heist, figuring to beat it back here for breakfast and then hightail it out.

Of course, Colin could have been too afraid to take the money or maybe there had been more and he left some to divert suspicion. That's the price you pay, I guess, for being a cop. Everyone is suspect, even for apparent honesty. You start wondering what angle the guy's playing. Then, sooner or later, you start wondering why you've stayed honest so long—or at least what passes for honest—when everyone else is bent.

I had my own definition of honest and it didn't include stealing a dead guy's cash, even if it had been left under an assumed identity and he was an outlaw. Those last two things tested me, but I left the money in the wallet. I tossed it aside and went through the rest of the stuff in the box Colin had stashed on a shelf in his storeroom. I moved the box to a small table under the single bare lightbulb that hung from a cord. There wasn't much to see. A shaving kit and a few toiletries. A roll of black electrical tape, a jackknife, and a fountain pen. A dog-eared paperback, *Appointment with Death* by Agatha Christie, waited for its reader to discover who the murderer was, a page toward the end folded down to mark where he'd left it.

Some objects hold nothing once a person dies. I'd handled his wallet and his toothbrush, and they were just things. But that folded page still held the aura of his hand, the feel of his fingernail on the crease, the expectation of life going on, of another day, the sun shining, a cup of tea, and a paperback waiting to be finished. It was the kind of thing that got to me, more than the big stuff, since life was really made up of little things. The things you kept on your night table. The jackknife in your pocket. The photo you kept in your wallet. The book you were reading.

I fanned the pages to see if anything was hidden but all I got was air. I stuffed the book in my pocket. Someone had to finish it.

A crumpled pack of Senior Service cigarettes still held a couple of butts. He'd probably taken a fresh pack with him. A few hard candies showed he had a sweet tooth, and the stub of a pencil and a crossword puzzle from a month-old London *Times* told me he was bright but not bright enough to finish it. The only thing left in the box was a book of matches. I grabbed it and idly turned it in my fingers, eyeing the suitcase next. I opened it on the chance something might be stuck inside but all I found were three lonely matches. I closed it and made to toss it into the box but something caught my eye. It was so familiar I almost didn't realize how out of place it was.

I held it under the light and stared at the picture of Warren Spahn, left-handed pitcher for the Boston Braves, our National League team. They gave out matchbooks with pictures of all their top players. They were a dime a dozen in Beantown but I never expected to see one east of Boston Harbor. Spahn had been in the news during his first season with the Braves in '42. He hadn't gotten along with their manager, a guy named Casey Stengel, and was sent down to the minors after refusing to hit a batter. Spahn had enlisted after that season, and for all I knew, he was somewhere in Northern Ireland. Maybe he'd left the matchbook in a bar and Eddie picked it up. However it got here, it was a little bit of home, and I tucked it away in my shirt pocket, thinking of Braves Field on a bright spring day, wondering how long it would be until I watched a game again.

Next was Eddie's suitcase. It was small, well used, scuffed, and worn at the corners. One pair of trousers and a shirt were neatly folded on top, nestled in among undergarments and socks. A scarf and one wool sweater, worn through at the elbows, completed Eddie Mahoney's wardrobe. He traveled light, and given the condition of the suitcase and clothes, I guessed they were secondhand props, used only while on this job for the IRA. Which meant that there wouldn't be anything of value, any evidence, left here. Eddie expected to be back but if he did have anything important in his possession, he would have hidden it. An IRA professional would take precautions out of habit.

"Colin," I shouted over my shoulder, "anyone in his room?"

"It's vacant. Go on up if you want a look," he said, sticking his head in the door. "It's open—just don't leave a mess, will you? First door on the left."

There were four rooms upstairs, two on each side of a narrow hall. I entered Eddie Mahoney's last abode, turned on a light switch, and surveyed the room. Bed against the wall to my left, bureau to my right. Washstand along the wall by the door, and a thick rug on a hardwood floor. A single curtained window straight ahead looked out over the harbor. Next to it was a wooden chair with wide arms and embroidered cushions. Is that where Eddie sat, reading his mystery, waiting?

I sat in the chair and looked around the room. He was going on a dangerous mission. If Eddie had anything to hide, where would he hide it? Under the mattress? No, that's the first place someone would look. He'd want to hide it from snooping landlords or cleaning ladies, so it would have to be somewhere a traveler wouldn't normally stash valuables.

I walked the floor, feeling for loose floorboards but everything seemed nailed down tight. I looked under the mattress, couldn't help myself. Nothing. I felt the cushions on the chair but came up empty. It wouldn't be that elaborate anyway; it would have to be someplace he could get to easily and quickly in case he needed to make a fast exit.

I opened the window and stuck my head out into the rain, looking for what I don't know. A hidey-hole in the brickwork maybe? The wall within reach was disappointingly solid, and all I came up with was a face full of water.

I wiped my eyes and looked at the room again, remembering that roll of electrical tape. There were only a few surfaces hidden from view so I started on those. Behind the bedboard: nothing. Behind the bureau: nothing except cobwebs. I felt along the bottom of the bureau and came up with nothing but thin, cracked wood, the underside of the bottom drawer. I opened that drawer and felt the bottom of the one above it. My hand brushed the dry wood, sweeping back and forth. At the back, my fingers caught on paper. I pulled at it, and a sealed blank envelope came out, dangling two strips of black tape.

It was a good hiding place. You couldn't see it but Eddie could reach in and grab it in a second. I sat in the chair and listened to the rain drive itself against the window for a minute, hoping this would finally tell me something useful. Maybe it would or maybe it contained dirty pictures or his last will and testament. I ripped the envelope open and read the top typewritten sheet.

DATE: 3 November 1943
FROM: Charlie Kerins, chief of staff, Irish Republican Army, Dublin
TO: IRA Northern Command

IRA units of the Northern Command are ordered to provide all necessary assistance to the bearer of this letter. His true identity will not be revealed for reasons of security. He is on a mission to gather evidence to determine the guilt, or innocence, of IRA member Jack Taggart, also known as Red Jack, in the matter of embezzlement of funds from Clan na Gael and the Irish Hospitals' Sweepstake.

Funds sent from America have gone missing, and the bearer of this letter is charged with determining if Jack Taggart is guilty, and if so, to recover the funds and apprehend him for an IRA court-martial.

Additionally, IRA Northern Command units are directed to assist in any other tactical operations these two men are engaged in, without reference to the above.

So the hunter had become the hunted. Red Jack must've tumbled to his game and decided all Mahoney was going to get was that single pound note. That was meant to throw us off track. The IRA in Dublin would know what had happened but not the northern IRA, if Eddie had not made contact yet. The last sentence was interesting. Apparently even embezzlement didn't trump fifty BARs. Eddie had thought he was using Red Jack, and all the time it was the other way around. I folded the letter and put it back in the envelope.

The second sheet was on different, cheaper paper, handwritten, probably with the fountain pen Eddie had left behind. Each entry was headed with a date and time, and it had the look of a surveillance record. I scanned the notes; most of them appeared to be about IRA meets or casing Ballykinler. There were several mentions of Clough, and I wondered if they'd stopped for a pint on the way back from driving by the base. Two entries for Armagh caught my eye. October 25 at 2:00 p.m., Eddie observed Red Jack meet an unidentified male carrying a briefcase outside the Northern Bank. They entered together but left separately half an hour later. Red Jack had told Eddie he was going to meet an American GI who had information about the layout of the base. He later claimed the GI failed to show. Eddie followed him to the bank again on the morning of November 3, and this time he recorded a description of the other man. Short, sandy-haired, midtwenties.

That description fit a lot of Irishmen. It also perfectly described Adrian Simms. But it made no sense at all. Adrian was probably in cahoots with Andrew Jenkins. Red Jack? It wasn't likely he'd be working both sides of the sectarian wars. Maybe he was undercover? I doubted it but I'd ask DI Carrick about it to be sure. I wondered about McBurney and what he hadn't told me. Maybe I could get Carrick to bring him in for questioning, Black Knight brothers or no.

The October date nagged at me. Hadn't Micheál said that McBurney gave him and a new teller the afternoon off about a month ago? Was there any connection? Red Jack Taggart entering a Protestant bank was unusual, that's for sure. Especially since it seemed like he was making a deposit, not robbing and shooting up the place. Then it hit me. What a perfect hiding place for embezzled IRA funds. An assumed identity, and the money is deposited under the watchful eye of a Royal Black Knight. Maybe the short guy he met had introduced him to McBurney and recommended the bank. Was he an accomplice or a dupe? Or was Red Jack simply saving his pennies?

I pocketed the papers and went back down to the bar. Colin had kept my dinner warm and I ate my sausages and boxty, hardly noticing what was on my plate. I had a whole new motive for Red Jack's actions now, and things were beginning to make sense. Except why had he gone through with the arms theft? If he knew the IRA Command was onto him, why bother? Why hadn't he simply taken the money and run?

CHAPTER ▪ TWENTY SIX

MORNING ARRIVED TOO soon but at least it brought sun-
light and blue skies. After yesterday's cold winds and rain it made everything seem fresh and new, scrubbed clean and verdant. The air was cool
and crisp as I drove from headquarters down the hill to the Slieve Donard
Hotel in Newcastle to meet Sláine O'Brien for our trip to Stormont
Castle. The Boston Irish part of me didn't like the sound of that one bit
but at least I was being taken there as an ally, not a prisoner.

Main Street was quiet, the shops and businesses not yet open. I
turned right on Railway Street, which led to the railroad station and the
hotel, driving close to waves lapping the hard-packed gray sand beach
as I slowed to enter the gravel drive. The hotel was an ornate, four-
story, red-brick affair, with a single tower jutting skyward above the
main entrance. Military and civilian vehicles were neatly parked along
the front but I could see a few jeeps and an ambulance farther down,
along the wing of the hotel that faced the sea, parked at angles to each
other on the lawn. The haphazard arrangement was out of place with
the studied elegance of the building and grounds, so I drove closer for
a look. I could see RUC and British Army uniforms among the men in
plainclothes standing around, looking up at something beyond my line
of vision. I got out and walked over, a feeling of dread washing over me.
This was a crime scene.

The wing of the hotel was angled to face the water, and as I drew
closer I saw orderly rows of double windows and dormers set against
red brick and gray slate. Except that one of those windows was blown
out, black streaks radiating from the edges. Debris lay strewn on the

ground, and firemen were rolling up hoses and putting away their gear. The air smelled of smoke and ashes.

"Stand back, sir," a British corporal said, his hand held up in a polite but firm command.

"What happened?" I asked. He looked away and stood at attention, as did the other soldiers, while a stretcher was brought out of the hotel bearing a figure covered in a white sheet. It looked like a body but it didn't lie right under the covering. It was uneven, as if pieces were missing or terribly twisted.

"A bomb," I said, not realizing I'd spoken. The stretcher was loaded into the ambulance. The breeze from the Irish Sea swirled the odor of burnt flesh around us, and I stood rooted to the spot, wondering who it was and hoping this was not the work of my childhood heroes.

"Aye, a bomb, sir," the corporal said once the body was on its way. "It blew up in his room. We think it was planted there earlier in the day."

"His? Who was that?"

"Sergeant Cyrus Lynch, Lieutenant. My sergeant. And what is your business here?" The corporal asked his question with a minimum of regard for my rank.

"My name is Boyle. I was to drive to Belfast today with the sergeant and Subaltern O'Brien."

"We've been expecting you. Did you tell anyone where you'd be meeting them this morning?"

"Who is 'we' exactly?"

"Special security detail, attached to MI-5. Please answer the question, Lieutenant Boyle."

"No. No one knew I was coming here this morning, and I didn't tell a soul where the meeting was."

"Very well. Please show me your identification." I showed him my orders and ID, which he went through carefully, studying my face as well as the paperwork. As he handed it back to me, I caught sight of DI Carrick.

"I'm not surprised to see you here, Boyle," he said. "Trouble seems to follow you about."

"I was supposed to meet someone," I said neutrally, glancing at the corporal.

"You can tell the bloody district inspector about it, especially since the bomb's already gone off," he muttered as walked away, "sir."

"Yes, I know. You seem to have entrée into the secret world of MI-5," Carrick said, studying the corporal's back.

"More than you do?" I asked, craning my neck up to the blown-out third-floor windows.

"I'm sure you're aware that there are conflicts between agencies. Sometimes their need for secrecy outweighs my need for information."

"Like Andrew Jenkins and his file?"

"Yes, like that. My presence here this morning is a formality. The RUC will not receive one ounce of cooperation from these louts."

"Louts? Aren't you on the same side? Don't you all go to the same church?"

"Subaltern O'Brien certainly doesn't, and I doubt these men have seen the inside of a church since baptism. Be careful, Boyle." Carrick spoke without looking at me, watching the flow of security men around us. I was surprised at his concern, until I thought about what he might need from me.

"You want me to snoop around for you, don't you? Try to find out what's so top secret about Jenkins."

"That would aid you in your investigation, wouldn't it?"

"It may confirm what I know already—that he's a thief, a black marketeer, and a killer."

"I'm already aware of that, and so is half of Ulster. What I want to know is why your Subaltern O'Brien deems him worthy of protection." I let the *your* slide by. I knew what he meant, and it was so ingrained I wasn't sure he was even aware of his implication.

"Fair question. If I find anything out, I may have some questions for you about your Constable Simms."

"What sort of questions?"

"For now, can you tell me if he's been assigned to any kind of undercover work?"

"No, he hasn't. What are the other questions?"

"Uncomfortable ones but I'm not ready to ask them yet. Until I am, I'd recommend not sharing any sensitive information with Simms. Keep him in the dark."

"I will let Constable Simms tend to his duties in Clough, which he does very well," Carrick said, folding his arms behind him and tilting his head back, the familiar anger and arrogance returning.

"I'll take that as agreement."

"As you wish."

"One more thing," I said.

"What is it, man?"

I knew he was frustrated at being frozen out by the security toughs, and by the fact that I had the ear of Sláine O'Brien. He couldn't take it out on them, and the act of being nice to me had drained him, so I made allowance for his irritated tone.

"They never took the guns into the Republic. They're close by."

"How do you know?"

Carrick sounded happier. I told him about the delivery of the empty truck the night of the theft to Warrenpoint. I didn't see much reason to tell him about Red Jack embezzling IRA funds; that had the feel of a family matter.

"There's a reason Red Jack is still around, and why they didn't want us to think the BARs were still in Ulster. That's what we've got to figure out." As well as who the mystery Yank was, what role Adrian Simms had played in the whole thing, if there were any Germans hiding in the woodwork, and who the hell else might be involved.

"Is that all?"

"Actually, it isn't. Do you know a banker named McBurney in Armagh? He's part of your Royal Black Knight outfit."

"Yes, what's he got to do with all this?"

"There's something strange going on at that bank. I think Red Jack may have stashed some money there for a rainy day."

"Taggart? But he's a wanted man and a Catholic! That bank is frequented by Protestants, good solid businessmen, not Republicans."

"Exactly." I let that thought settle, and as it did I saw that Carrick had put two and two together.

"Very well. I shall have a talk with Mr. McBurney. And I'll not tell Constable Simms about it. But I want to hear from you very soon if you have any evidence of his wrongdoing."

"The wrongdoing outweighs the evidence at the moment. But I'll do my best."

"I shall be at RUC headquarters if you find out anything. It's on Waring Street in Belfast center, near the Albert Memorial Clock Tower. Just ask, everyone knows where that is." With that, Carrick motioned to his men, and they went to their vehicles, leaving the investigation to the security force and me on my own.

I asked the corporal to take me to Subaltern O'Brien. He led me into the hotel past one guard and down a hallway with men posted at either end. He knocked on a door, two short raps that sounded like a signal. He entered, I followed.

Sláine O'Brien sat at a desk, facing the door. In one hand she held a telephone, in the other a revolver. Only after the corporal shut the door after himself did she set down the gun.

"Yes, he's here now. I'll tell him . . . yes. I understand . . . I'll ring you later." She hung up the phone and rested her head in her hands, the big black telephone and the handgun at each elbow. "It was supposed to be me."

"What was?"

"In that room. It was supposed to be me. Cyrus said he had a bad feeling about being here without an escort, and we should switch rooms. He was going to sit up all night, he said, with his Thompson, and wait for them."

"Why? I mean, why not go somewhere else or get new rooms?"

"Because it's what we do, Lieutenant Boyle. We hunt extremists. Cyrus thought they'd come during the night, and that he could take them. He was usually right about these things." She pushed back in her chair, taking a deep breath. She looked exhausted. She motioned to a chair.

"There's tea," she said, nodding to a tray. "Still hot enough, I think."

"No thanks," I said. "What did you mean about being here without an escort? How did that make Cyrus nervous?"

"The IRA has a price on my head. It was five hundred pounds, last I heard. To them I'm a traitor, and somehow they find the notion of a woman hunting them especially despicable."

"Then why didn't you have an escort?"

"Sometimes my job requires discretion. Sergeant Lynch was my bodyguard, and he was very good at it. I had to visit a few contacts, and a motorcycle escort would have attracted too much attention."

"Looks like you got someone's attention," I said.

"Evidently. Did Corporal Finch ask if you'd told anyone about meeting me here?"

"Yes he did. I was glad to be able to tell him I hadn't. He looks like a tough customer."

"Otherwise you don't survive long in this business."

"Sláine, why *are* you in this business?"

"Do you have a problem with women in the service, Billy?"

"No," I said, thinking how complicated that question was for me. "It's not unfamiliar ground. I know it can be tough. But I'm not talking about doing your bit for the war effort. I mean, why are you in the business of hunting extremists? Or Republicans, depending on your viewpoint."

"Or Unionists. They have their own brand of extremists, as you know."

"OK, I get your point. But why you?" She poured herself tea and stirred in a cube of sugar. I thought I could use some caffeine too, and joined her.

"You know that there used to be one police force for all of Ireland, before the partition," she said. "The Royal Irish Constabulary."

"Sure. Up here it became the Royal Ulster Constabulary, and in the Republic, the Garda."

"Right. My father was an RIC constable in Dublin. He never rose far in the ranks, he just did his duty and kept the peace of the city, much like your father does in Boston. Anyway, one spring day, he drew Sunday duty at Dublin Castle. You know what that is?"

"Yeah, it's where the British had their headquarters. Police, intelligence, government."

"Yes. I was just a wee girl at the time but I swear I remember him leaving the house that morning, his buttons shined and his big shoes gleaming. But no sidearm. The RIC constables did not go armed, just like the bobbies in England. I remember that morning because I was so excited about my new Easter dress."

"Was this 1916?"

"Aye, Billy. It was the Easter Rising, which so many of our kind celebrate in song. But to me, every Easter is bitter. You see, there was hardly anyone at the castle, so they only had one constable on duty. Other than a few clerks, the place was empty, except for my da, standing guard in the courtyard. The Irish Volunteers sent a flying column in. Through the gate they came, men running with rifles at the ready, charging right at Constable O'Brien."

"What happened?" I could see the picture in my mind, since I'd seen so many illustrations of that day. Dublin Castle was small, a stone turret and attached building, right in the middle of the city.

"He did his duty. He stood his ground. He held up his hand, palm toward the gunmen, and ordered them to stop. Can you believe that? Can you imagine yourself unarmed in Boston, a gang of armed men charging you?"

"No, I can't. What happened?"

"They shot him dead. I learned later that one bullet pierced his hand."

"I'm sorry. That must have been terrible."

"Oh, that's not even the really terrible part. Do you know your history? Do you know what happened then?"

"At the castle? No."

"I'll tell you then. Nothing. Those brave Volunteers who had just gunned down an unarmed man stood in the courtyard, looking at the great stone fortress, and saw no one else. It was theirs for the taking. Having come that far, all they needed to do was take a few more steps and they could have held it. But they didn't. They turned and ran, leaving my poor da dead on the cobblestones, for nothing. They killed him for nothing, and they lost the great prize. That's why I'm in this business, Billy. If they had taken the castle and won the day, I would have been a little girl who'd lost her father in that great battle, and that's all. But I grew up despising the rabble who killed without thought, and then ran from victory. I hate them for what I lost, and for what they lost. I can't bear the thought of them."

She drank her tea, made a face, and set the cup down. "It's cold," she said. I couldn't argue.

"Who was that on the phone when I came in?" I wanted to get back to the here and now, and leave the dead of 1916 in peace. It seemed to me that those who'd died in that fight had at least been spared the agony of witnessing civil war, assassinations, bombings, and the divided loyalties that the struggle had brought about.

"Major Cosgrove. He's anxious to hear about your progress. Have you learned anything since yesterday?"

"I'm certain the BARs were not driven south into the Republic. That was a ruse. Jenkins's truck was delivered empty to Warrenpoint a few hours after the theft. So the weapons are still close by, somewhere between Ballykinler and Warrenpoint."

"That's not good news. Anything else?"

"A lot of little things but nothing that makes sense yet. About this case, anyway. Once I get a look through your files, I might be able to put two and two together. The problem is, everything here is so complex.

It's not just tracking down suspects, it's thinking about their religion and their politics. It makes everything ten times more difficult."

"What about Negroes in America? Don't you have to think about race in the same way? Doesn't that complicate things for the police? You don't have any Negro parishioners in your church, do you? "

"No. But we understand where the lines are drawn. And we don't murder each other just because we're different."

"Really? Don't you mean they don't murder *you* because you're different? What about your Ku Klux Klan?"

"It's not *my* Ku Klux Klan! And that's different." It seemed like everyone over here wanted to slot me into some group so they'd know who I was. It didn't strike me as a useful system.

"No, it isn't. The only difference is you've grown up with all those rules and you understand them. You know how to navigate the boundaries of skin color in your own land so that it seems natural to you. Then you come here, saddled with your preconceived notions, and wonder why you have such a difficult time. It would be the same for me if I went to Boston, don't you see? Here, I understand where the lines of religion and class are drawn. I know how to step around them when I need to. I can deal with the extremists when I must, because I understand each side. I see each side and feel for them, more's the pity."

See each side. Sláine's words faded away until that phrase was all that was left. See each side. Ballykinler and Warrenpoint. The start and end point for the delivery truck's route after the arms theft. See each side. Why? Something was wrong, something was nagging at me about each side of that trip. What?

"Wait a minute!" I snapped my fingers as it came to me. "The BARs aren't anywhere near Warrenpoint. It wouldn't make any sense."

"What?"

"Listen. Red Jack shot Eddie Mahoney the night of the theft, right outside Clough. We agreed he needed Mahoney to help load the weapons at the depot, right?"

"Yes. So the same would hold for the unloading?"

"It would have to, especially given the short turnaround time. The truck was dropped off about 3:00 a.m. near the Warrenpoint ferry. I was assuming that since the truck was found in the Republic, Red Jack would have had help at that end with the unloading. But that wasn't the case."

"So you're thinking he needed Mahoney's help to unload? Then he killed him. But why would he? It still doesn't make sense."

"Mahoney was investigating Taggart on behalf of the IRA for skimming funds." I decided it would be best to keep the details to myself. I didn't want the heavy hand of the security forces interfering with my investigation of the murders of Pete Brennan and Sam Burnham. But I needed Sláine to believe my theory of the crime. She did.

"The guns are very close then."

"I'd guess within ten miles of Clough, if my calculations are right about driving time at night." I watched her eyes narrow as she thought this through. It seemed to trouble her, as if it signaled something else to worry about.

"There's one other thing. Major Cosgrove told me to inform you that we had a report of a German seaplane landing in Lough Neagh. The RAF shot it down over the Irish Sea. There were no survivors but it had been gaining altitude just east of the lough. And last night, on the coast near Bangor, north of Belfast, there was a confirmed sighting of a U-boat on the surface. We're searching now for signs that anyone was put ashore."

"What does that mean?"

"It means something is happening. There may be two teams of German agents or commandos and the IRA Northern Command with fifty BARs on our doorstep. It means we need to get to work."

Sláine rose and began gathering papers. As she opened her briefcase, I saw her hands were shaking. I reached out to hold the briefcase open and my fingers brushed against her trembling hand. She jumped, as if she'd been startled.

"I'm just trying to help. You've had a tough night," I said softly, as if soothing a frightened child. She avoided my eyes. Then her hand returned to mine and grasped it, the warmth of her skin surprising me. The briefcase fell to the floor and her arms were around my waist, her face pressed against my chest. I felt her body beneath the wool uniform jacket press against mine and I was caught up in her scent. Her eyes looked up into mine, rich with tears that seemed ready to be released.

Two raps sounded on the door, and before the knob turned we were apart, picking up papers that had fallen to the floor, forcing our bodies away from each other out of fear they'd fly together again.

"Ma'am?"

"Yes, Corporal Finch?"

"We found a few pieces of the device," he said, his eyes darting back and forth between us, finally settling on Sláine as she dabbed at her eyes with a handkerchief. "It was a timer, set to go off during the night. Plastic explosive, under the bed. Sarge was in a chair, right next to it."

"Who had access to the room?" Sláine was all business now, the sharp officer questioning her noncom. Finch didn't show resentment at having to deal with these questions coming from a woman. He looked like a hard case but he gave her the respect she must've earned. I wondered what life was like for her, forever punishing killers and fools.

"Just about all the hotel staff, since any of the passkeys would work. We're going through the list of employees and questioning them but frankly our only hope is that someone saw something and will tell us. Whoever set the explosive isn't going to volunteer the information."

"Focus on whoever knew we were coming here. Cyrus called from Portadown around noon. Find out whom he talked to."

"Yes, ma'am. Lieutenant, if you don't mind my asking again, are you positive you didn't speak to anyone about your purpose in coming here?"

"I'm sure," I said. *The curse of his own weapons upon him*, I heard Grady O'Brick say to Lynch's back. "Positive." Had I said anything to Grady? He'd gotten a face full of Sergeant Lynch but was that encounter enough to set off a chain of events that placed a bomb under Sláine's bed hours later? No, it couldn't have been. But I had said something else to Grady, back at his house. That I was going up to Belfast the next day with Sergeant Lynch and another officer. But I never mentioned where they'd be staying, I was certain. Maybe Grady had mentioned his run-in with Lynch at the pub. The walls had ears here, they'd told me.

I'd ask Grady about it later, but I decided not to share this tidbit. There was no way I was going to subject him to a single question from the likes of the late Sergeant Lynch's crew. He had no more fingernails left to give.

"The boys are on it, ma'am," Finch was saying to Sláine. "I'll drive you to Stormont."

"Right," she said. "I'm afraid I'm not thinking clearly. Let's go." She gave me a look. A message that she'd been temporarily deranged? Or that there was more where that had come from? I had no idea, and felt a sinking feeling in my stomach when I realized I wasn't sure which I wanted it to be.

The corporal carried her overnight bag. Sláine seized her briefcase and stuffed her revolver into her uniform jacket pocket. I followed them to the main lobby, where they went to the manager's office, currently in use as an interrogation chamber. A cleaning woman sat in a straight-backed chair, facing two large British soldiers who stood before her. Their jackets were off, their sleeves rolled up. The three of them looked up as we entered, the faces of the two men blank, the woman's pleading.

"I've told them, miss, I don't know a thing about what happened. 'Tis true, I swear."

"Mrs. Delaney," one of the men said, consulting a clipboard. "She last cleaned the room yesterday."

"And?" Sláine asked, no trace of pity wasted on Mrs. Delaney.

"She went home when she was done at 1400 hours."

"Did you see any strangers about, Mrs. Delaney?" Sláine asked, now in a pleasant tone of voice, as if they were discussing the weather.

"Of course, 'tis a hotel. But you mean skulking about, pretending to be staff? No, I didn't, miss, I swear."

"Do you have a time clock here?"

"A what, miss?"

"How do you account for your hours? Do you simply come and go?"

"Oh, no, we have to see Mr. McGregor in the morning and then when we leave. He signs us in and out."

"Verified with McGregor?" Sláine asked the man with the clipboard. He nodded yes.

"Let her go unless you've heard of a thirteen-hour timer. The bomb went off just past three." She turned on her heel and strode out of the room, shaking her head. Finch shot the two men a dark look and followed her. I waited until Mrs. Delaney got up and walked her down the hall.

"They didn't mistreat you, did they, Mrs. Delaney?"

"They asked their questions rough, I don't mind saying, but they never so much as touched me. Not that they wouldn't if they were told to. A nice young American lad like you shouldn't associate with them ruffians, if you don't mind me saying so."

"I'd rather be back in Boston myself but those ruffians are our allies."

"Boston, is it? I thought you had Irish in you; it shows on your face, it does. I turn here, dear, it's the servants' entrance. They don't want us traipsing in and out through that grand lobby of theirs." She patted my arm and descended a staircase that led to the rear of the hotel. As she opened the door I heard an engine start, and voices rising above the sound. I took the stairs and stepped outside. Delivery trucks stood at a small loading dock, the familiar name of Jenkins printed on the side. Crates of potatoes and beets were being carried in. Beyond the loading dock was a garage with three large bays, spaces for two vehicles in each. Backing out of one was the Ford Fordor staff car Sergeant Lynch had driven in yesterday. Corporal Finch must have called for it from the front desk. It made sense that they'd have it parked in the garage; it was distinctive, and there'd be no percentage in advertising their presence by parking it out front. A guy wearing a blue coverall was at the wheel, probably a mechanic or janitor. I watched the scene for a minute: employees walking by the garage, coming and going to work. Jenkins's men finished unloading and the two of them leaned against the truck, smoking, in no hurry to rush back for more heavy lifting.

The garage doors were open. I walked over and went in, no one paying me much mind. The first bay held only one vehicle, a Rolls-Royce being waxed by two kids using elbow grease, too focused on getting a glossy shine to notice me. I walked to a workbench where a telephone was mounted on the wall. There was no dial so it must have been a house phone. Next to it was a clipboard hanging from a nail pounded into a stud. Greasy fingerprints stained the pages but the entries were readable. There were columns for vehicle description, license plate, bay number, and guest name and room number.

Next to the Ford Fordor entry was the name Miss S. Howard, Room 314. Who was S. Howard? Did Sláine use a false name? Probably; she had a price on her head. I pulled the sheet from the clipboard and made my way out of the main lobby.

"Lieutenant, we've been waiting," Finch said impatiently. I ignored him and got in the back with Sláine.

"What was your room number? The room Sergeant Lynch took?"

"It was 314. Why?" I handed her the sheet.

"Howard was the name you used, right? This was hanging in full view of dozens of people. No one even noticed me take it. All someone had to know was what your car looked like. There's not many of those driving around the countryside."

"Damn! We always use false names when booking rooms. And we

always have the car parked under cover when we can for that very reason. And now it's gotten poor Cyrus killed."

"Ma'am? Should we go back inside?" Finch wanted to know.

"No. It's too late for that. Let's get to Stormont. Lieutenant Boyle has a lot of reading to do. I shall miss this automobile. Get me a new car, Sergeant Finch. You're promoted."

Finch accelerated and she leaned back in her seat, closing her eyes as she let out a long sigh. New car, new sergeant, and off we go. I wondered what she was thinking, dealing with the fact that she had narrowly missed an assassination attempt and had lost her trusted noncom in the bargain? Was she plotting her next move in the secret war against Irish extremists, holding her hand up, forcing them to stop, never knowing when the bullet would pierce her palm, wedding her to her family's stubborn history? And I wondered about that car. It did stand out but someone would have had to see it and know she and Lynch were staying in the area. Then check the hotels, waiting for the vehicle to turn up. Get the room number and plant the bomb.

"Did you leave your rooms after you checked in?" I said.

"We got in about six o'clock. We met in the dining room at seven. We were there about two hours. We had work to do, so we stayed after the meal. That's when Cyrus said he wanted to switch rooms."

"And that's when the bomb was planted. It gave them enough time to get your room number, wait for you to leave, and set the timer."

"That implies a number of people involved. They'd have to watch several hotels."

"Do you always stay at the same hotel in Newcastle?"

"No, we've used several. This one more than others, since there's a garage for the car. The IRA must have noticed a pattern."

"Why limit it to the IRA? What about the Red Hand? Aren't they on your list of extremists?"

"They are, but the only group on that list allied with the Nazis is the IRA. This may be linked to the two German teams."

Was this the opening salvo in an IRA uprising in Ulster, aided by fifty American BARs and German commandos? What would the IRA in the Republic do? Cross the border probably. Launch hit-and-run attacks, tying down the American and British forces here. Lots of people would die, and there would be cries for more blood. Vengeance. Reprisals. Would we strike back across the border, to hit at the IRA?

Would the Republic attack Ulster, coming to the aid of the IRA with the hope of uniting Ireland? My mind swirled with the possibilities, all of them awful. Ireland stumbling into an alliance with Nazi Germany, guerrilla war across the border, ambushes of American troops training for the invasion, and the grim work of men like Finch, Jenkins, and Taggart going on and on.

CHAPTER ▪ TWENTY SEVEN

MY BOOT HEELS fell softly on the marble floor as we crossed the foyer of Stormont Castle. Sláine's dress shoes clacked loudly ahead of me, echoing off the stone walls as we approached another set of sentries. This was the seat of Ulster rule, the fortress of loyalty to the British crown. On the outskirts of Belfast, it felt like a castle, set in a large park, green lawns all around it giving a clear view from any direction. The intelligence services had their headquarters here and their secret cells too, places into which suspected IRA men and their sympathizers disappeared. The very name had sounded evil to me as I was growing up, hearing it cursed as if it were a living thing, a beast. And now I walked through it, British soldiers opening doors for me, as I followed a strange and beautiful Irish woman deeper and deeper into its cold stone interior.

We took a circular iron staircase to a narrow corridor. Steel beams were visible above our heads. Metal doors ran along one side. Sláine knocked at the first. A small peephole appeared at a Judas window and a set of eyes looked us over. Locks tumbled open and we were admitted by a Royal Marine sergeant with a Sten gun hanging from a strap over his shoulder.

"Ah, there you are," said Major Charles Cosgrove. "So glad to see you in one piece, my dear." Cosgrove sat behind a huge, ornately carved wooden desk that seemed out of place in a basement office. The whole room was a surprise, with thick carpets, several easy chairs, and a fireplace. But no windows. A row of telephones sat on a shelf behind Cosgrove, three black, one green, and one red. Above them was a map of Northern Ireland and the border counties of the Republic. "Sit, please. Good to see you too, Boyle. Getting on all right, are you?"

"Fine, except for all the dead bodies."

"Yes, terrible. What a waste. Sergeant Lynch was a good man."

"I wouldn't know about him. I mean Sam Burnham and Pete Brennan."

"Ah, yes," Cosgrove said, flipping through an open file on his desk, licking his finger as he turned each sheet. "Lieutenant Burnham was killed in an IRA ambush, am I correct? And this enlisted man, Brennan, wasn't he mixed up in the black market? Has the look of a falling-out among thieves, doesn't it?"

"Who suggested that?" I said.

"It suggests itself. Now, if these killings have anything to do with the task you were sent here to complete, please do tell all. If not, leave the matter to the authorities."

I was about to argue with Cosgrove that Jenkins was involved and the authorities weren't allowed to touch him but managed to stop myself. My main reason for being here was to find out more about Jenkins and why he was off-limits. Cracking wise with Cosgrove might be fun but it wouldn't get me what I wanted.

"Yes, sir," I said, with the right combination of resentment and obedience.

"Good. Now give me a summary of what you've learned. Then I shall brief you both on the hunt for these Germans."

I went through my reasons for believing the weapons were still in the Clough-Ballykinler area. I told Cosgrove an informant had given me the dope on Eddie Mahoney being sent by the IRA chief of staff to keep an eye on Red Jack, who was suspected of stealing IRA funds. With the unknown Yank still out there, I wanted to play that one close to the vest, so I kept mum about the letter and notes I'd found in Mahoney's room.

"What is your opinion of all this, Subaltern O'Brien?" Cosgrove asked as he lit up his pipe. The smoke floated above him, then disappeared as a vent soundlessly sucked it out of the room.

"There is no hard evidence other than the empty truck in Warrenpoint but it is a very good theory. It explains everything, and there is no other rational explanation for why Mahoney was killed."

"The IRA could simply have mistakenly believed he was an informant," Cosgrove said.

"True," she said. "And it's happened before. But would they let an informant in on such an important operation? He might've slipped away. It doesn't add up."

"Very well. But where does that get us? It leaves us with a very large area to search for the arms cache. Boyle, what else have you found out?"

"I was sidetracked at first by the black market activity and the fact that one of Jenkins's trucks was used in the robbery. I thought there might be a link but all I found there was a crooked U.S. Army major. The military police have him. Pete Brennan was involved in a lesser way. He asked for a transfer to Italy and was about to ship out when he was killed. His body was found in the car Red Jack Taggart had used for his getaway vehicle after shooting up the RUC station and killing Sam Burnham."

"That is odd. Any idea why the vehicle was used?"

"No. That's one reason I wanted to get a look at the files you have here on Jenkins and Taggart. Maybe there's something we're missing. Jenkins had a motive for killing Brennan but not much of one. Only a few hundred bucks. It would have been easier to let him get on the boat to Italy."

"Indeed. Italy is proving to be a tough old boot and might have been the end of Sergeant Brennan in any case."

"And I think that Sam was the target at the RUC station, not me. Taggart shot him first then sprayed the windows with fire to keep everyone down. But why shoot a U.S. Army officer? There's no percentage."

"Be glad you can't understand the motivations of killers like Taggart, Boyle. He obviously enjoys killing for its own sake. Anything else?"

"There's something fishy going on at a Protestant bank in Armagh. Brennan was kidnapped near there, and a local constable named Simms was in on it. It's where Jenkins does his banking, and Sam Burnham was seen nearby before he was killed."

"My God, Boyle. What a mishmash of conjectures. Who cares where Andrew Jenkins keeps his money? Perhaps this Simms fellow is in the black market business himself and had a score to settle. As I said, leave local corruption to the police. District Inspector Carrick is on the case, is he not?"

"Yes. He's looking into the bank. He knows the manager."

"Then leave it to him."

"Yes, sir." Leave it to the man who isn't allowed to look at Jenkins's file. Perfect. "Say, Major, you wouldn't happen to be a member of the Royal Black Knights of the British Commonwealth, would you?"

"And if I were?" Cosgrove growled.

"Nothing, just curious. I'd never heard of them before, and they seem to be everywhere in this case."

"It so happens I am proud to be a member. I was invited to join several years ago, when I was originally posted here. I was inducted at Brownlow House."

"The headquarters of the society. I've been there. Not a member myself, though."

"I should say—" Cosgrove stopped himself. "Never mind. Does this have anything to do with what we are discussing?"

"No, sir." I decided it was time to clam up.

"Any luck tracking the Germans, Major?" Sláine asked, helpfully filling in the silence.

"None. We did find two rubber rafts hidden among the weeds at the edge of Lough Neagh. They had been sunk in shallow water. A few footprints in the mud, nothing else. Up the coast, by Bangor, we've had reports of three strangers with knapsacks boarding a train to Belfast. Their trousers and shoes were wet, but it had been raining. No one thought much of it at the time but a conductor remembered when the police asked about suspicious strangers. They could be from the U-boat or they could be bird-watchers out for a holiday. No trace of them since."

"Any idea of what the target might be? If all these events are related, it adds up to a major operation. Pulling off the arms theft, coordinating with Germans, it had to be carefully planned in advance," I said. "What are they after?"

"It almost doesn't matter what the target is," Cosgrove said. "That's the devil of it. There are so many places to strike, they can have their pick. There are U.S. Army convoys on most main roads every day. Units in the field on maneuvers. RAF bases. The Belfast shipyards. Seaplane bases on the west coast. Give me one hundred well-armed men and I could raise havoc long before a sufficient force was dispatched to stop me. Then I'd fall back into the hills and dare them to give chase."

"And all the while, the world cheers on the brave lads striking a blow for freedom. The American Irish ponder their loyalties, and the

Republicans in the south begin to act on theirs. Soon we have a crisis in the alliance between the United States and Great Britain," Sláine said.

"That may be the best-case scenario. Imagine if de Valera is pressured into aiding the IRA in the north, even clandestinely? Great Britain could not stand for it. There would be war again across all of Ireland. It would be terrible for the Irish, and possibly delay the Allies' invasion of the continent, giving the Nazis another year to prepare their defenses. Unthinkable."

A telephone rang. One of the black ones. I wondered who called on the red phone.

"Yes" was all Cosgrove said. He listened for a minute and then hung up. "We've intercepted a dispatch—don't bother asking how— that gives the code name for the German agents landing in Northern Ireland. Operation Sea Eagle II. The Nazis are absolute dolts when it comes to code names; there was an Operation Sea Eagle two years ago, landing agents by seaplane in the Republic. Obviously Sea Eagle II is more of the same but here in the north."

"Any indication of the target?" Sláine asked.

"None. But another team is expected to be dropped in tonight. We've no idea where. The RAF will have their night fighters up but it's impossible to cover every location. They could use another seaplane or they could make a parachute drop. If they fly low and evade our radar, they stand a good chance of getting in and out."

"If we could capture them, we might discover the target," I said.

"We have a surfeit of ifs, young man, and very few facts. If going through the files will help you with the latter, by all means, get to it. I've arranged for you to view the files on the three individuals you requested, and I also had one put together noting any unsolved killings during the last month, in case any of those incidents are related."

"LEAVE YOUR COAT and jacket in this outer room, sir," said a Royal Marine private, his hand resting on his sidearm as if I might respond violently to the suggestion. He pointed to a coat stand and I hung up my trench coat and my tanker's jacket.

"Your belt and weapon then empty your pockets onto this table," he said.

I handed him my web belt and .45, and dumped out a few coins and chewing gum onto the table. I took a pen from my shirt pocket and left it as well, along with my ID and a few pound notes.

"Is that everything, sir? You are not permitted to bring anything in with you or anything out." He had escorted me from Cosgrove's office and through another metal doorway. This one led to a small antechamber, where I was relieved of about everything except my shoelaces. "No writing implements of any kind. No paper or any item on which you could take notes. Is that understood, sir?"

"Nothing up my sleeve," I said, pushing up my shirtsleeves.

"Is that understood, sir?"

"Understood, Private. Just kidding around."

"The major doesn't appreciate kidding, sir."

"Tell me about it. What next?"

"I will take you into the file room. You will find a table with the files you requested. You may sit and read. You may not get up from your seat. When you are done, tell the guard behind the desk. He will summon me, and I will escort you out. You will be searched. Is that understood, sir?" He spoke in a monotone that told me he'd given this speech many times before.

"Sure. Does Subaltern O'Brien conduct the search?"

"Quite the kidder you are, sir. Follow me."

He unlocked the inner door. Straight ahead of me was a table and one chair. Four file folders sat in a row in front of the chair. To the right was a counter behind steel bars. Beyond the counter were rows of file cabinets, single lightblubs dangling from the ceiling every couple of yards. There were hundreds of file cabinets, and I couldn't see how far the rows extended around the corner. Seated behind the counter and behind the bars was another Royal Marine. Or was I the one behind the bars? As my escort shut the door, I saw there was no knob on my side. Basically, I was in a cell.

"How long do you have to stay down here?" I hollered to the marine on the other side of the bars.

"Doesn't matter, sir. Please read your files and inform me when you are done."

I decided I'd be testy too if I had to spend more than an hour down here. Cold concrete floors, army green paint job, and black iron bars. What a cheery place to work.

I grabbed the first file. Jenkins, Andrew. A strip of blue tape across the top and the word RESTRICTED in bright yellow. Beneath that was a memo stapled to the file folder. It said the file was not to leave the file room, and that access was restricted to MI-5 personnel. I felt honored.

Jenkins's file contained a section on his personal history. Evidently the Jenkins clan had lived in Armagh for generations, and his grandfather had started the family business. During the War of Independence, Andrew's father had targeted the Catholic competition, creating opportunity out of chaos. After the partition, the more prosperous Catholic farmers had been burned out, and the only other vegetable wholesaler was dead. Andrew Jenkins inherited a thriving business and the thanks of the Protestant farmers who had divided the spoils. Not very pleasant or too surprising.

Another section dealt with his association with the Red Hand. Each page was headed by dates. The first was 1925–1929. He had joined as a young boy after the partition, and enthusiastically took part in suppressing the Catholic minority. He was a suspect in the murder of a Catholic whose body was found beaten to a pulp in 1928. No arrest, lack of evidence. Another run-in with the law in 1930 over the shooting of an IRA suspect who had turned out to be a businessman from south of the border with no known IRA links. Again, no witnesses, no evidence, no arrest. By 1938, Andrew Jenkins was a well-respected businessman himself, and commander of the Red Hand. He had risen within the ranks through a combination of brutality and the ability to evade the law. The RUC did arrest some of the Red Hand mob when the killings were too public and distasteful even for them. As I read the file, I noticed some of those arrested had been Jenkins's competition within the Red Hand. Like his father before him, he was good at coming out on top.

I turned to the page headed 1938–1940, where the file ended. There was no entry for any of the last three years. The final note was dated March 1940. Jenkins had been brought to Stormont for questioning in the death of a British soldier, a Catholic from Birmingham, suspected of selling arms to the IRA. He hadn't been taken by the police but by MI-5. Why?

They had his bank records too. According to the Northern Bank, he had a fair-sized savings account. Nothing out of the ordinary for a successful businessman. If he had dirty money, and I was sure he did, it was probably in his mattress or an overseas account.

The door opened and I watched a private wearing an apron carry a stack of photographs to the counter. They looked shiny and new, as if he'd just pulled them from the developing tray. He handed them to the marine through a slot in the steel mesh.

"Here you go, Hawkins. More photos for your collection, all ready to be signed off. Some of my best work, I think."

Hawkins barely nodded, apparently not in the mood for conversation with this guy either. The private shrugged and left. Hawkins shuffled through the photos, checking the back of each and sorting them into separate piles.

I went back to the file, working through a section labeled SURVEILLANCE. Notes and photos from various stakeouts, including one taken in Portadown, similar to the RUC surveillance photo that had caught Subaltern O'Brien meeting with Jenkins. It showed her and Jenkins entering the pub but from a different angle. On the back was a label marked FILE: JENKINS, ANDREW. Below that a written notation: Meeting with A. Jenkins, the location, and the date, three days before the arms heist. Plus a section for "Officer's Name." Subaltern S. O'Brien had been typed in, and beneath that was the signature of Sláine O'Brien. It looked like MI-5 documented contacts with characters like Jenkins, probably so no one later could accuse them of unauthorized activities. And for their own protection. I looked at the photos Hawkins still had in his hands. They seemed to bear the same filing label as the ones in front of me.

"Here's another for one of your files, Lieutenant," Hawkins said. He held out a glossy through the slot. I got up and took it. It was the same pub, the same two people. The same notations were on the back, except it was dated yesterday. Sláine hadn't signed it yet. I gathered that she and Lynch had gone to Portadown after I'd seen her at Clough. Why hadn't she mentioned meeting Jenkins again?

"Do you want this back or should I put it in the Jenkins file?" I asked, looking up from the photo. Hawkins had taken one of the piles he'd sorted and was bent over a file drawer a few rows to the right.

"In the file, Lieutenant." He didn't waste a word or look up as he pawed through the drawer, which was crammed with manila folders.

I looked at the piles of photographs he'd left on the counter. There were five, facedown, in alphabetical order. The first was Connolly, the last Wilson. Right next to Wilson was a label that read FILE: TAGGART,

JACK. Hawkins seemed all business, not the type to forget he'd pulled Taggart's file for me. I gave the Taggart file on the table a quick glance. No blue label, no filing indicator of any kind. I figured that meant Taggart's file was also restricted but they didn't want anyone to know.

Hawkins had two files pulled and was placing photos in each. I reached through the slot and took the Taggart photos, two of them, looking as brand-new as the one he'd handed me. The scene was darker, maybe late afternoon. The note on the back gave the location as Castlewellan. I recognized it as one of the towns I'd driven through on my trip to Lurgan a few days ago. It was outside a restaurant. The first shot showed Sláine and Sergeant Lynch entering together. Behind them was a tall man with the brim of his hat pulled down low over one side of his face. His hand was up, scratching his nose, so his face was unrecognizable.

I saw what the photographer had done. The guy must have spotted him, so he changed positions and waited for the man to emerge from the restaurant. This time his cap was pulled down to conceal his face in the direction where the photographer had been, revealing his full profile to the hidden photographer's new angle. He'd gotten a clear shot of Red Jack Taggart, fresh from sharing a meal with Sláine O'Brien and the late Sergeant Cyrus Lynch.

I put the Taggart photos back just as Hawkins closed the file cabinet drawer. He walked back stiffly, as if he had a cramp in his leg.

"In the file, did you say? Couldn't hear you," I said, holding up the Jenkins photo.

"Yes, Lieutenant. In the file, please." He looked at the piles on his counter and back at me, his forehead wrinkled in thought. I smiled my best dumb smile, which must have been convincing, since he picked up the Connolly photos and went limping off to do more filing.

Jenkins and Taggart. One a thieving brute and likely murderer, the other the very man we were after. And Sláine O'Brien breaking bread with him on the same day she complained that I hadn't found him yet. I'd had the evidence in my hands. But I never would have gotten it out of this room and would probably have been tossed in an even deeper cell if I had tried. I had to figure some way to find out what she and Taggart were up to, and whose side each of them was on. The prospect made me dizzy.

I went through the Taggart file I had been provided. It was obvious it was only part of what they had on him. The file cover was blank and smelled of fresh-cut paper along the edges, as if it had just come out of the box. I thumbed through what they'd given me, certain that anything important was sitting in the original restricted file on the other side of those iron bars.

There was the standard background history about his family in Dublin. The first surprise was that his mother, Polly, had been Protestant, disowned by her family when she married Brian Taggart, a Catholic. Jack Taggart had been raised a Roman Catholic and left home in 1916 when he joined the Irish Volunteers to fight for independence. His father died two years later in the influenza epidemic, and in 1920 his mother remarried—to a Protestant this time. The report noted that the marriage had been arranged by her family, so she must have been taken back into the fold at some point.

In 1921, shortly after the birth of their new child, Polly and her husband were caught in a cross fire on a Dublin street between the IRA and the Royal Irish Constabulary. Both were killed. Not an uncommon event, unfortunately. I wondered what share of the hatred Red Jack carried came from the losses he endured in the first two decades of his life.

There were blank spaces in the chronological record before his service in the Spanish Civil War. After his return, minus most of the men he'd brought with him to fight in the Republican Brigade, he recovered from his physical wounds and drank his way through his emotional ones. He married and cleaned himself up. His wife had twins, and he obtained his position with the Irish Hospitals' Sweepstake. The report noted matter-of-factly that the sweepstake tickets sold in the U.S. provided a conduit for funds to be channeled back to the IRA, as Clan na Gael added significant sums to wire transfers as well as to the hard cash delivered across the Atlantic. Jack Taggart seemed to have been tamed by his marriage and his nearly legitimate job.

In early 1941, he dropped out of sight. His wife and two children no longer lived in Dublin, and the file showed no trace of their whereabouts. There were no surveillance photos. All the good stuff was hidden away. I figured that's when the IRA chief of staff sent him to Ulster to work with the IRA Northern Command. Maybe he brought his family with him, under an assumed name. Or perhaps they'd moved to one of the border counties, so he could slip across for a visit when things got too hot in Ulster. Wherever his family was, it must have been before the IRA chief of staff found out Red Jack had been cooking the books.

Two years later, Eddie Mahoney is sent north to set things right, and nothing works out the way anyone planned. Sláine O'Brien hob-nobs with the likes of Jenkins and Taggart at the same time she's trying to keep a lid on sectarian violence. Mahoney is just doing his job, and before he can finish his Agatha Christie, he's facedown in a ditch. Sam Burnham and Pete Brennan are caught up in it somehow, and they end up dead before their time.

I opened the next file, the one Major Cosgrove had assembled containing details of unsolved incidents. The most recent was the murder of the RUC constable in Dromara. DI Carrick had just come from his funeral when I first met him. Four shots in the back, almost on his doorstep. Attributed to the IRA. No suspects.

A week before, the body of a Protestant member of the Ulster Volunteer Force—not that there were any Catholic members—was found on the outskirts of Castlereagh, just to the east of Belfast. A hood was tied over his head and he'd been shot twice in the heart. The report mentioned that he was thought to have split off from the Red Hand, dissatisfied with what he considered to be a lukewarm response to Republican violence. No suspects.

A garage had blown up in Shankill, the Catholic neighborhood in Belfast. The body of a man, burned beyond recognition, was found along with bits and pieces of bomb-making equipment. It appeared he had been bound to a chair and left to watch his own bomb explode. No suspects.

A British soldier killed, struck by a vehicle on a deserted road. Catholic, no suspects, may or may not have been connected with sectarian violence. The reports went on and on, about evenly divided between sides, the Catholics slightly higher in the corpse count. Some were obvious targets of opportunity, in the wrong place, presenting an easy kill. Others, like the bomb maker and the UVF man, were definite extremists, killers who would have taken many more lives. I could feel sorry for the poor soldier, run down walking a country road at night. But a guy making bombs? No, that was beyond me. IRA bombs had killed too many innocent civilians during their S-Plan, and I didn't want to read about any more mothers getting blown up while pushing baby carriages to market. The same went for the UVF guy, breaking away from the Red Hand. If they were too tame for him, he would have been certain to spark another wave of reprisal killings.

There were two other killings among all the other deaths that matched these two. Dangerous, extremists both, one IRA and one Red Hand. If I eliminated those, and the deaths that were possible accidents or attributed to more personal motives, there were very few left. The constable from Dromara and a Catholic dockworker from Belfast, beaten to death, the letters IRA carved in his forehead. Maybe one was payback for the other, or maybe the whole chain of events went back to the last century.

What was important was the pattern. Bad guys with big plans on both sides were ending up dead. And Sláine O'Brien was working with both Red Jack Taggart and Andrew Jenkins. Was she running her own assassination bureau? Who would be better at getting close to Republican or Unionist extremists? Were Jenkins and Taggart killing their own or sharing information, letting each other do the dirty work for MI-5?

And most important, was that such a bad idea? I couldn't say. Nothing was as it should be here. It was not the Ireland I had expected. I shut this file.

Adrian Simms's was last. His dossier wasn't restricted and looked worn at the edges, like any cop's personnel file. I leafed through copies of his application to join the RUC, a few minor commendations, and other police forms for expenses, lost property, all the usual chickenshit paperwork law enforcement bureaucracies love. But this wasn't his official RUC file. MI-5 seemed to be keeping tabs on the RUC. There was a report on his bank records, about a year old. He had nearly two hundred pounds saved, a nice sum, but nothing that signaled payoffs. One sheet was headed "Known Associations" and listed the County Down Orange Society, which nearly every Protestant belonged to. He'd worked for Jenkins Foods Ltd. when he first moved to the area. So that's how he'd come to be so chummy with Andrew Jenkins. There were several entries about his attempt to join the Royal Black Knights. Poor Adrian. I wondered if he was surprised to find he was ineligible because he had a Catholic skeleton in his closet.

Then I saw a familiar name. McBurney, my pal the snotty Protestant bank manager. A letter to him detailed the background check the Royal Black Knights had conducted into Adrian's family history in Dublin. He had been raised from the age of two by a widowed aunt after the death of his parents. He'd been brought up as a good Protestant in the Church of Ireland. His aunt and both parents had been Protestants, as well as his grandparents on both sides. It even noted that he moved north to Ulster when he was old enough to leave the care of his aunt, in order to live and work under British rule. The letter writer—it was unsigned—concluded that Adrian Simms would be an excellent candidate, except for one thing. There was a step-brother from an earlier marriage, and that connection, even though no fault of Adrian's, precluded his acceptance. He went on to say that copies of birth certificates and other documents would follow. McBurney had mentioned those as well, but they weren't included in this file.

It didn't say which Protestant parent had committed the youthful indiscretion. It hadn't mattered; Simms was out, and his social-climbing wife had been unhappy. I guess he'd hoped that they wouldn't dig that far back. Maybe that was the reason he went north, to escape the Holy Roman stain on his family history.

No bank records, no photos, nothing to link Adrian Simms to anything incriminating. But I did have the word of a Catholic janitor that he'd seen Simms kidnap Pete Brennan near the Northern Bank in Armagh. It would probably be the end of Micheál, or at least his job, if he spoke up against a Protestant RUC man who was friendly with Andrew Jenkins. I had to find another way. Simms was not going to escape justice. I shivered, the chill of the enclosed room seeping into my bones. I was sick at heart, wishing I didn't have to read these secret histories of betrayals, death, hate, and lost hope.

I thought again about the matched killings of extremists from both sides. It had a logic, a symmetry that made terrible sense to me. Balance. It was all about a very delicate balance.

Less than two years ago, back in Beantown, I would've thought such a thing crazy. Now I was in the lair of my family's sworn enemies, nodding my head at the soundness of the idea. Sláine O'Brien was doing her job, and doing it well. Did Cosgrove know? Or didn't he care how she got it done? There must have been lots of money involved but that probably wasn't important to MI-5. Getting the job done was. Keeping a lid on things so Allied troops could move peacefully through Northern Ireland on their way to the next invasion. But now somebody had thrown a monkey wrench into the works, and we had Krauts and a well-armed IRA faction to worry about.

I was going to have to confront Sláine about Taggart. Why hadn't she used her relationship with Taggart to recover the BARs? Was it possible that she had an arrangement to turn a blind eye when she needed him to carry out a killing? Or maybe he no longer had possession of the guns, didn't know where they were, and she saw no reason to end a useful arrangement. I thought it might be possible. But she'd nearly broken down when we were alone. Did that signal a more vulnerable side of her? Could the Sláine O'Brien I'd held in my arms do all this, conceive of all this, and see it through?

I might have to find out. I pushed back from the table, a feeling of intense weariness washing over me. I could have laid my head down on the hard wood surface and fallen asleep. I looked at my watch, and it was half past one. I was hungry and needed a cup of coffee.

"You want me to give these to you?" I said to Hawkins, gathering up the files.

"Yes, sir. Please pass them through the slot."

"Must be a lonely job down here," I said, still trying to get a response from the man.

"The day does sometimes go slowly, sir, but I don't mind. Not much else to do."

"Why not ask for a transfer?"

"Here's why," he said, rapping on his right leg, the sound of knuckles on wood echoing in the room. "Lost my leg at Narvik. Lost my wife and son in Coventry when the Germans bombed it. There's not much for me to do but file papers and be glad I still have a job to do. Anything else, Lieutenant?"

"No, nothing. Thanks for your help. Sorry, about everything."

"Same here," he said, and with that I understood why he said so little.

CHAPTER TWENTY EIGHT

I FOUND MAJOR Cosgrove and Sláine waiting for me. In a rare moment of courtesy, the major invited me to lunch in the Stormont officers' mess. I followed them upstairs to more open and elegant surroundings. The dining room was paneled in dark walnut, buffed to a high shine. Soft carpets graced the floor and paintings hung along one wall, huge landscapes of castles and knights on horseback. Probably Irish lands and English castles.

It was very civilized, so civilized that it was hard to believe we were only two floors above evidence linking Sláine O'Brien, if not all of MI-5, to murder. I stared at an English knight on one of the canvases, his black armor gleaming and a long sword held out before him. He was right over Cosgrove's head, one black knight watching over the other. I decided this was not the time or place to accuse either of them of their crimes.

"Well, Boyle, did you find anything of value?"

"There's very good background material in those files. Could be helpful, I suppose. But no smoking gun."

"What did you expect to find in our file on Constable Simms?" Sláine asked. "He's never been investigated for anything; there's just the usual accumulation of data."

"You've looked at it?"

"Yes, to see what you found so interesting about the man. There's not much, I'm afraid."

"No. Major Cosgrove, did you know Adrian Simms was blackballed when he asked to join the Royal Black Knights?" A waiter appeared with the wine Cosgrove had ordered, and we waited in silence as he poured.

"I had no idea. I am not an active member. I travel too much and I can only attend meetings sporadically. But membership is useful for staying in touch with that stratum of Ulster society."

"Which stratum is that?"

"Those Unionists who are not bomb throwers. They want to maintain their connection with Great Britain but at the same time they wish for a stable society here, for all."

"Like the banker, McBurney," I said.

"Exactly. Good man, McBurney."

"He actually employs a Catholic. The bank janitor."

"Things won't change overnight, Boyle. Hiring one is better than killing one, I say. Don't you agree?"

I didn't answer. I raised my glass, thought of a few Irish toasts, then thought better of it and downed half the wine.

"I may see McBurney tomorrow evening at Brownlow House, if I can get away. Some sort of event honoring members from the American lodges. I shall ask him about your suspicions."

"I hope you have better luck than I did."

"So were the files a waste of time, Billy?" Sláine asked.

"No, I got to see a nice picture of you. They brought in the surveillance photo of your meeting with Jenkins. Do you document all your contacts like that?"

"Yes. It's part of our record keeping. It comes in handy if we're building a case file. And photographs can be used in other ways if the informant ceases to be cooperative."

"Blackmail?"

"Don't be melodramatic, Boyle!" Cosgrove said. "Once an informant betrays his organization, we need to keep him on a tight leash. He needs to know if he tries to run, we will show the photographs to those who will be interested. It's all part of the game. They come to us in the first place, after all."

The soup arrived. It was potato and leek, steaming hot, and very good.

"How did Jenkins become your informant?"

"Ancient history, Billy. The soup is good, isn't it?"

"So he's been one a long time?"

"Boyle, it is bad form to discuss informants, even here in the officers' mess. One never knows," Cosgrove said, glancing at a passing waiter.

"Sorry. Professional curiosity, that's all. Without mentioning any names, how do you feel about depending on informants? Back in Boston I was always worried that they might turn on me, and the next meeting would be a setup."

"You have to be careful, it's true," Sláine said. "We have many sources of information, though. I think I'd hear if something was afoot. And you forget, Billy, we are not the police."

"Meaning?"

"Meaning that retribution would be mine," Cosgrove said, slurping down the last of his soup.

"Did one of those sources tell you about the murder of Pete Brennan?" I asked. "You never said how you got word so quickly. Was it the RUC?"

"Ha! Do you call your FBI every time there is a murder in Boston? I think not," Cosgrove said.

Sláine stayed quiet as the waiter removed the soup bowls.

"So who was it?" I asked.

"Excuse me, sir," a waiter said, handing Cosgrove an envelope. "Your office said to give this to you straightaway." Cosgrove tore it open, read it, and handed the paper to Sláine.

"Speak of the devil," he said. "Andrew Jenkins is dead."

"Oh, that can't be true," Sláine said.

"What can't be true? That's he's dead?" I asked.

"No," she said, looking me in the eye. "That he killed himself. It says he was found hung from a rafter in a small warehouse in Lisburn. Andrew Jenkins will have a lot of things to answer for in the next life but the sin of suicide will not be one of them."

"How can you be so sure?"

"Mr. Jenkins spent his life clawing his way to the top," Cosgrove said. "As you've discovered, he provided us with certain information. Often that information benefited us, and he was well paid for it. Other times, the information he gave us benefited him. He was a man who held only one life dear. His. I quite agree—he was not the suicidal type."

A waiter came to the table, three plates of lamb chops and boiled potatoes at the ready.

"Oh dear," said Cosgrove as he pushed his chair back. "Those look delicious."

■ ■ ■

ON A PERSONAL level, I thought Cosgrove was more dis-
traught over the idea of the lamb chops going back to the kitchen
than the image of Jenkins dangling at the end of a rope. I was
wistful about them myself. It took him about five minutes to get a
staff car and driver for us, and then we were off, exiting the formal
gardens surrounding Stormont and heading for the main road that
would take us south to Lisburn.

One of the first things I saw was a bombed-out stadium. It looked
like it had just been hit.

"What's that?" I asked.

"The Oval. It's a football stadium. Not American football, the real
thing," Sláine said. "The Germans bombed it in 1941. They were probably aiming for the dockyards or the railway station and released their
bombs too early."

"Bad luck for Glentoran," the driver said. "I'm a supporter."

"That's a team, Billy, and he's a fan," Sláine explained.

"Thanks. I'm a Red Sox supporter myself. Ever hear of them?"

"You mean like garters?" the driver asked.

"Never mind."

Cosgrove laughed and I gazed at the gritty city landscape. We were
nearing the Belfast dockyards, one of the busiest harbor areas in Europe
now. Troopships, tankers, Liberty Ships, and destroyers were lined up
to unload or refuel. Trucks rumbled by, heavy with the material of war
brought by ships. A column of GIs crossed the road in front of us until
finally an MP let us through.

"Have you seen all this before, Boyle?"

"No, sir. First time in Belfast."

"It's rather amazing. They have a runway built right up to the
docks. After they unload the planes, they take off, right from the ship.
Wizard, simply wizard."

"More bomb damage?" I said, pointing to piles of rubble where
workers were loading debris onto trucks.

"Yes. The Luftwaffe gave Belfast the full treatment early on. They
went for the dockyards regularly, the railroads, and the city in general.
Some neighborhoods were hit quite badly. There are not enough
resources at present to rebuild everything, so some of the damaged

buildings are taken down and the rubble hauled away, as they are doing there. They still find bodies underneath."

"Do they still hit the city?"

"No, not for a while. With you Yanks coming in, with your aircraft added to ours, and our increased defenses, it's too risky for them. It's a long flight, navigating at night, across England, avoiding the Republic of Ireland, and then finding Belfast. It's a wonder they ever tried. Do you know they accidentally bombed Dublin? Blighters got lost and thought they were over Ulster! I'd say those particular boys are shivering at the Russian front, if they're still alive."

"I never heard about that."

"De Valera kept it as quiet as he could. Embarrassing for him not to retaliate in any way but he didn't want to antagonize the Germans or encourage us. He's walking a tightrope. One slip and he'll have us, the Germans, or both over his border."

We left the city, occasional gaps in the rows of buildings showing where German bombs had fallen. A few new buildings were going up but mostly it was bricks and concrete going out, leaving small fields of weeds sprouting between structures, marking the place where homes and lives had once flourished.

Convoy traffic lightened up and we made it into Lisburn in forty minutes. Sláine gave the driver directions to Jenkins's warehouse, one of a number of small facilities he owned as part of his distribution network. Had owned, I should say. We drove up to where two RUC constables had set up a roadblock with their vehicle at the entrance to a fenced-in yard containing a few large garages, some open sheds, and a few sheet-metal-roofed wooden buildings. The main gate was open, a chain with an open padlock hanging from one side.

"Here to see DI Carrick," the driver said.

We were waved through, the constable pointing to the row of buildings on our left. We drove across the dirt drive, still wet and churned up from the recent rains. Ahead of us were an ambulance and three police cars. It occurred to me I'd seen several ambulances in Northern Ireland, and they all had been used to transport murder victims. Wasn't anybody ever simply injured here?

Jenkins's warehouse was the last building. The double doors were open and one of the police cars was parked in front, its lights on, illuminating the dark interior. Two thick wooden beams ran across the interior space. From the second hung the limp body of Andrew Jenkins, his head tilted sideways at a sickening angle. Those who hang themselves are not pretty to behold, and I'd give odds that no one would do so who had ever seen such a sight.

"Lieutenant Boyle," DI Carrick said with the solemn tone appropriate to a crime scene. He shook Major Cosgrove's hand and suggested to Sláine that she might wish to wait outside.

She ignored his concern and glanced around the space. Beneath Jenkins was a flatbed truck and a single wooden chair on the ground next to it. Crates of vegetables were stacked along one wall, and an empty workbench adorned the other.

"Nothing's been moved?"

"Nothing. We thought you might have an interest, and were sure Lieutenant Boyle would."

"Do you mind?" I asked, stepping forward. Carrick nodded his assent, and I walked over to the truck, watching where I stepped across the dirt floor. The truck had been driven in recently, the wet mud showing clearly in its tracks. A rope was secured to the truck bed, tied through one of several clamps used to tie down crates. The truck looked like it had come straight from a farm.

"It appears that Mr. Jenkins secured the rope, threw it over the rafter, put the chair on the truck bed, and then kicked it out from under him," Carrick said, raising his voice for all to hear.

"It does," I said, looking inside the truck cab. "There's no note. Did you see any paper in here?"

"None."

I walked around the truck, searching the ground. I looked inside the cab. The seat was cracked and torn, the interior caked with mud and dust. The key was in the ignition. I put the chair on the truck bed and jumped up. I could see the rope wasn't long enough to reach the rafter from the ground, so he'd used the truck for extra height. I stood on the chair, close to Jenkins. His feet dangled several inches above the seat where my feet were. I had to look up at his face, which was distended, eyes and tongue bulging out. I didn't linger long. He hadn't been much to look at when alive.

I felt his arm and noticed the beginnings of rigor. "Who called it in?" I asked.

"Anonymous phone call," Carrick said. "To the local station, saying that Andrew Jenkins had hung himself."

"The caller used that name specifically?" Carrick consulted with a constable, who nodded his head emphatically.

"Yes."

Why? Why would someone who knew Jenkins call in his suicide? Why mention his name? I turned the body, listening to the creak of the rope on wood as I did. The back of his head was dark. I turned the body more, bringing his head into the full light of the headlamps. Dried blood. Andrew Jenkins had been hit over the head before this noose had gone around his neck. I looked at the rope again, and I saw how it had been done. Knock Jenkins out, and then throw him up on the truck bed, parked right below the rafter. Toss the rope over, tie it to the truck, and put the noose around his neck. Then drive the truck forward about four feet, and Jenkins is swaying in the air. Throw the chair down near the truck, and we're ready to jump to the suicide conclusion.

"He was murdered," I said. Jenkins spun around once or twice, then settled into a gentle back-and-forth motion. I saw Sláine turn away, her hand over her mouth. Not quite one of the hard-case boys yet. I got down from the truck and told them about the blood on the back of his head.

"And his feet don't quite reach the chair," I said. "I doubt he hit himself on the head and then jumped up into the noose."

"Why stage a suicide then? It doesn't make sense. A man like Jenkins was bound to come to a violent end," Carrick said. "It wouldn't have surprised me to find him shot or beaten to death and left by the side of the road. But this seems like an elaborate ruse for no purpose."

"Perhaps the killer wanted to divert suspicion from himself," Cosgrove said.

"No need to, sir," Sláine said. "There are any number of IRA types who would gladly have strung him up. We'd be hard-pressed to limit ourselves to a dozen suspects offhand."

"Then why?" Carrick asked. "Drive the truck forward slowly, so we can let the body down," he said, pointing to two constables who stood by the cars. "One of you hop up and get that noose off him."

The constables acknowledged his order and walked to the truck.

The silence was broken by the throaty sound of a motorcycle on the main road, downshifting, followed by a short, sharp screech of tires. Shouts came from the direction of the main gate, and heads turned in that direction. The motorcycle engine revved high and I saw it turn the corner, followed by the two RUC men from the gate, their pistols drawn, yelling for the man to halt.

Carrick drew his revolver, and I followed suit with my automatic. One of the guards fired a warning shot over the motorcyclist's head, and I saw him scrunch down, making himself a smaller target.

"Get back," Carrick shouted to all of us. "Inside!" We were in the line of fire. He dropped to one knee and held his pistol level as the motorcycle drew closer. Two shots rang out, the men from the gate firing and missing. The motorcycle swerved left and right, then turned hard to drive straight at us. The driver wore a leather helmet and goggles, and his mouth was open, yelling something. He looked like a crazy man, his face contorted in rage or frustration.

"No!" he shouted as he braked and slid the bike sideways, spraying Carrick and me with mud. Carrick kept his revolver aimed at the man, but didn't fire. He stood and raised his free hand in the direction of the men giving chase. I kept my .45 aimed at the motorcyclist. He looked familiar. This had to be the mystery Yank: same motorcycle, same trench coat.

"For God's sake, don't start that truck!" He pulled off his goggles and helmet, his American accent ringing out loud and clear. And then I knew why he'd looked so familiar. I lowered my automatic, not believing what my eyes were seeing.

"Who the hell are you?" Cosgrove said, emerging from the warehouse.

"I'm the man who just saved your goddamn life," he said. "Want to tell them who I am, Billy, as soon as you point that cannon away from me?" His face lit up in a hell-raiser's grin, one I'd seen many times, and I couldn't help but smile back at him, even as the impossibility of it rattled around inside my head.

"This is Daniel Boyle. He's a homicide detective with the Boston Police Department. And my uncle."

"Explain yourself," Carrick said, not showing much interest in this Boyle family reunion.

"Call your bomb squad. That truck is wired with plastic explosive, enough to destroy this place and anyone close to it," Uncle Dan said as he gave me a bear hug. "It's probably wired to the ignition but I wouldn't recommend trying the doors until the experts look at it."

"I don't mean that," Carrick said. "I mean explain what you are doing here, and how you come by this information."

"This is District Inspector Hugh Carrick," I said, and introduced Uncle Dan to the others. I wanted to know what the hell he was doing here myself but I sensed his presence might not be entirely on the up-and-up.

"An explanation is in order," Cosgrove said.

"I'd like to have a word with Billy, if you don't mind," Uncle Dan said.

"No," Carrick said. "There will be time enough for a chat later, at headquarters. What I want to know right now is how you got by this information."

"Well, let's see if I'm right," Uncle Dan said, walking over to the truck. "Billy, can you slide under and take a look at the engine? Don't open the hood. Don't touch anything."

"Don't worry," I said, getting down on my back and pushing with my heels. Carrick and the others crowded around, their curiosity overcoming their qualms. It was dark under the truck but not so dark that I couldn't see bricks of plastic explosive tucked in the wheel wells and in various places around the frame and engine. Detonators were wired to each, and seemed to lead to the ignition switch. I could see above the radiator to the hood latch, and there were no wires or explosives there. I pulled myself out.

"The hood is clear," I said. "But look at this." I opened the hood and propped it up. Even more of the plastic explosive was visible. It looked like enough to sink a battleship.

"That's why the killer faked a suicide," Carrick said. "So we would all be called to the scene, stand around trying to figure things out, and then blow ourselves to smithereens."

"The rope was short so that we'd have to start up the truck to lower the body. If Uncle Dan had been just a few minutes late—"

"This would have been one big hole in the ground," he finished for me.

"We owe you our thanks, to be sure," Carrick said. "If you're a policeman, as your nephew says, then you will understand we need to speak with you further about this matter and your presence here. It is not official, I take it."

"The jurisdiction of the Boston PD does not extend over the Atlantic, to be sure," Uncle Dan said. "As for right now, I'd be happy to answer your questions but I have an appointment. Saving all your lives has made me late, and this much explosive makes me nervous, so I'll be leaving."

"I agree with you about the explosive, Mr. Boyle. But not about your leaving. Constable," Carrick said, pointing at Uncle Dan, "search him."

They found a .38 Special, brass knuckles, and a switchblade, but no passport or identification. But it was obvious he wasn't here to tour the old country. Cosgrove and Carrick argued over whether this was a police matter or one for MI-5. Carrick responded by informing Uncle Dan that he was under arrest for reckless driving and vagrancy, and put him in the back of one of the police cars with a constable on either side. Uncle Dan nodded and smiled in appreciation of the maneuver as he settled in for the ride between two cops who owed him their lives. I figured these Ulster cops were a better bet than MI-5 at Stormont Castle. Our driver followed us on Uncle Dan's motorcycle, and we all drove north, back to Belfast and RUC headquarters, me at the wheel with Cosgrove and Sláine in back.

"They should give him a medal, not take him in," I said, probably for the tenth time.

"You had no idea he was here?" Sláine asked.

"None. I'd seen a guy on a motorcycle shadowing me, and a few people I talked to mentioned another American asking the same sort of questions I was. That must have been Uncle Dan. Remember, I asked you if you had another American working on this?"

"Yes, I do. It rather looks like you had the other American, not I."

"I had no idea it was him. How could I?" I thought about the Boston Braves matchbook in my pocket. That would have come from Uncle Dan. He was a Braves fan and could easily have grabbed a few packs of smokes and matches for the trip, without even thinking about it. Then he and Eddie Mahoney meet for a pint, the cigarettes and matches are out on the table, and Eddie ends up with Warren Spahn in his pocket. But what had Uncle Dan been up to with Eddie Mahoney, and why was he following me around in secret?

I could think of one reason. Given Uncle Dan's membership in the North American IRA and his connections with Clan na Gael, I could make a pretty good guess, especially since he'd been in touch with Eddie Mahoney. The Dublin IRA wouldn't be the only ones out for blood when they learned about Red Jack stealing from them. Joe McGarrity, the head of Clan na Gael, and good friend of the Boyles, would be upset too. Upset enough to send someone to eliminate the thief, and set an example. Upset enough to send a hit man. A man loyal enough to do what had to be done and keep quiet about it. A man like Daniel Boyle.

WE PULLED INTO the rear of the brick RUC station on Musgrave Road as DI Carrick took Uncle Dan by the arm and led him up the steps. It wasn't a tight grip and he didn't use handcuffs. Professional courtesy, I guess.

"Major Cosgrove?" a constable asked as we stepped out of the vehicle. "Message for you, sir. Follow me." We did, turning right as we entered the building. I watched Uncle Dan and Carrick disappear down the opposite corridor. We were taken to a radio room. An operator handed Cosgrove a dispatch, which he read carefully then held over an ashtray and lit with his lighter. He held it until flames licked his fingers, and then dropped it.

"Operation Sea Eagle II," he said in a whisper. "A Focke-Wulf Condor will take off from Saint-Servais in Brittany this evening. Two men will be dropped by parachute tonight, somewhere near the border."

"How do you know—?"

"Never mind that, Boyle. What matters is we do know."

"Are you going to intercept it?"

"What would you suggest, Subaltern O'Brien?" Cosgrove said, ushering us out into the deserted hallway.

"I'd prefer those two men alive. Let them come."

"Of course. Only sensible thing to do at this point. Now let's find out what your relative has been up to and then work out this little puzzle."

A little puzzle. That's all this was to the old men of the British Empire, the riddle of the Irish. I didn't have much sympathy for the Luftwaffe, based on recent experiences, but I did feel sorry for those guys, gearing up for their flight, not knowing that their lives were being weighed in the balance. Was their part of the puzzle to live or die? I hoped no one was thinking about me that way, and then I remembered Sláine and her secret meetings. Was I part of her puzzle? And if so, was I her solution?

We entered what looked like home. A big room, desks pushed together, guys pecking at typewriters, talking on telephones with receivers scrunched between cheek and shoulder as they took notes, the low buzz of talk and back talk and all the familiar noises of a big city stationhouse. Rising above the Ulster Irish accents was one pure American voice.

". . . so then I says to him, 'Either way is fine with me!'"

Laughter broke out at the punch line from a group of constables crowded around Uncle Dan, who took a sip of tea from a mug one of them handed him. He was grinning ear to ear as he winked at me, charming everyone around him as usual. I watched DI Carrick in his office, through the open door, as he spoke on the telephone, one eye on Uncle Dan.

"Billy, come here and tell our brother officers about your first arrest, that Frenchman who couldn't keep his pants on, wasn't it?" He set down the mug and hitched his trousers up, the way he always did when he carried a pistol, badge, and cuffs. Cop force of habit. He rocked on his heels, his head tilted back as he brushed his thick brown hair off his forehead. He looked good, still strong, broad in the shoulders with blue eyes that drank in everything around him.

The constables looked eagerly at me but I wasn't the storyteller Uncle Dan was. I saw Carrick hang up.

"I think we're keeping DI Carrick waiting," I said.

The group broke up, a few of the men wishing Uncle Dan luck before moving back to their desks and duties. Carrick motioned us in. His office was long and narrow, a conference table to the right of his desk, along a window that overlooked the room. He sat at the head under a portrait of King George VI, gazing serenely over us in his naval uniform, one hand languidly resting on a chair, gold braid up the elbow. Uncle Dan looked at it, then turned away to face Major Cosgrove and Sláine across the table. He shook his head slowly and muttered something under his breath. I didn't dare ask him what he'd said.

"I have many questions for you," Carrick said as he opened a small notepad. "But please begin with how you came to know about the bomb in the truck."

"I'll not speak further in front of this lot," Uncle Dan said, gesturing dismissively with his thumb toward Sláine and Cosgrove.

"You certainly will, and answer every question put to you," Cosgrove said, his cheeks puffed out in indignation. "I've half a mind to take you in for espionage as it is."

"The old man has only half a mind, as he says," Uncle Dan said, turning to face Sláine. "What's your excuse?"

"Hold on," I said, watching Cosgrove's face redden. "I think we're all after the same thing here, so let's not fight each other. OK?" I laid my hand on Uncle Dan's arm and held my breath. Dad always said I got my wiseacre mouth from his brother Dan, and he was right. Problem was, right now we needed some of Dad's calm diplomacy, and this branch of the Boyle clan was short on both.

"Allow me to suggest that Mr. Boyle need not worry about the security services carting him off if there is no proof of actual espionage," Carrick said. "I would remind you that we would all be in very small pieces right now if not for his arrival, which was at great risk to himself."

"Yes," Cosgrove said. "I suppose we do owe him that. Very well."

"Mr. Boyle, your nephew has been working with Major Cosgrove and his section. As a ranking detective yourself, I am sure you understand they must be involved."

"I can't fault you there. I can see why you're a district inspector, you've got a fair hand," Uncle Dan said. "OK, I'll lay it out for you, as best I can."

"The bomb?" Carrick said, his pen poised.

"Well, now, I have to start back a ways first. Without revealing unnecessary details of names and identities, I'll just say that I was asked by an organization in the States to pay a visit to Ireland—the Republic of Ireland—and investigate charges of embezzlement against one Jack Taggart."

"Was it Clan na Gael?" Sláine said. "Such an assignment must've come from Joe McGarrity himself."

"There's no need for names, young lady. And it was a request, not an assignment, from an organization that sends funds to Dublin to benefit hospitals and to care for the sick. I work for the Boston Police Department. I had plenty of vacation due me, so I decided it was time to see the world. I booked passage on a neutral steamer to Cork, all nice and legal."

"Proceeds from illegal Irish Hospitals' Sweepstake tickets sold in the United States," Sláine offered. "Funds for IRA activities are often conveyed along with their proceeds."

"That's a fine story, but certain details are not necessary," Uncle Dan said. "What's important is that this fine fraternal organization was concerned that Taggart was siphoning off funds."

"We understand, Mr. Boyle. I am not concerned with the legality of sweepstakes tickets at the moment. Please continue," Carrick said, with a quick glance at Sláine. I could tell Carrick wanted her to shut up and let the story come out.

"All right then. I get to Dublin and find that Taggart is no longer at the Sweepstake—I mean his place of employment—although they still carry him on their books. I ask questions in certain quarters that the young lady does not need to mention, and I find out that he's gone north, over the border. That presents me with a problem. The border's closed up tighter than a spinster's knees, and I have no idea where to look. So, I do two things. I search for his relatives, and I buy a motorcycle."

"For slipping across the border," Cosgrove said.

"And then saving your hide, yes. Taggart's parents are both dead but I find an aunt, his father's sister. I tell her I was with Jack in Spain, that we served together in the International Brigade, and I wanted to get in touch. It took a bit of charm and a damn lot of tea, but finally she said it couldn't do any harm to tell an old comrade that Jack was somewhere in County Down, about to do something grand for the cause."

I leaned forward, about to ask a question, but stopped when I realized I didn't know what it was. Something in what he'd said triggered a question in my mind but it was so far down I couldn't even put it into words. Like Dad said, sometimes your subconscious does its job but it takes its own sweet time about it.

"So I make my way north, crossing over fields and through farm lanes, until I'm in occupied Ireland. No offense intended," Uncle Dan said, grinning. "Then I proceed with good old-fashioned detective work, real gumshoe stuff. I ask certain unnamed contacts about Taggart but they all deny any knowledge of the man. It's as if he went underground from the underground, if you know what I mean. Finally, I get a message to meet a man."

"In Annalong," I said.

"Well, well, Billy! You may become a real detective yet! How did you find that out?"

"These were in Mahoney's room, along with all his personal effects. He left everything behind the night he went off with Taggart to steal the BARs." I handed him the Boston Braves matchbook.

"Whose room?"

"You may have known him as John Davies. That was the name on the driver's license he carried."

"Jesus, that'll teach me to empty my pockets next time I do this cloak-and-dagger stuff. I never even thought about it. We had a few pints and smoked. He must've picked them up."

"So the man you met—Eddie Mahoney—called himself Davies?"

"Yes. He told me Dublin had sent him north as well, on a similar mission, to keep tabs on Taggart."

"By Dublin you mean the IRA?" Carrick asked.

"It wasn't the organization that sent me. Remember, my group raised and sent the money. We had our own suspicions, and wanted to find out if Taggart was implicated before contacting Dublin."

That sounded like Joe McGarrity. He'd tell his left hand a lie to keep it from meeting his right.

"Why did Mahoney want to meet you?"

"Word had gotten back that I was asking questions. His bosses in Dublin had checked me out and learned I was here at the request of my American group. Davies—or Mahoney, rather—wanted to exchange information but also to tell me to keep my hands off for a while. Something big was in the works."

"What happened next?"

"He was supposed to meet me again in four days but he never showed. I heard about the arms theft and guessed that was the big deal he'd talked about. I kept asking questions, until one day, who do I see driving by in a jeep but my own nephew. Knowing he works for Ike, I start following him. Wasn't much left for me to do at that point anyway. Taggart had gone to ground, and no one had heard a thing from him."

"I heard from him. He killed a U.S. Army MP and almost got me too. With a BAR."

"Yes, I know. Word travels. That's when I decided you needed a bodyguard as well as a tail. I kept as close as I could without tipping my hand."

"Are we getting close to how you learned of the bomb?"

"In a way, yes. I've said several times I won't mention names. One of those I won't mention said there was some sort of operation going on, and that Taggart had asked for plastic explosive. The IRA Northern Command provided it, as well as a bomb maker to wire it up. I didn't know where the explosion was going to happen. I feared for you, Billy, since he'd tried to kill you once already. But when I saw you heading into Stormont, not looking like a prisoner, I thought you'd be safe for a while. Then the grapevine started chattering."

"About Jenkins?" I asked.

"Yes. Taggart had taken him, I learned, in Lisburn, part of the same operation. Guaranteed to take out RUC and MI-5 personnel, my contact said. It was the combination that had me worried. I knew you'd be working the case with them, so I used my charms on the fellow who'd told me, and got the whole story."

"Brass-knuckle charm?" Carrick asked.

"It gave him the gift of the gab," Uncle Dan said. "I wasn't far away, so I hightailed it straight to Jenkins's warehouse, dodged a few poorly aimed shots, and saved the RUC from a manpower shortage."

"I have to ask," said Carrick, laying down his pen, "for the names of all concerned."

"Yes, you do," said Uncle Dan. They stared at each other for five seconds that felt like five hours, and then Carrick nodded slightly.

"Very well. I owe you my personal thanks as well as those of the Royal Ulster Constabulary."

"Glad to assist another police force, even in Ulster," Uncle Dan said. "One other thing. I found out that Taggart didn't exactly give the weapons to the IRA. He sold them."

"How much?" I said.

"One thousand dollars each, and another ten grand for the ammo. They paid too. Sixty thousand smackers."

"Good lord," said Carrick. "A fortune."

"Yeah, it is," Uncle Dan agreed. "It shows how important this operation is. No wonder he set up the bomb in the truck."

"Why now?" Sláine asked.

"What?" We all spoke at the same time.

"Why now?" she repeated. "Why go through all this trouble today, now? Why not four days ago or three days from now?"

"Obviously, because Taggart felt us closing in," Cosgrove said.

"But we weren't," she said. "We had no idea where he was. So why lure us in at this moment?"

Uncle Dan whistled. "I wish a woman of your brains and beauty was serving a better cause than English dominion over Ireland," he said. "You have a sharp mind. While I sit here playing the hero and accepting thanks for my great deeds, it escaped me completely. He wanted to eliminate everyone connected to the investigation of the BARs. In case you were getting close. Which means that something is about to happen, something he didn't want to take any chances with."

Sláine, Cosgrove, and I exchanged glances. Carrick furrowed his brow and watched us. "Something *is* happening, isn't it?"

"Ah, I think it's time for Mr. Boyle to be removed from the conversation," Cosgrove said.

"It appears Mr. Boyle has been more straightforward than you have, Major Cosgrove. As a guest of the RUC, he will remain with me for the time being, so there is no need to worry about security. A guest, not a prisoner," Carrick added, for Uncle Dan's enlightenment.

Cosgrove said, "We have information concerning two teams of German agents, possibly commandos, landing separately in the north within the past few days. One more two-man team is due to parachute in tonight, somewhere along the border. It seems the timing is right for a joint IRA/Abwehr operation. Eliminating us would have helped them by creating chaos." Cosgrove sank back into his chair, all the bluff and bluster blown out of him as he considered the possibilities.

"What's the target?" Uncle Dan asked.

"We don't know," I said. "What matters is that if the IRA and the Germans launch a major joint attack in Northern Ireland, it could affect the course of the war."

"Would it pull the Republic in?" Uncle Dan said.

"Either willingly or not. You know there'd be pressure to come to the aid of the IRA in the north. The British might retaliate. Our troops would certainly be involved; they're everywhere. Chaos pretty well describes it."

"Mr. Boyle, your political sympathies are quite clear," Carrick said. "Even so, you seem to be an honorable man. I ask you now, if you have any inclination to support those extremists who are laboring to bring this about, to tell us."

"And if I did?"

"I already have arranged with the U.S. Army Air Force to have you brought to the Greencastle Aerodrome and flown back to America on the first available flight. As a courtesy, of course," he added with a smile.

"Since you've spoke true with me, I'll do the same. Yes, I wish Ireland united as one free nation. If I saw this plan as a way to accomplish that, I'd be off in the mountains with a weapon in my hand right now. But this is madness. I saw enough carnage to last me a lifetime in the First World War, and we're due for much more in this one. No need to add to it. The people of Ireland don't deserve to be used as pawns. And I mean all of them, north and south."

The room was silent. Cosgrove grunted as he nodded, giving his grudging consent. I waited. Carrick signaled to a constable sitting outside near the window, who opened the door.

"Yes, sir?"

"Hayes, please return Mr. Boyle's weapon to him. He is on loan to us from the Boston police."

"The lot, sir?"

"Yes. We may have need of all his charms."

CHAPTER ▪ TWENTY NINE

COSGROVE HAD LEFT for Stormont to coordinate the tracking of the Luftwaffe flight. Radar stations in Cornwall, Wales, and the Isle of Man as well as on ships in the Irish Sea were being alerted to report on the course of the Focke-Wulf Condor. Carrick was at his desk making phone calls, organizing roadblocks at all major intersections. A pot of tea and a tray of sandwiches had been brought in, which Sláine, Uncle Dan, and I dug into. I waited to be sure Carrick was deeply involved in his phone call before I edged closer to Uncle Dan and spoke in a low voice.

"Was it you who warned me about Constable Simms?"

"The note in the jeep? Yes. Did you know he'd been following you? And the day you stopped at his house in Clough, he was at home. I'd followed him there myself. Now why would he have his wife say he wasn't at home?"

"How do you know he followed me? Were you behind me every second?"

"Don't get hot under the collar, Billy. I figured I'd keep an eye on you and let you lead me to Taggart. Meanwhile, I noticed Simms shadowing you."

"He must have seen me in Armagh then."

"What's this about?" Sláine asked, glancing at Carrick.

"Not sure yet," I said. "I think Simms was involved with the killing of Pete Brennan, the GI whose body turned up in the trunk of that Austin the day I met you on the road. But I need to be certain before I say anything to the district inspector. Hey, you never told me how you came to be there so early in the morning, did you?"

"No, I didn't," she said.

"Was it Jenkins or Taggart who informed you?"

"Jenkins didn't. How could Taggart have?"

"Right," I said, watching her eyes. They blinked twice.

"Roadblocks will be in place within thirty minutes," Carrick said as he poured himself some tea. "Any suggestions for our next move?"

"Nothing," I said. "Is there, Subaltern O'Brien?"

"No, sorry. I was famished, I'm afraid I lost focus for a moment. Mr. Boyle, is there anything else you saw or heard that might be of use?"

"Did you know Taggart moved his family up here under an assumed name?"

"No, we didn't," Sláine said. "Do you know where they are?"

"Dead," Uncle Dan said. "Killed in the German bombings in 1941, right after he brought them up here. His wife, Breeda, and their twins, Polly and Adrian. Sweet-looking children too. Named after his mother and half brother."

"How do you know their given names?" Carrick asked. I could barely pay attention. A little voice in my head was trying to tell me something.

"Taggart's aunt told me. Showed me pictures of the three of them. The poor thing obviously hadn't heard yet. It'll break her heart."

"Were there pictures of any other relatives? The half brother?"

"Yeah. As a young fellow."

"Is this him?" I asked, pulling a picture from my pocket, the one from the newspaper, showing Sam Burnham and Constable Simms directing traffic in Clough during maneuvers. Uncle Dan squinted, holding the paper at arm's length. Then he closed his eyes to draw out the memory, like I'd seen him do in years past. Cleared out the cobwebs, he said.

"Yes, that's him," he said, his finger tapping on the picture of Adrian Simms.

"What do you mean?" Carrick asked.

"What I mean is that this Simms fellow is the half brother of Red Jack Taggart, at least according to Taggart's aunt."

"Impossible!" Carrick said.

"Why?"

"It just isn't . . . possible."

"This morning I reviewed Taggart's and Simms's files at Stormont," I said. "I think it is."

"Why does MI-5 have a file on Simms? Did you suspect him of anything? Why wasn't I told?" Carrick was fuming, directing his anger at Sláine. Uncle Dan looked amused.

"We have files on many people, just for reference. He wasn't suspected of anything, and his file was little more than biographical," she said.

"That's right," I said. "I didn't think the family details were important but Taggart's mother, Polly, was Protestant. She married a Catholic and raised their son in the father's faith. That was Jack. He left home in 1916 to join the Volunteers. His father died from the Spanish flu, and Polly later remarried, this time to a Protestant named Simms."

"That must be why Simms was not admitted to the Royal Knights," Carrick said, half to himself.

"Who the hell are they?" Uncle Dan asked.

"Long story," I said. "Right after young Adrian was born, Polly and her second husband were caught in a cross fire between the RIC and the IRA. Both were killed, and Adrian ended up being brought up by his aunt. I'd guess that she knew Polly and her husband would have wanted him brought up Protestant, so she obliged."

"What would Red Jack have thought about that?" Uncle Dan asked.

"We know he's an atheist—that's part of his Marxist beliefs," Sláine said. "It's not about religion with him; he'd abolish all churches if he could."

I stared at the picture of Sam with Adrian Simms. What had Sam said to me just before Taggart opened fire? That Adrian had told him about the funeral, and to dress in his Class A uniform. I remembered Adrian leaving the room, just before the shots.

"Taggart and Simms are working together," I said.

"I can't accept that Simms would work with the IRA simply because he shares a parent with Taggart," Carrick said.

"He isn't. They're both working for themselves."

"Explain yourself," Carrick said as his back went rigid and his eyes narrowed in righteous disbelief.

"I think Adrian Simms brought Sam Burnham to the wake to be killed. It always seemed to me that Taggart targeted Sam deliberately, then shot up the house without hitting anyone else."

"Why, in God's name? Why would Simms do such a thing?" Carrick said.

"Because he was crooked. He worked with Jenkins and was involved in the black market and any other rackets he had going on. He had a lot of secrets."

"Even if that were true," Carrick said, the disbelief fading from his voice as his policeman's mind started turning over the details, "why would Simms have a hand in killing Lieutenant Burnham?"

"Sam Burnham spent a day wandering around Armagh and was identified by a grocer near the Northern Bank. That's Jenkins's bank but it's also where Simms has his accounts. I had a conversation with a fellow there—the janitor, a Catholic—who told me that recently the bank manager gave him and a new teller the afternoon off. I described Taggart, and he said a man like that had been to see McBurney but his name was Lawson. He wasn't sure if it was Taggart. He was afraid to say more. When I described him to McBurney, he wasn't eager to answer questions. Said the Black Knights were everywhere."

"Where does the afternoon off come in?" Sláine said.

"That was Lawson's second appointment with McBurney. It could well have been the same day Sam was in Armagh. My guess is that Simms brought his half brother into the bank as Mr. Lawson, telling McBurney some story about him, and that only trusted employees should be allowed to see him. I'd guess that visit was a surprise. And an even bigger surprise was when Simms and Taggart, posing as Lawson, ran into Sam on the street. It was his death sentence."

"Because Simms knew that sooner or later, Lieutenant Burnham would see a picture of Taggart," Sláine said.

"Exactly," I said. "And he couldn't afford for his link to Taggart to be known. He also had a hand in kidnapping Pete Brennan as he was about to be paid off by Jenkins. Another loose end cleaned up, since Brennan had both seen Taggart in Clough with Eddie Mahoney and had evidence against Jenkins."

"And you say Simms was working with Jenkins?" Carrick said.

"Yes. Jenkins might have been happy to let Brennan go but I bet Simms talked him into saving his money. That way there was no risk that Brennan could place Taggart anywhere near Simms. The sighting at Clough must have been too close for comfort."

"How does this bank figure into everything?" Uncle Dan asked.

"It's the perfect cover for a Catholic extremist," Sláine said. "Create a new identity, have a customer vouch for you, and you've got your money hidden away in a Protestant bank, protected by a Royal Black Knight, no less. Perhaps Simms alluded to the Red Hand, or something equally secretive, so that McBurney would handle everything discreetly."

"So that's where the money is, the money that Taggart embezzled," Uncle Dan said. Clan na Gael money.

"Yes," Carrick said, drumming his fingers on the table, his tea long gone cold. "That seems likely. But at the moment, money is not our main concern. The guns, Taggart, and the German agents are."

"Does it seem likely that on the one hand, Taggart would steal from the IRA," Sláine said, "and on the other hand, work with the Germans on their behalf?"

"The same Germans who killed his family," I said, half to myself. A picture started to form in my mind. A picture of two half brothers, united in death, despair, and disillusionment. "Forget the politics. Taggart and Simms both lost their mother to a gun battle, no telling which side fired the killing shots. Then Taggart serves in the Spanish Civil War and loses his idealism. He returns to Ireland, drinks heavily for a while, and is finally able to start a normal life. He's still working for the cause but he has a regular job, marries, starts a family."

"Then they send him north," Sláine said, picking up on the thread I was weaving. "He brings his family under an assumed identity, thinking they'll be safe. But they're not. German bombs find them, and he's lost everything. Again."

"Maybe he started skimming the sweepstake money before, or maybe that was the trigger," I said. "Either way, I think he got in touch with his half brother, Adrian Simms, and made common cause with him."

"Them against the world," Uncle Dan said. "Against the Brits, the Americans, the Germans, the rest of the Irish, damn all in their eyes."

"Did you notice a change in him, Sláine?" I said it softly, watching her eyes. She didn't look at me. She didn't answer.

"What do you mean?" Carrick said.

"Tell them," I said to her. She raised her face, a small twitch at one corner of her mouth betraying her emotions. Her eyes glistened for a moment but she sat up straight, one hand laid flat on the table as if to steady herself.

"Taggart and Jenkins, they both work for me," she said. "Worked, I should say."

"That's insane," Carrick said. "What could those two do for you?"

"Maintain a balance," I said. "Each of them taking care of the worst of their own lot. Or did they kill each other's rotten apples?"

"They took care of their own," she said. "Jenkins was easy. What he wanted most was protection and to eliminate his rivals. Taggart was more difficult to manage. He wanted money."

"Does MI-5 have money problems?" Uncle Dan said.

"He wanted a good deal of money. I needed to keep it a secret, and the greater the sums, the more likely someone would question it."

"You sanctioned murder? Actually paid them to assassinate their own people? In my jurisdiction?" Carrick sounded astounded at the scope of it.

"It was necessary," she said, making a fist and pounding the table, rattling teacups. "You have no idea how many revenge killings we stopped. The more brutal the attacks, the more necessary it was to eliminate the attacker. Like stopping an infection before it spreads."

"And you kept on meeting with Taggart, even after the theft of the BARs? Even after he killed Sam Burnham?"

"It was all part of the agreement, with both of them. That was separate from everything else. They understood that I might need to investigate them with one hand and pay them with the other."

"You can't separate murder from everything else. You can't deal with men like Jenkins and Taggart and expect them to maintain some sort of code of honor," I said. "Jenkins wound up hanging from a rafter, and you almost got blown up, twice."

"I didn't expect honor. I thought I knew what each of them wanted. With Jenkins, I think I did. He needed to be the top man, to have the respect and fear of all those around him. I insured he'd be untouchable, and he did the rest. I never really understood with Taggart, although he seemed to be satisfied. Pleased with himself actually. He took large sums from MI-5 and still played the IRA rogue."

"And you never questioned him about the weapons theft?" Carrick said.

"No. It was part of the agreement. When we met it was always about the task at hand. It was understood that neither would use the situation for any other purpose. We used a drop, a different one for each of them. Sergeant Lynch would leave a message whenever we needed to meet."

"One of them told you about Brennan, didn't he? How else would you have known about it?"

"Yes. Jenkins did. He said he had nothing to do with it. He was afraid the Americans would think he had killed their soldier, and that I wouldn't be able to protect him."

"Now we know why the same car was used by Taggart and Brennan's killer," Carrick said. "Simms had easy access to the vehicle. It confused us, which was probably the intent. Do you think Jenkins was in on it?"

"Just a guess but I'd say Simms talked him into going along. Which may be why he ended up in that noose," I said.

"Well, it seems to me that Red Jack is a man on the edge," Uncle Dan said. "Playing each side against the other, and planning something big. If he were simply in it for the money, he'd be long gone by now, wouldn't he?"

"Both he and Simms," I said.

"He hasn't legged it. Why is he still here? He's got his sixty grand, plus all the money from the sweepstake, tens of thousands of dollars. He could have the Northern Bank wire it where he wants. He could be in Switzerland or Rio, anywhere. What's keeping him here?"

"He's waiting for the other thing he wants, if you're right." Carrick said. "He has money; all that is left to him is revenge."

"Revenge for his family, for his losses in life," Sláine said. "But revenge visited upon whom exactly?"

"All of us," Carrick said. "God help us, all of us."

CHAPTER ■ THIRTY

CARRICK HAD SENT a squad out to round up Simms but he was nowhere to be found. He had set the wheels in motion for a Crown prosecutor to investigate the Armagh bank, McBurney, and the accounts of the mysterious Mr. Lawson but that wasn't going to help us right now. He'd also put in a call to Major Cosgrove, then pointedly asked us to leave his office. Uncle Dan was stuck with Constable Porter, one of the men who had been at Jenkins's warehouse. Carrick had called Porter his "escort," but it was clear he was also a minder, charged with keeping Uncle Dan on a short leash.

Sláine had watched Carrick on the telephone with Cosgrove through the office window, lines of worry furrowing her brow. I wondered if Carrick was considering charges against her, then decided he was actually wondering if he could make them stick. In time of war, MI-5 personnel were not likely to be brought into a courtroom. But it was easy to see that Sláine's schemes went far beyond what Carrick was willing to condone. He was a straight arrow, maybe not a great friend of the Irish Republic but a policeman you could count on to go by the book. And the book didn't countenance assassinations, no matter how carefully balanced between extremist groups. Still, he didn't strike me as naive, and unless he had a couple of aces up his sleeve, he wasn't going to handcuff Sláine O'Brien anytime soon.

Sláine was the one with the worries. She was quick to come up with a reason to leave RUC headquarters. The only link we had to Simms was his wife, and we both thought it worth a visit to see if we could shake any information out of her. It was better than sitting around waiting for reports from a string of radar stations, so I told Uncle Dan and Constable Porter where we were headed, and that we'd call in after we talked with Mrs. Simms.

Former Corporal Finch had been quick about finding sergeant's stripes, and he gave them the occasional glance as he drove us south, through Carryduff and Ballynahinch, small market towns with gray granite buildings marked by rows of four-stacker chimneys. Rain splattered on the windshield as the sky darkened. We had a wet and cold night of waiting ahead of us.

"I never should have let you see those files," Sláine said. She stared out the window, streaks of rain making tiny rivers across the glass. She tapped a finger against her lips, calculating where she'd gone wrong, granted me too much, and revealed her dealings with Catholic and Protestant devils.

"Then we wouldn't have made the connection between Taggart and Simms," I said.

"I'm not sure how important that is in the larger scheme of things. What you have to understand is that there always will be a divide in Ireland. The solution is managing it."

"And managing it is more important than recovering the stolen weapons?"

"Fifty automatic weapons are serious, I grant you. But I had an opportunity to maintain an equilibrium, possibly for years. What's fifty guns, which may or may not ever be used, against that?"

"I get nervous when people who work for outfits like MI-5 use words like equilibrium when they mean murder, even if the victims are killers themselves. Call it what it is; don't try to dress it up. At best, you're a vigilante," I said.

"And at worst?" She traced a line on the glass, her finger leaving an arc in the condensation.

"That's not for me to say. Uncle Dan once told me that we all know the worst of ourselves, and that it's only the truly evil who let themselves off the hook."

"I saved lives. I did."

"Yes," I said, but at what cost to her soul? I wasn't the one to judge her, I knew that much.

We stopped at an intersection as a column of trucks crossed in front of us. A sign pointed toward Lurgan, where tomorrow at this time the

Royal Black Knights would be gathering at Brownlow House to honor their American cousins and do whatever secret societies did. Some sort of ritual perhaps? Funny clothes, handshakes, odd titles? I wondered if Cosgrove was a worshipful master of some sort, and if he'd enjoy being saluted as such. Maybe I should drop in and give all those Protestant bigwigs a real Boston Irish surprise.

"What do you know about the Royal Black Knights? Are they really a harmless bunch of lodge brothers?"

"Harmless implies a lack of power, which they are not short of. They are a step above the Orange societies and provide stability among the professional classes. Not dangerous but hardly harmless."

"All heavy hitters?"

"Pardon me?"

"Important men. Movers and shakers."

"Ah, I see. Yes. I can't think of any leader in business or government, not to mention the military, who isn't a member."

"And you would know. You probably have files on all of them."

"Lists of members, certainly. Some names are too important to keep dossiers on. At least in the official files."

"Really? Well, maybe you won't have to worry about losing your job if you know all those secrets."

"It wouldn't be my job I'd be worried about," Sláine said.

"What do you mean?"

"My position offers certain protections. But I do have enemies, and it might be difficult to sort out who was responsible if one of them got to me. After what happened today, have you rethought the matter of the bomb at the hotel?"

"No. It must have been Taggart, right? He had a supply of plastic explosive."

"I don't buy it. Think about it. He must have already set up Jenkins's death and planned the trap for all of us. Then why go through all the trouble of planting that bomb to kill me the night before? It doesn't make sense. He's the one suspect we can eliminate."

"You're right," I said. "Simms?"

"I don't see why. He's already taken care of Brennan and Burnham. As far as he knows, we haven't made the connection between him and Taggart yet."

"So who else wants you dead?"

"That could be a long list. The real question is who needed me dead *now*?"

I didn't have an answer for that. Thinking about all the people who'd like to kill you doesn't make for cheery conversation, so I let it drop as Sláine gazed at her reflection in the window. I couldn't tell if there were tears in her eyes or if it was the rain splattering against the glass.

We passed the Lug o' the Tub Pub and the boreen leading to Grady O'Brick's cottage. We pulled up in front of Simms's house. Rain dripped off the thatch but the smell of a fire promised warmth. I knocked on the heavy wooden door as Sláine and I huddled beneath the overhanging thatch, water catching our backs.

"Yes?" Mrs. Simms said, opening the door wide. "Are you looking for Adrian?"

"Yes, ma'am, we are. May we come in?" She stood there, the wind blowing rain into the house and carrying her loose black hair into swirls around her head.

"Of course, forgive me," she finally said, as if she'd just woken up. "Lieutenant Boyle, isn't it? Here, let me take your coats, it's a sinful night to be out."

"This is Subaltern Sláine O'Brien," I said, shaking the water off my trench coat. She nodded at Sláine as she helped her with her raincoat with no trace of animosity. From the little I'd seen of her, and from what I'd heard about her, I didn't expect a warm welcome for two Catholics. But Sláine was in a British uniform, and that probably helped. She hung our coats on pegs near the door, and gestured to chairs near the fire.

"Please, sit." She clutched a shawl at her breast as she sat on a straight-back chair, leaving the two cushioned seats for her guests. It was all very cordial but there was something about her hair and the way she gripped the shawl that looked wrong. Before, she had been very prim and tidy. Now she looked like a wild woman, her hand crushing the shawl in her grip.

"We need Adrian's help," Sláine said, smoothing out her skirt. "Have you seen him today?"

"He's my husband, isn't he?" she said, evading the question. "All the same, I don't think you should count on him for much help."

"We're all on the same side, Mrs. Simms," I said. "I know there are differences here that go back centuries but we do have a common enemy."

"You know, I said the same thing to Adrian just this morning. That whatever happened in the past, we all have to do our part now."

"This morning?" Sláine said. "Was that when you saw him last?"

"Oh no, I've seen him since then. What do you need him for?"

"It's important," Sláine said.

"German agents," I said. "We need him to help us find German agents." I watched her face as she looked back and forth, at us, around the room, to the door leading to what had to be the kitchen, as if she expected Adrian to walk in at any moment. "Are you expecting someone? Is Adrian here?"

"Do you think I don't know where my own husband is? Do you think I'm mad, is that it? He's my husband, he is. A good, God-fearing Protestant. No more, no less. A man I'll spend my life with, right here, in this house. Not off to some other land."

"Mrs. Simms?" Sláine prompted. Something about the woman's conversation was odd.

A faint odor penetrated my senses. Not the scent of the peat fire, not the smell of a cigarette. Something else.

"When you marry," Mrs. Simms said, cautioning Sláine, "you expect your husband to be who he says he is. But all men have secrets, I suppose. One secret, even a shameful one, could be forgiven. But not another. Not one that betrays everything you hold dear."

She began to cry, with big gulping sobs. She let go of the shawl, her hand covered her mouth, and the shawl slipped from her heaving shoulders. Her blouse was stained dark red between her breasts, but there was no wound. Then I recognized the odor. Cordite lingered in the air, the faintly peppery smell of spent gunpowder drawing out another terrible and familiar scent.

"Have Finch drive to the pub and call Carrick," I said to Sláine as I walked to the kitchen door. Mrs. Simms was hunched over now, silent, her head buried in her hands. I entered the narrow room, the smell of death heavy in the air. Gunpowder and blood, whiskey and piss. Adrian Simms faced me, seated at the end of a small kitchen table, his face tilted toward the ceiling, his mouth slack. His revolver lay on the table, surrounded by a box of shells and cleaning gear. Bore brush, rags, an old toothbrush, and solvent. A bottle of whiskey had been tipped over, the amber liquid soaking into the tabletop. A broken glass lay on the floor.

One shot to the heart. Simms wasn't in uniform. He had on a white shirt, sleeves rolled up. A dark hole above his shirt pocket was tattooed with gunpowder marks, the dried blood coating his shirt and soaking his trousers. He hadn't died right away; he'd had a minute, maybe two, as his blood flowed.

"He told me we had to leave," Mrs. Simms said, coming up behind me. She was wringing her hands, her eyes darting from me to her dead husband. "Leave, can you believe it? Hide, like criminals, all because of his hideous half brother, that Bolshevik killer. He said we would go to South America. South America!"

"With Jack Taggart?"

"I said, 'No, I am not leaving this house!'" She hadn't heard me, wasn't speaking to me. She pushed against my chest, her arm extended, pointing at her husband, continuing the argument that had ended with a bullet. "'And neither are you. Would you make a laughingstock of me again, you liar? How dare you!'"

I could see it all, Adrian telling her that they had to go. Maybe he said the money was all for her, so she could be a high-society lady somewhere south of the equator. He'd laid his revolver down, finished with cleaning and loading it, ready for whatever the night held—German agents, the U.S. Army, everyone except his own dear wife. Maybe as he raised the glass to his lips, she'd grabbed the revolver, two-handed it, and pulled the trigger, less than a foot from his chest.

"Gold, he said, hard cash and gold, just a few hours away. Well, no one from my family ever ran off like a thief in the night, gold or no gold," she said, her eyes fixed on her husband's once-white shirt.

"What gold?" I asked, easing her out of the kitchen.

"German gold, he said it was. That wasn't Adrian, that was his bad blood speaking. Catholics, Communists, and Germans. Did he think I'd consort with them? Take their money and flee my own nation, my family, my church? He was insane, don't you see? It wasn't his fault."

Her face softened as some memory of the man she loved crept in and dissolved her hate and anger for a moment. I could imagine her placing the revolver on the table, hugging Adrian as he gasped for breath, the shock widening his eyes as his shattered heart pumped the last of his blood, staining his wife's blouse, his dreams of revenge and wealth fading with each pulse, then gone.

"What will I do now?" Mrs. Simms said, seating herself in one of the good armchairs by the fire. Her chair, next to her husband's.

"We'll get this all sorted out," I said as soothingly as I could, as if it were all a matter of paperwork. "Tell me, did he say anything about where the gold was? Was he going to meet Taggart tonight?"

"Don't speak that name in my house," she said, drawing the shawl around her.

"I'm sorry. The gold, that he said was only a few hours away. Do you know where?"

"He didn't make any sense, he must have been off his head. He wasn't responsible, you know; it was that terrible half brother of his."

I heard the door open, and Sláine walked in ahead of Finch, who stood guard at the entrance. There was no wind now and his coat was dry.

"Have you come to take him away?" Mrs. Simms asked. "I have to clean up, I don't like a messy house."

"What was it that didn't make sense?" I asked. I smiled, trying to keep her with me for another minute or so. She was retreating, falling back on memories and delusions, blotting out the present of betrayals and failures, her visions turned inward. "What did Adrian say?"

"That it was above us. Right above us. Do you think he meant in the attic?"

"I don't know. Didn't he say it was a few hours from here? It has to be someplace else."

"Oh dear, I suppose you're right. You can ask Adrian when he gets home." With that, she relaxed, staring at the glowing peat, and sighed.

"A few hours away, and above us," I said to Sláine. "What does that mean?"

"The German Focke-Wulf 200? It should make landfall within a few hours."

"But we don't know where," I said.

"There's only one place above us and a few hours away," Finch said from his post by the door. "Slieve Donard, that great bloody mountain that's at our backs. About half a mile up."

CHAPTER · THIRTY ONE

I STOOD OUTSIDE the house, watching the clouds break up and stars begin to show in the east. The rain had passed. By the time the Focke-Wulf made landfall, the half-moon would give enough light to find the drop zone, probably with the aid of a signal fire courtesy of Red Jack.

"You should be able to make out Slieve Donard soon," Sláine said, pointing south. "It's the closest peak to Newcastle, and the highest of the Mournes. It blots out the stars."

"Have you been up it?"

"Yes, it's a pleasant climb in daylight and good weather. Steep but not difficult. There's a bit of a plateau just before the last stretch up to the summit. That's where I'd look for parachutists. Tricky but if the pilot gets close enough, he should be able to put them spot-on."

"Red Jack could be up there right now, preparing a signal fire," I said.

"More likely a torch—what you Yanks call a flashlight. It's above the tree line and he'd have to drag an awful lot of wood up there for a sustained fire. But the plateau is protected by mountain walls, Slieve Donard on one side and Slieve Commedagh on the other. The Glen River runs between them, and that's the route we'll follow. Beyond the river the terrain flattens out before the final ascent."

"We?"

"Of course. You're coming, aren't you?" She opened the trunk of the car and pulled out boots, clothing, and a Sten gun. "Finch called the RUC from the pub. They're sending a constable from the next village, and Carrick is on his way, probably with your uncle. You drive while I change in the backseat. And keep your eyes on the road."

I backed out of the drive, listening to the sound of fabric being pulled off and on, resisting the temptation to risk a backward glance. She had a submachine gun.

"I'm going to make a call for reinforcement," I said, stopping at the pub. "Where should they meet us?"

"We don't need a company of gum-chewing, heavy-footed GIs getting in our way," she said. "No offense."

"Not a problem," I said. "But I know some guys who have been training up and down those mountains. A reconnaissance platoon."

She came in with me, now wearing sturdy boots, camouflage jacket and trousers, with a web belt and revolver. I was glad she'd left the Sten gun in the car.

"What's going on?" Tom asked, staring at Sláine in her combat duds as she adjusted her beret. "That sergeant burst in here and demanded to use the telephone, said it was an emergency."

"It was. Still is, so I need the phone too."

"What emergency, Billy Boyle?" Grady O'Brick asked from the end of the bar. "What trouble have you got yourself in now?"

"Not me, Grady. Adrian Simms is dead."

"Jesus," Grady and Tom said at the same moment. I went behind the bar and called the division HQ, speaking to the new executive officer, Thornton's replacement. He was eager to please.

"He said there's a stone bridge across Glen River. They'll meet us there," I said to Sláine.

"How did he die then?" Grady asked me, ignoring Sláine.

"Bullet to the heart," I said.

"IRA? Red Hand? Smugglers?" Tom asked.

"His wife."

"Jesus," they said again.

"We have to go," Sláine said, cutting the conversation short. "There will be a lot of RUC men by shortly; they may need directions to Constable Simms's house."

"And where are you going, lass?" Grady said, his first acknowledgment of her presence. He raised his glass to his lips, watching her as he drank. I saw her eyes on his fingers, and wondered if she knew his story. If not his story, then if she knew what it meant.

"Away from here, old man."

I glanced at Grady as I followed her out. He was laughing, a wheezy, ancient laugh, and I wondered what could possibly have struck him as funny, having just heard of the death of Adrian Simms by his wife's hand, and then been insulted by an Irish girl in a British uniform.

We drove through Newcastle, into Donard Wood, past HQ, and along a dirt track until we came to the stone bridge. Three jeeps were parked off the track. I didn't see anyone until armed men appeared from nowhere, surrounding the car, blackened faces staring through the windows, weapons pointed at us.

"Lieutenant Boyle? I'm Sergeant Farrell, follow me please," one of them said, lowering his weapon.

"Here's your gum-chewing Yanks, Subaltern," I said as we got out of the jeep.

"My mistake, Billy. They appear fairly competent."

"Is that you, Billy?" Bob Masters said, shining a flashlight with a red night-vision lens in my face. "Who's that with you?"

"Yep, that's me. Thanks for joining the party. Lieutenant Bob Masters, this is Subaltern Sláine O'Brien. British Army."

"Sláine?" he said, pronouncing it carefully, to be sure he understood. "That's a girl's name, I thought." He shined the flashlight beam on her, and one of his men whistled.

"Shaddup," Masters said in a low growl. "Beg your pardon, Subaltern. I didn't expect a female, that's all. I assume this is not a drill?"

"Not a problem, Lieutenant. And this is for real." Sláine briefed Masters and his men, giving them Taggart's description, telling them about the FW-200 and the German agents.

"There may be other IRA men, or Taggart may be alone. We've no way of knowing," she said.

"This is the guy who stole the BARs?" Masters asked.

"Yes. He may be armed with one," Sláine said.

"Not if he's as smart as you say. I wouldn't hump one of those things up a mountain, an M1 is heavy enough. There are extra canteens, wool caps, and gloves in the jeep if you need them. Billy, you want some extra armament?" Bob asked as he watched Sláine check her clip.

"No, I have my .45. I think we have enough firepower as it is."

I took a canteen and gloves, and we headed up a rocky path that followed the river, which was swollen and overflowing from the recent rains. Water splashed down the hillside. The path was narrow, and at times it was easier to go rock to rock in the water, catching a bit of moonlight outside of the canopy of trees. The only sounds were boots on hard earth and smooth stone, gurgling water, and the labored gasps of my own breathing. In no time I was soaked in sweat, my thighs aching from climbing the steady incline and my lungs heaving to draw in enough breath for the next step. I looked at my watch. We'd only been at it for fifteen minutes. I stopped to take a drink and splash cold water on my face.

"You OK, Lieutenant?" It was Callahan, the Irish kid in Masters's platoon. I remembered his voice from the mess hall but I wouldn't have recognized him in broad daylight. His face was blackened and a GI wool cap was pulled down tight.

"Yeah," I said, trying to sound normal. "Little out of shape maybe."

"Hell, we've run up this thing a few times. A walk in the park."

Then he was gone. I moved as quickly as I could, not wanting to be overtaken by the Tail End Charlie or to be outpaced by Sláine, both of which were distinctly possible. Pride won out over exhaustion, and I caught up to her about thirty minutes later. Masters had called a halt and was signaling two men to move ahead as I came upon them.

"Tree line ends ahead," he said in a whisper. "They're on point. Not a lot of room to spread out up there, steep walls on either side of the valley. We move out as soon as they check out the icehouse."

"Icehouse?"

"Yeah, you'll see it. Like a big stone igloo, built a hundred years ago, they say, over an underground chamber they kept filled with ice where they stored food all year round. Be a hell of a hiding place now."

We waited. I didn't hear a thing but after a couple of minutes a GI appeared in front of us and gave the all clear signal. Then he was gone, and Masters had us head up the treeless path one by one, spaced out so we could see the person ahead of us but not make easy targets. I began to wish I did have a rifle so I could use it for a crutch. I began to hate Red Jack Taggart all over again. This was worse than being shot at.

I cursed silently as sweat dripped into my eyes. I cursed Taggart, I cursed Sláine O'Brien for coming along and having legs like a jackrabbit. I cursed Major Cosgrove and Uncle Ike for sending me here. I cursed the highest mountain in Northern Ireland, and I cursed Andrew Jenkins for getting himself killed before I had time to eat my lunch. I got into a rhythm of cursing, damning the Irish for their feuds and the

English for being here. I cursed Pete Brennan for his greed and Sam Burnham for standing in front of the window. I cursed a blue streak at Diana for wanting to be a spy and at Adrian Simms for not being satisfied with his life as a cop. I cursed his wife for wanting him to be something he wasn't, but found I was cussed out when I thought about her shooting him. That at least was logical, as terrible as it was. He should have known her better.

Who was left? Should I curse myself? Grady O'Brick came to mind, and what he'd said when Sergeant Lynch drove by. *The curse of his own weapons upon him.* And the next morning, he was dead. Maybe I should lay off the cursing. Sooner or later I'd come to yours truly, and to be honest, I had some coming. I'd been a bum with Diana, I knew that. It didn't change how I felt about her taking chances with a Gestapo interrogation but it hadn't been my best moment.

And I felt like a traitor to everything my dad and uncle had taught me about the struggle to free Ireland. I hadn't changed my mind about the British overlords but I saw things from a different angle, one that revealed the suffering that comes with unresolved hate. God help me, Sláine's plan to kill off the worst of each side had made sense to me, at least in the early stages. But I knew that when people in uniform started playing God, sooner than later they unleashed demons beyond their control.

So I cursed myself among all the other Irish. For believing in fairy tales that masked sectarian slaughter. For not thinking about where things led. And for failing my grandfather, Liam O'Baoighill, who wished to send an avenging warrior back to the old country, to strike hard at the British masters. Instead, here I was, gasping for air about a quarter mile up, scrambling over rocks by the light of a half-moon to put a stop to an IRA plot to do just that.

Damn my eyes.

Crack. Crack. Two sharp sounds, pistol shots maybe, echoed off the rock slopes on either side of us. Impossible to pinpoint the source. We all froze, waiting for the next shots, wondering if they'd be aimed our way. All my curses were forgotten, as an unspoken truth flashed through my mind: *I'm glad it wasn't me.*

Callahan was in front of me, and I could see him ease himself down, slowly, quietly, making a smaller target. His head swiveled, eyes and ears searching for the sound of boots or metal, maybe a wood stock laid down on granite to steady the aim. I did the same, except that the climb, altitude, and fear all combined to keep my breathing ragged, my nose running, and my heart pumping so hard I couldn't see anything beyond dark, gray rocks. Sláine appeared at my side, pointing up to the right. Her arm pulled at my shoulder, her lips next to my ear. I could feel her hot breath and excitement.

"Pistol shots, up by the wall." And then she was gone, holding her Sten gun close to her chest, cradling it so it wouldn't scrape against a rock. I'd never seen a woman so at home with cold metal, even Diana. At this point, it was her only salvation. Even Major Cosgrove of MI-5 couldn't let her contract killings go unpunished, especially since a straight arrow like DI Carrick knew about them now. She had to bring back Taggart, if only to enable her to go out with her head held high. Taggart dead, that is. Alive, he knew too much. Personally, once a guy fires an automatic weapon at me, I take a dim view of his longevity. But I didn't want Taggart shot full of lead before we got everything he knew out of him and found the BARs. Then Uncle Dan or Sláine could do what they needed to do. I owed Red Jack Taggart no justice, no day in court, no sympathy for his politics. He had killed a friend, had tried to kill me, and now maybe he was killing someone a few hundred yards above us.

It was time. I gasped for air, and took off after Sláine. I caught up to her huddled with Masters. He pointed to two men and they went off the trail, hunched low, to hide among the rocks.

"Rear guard," Masters whispered to me. "They'll block the path in case he gets past us. That shot came from Slieve Commedagh, the peak to our right. If we get up to the Saddle—the ridge that connects the two mountains—we might be able to nab him as he comes down."

I nodded. I didn't have enough air in my lungs to ask questions: What if he hears us coming? What if he does have a BAR with him? What if it was a shepherd shooting at a fox? None of the answers mattered. Shots had been fired, and we had good reason to believe Taggart was up there. If we were right, odds were he had pulled the trigger.

"Let's go," I said, trying to sound as if I'd caught my breath. Masters rose and started off at a slow trot, taking rocks like stairs as the trail rose from the plateau, curving up to the Saddle, where the Mourne Wall ran between the peaks. It marked some sort of reservoir system, twenty or more miles of stone wall, over five feet high and nearly three feet thick.

It wasn't the Great Wall of China but it was impressive. I'd never expected to see it, much less while hunting a killer in the dark.

It seemed easier taken at a run. I felt lighter jumping from rock to rock than carefully picking my way. My fatigue faded and everything around me grew clearer by the faint light of the partial moon. At my back I could hear the wind blowing up from the sea, rushing over the landscape. The stars were sparkling against the blue-black sky, the ridgeline a smooth black line beneath them. As we neared the top of the Saddle, I looked down, taking in the wide bowl we'd just come through, the place we thought the parachutists would aim for. Maybe they'd been blown off course or maybe they hadn't shown up yet. Maybe the plane had gone down or gone home, a malfunctioning engine saving everyone a lot of trouble. Maybe this, maybe that; it didn't feel right to me.

Masters signaled us to halt. He sent Callahan ahead at a crawl to peek over the top where the path led to an open area. Then he signaled us one by one to follow, motioning with his hand, palm flat to the ground, to keep low. I followed Sláine, head bent, watching for loose rocks, one hand gripping my automatic. We gathered in the lee of the wall, the wind surging against it, breaking over it, swirling loudly around us. We were at the lowest point of the Saddle. The Mourne Wall rose in either direction, up Slieve Donard to our left and Slieve Commedagh, where the shots had come from, on the right. Masters sent two men scrambling up the Slieve Donard side, left two behind to block the path, and signaled Callahan to take point, moving up, up, up, along the incredibly straight wall, heading directly for the peak. The terrain dipped and then rose again. Callahan held his hand up for us to halt as he raised his head, scanning the remaining distance to the top.

A shot boomed out, and Callahan's head snapped back, blood coating the wall as he fell against it, limp as a rag doll.

"Spread out," Masters yelled as he ran to Callahan, saw he was beyond help, and raced to the right to peer over the edge. He gave one of his men some quick hand signals I couldn't make out, and in a second he was over the top of the wall, covering our other side. Another shot came, loud enough to be recognizable as coming from a high-velocity rifle. This one missed, but sent rock chips flying.

In silent understanding, Masters and his men stood at the same moment and unleashed a fusillade, then ducked, reloaded, and without a glance at each other, rose again, firing M1s and Thompsons in a second thunderous response. Again they went down and reloaded but this time when they rose they ran, without a word, to the top. I followed, figuring the idea was that Taggart would lie low, expecting a third volley.

I came to the crest, .45 in hand, pointing it at every shadow I saw, gasping for air, each breath a deep, rasping struggle. I blinked sweat from my eyes. Masters and his men spread out, and I went straight, feeling as if I were at the center of a bull's-eye. A howling roar rolled up from beneath us, a churning wind from the sea blowing itself a half mile up, low and insistent, like a freight train with its horn blasting. When it hit, it almost bowled me over, knocking me down on one knee. A white form jumped up in front of me, towering over my head, snapping at my face and enveloping me. I fell back, recoiling from a demon, a ghost, a killer, a mountain wraith, I had no idea. The wind gusted again, loud and insistent, and the whiteness descended on me. Without thinking I fired three quick shots, not knowing what I was shooting at or if the bullets would take it down.

The wind dropped, and I felt the smooth silk of a parachute as it fell limp across my face. I'd shot a German parachute. Hands pulled at me, helping me up and bundling the parachute. Masters signaled silence, and the group formed a circle, facing out in every direction, squinting in the darkness for a sign of movement, listening for a footstep. Nothing but the sound of a dying wind over rocks. Our own breathing. The soft flap of silk in the breeze. Moonlight and stars, the sea below us. It was as if no one else existed, except for Callahan, dead, and Taggart, alive.

"Look," I whispered. The parachute had been half buried beneath rocks. The wind had blown the exposed section in my face. In another second I would've stepped on it.

"Over here," Sláine said in the same low voice. A few feet away lay a body.

"Fallschirmjäger," Masters said pointing to the distinctive helmet of a German paratrooper. He checked for a pulse but he didn't need to bother. Two blackened bullet holes were clustered over the heart. No blood was visible; the paratrooper had been dead before he hit the ground. His belt was off, his long smock unbuttoned, and pockets turned inside out. His pistol was still in its holster, and one of the GIs grabbed it, an unexpected souvenir.

"Looks like Taggart searched him after he shot him," I said.

"For gold," Sláine said. "He must've found it."

"I wonder if he went off course?" Masters said.

"No, I don't think so. I think Taggart signaled them to drop here instead of the flat area below. It would be easier for him if they were dead or injured when they landed."

"So where is the other man?" Sláine asked. It was a good question.

A sharp *crack* tore through the night, followed by *zing* as a bullet hit rock and ricocheted, inches from her head. We dove for cover as a second shot followed from the direction of Slieve Donard.

"Move down, along the wall," Masters said. "We're silhouetted up here. Move!"

Firing broke out as we slid our way down, hiding in the gloom along the base of the thick wall. The shooting stopped as we met up with our rear guard, joined by the two GIs Masters had sent up Slieve Donard.

"Dead Kraut up there, about halfway to the top," one of them told Masters.

"Shot?"

"Nope. Neck broke, I think. His chute was ripped to pieces, looked like the wind dragged him along the ground. We checked him for papers, and look what we found. C'mon, Sweeney, show him."

"Jeez, some guys have no sense of larceny," Sweeney said. With a show of reluctance, he lifted a heavily laden bandolier from around his neck, an ammo bandolier, in the same camouflage pattern as the paratrooper's smock. There were six pockets on each side, secured by metal snaps. Sweeney opened one, and even in the dark, by dim moonlight, it glittered, filled with gold coins, the German eagle on one side, Kaiser Wilhelm on the other. Kaiser Bill, my dad would have called him. There were lots of Kaiser Bills, and I understood the look on Sweeney's face.

"Don't worry," I said to him. "I knew about the gold. There wasn't a chance you could've gotten away with it."

"That's a relief, Lieutenant. They're all yours then. Damn things are heavy." I put on the bandolier and felt the straps dig into my shoulders. That was a big drawback to gold. It was valuable, sure, but in any quantity it was like lugging around a cast-iron stove.

"Anything else?" Masters asked.

"Yeah, sniper rifle," Sweeney said. He held out a Kar98k, the standard German infantry rifle, fitted with a Zeiss scope.

"The other Kraut must have had one too," Masters said. "And Taggart has had us in his sights."

"Think he got around the rear guard?" I said. Masters looked down into the valley, the dark mountainsides vanishing into murky gloom beneath us. Then he looked to the east, where a thin line of pink light showed at the horizon.

"He knows what he's doing, so, yeah, we should count on his being below us. And dawn isn't far away. We need to hustle after him right now or else stay put. It'll be light enough for him to pick us off in thirty minutes, unless he's hightailing it out of here. What do you think?"

"Taggart won't be able to resist taking another shot at us," Sláine said. "Especially since we have half his money."

I nodded. There were ten of us now but that wouldn't seem like impossible odds to a guy with a sniper rifle hidden in the rocks, a few hundred yards separating us from him. Throw in a touch of derangement, and it would seem like a sure thing.

"OK. Let's go." Masters led this time, point being the most dangerous spot. We ran in the darkness, against the dawn that would illuminate us, keeping our heads down, watching the ground and risking glances at the terrain ahead, waiting for a shot to find us. We passed the icehouse and went into the trees, hopping from rock to rock in the stream until that became impossible. We caught our breath in the woods off the path, soaked in sweat, gulping in mouthfuls of air.

Pop pop pop. Pop pop. Gunfire sounded below us. It was too far away to be aimed at us, but each of us tightened our shoulders and hunched low. The shots increased; the loud, rapid fire of a BAR stood out.

"The jeeps," Masters said. "It's coming from the jeeps, by the bridge."

"But we didn't leave anyone there," I said. "Who's being shot at?"

"I don't know," Masters said, "but I'm tired of this bastard running rings around us. If he's caught up in a firefight, we have a chance to take him."

Masters had a plan. He split his men into two groups, each taking one side of the trail, heading for the jeeps. He took one, Sergeant Farrell the other; one of them was bound to outflank Taggart. Sláine and I were to wait two minutes then go straight down the path. I think we were an afterthought, and Masters simply wanted us out of the way. They vanished into the woods, and I checked my watch. The gunfire continued, small bursts punctuated by single shots, the kind of shooting that goes on when both sides are under cover and no one wants to expose themselves.

"Do you think all will be forgiven if you bring in Taggart?" I asked Sláine.

"Accounts will be settled as far as I'm concerned," she said. "Then they can chuck me out of the service or assign me to file papers and make tea, I don't care."

"But you did care about keeping things in balance."

"In case you haven't noticed, the world becomes an awful place otherwise. Someone has to do something to maintain order. I did, and ultimately I failed. But I did try."

A breeze rustled the leaves around us, and I thought of the ghosts of Ireland, all the souls lost in the struggles with the British, and with our own people. Some of those ghosts were my ancestors, and one was Sláine's father, shot dead for ordering armed men to halt as they sought to alter balance. The breeze gusted, turning into a howl, swirling the branches around us. Sláine put her hand out and held onto my arm. Her touch was electric. I took her hand. I kissed her, felt her press against me, and then we broke apart. We stared at each other a moment, the branches still whipping around our faces. We didn't speak as we started down the path, to the place where people were killing each other.

CHAPTER ▪ THIRTY TWO

ONE OF THE jeeps was in flames. The smell of burning tires and gasoline drifted into the trees. Rolling black smoke surrounded us, giving us added cover as we slowly crept down the path, trying to puzzle out who was doing the shooting. Occasionally a round zipped through the trees around us or a yell emerged from the chaos below, curses laced with Irish accents between bursts of lead. We edged closer, the emerging sun and the light of the fire revealing at least one body near the burning jeep. It looked like it wore an RUC uniform but in the murky smoke I couldn't be sure.

Rapid bursts came from our left. Sláine tapped my arm and pointed. I could see the muzzle flashes across the small stone bridge, coming from a jumble of boulders on the far side. BARs. Pistols and rifles responded from behind the jeeps, but that group seemed outnumbered and outgunned. Sláine ran ahead to a better vantage point, rose from a crouch, and fired her Sten gun at the BARs, guessing that was Taggart and his gang. She emptied her clip, and as she ducked to reload, both groups aimed their fire in our direction, unsure of who we were, and worried about their flanks. We were showered with leaves and small branches until the firing let up.

"Wait," I said. "Wait until Masters opens up. They're too far away. He'll drive them out into the open." She worked the bolt on her Sten, giving me an icy look. She wanted blood, and she wanted it *now*.

"Taggart!" a voice yelled out. "Give yourself up in the name of the Crown!"

That was Carrick, and although I thought him a smart policeman,

I wasn't sure this was the best choice of words. The only reply was a volley of fire.

"Taggart," another voice boomed out. "This is Dan Boyle. Give up now, man, there's nowhere for you to go!"

"Damn you all," Taggart screamed back and began firing again. This time it was an assault, not a standoff. I caught a glimpse of Taggart, waving men on. He had the sniper rifle and a half dozen or so BAR-wielding gunmen followed him, blasting away at the jeeps and the few RUC huddled behind them, along with my Uncle Dan. I stood and fired at Taggart, and Sláine did the same, but the distance was too great for accuracy. We dove for cover as one man sprayed BAR fire in our direction. Bullets smacked into tree trunks and ricocheted off rocks as we covered our heads.

A new source of heavy fire broke out, driving the IRA men back. It was Masters's group, running and firing as they came alongside the RUC, dropping two BAR men in their tracks. Then Sergeant Farrell's men arrived from the other direction, creating a deadly cross fire. The IRA gunmen scattered, seeking shelter among the rocks.

"Get down," I said, pulling on Sláine. "There's too much lead flying around."

"My bloody weapon is jammed anyway," she said, banging on the bolt. We kept our heads down, listening to yells and howling voices while M1s and Thompsons overwhelmed the staccato sound of the BARs. It was extraordinarily loud, the way combat is when men shoot at each other up close, seeing the look on their enemy's face as they pull the trigger, rage, fear, and blood lust ripping screams from the throats of the living and the dying. Emerging from the all-enveloping sound was a new one, a man thrashing his way through the undergrowth, branches snapping, boots pounding on uneven ground, grunts and gasps as he strained at vegetation in his way, drawing nearer as the sounds of the fight below dwindled. I held my automatic at the ready, trying to pinpoint the direction of the sound, swinging it back and forth as to ward off a wild beast from the woods. Sláine ejected the jammed rounds from her weapon and scrambled to put in a new clip, her eyes wide with fear.

Taggart burst through the bushes, his face covered in blood, his mouth twisted in rage. He held a revolver in one hand, the other covered with a hasty bandage, soaked red.

"You! Goddamn you both!" Spit flew from his mouth as he cursed us. He looked like the devil, blood staining his skin red, the wild look in his eyes as maniacal as it was gleeful. I pulled the trigger but the shot went wide. I pulled it again and got nothing but the *click* of an empty magazine. Taggart grinned, and then pointed his revolver at Sláine, empty Sten gun in one hand, full clip in the other. He pulled the trigger, shot her in the chest, and grinned even wider. I watched her fall as he aimed the pistol at me and fired. I saw the blast, a bright orange flame shooting out, but I didn't feel a thing. I looked at my left arm and saw a neat hole just above the elbow, black scorched edges turning red.

"Next one will be in the head," Taggart said as he grabbed me by the collar, dragging me along with him. I tried to find Sláine but everything was hazy. I've been shot, I kept saying to myself. He shot me. I felt blood dripping thickly down my arm. He did it on purpose, I thought. Just enough to put me in shock yet keep me on my feet. Smart guy, I had to give him that, as he propelled me down the path, right to a gaggle of armed men who wanted him dead. I felt the hot barrel of his revolver pressed behind my ear as he jammed it against my head, his other hand firm on my shoulder. "Try anything funny and I'll take you with me," he hissed.

"Don't shoot!" Taggart yelled. "Don't shoot or the Yank is dead." He hid behind me as much as he could, tightening his grip on my shoulder. As sweat streamed across my face I felt his hot breath, smelled blood. His hand was covered in it. It was warm and sticky against my neck, and for a second I wondered if he really was the devil, carrying me off to hell. I knew it was shock but I felt strangely in his power, this bleeding demon driving me through the woods.

"Hold," Carrick said. "Don't move."

"Oh, I'll move, I will, or you'll be picking up the pieces of this bastard Yank's skull."

"You'll be dead within seconds if you do that," Carrick said reasonably as he walked closer, casually reloading his Webley revolver. Uncle Dan was behind him, his gun hand down at his side, his eyes darting everywhere. He moved two steps to his left.

"We all have to die," Taggart said. "I don't care, it's as simple as that. It would bring me joy."

"Why don't you care?" Uncle Dan asked. "You have all that money you stole."

"Ah, you must be the enforcer from Boston. I've heard about you. Working with the RUC, are you? Strange bedfellows, eh? Now put down your weapons, and order your men to do the same."

"Where can you go?" Carrick asked. "We'll find you." He hadn't put his gun down.

Masters and his men had rounded up the wounded IRA men and those who hadn't gotten away. They were on the other side of the bridge, too far away to intercede. Two RUC constables were closer, and looked to Carrick for direction.

"No, I'll find *you*," Taggart said. "And you'll pay, you'll all pay."

"For your wife and children?" I asked, struggling to get the words out. He ground the barrel of the pistol against my skull.

"No, he's nothing more than a crook," Uncle Dan said, taking one step forward. "He was stealing from us long before they died."

"Stop!" Taggart said. "It's everything, all of my wrongs. My family, my mother, killed. My half brother, hounded out of Dublin for who he was. We were going to get even for all the failures, all the deaths, the senseless brutality. You have no idea what I saw in Spain. What I did there, what I did here. What was it for? So the Irish could live like contented sheep? Or serve the British? When Breeda and the kids were killed by the bloody Germans, that's when I decided to bring you all down, to let you all feel the pain. And you will, whether I live or die. The money would have been nice but you can't have everything. I've come to prefer chaos myself."

"Just one question, Taggart," Uncle Dan said. "Just one."

"What?" He spoke through gritted teeth, eager to get on either with his escape or his big exit.

"Do you know Sammy Bazzinoti?"

I felt the muscles in Taggart's hand tighten. I went slack, dropping my head and letting my feet fold at the ankles, trying to be deadweight. I saw Uncle Dan raise his gun hand, closed my eyes, and waited. I heard the shot, thunderously loud, and felt the spray of hot blood at the back of my head. I fell out of Taggart's iron grip and went down on my knees, praying the blood wasn't mine.

"My God," I heard Carrick say. "Quite a shot."

"Sláine," I managed to get out. "He shot her, up there." I tried to point but pain stabbed through my left arm as I tried to raise it. I turned to use the other. Carrick sent out a constable, followed by a couple of GIs with medic packs. Uncle Dan kicked the pistol from Taggart's hand but it was nothing more than a routine cop gesture. The shot had gone neatly through his right eye, exploding out the back in a much messier fashion.

"How bad is Subaltern O'Brien?" Carrick asked. I noticed he was bleeding too, holding a handkerchief to one leg.

"I don't know. He shot her point-blank, then hit me in the arm and dragged me down here."

"And who is this Sammy character?" Carrick asked Uncle Dan.

"Sammy Bazzinoti owns a nice deli back in Boston. He was robbed at gunpoint, and it went bad. A cop was coming in just as the guy was pulling his gun. Young rookie name of Billy. The guy takes Sammy hostage, puts a gun to his head. I get called to the scene, and Billy's got it all contained, all the other customers are out. So I go in to see what I can do. Sammy sees me with my gun out and faints dead away. The guy loses his grip and I plug him. End of story."

"He shot him in the right eye," I said.

"Steady hand you've got there," Carrick said as he stared at Taggart's corpse. "Too bad you didn't get to recover the money you came for."

"I didn't come for money," Uncle Dan said, gazing at the corpse.

Then I felt dizzy. Someone tried to keep me from falling but it was lights-out.

CHAPTER THIRTY THREE

I WOKE IN an ambulance, Uncle Dan by my side, supporting me. We were perched on a fold-down bench seat. Opposite us I made out Sláine on a stretcher, being attended to by a nurse. Her face was white. Her shirt had been cut away, and there was a compress bandage pressed to her chest, far enough to the right that it looked like the bullet had missed her heart. Maybe. The nurse had an IV working and held the stretcher steady as the ambulance rumbled over an uneven road. My coat and shirt had disappeared. I looked at my arm, saw the bandage. It started to hurt. The pain cut through the hazy veil of shock and fatigue.

"How is she?" I asked, surprised that my voice came out in a tight croak. Uncle Dan put a canteen in my good hand and I drank.

"She's alive but I can't tell how bad the damage is. Still, alive is good, and we should be at the base hospital in a minute."

"Which base?"

"Ballykinler. It's the closest hospital."

Ballykinler. Where it all started. The theft of the BARs, Pete Brennan, Thornton, Andrew Jenkins, Carrick, Taggart, Sam Burnham, all the names involved in this mess had passed through Ballykinler at some point. But the list seemed incomplete. I was missing somebody, something, and I tried to fix a face in my mind, but all I saw was Uncle Dan, leaning close, his hand on mine.

"You did good, Billy. Your father'll be proud when I tell him, he will."

His words felt like water, cleansing me, washing over me and carrying me home. I rested my head on his shoulder and wondered if

Sláine felt her father's distant pride. If she lived, I could ask her. And if I could remember who the missing face was, everything might be OK. But I couldn't keep my eyes open and fell asleep in my uncle's arms, as I had so long ago, chugging back into Cohasset Harbor, into the setting sun, the silence of men sweet in my dreams.

"WHAT . . . where am I?" My eyelids were heavy with deep sleep and I blinked, trying to pry them apart and figure out what this place was. I was in bed on a nice soft mattress and under white sheets. I was wearing pajamas, and after the last day and night I was ready to stop fighting and lie back. Enjoy it, a small voice told me. But then a more insistent sound clamored inside my head, asking who I was missing. Who was the missing link? Just to shut the voice up so I could sleep, I gathered enough energy to open both eyes and look around, hoisting myself up on my good arm.

I was in a hospital room. Bandaged arm, I remembered that. Everything else seemed OK. I rubbed my hand on my neck where Taggart had pressed the barrel of his pistol. It was bruised and sore. I swung my feet off the bed and let them hang there as I stared at the other bed in the room, occupied by Uncle Dan, shoes off, tie loose, softly snoring. I looked around for a clock, then saw my wristwatch on the table. It was after one o'clock. Five or six hours, maybe, since the fight at the bridge.

The fight. That was one of the things bothering me. How did Taggart's men know to be there? When had he summoned them? No one else knew we were going after him. For that matter, how did Carrick find us? Sláine hadn't told anyone where we were going. I wanted to know how she was doing too, but business came first.

"Uncle Dan," I said. He snored even louder. I sat on the edge of his bed, to shake him awake.

"What? Billy, how are you feeling? How's the arm?"

"It hurts like the devil. Never mind that now. How did you know where to look for us? At the bridge."

"Hugh brought me along when we got the call about Simms. When I couldn't find you, I asked him to call the base over in Newcastle, and the officer there said you'd gone up the mountain with a squad of men. When we got to the jeeps, they opened fire. They must have been waiting for you."

"But they couldn't have been. Except for the executive officer, no one else knew where we were headed, and even he didn't know why we were going or who we were after."

He sat up, crossing his arms behind his head. It was his usual position for conjecture. "Perhaps Taggart's men thought he was going to double-cross them, so they sent a security detail. They were expecting gold, weren't they?"

"Maybe. But it's more likely that only Taggart and Simms knew about the gold."

"Now what exactly was their plan, Billy boy? I understand Taggart was out for revenge and all—"

"I think Taggart and Simms were close, closer than half brothers divided by religion might be expected to be. They both lost their mother to sectarian violence, and both lived on, damaged. Simms never fit in up north, and Taggart lost his ideals in Spain, then his whole family here. He'd given everything for the cause, and all he got out of it, at the end, was pain and grief. By now, most of the Irish are content with things the way they are. Exhausted, if content isn't the right word. Either way, they've settled into neutrality in the south and accommodation in the north."

"I see what you mean. It would be a powerful disillusionment for a man who'd given everything to the cause. So they set up a scheme to steal from all sides—the army, the IRA, the Germans, whoever they could—and leave Ireland behind them."

"Yeah. Simms planned to take his wife along, and that was his big mistake. No beach in Rio for her. But Taggart wanted something more. He wanted the money but with him, I think, there was a desire to strike at the people who failed him."

"The Irish people."

"I think so. It's exactly what I was sent here to investigate. A plan that involved the IRA and the Germans, an uprising in the north that might draw the Republic into the war. That's what the fifty BARs were for."

"At least it's down to forty-four now. We recovered six at the bridge. Three lads dropped them and skedaddled, two died with their boots on, and one was shot through the lungs. He was alive an hour ago but barely."

"How's Sláine?"

"Still in surgery. The head doc said he'd stop by once they were done. Said she had a chance, a fair one. Can't say I think much of an Irish lass working for the Brits like that but still, that's quite a woman. If anyone can survive, she will. Are you two, ah . . ." He waved his hand back and forth, a motion that meant anything from holding hands to a romp in the hay.

"Strictly business, and none of it yours."

"Whoa, Billy, can't you tell your old uncle what you're up to?"

"You'd never believe it. Tell me, did Carrick know any of the IRA men?"

"No," he said, serious again. "He said they didn't seem to be from around here. No identification, not even a wallet or a watch. Probably brought in from cells in other counties."

"Did you hear about the Germans?"

"Aye, the Germans and the gold. They sent a party up to recover the bodies. Hugh and I searched them thoroughly, the Germans and the IRA boys. No evidence. Nothing except this." He drew a gold coin from his coat pocket. One of the Kaiser Bills.

"Jesus! Does Carrick know you took that?"

"Now, Billy, it's not like I stole it. That dead German had it in his pocket. Maybe he wanted a little insurance or maybe it was his own souvenir, I don't know. But since it had become his personal property, I see no reason why it shouldn't be mine. Booty of war, it is. It'll make a nice present for your mother. She doesn't always look kindly upon me, to tell you the truth."

They said philosophers split hairs. "OK, OK. Keep it out of sight. And when did DI Carrick become Hugh? Are you guys pals now?"

"Don't get your knickers in a twist, Billy. He's not a bad sort for a Scots-Irishman. Not that they're my favorite bunch but he's a fair cop, I'll give him that."

"Is he around?"

"No, he left about an hour ago. Said he had to get into his fancy dress for some lodge meeting tonight. He's got roadblocks set up everywhere, and they're checking IDs at train stations, buses, that sort of thing, still looking for those other two Germans who came ashore."

"And forty-four IRA men carrying BARs."

"Them too, but with Taggart dead they've no leader. And they'll be hard to miss, especially if any of them stop off in a pub. I've had a close association with that group, you might say, and they're not the most close-lipped bunch. I'll bet you we'll hear something soon."

"Odd we haven't, isn't it?"

"How do you mean?"

"Well, obviously MI-5 and the RUC have informers."

"All cops have informants. So?"

"But no one has reported a thing about the BARs. And you haven't heard either, even with your connections."

"Right," Uncle Dan said.

"And Taggart himself was the flamboyant type, not the type to plan something quietly, keeping it under his hat. Remember, he already had openly used a BAR."

"You think maybe there's someone else? The quiet brains behind the operation?"

"It makes sense, doesn't it?"

"In a crazy sort of way, I get your point. But what is the operation? And how do we find out who's really behind it?"

"You sure there was nothing on the bodies that might give us a clue? Or anything that happened during the fight? Could you tell if they had a leader?"

"All I knew was that they were shooting at me. Taggart sounded off a few times but as you said, he was half mad. No one else stood out."

The door opened and a doctor in an operating gown came in, faint sprays of blood across his chest. "Lieutenant Boyle? We just finished with Miss O'Brien. She's come through the worst. She's lost a lot of blood but if she remains stable for the next twenty-four hours, she should fully recover."

"Should?"

"There was a lot of damage, a good deal of internal bleeding. The next day or two will tell."

"Can I see her?"

"Later. Right now she needs to rest. She wouldn't know you were in the room anyway."

The doctor left. I was glad I didn't have to see her right away. I'd visited enough wounded cops half dead in hospital beds already, and I preferred to see her semi-upright and talking.

"Let's get out of here," I said. "Where are my clothes?"

"Oh, I almost forgot. Bob Masters, that lieutenant you took up the mountain, he came by earlier with some things for you. Everything you had was muddy and bloodstained so he brought what you'd need. I took your lieutenant's bars off your old clothes and put them on the new duds. And I got your boots and automatic when they brought you in. Didn't want some orderly walking off with your armament."

"Thanks. Is Masters still around?"

"No. He went back up Slieve Donard with a Graves Registration detail. To bring the bodies down."

"Too many dead bodies around here, before these guys even reach the shooting war," I said as I pulled on my shirt, wincing as I lifted my arm.

"There are places where the ground calls out for death, Billy, and this is one of them," Uncle Dan said, helping me with my web belt as he might help a child to dress. "And they'll be more if we don't finish this thing. Oh, I almost forgot it. There was this little wooden pig in your pocket too. What the hell is that?"

"A good luck charm that lost its power," I said as he handed Pig to me. I put him in my shirt pocket, and it felt like he belonged there. No harm in keeping him, I thought, as long as I don't start talking to him.

"Where to next?"

"The bodies," I said. "Are they here?"

"Yeah. In the morgue. You can always count on an army hospital to make room for the dead."

It might have been the few hours of sleep or the clean clothes but it was most likely walking out of a hospital room under my own power that gave me a thrill, that survivor's joy at having lungs, legs, and eyes that worked and moved as they should. I owed most of that to Taggart for not killing me. He had needed me mobile but subdued, and a through-and-through flesh wound was the quick and smart way to do it. I was lucky, I knew it. I also knew not to say it out loud, since Uncle Dan was famous for his thinking on the subject of luck. If you were really lucky, I could hear him say, you would have shot him dead first and been done with it.

They'd stripped the bodies. I looked at each man, naked and laid out on cold stainless-steel tables in the morgue. Washed down, their bodies looked pale, the whiteness punctuated by gaping bullet wounds. Each was small and wiry, the descendants of the famine generation, their frames a testament to rule by Britannia. Two had healed wounds, bullet holes in a leg and shoulder.

"They have the look, don't they?" Uncle Dan said in a quiet voice.

It was tinged with admiration, even though they'd tried to take his life the night before.

"Yeah. Their hands are rough but not callused like farmworkers."

I sorted through their clothes, laid out on a table opposite the bodies. Typical wool pants, collarless shirts, caps, and shoes that you'd see on any man on the street, in a pub, or at work. Not their Sunday best. The pants were spattered with mud—no surprise there, since they'd been out in the wet weather.

"Not a single piece of identification but that's standard practice. Even the labels were cut out," Uncle Dan said, showing me the inside of a shirt.

"I don't think Red Jack Taggart would have thought of that. Why isn't he here?"

"Hugh—DI Carrick to you—moved the body to Belfast. Proof that he'd been taken."

"Did you get a look at his clothes?"

"Yes, we went through everything. Now that you mention it, his tags were not cut out."

"I'd say that means someone else was in charge of the IRA men. You checked everything?" I knew it was a dumb question, and I avoided Uncle Dan's eyes as I felt along seams for anything hidden.

"Of course, what am I, a rookie? Jesus, Billy, you take nothing for granted, do you? I taught you well." He gave me a playful push on my arm, and I winced. "Sorry, lad, I forgot about the arm. Well, here's one small thing I did notice. These boys must have been doing some sort of farmwork before they came hunting you. Look."

He turned out the cuffs on several pants. A fine, gritty line of dark brown powder and fibrous material fell from each. I rubbed it together between my fingers and smelt it.

"Is it fertilizer?" Uncle Dan asked.

"You're no farmer, that's for sure. But you are an Irishman. Don't you know the smell of dried peat?"

"Jesus," he said. "I've heard of it all my life but never ran across it in Boston. I've smelled it burning here but never paid it much mind. So these boys all had been handling peat? Maybe working for some farmer as a cover, you think?"

I stared at the peat on my fingertips. Was it possible? I thought it through, and everything fell into place. No, I finally saw what had been right in front of me all along. It was all there—logical, deliberate, deadly, and cunning.

"You still have your revolver?"

"Yes and a new box of shells, courtesy of the RUC. Why?"

"I know where the BARs were hidden. They're probably gone by now but it's worth a shot."

"You could do with a better choice of words, Billy. Lead on."

CHAPTER ▪ THIRTY FOUR

WE STOPPED AT the hospital switchboard and I put some calls through. First to the executive officer at division HQ. I had him organize the I&R Platoon to meet Masters when he came down the mountain, and told him where the platoon was to rendezvous with us. Then DI Carrick's office but he wasn't in. I left the same information and thought for a minute about calling Major Cosgrove but I didn't. Either he wouldn't believe me or he'd send in his heavy-handed goons.

"We're on our own for the moment," I said. "Come on, let's find a jeep."

"Don't you sign them out from the motor pool?"

"Yeah, well, that takes paperwork, and paperwork takes time."

Once outside, I checked the jeeps parked in front. They all had drivers, sitting in them or leaning against fenders, smoking and passing the time as they waited for their officers. I signaled Uncle Dan to follow me around back, where a row of ambulances stood without drivers or anyone who might care if we borrowed one. One was still parked by the rear doors, maybe the one that brought me in. A medic's helmet with the distinctive red cross was on the seat. I opened the car door and signaled to Uncle Dan.

"Get in, you're driving. Button up your trench coat and put the helmet on."

"I wonder what you get for grand theft auto in Ulster," he said as he pushed the starter pedal.

"Don't worry about the RUC; this is army property. They'll probably shoot you."

"So where are we headed?" He turned onto the main road leading to the gate, grinding the gears as he got used to the three-quarter-ton vehicle.

I told the sentry at the gate we were headed to a convoy accident on the road to Lurgan, hoping he wouldn't look too closely at Uncle Dan and notice his nonregulation shoes and pants, not to mention his age. He managed to look bored, like any GI driver with a second louie in the passenger's seat.

"OK, what's the deal?" he said as we pulled through the gate, opened by another bored private not at all impressed by my state of urgency.

"Take this left," I said, pointing to the road to Clough. "There's a reason those guys had peat in their cuffs. The BARs were buried in stacks of the stuff, in a croft a few miles from here. I knew the BARs had to be close by but I never guessed I'd been within feet of them myself. There's an old fellow, Grady O'Brick, who lives in a cottage not far from the Lug o' the Tub Pub in the village."

"Poor old boy with his fingernails gone, right? Courtesy of the Black and Tans is the story I heard. Drummed out of the IRA for giving up an arms cache back during the war. After seeing what they'd done to him, it seemed a bit harsh to me."

"That's his story. But I think it was a ruse, an excuse for him to go underground. He told me, and others confirmed it, that his IRA cell had a reputation for keeping quiet, planning and carrying out operations without the Brits getting wind of a thing."

"This is beginning to sound familiar."

"When I first visited Grady, I drove down the boreen—that's a dirt track—and I noticed broken branches all along the shoulder. I'll bet that was from Jenkins's truck bringing the BARs there to hide them beneath the stacks of peat bricks drying in the croft. And I'll lay odds that there are newly broken branches there now that they've just been taken away."

"I know what a boreen is, lad; do you think I just came up the Liffey? But why Grady O'Brick? There's got to be dozens of peat crofts around here."

"I didn't put it all together at first but he was there when we found Pete Brennan's body. He drove his cart by, and had words with Sergeant Lynch. I think Grady recognized him, and maybe even the staff car. I mentioned to him in passing that I was going up to Belfast with a

British officer the next day. He could've easily had Lynch and Sláine followed, and planted the bomb, or had it planted, since we know the IRA has plenty of plastic explosive. Plus, he was in the pub when we stopped to call the base. He saw Sláine with me, probably overheard the call. He must have known Taggart was up the mountain and called out the reinforcements when he found out we were going up after him."

"He seems like a harmless old gent, Billy. Are you sure?"

"It's the only thing that fits. He was present when I met Sláine and Sergeant Lynch on the road, and he was in the pub when we called the base on our way to Slieve Donard. So he was behind the hotel bomb and the ambush at the bridge. Everything that happened had the hallmark of a careful planner, which by his own admission, he is. But most of all, it would be the perfect revenge. He was tortured over a Lewis gun, did you know that?"

"No, I didn't."

"He gave it up after they pulled out nine fingernails. The Brit pulled the tenth for the hell of it."

"Jesus, they are a bunch of bastards for all their grand civilization, aren't they? So now he's taking an old man's revenge, turning automatic weapons on them in repayment for one Lewis gun. And he was in league with the devil himself, mad Jack Taggart, to get his revenge."

"Turn here," I said as we passed the pub.

"Why are you so sure the weapons will be gone?"

"Because they need to get into position before everyone arrives at Brownlow House, for the shindig the Royal Black Knights of the British Commonwealth are throwing tonight. Black tie and dress uniforms. Americans and British, armed services and the RUC. The cream of Protestant Ulster society and their Yank guests. How's that for an opportunity to start a shooting war?"

"God, the man's a genius," Uncle Dan said with fervent awe. "You know those so-called knights are not the firebrands, Billy. Most of them will look down their noses at us and try to put us in our places but they like things neat and stable. Yet if you kill enough of them, the ones left will be crying for blood in the streets."

"I know. And if that happens, what will the IRA do?"

"Accept about ten thousand new recruits and head north. Then the Republic will have to step in, and God knows where it will all end."

"It's what Sláine warned me about in Jerusalem. Here it is, turn left."

"Jerusalem? You do get around in this war."

He slowed the ambulance to a crawl as he turned the wheel to enter the boreen. The wheels straddled the track, rolling over the gorse with its yellow flowers and spiky vines. Stretching ahead of us was proof of what I'd suspected. The gorse had been flattened the whole way, the ground beneath still muddy and churned up from yesterday's rain. Another vehicle, larger than Grady's horse cart, had been through here today.

We parked in front of Grady's cottage and got out, guns drawn. But I wasn't worried about an ambush; I was certain the IRA men were gone. We checked the house and it was empty, the picture of the bloody rabbit still next to Jesus carrying his cross down the Via Dolorosa. His choice of artworks had seemed strange when I first saw them but now they seemed the perfect pair of pictures for Grady to stare at during his long nights by the fire, planning his retribution. A small animal, hunted and mutilated, next to a man whipped and tormented, carrying a heavy burden to his death. It's a strange world, that place inhabited by those who have been harmed and plan harm to others. A house of sadness, pity, and terror, drenched in dreams of blood. I shivered as I turned from the pictures.

"Look at this," Uncle Dan said, moving some papers on a rough wood table with the barrel of his revolver. It was a copy of the *Ulster Gazette* about five years old, opened to a photo spread of Brownlow House, a history of its architecture, and pictures of the adjacent park. "You were right. We better get over there with backup."

There was nothing else in the cottage, no evidence other than an old yellowed newspaper. The croft was a different story. Peat bricks were strewn and trampled down everywhere. Piles had been taken down and open sections revealed the perfect hiding places for crates of BARs and ammunition. Broken wood planks were scattered about, the military nomenclature spelling out *Rifle, Caliber .30, Automatic, Browning, M1918* in dozens of pieces. An empty bandolier and a few bullets dropped in haste were all that was left.

"I have to say, Billy, I'm feeling a bit outgunned here. Is the cavalry on its way?"

"I don't think Masters is back down the mountain yet. Hopefully, DI Carrick will get the message before it's too late." I holstered my automatic and leaned against the truck, cradling my arm and lifting my head to the sun. The sky was a brilliant blue, everything washed clean from the rains. There was a chill from the damp ground but the sun warmed my face. Uncle Dan stuffed the revolver in his pocket and sat on the bumper.

"We've got to do more than hope, boy. Why not call out more troops? Brownlow House is an army headquarters, after all."

"Same reason I didn't called Cosgrove. If GIs and a security detail show up, Grady will go to ground. We can't let him get away. He'll simply plan something else."

"So how do we catch him?" Uncle Dan lit a cigarette, spitting out a piece of stray tobacco. "The two of us surround forty-odd armed men and tell them to give up, it's hopeless?"

"How would you get that many men with BARs close enough to attack Brownlow House? I mean close enough for them to have a chance of getting inside."

"Two things to take care of first," he said. "Take out the security in place, and then secure against reinforcements."

"OK, how would you do that?"

"Well, a diversion maybe. Something to attract the attention of the guards. Draw them in, cut them down. And I'd place a team on either side of the main drive to take out any vehicles bringing in reinforcements. BARs would be just the thing."

"All this assumes the main assault group is close by, ready to take advantage of the diversion and move in."

"Sure. Otherwise it's a waste of time. But how?"

How? How could you smuggle that many armed men into a guarded military facility?

"Jesus H. Christ on a crutch," I said, borrowing one of General Eisenhower's favorite curses. "They do it the same damn way they stole the BARs in the first place. Waltz right in!"

"Use a Jenkins truck?" Uncle Dan asked.

"You said the man was a genius. When he had Taggart kill Jenkins, it was for two reasons. One was to get us together and kill us with one booby trap, but the other was to get Jenkins out of the way to make it easier to steal a couple of his trucks in the confusion after his death. His firm is bound to be one of the suppliers for the event, so no one would think to check them."

"You know, Billy, I never believed what they said about you. You're a smart one after all, you are."

CHAPTER ▪ THIRTY FIVE

WE PARKED THE ambulance in an alley with a view of the entrance to Brownlow House. A black wrought-iron fence surrounded the property, but the gate was wide open. We watched a few jeeps come and go, and endured the stares of civilians passing by. With the ambulance's Red Cross markings, we were fairly conspicuous. A few buildings down, on our side of the street, cars began to park near a church, and men in black suits began to gather out front. Uncle Dan got out and strolled down the sidewalk for a look.

"That's a Protestant, Church of Ireland, crowd," he said when he returned. "Those fellows look like they could be with the Royal Black Knights. Might be getting ready for a parade or some lodge ceremony, although there's only nine of them so far, talking and having a smoke. They have rolled-up banners and the like."

"Maybe they're going to have a procession, from the church to Brownlow House. They'd make nice targets, like ducks in a line."

A few minutes later they'd gone inside the church, and two deuce-and-half trucks pulled over to the side of the road. Sergeant Farrell got out of the lead truck and I signaled him to come over to us.

"Where's Masters?" I said.

"We got in touch by walkie-talkie, and he told us to go ahead, to meet you right away. He's maybe thirty minutes behind us."

I gave him a brief explanation of what we expected, and told him to send in teams to sweep the woods on either side of the main drive. "Stash the trucks out of sight somewhere, and radio Masters to meet us on the grounds. We'll probably be with DI Carrick."

We drove in past the iron gates, slowly enough to check the terrain. A gravel drive crunched beneath our tires as Uncle Dan kept in first gear, his arm hanging nonchalantly out the window. I saw his eyes moving from tree to tree, up and down the road, into the woods. I'd seen him like that in Boston, in tenement buildings and back alleys. But this was different. This was combat, and the last time he'd faced this many automatic weapons had been in World War I in No-Man's-Land.

"There," he said, nodding his head forward. "That's where I'd put them. On the curve ahead. Clear line of fire down the road. Probably a couple of them there right now."

His face was blank, no emotion, no hint of fear, turmoil, or remembrance. Nothing but steely eyes and white knuckles on the wheel. He whistled a tune, "I've Heard That Song Before," as he took the curve. I bet he had.

It was late afternoon, and the sun sparkled off the sandstone building with its forest of chimneys stark against the deep blue sky. British and American flags flew from the lantern-shaped main tower, and dress uniforms of all types were evident as small groups of officers in blue, brown, and khaki strolled the grounds. I spotted DI Carrick in his dark green RUC uniform, walking with a plainclothesman. They were eyeing the perimeter, where the woods met the manicured lawns of Brownlow House. Uncle Dan parked the ambulance, backing it in next to a deuce-and-half as if he did it for a living. Carrick had seen us, sent the other man off, and waited for us near the steps leading into the main entrance.

"Did I understand correctly? You think they're here already?"

"Yes, or will be soon if they aren't. I have Lieutenant Masters's platoon conducting a sweep through the woods, looking for a rear guard to keep reinforcements at bay. His idea," I said, hooking a thumb in Uncle Dan's direction. He'd stepped away for better view of the grounds.

"Not a bad one. With that much firepower, half a dozen men could hold up a company on that narrow drive. I have some men in uniform patrolling the grounds, not any more than would be usual for such an event. Others are in plainclothes or dressed as waiters."

"Have trucks from Jenkins's firm shown up?"

"I saw two of them leaving as I came in. Why?"

I told him my theory about Grady O'Brick and my insight into the death of Andrew Jenkins and the use of the trucks to smuggle in the men and weapons. DI Carrick didn't seem impressed.

"A Jenkins vehicle delivering food for a large dinner, well, that's not out of the ordinary. And I've been through most of the house, and my men have checked every room by now. I don't know where they're hiding if they were brought in in those trucks."

"Are all your men accounted for?"

"I'll have a count made," he said. The sound of drums rolled in from the main road.

"Is there some sort of parade?" I said.

"A short procession, from the church and through the park, in honor of our guests, members from lodges in England, Canada, and the U.S. There will be a brief welcoming speech by the Grand Master on the veranda. Then inside for the dinner. That'll be them now, forming up."

"How many?" Uncle Dan asked, rejoining us.

"Two hundred for the dinner, probably twice as many in the procession. Many of the local lodges have sent members to take part in the parade."

"Plus all the brass here to watch it. It'll be a turkey shoot if we're right," Uncle Dan said.

"I'll be back with a count," Carrick said, a worried look crossing his face as he gazed out over the flat, open lawn.

"Let's walk once around the place," Uncle Dan said. We took off, trying to blend in with the officers enjoying the late autumn sunshine, GIs, and workers scurrying around, setting up inside and out for the festivities.

"Everyone looks like a genuine GI or an unarmed waiter," I said. "You heard that the Jenkins trucks have been and gone?"

"Yeah. Let's check the kitchen, see if there's food enough for two truckloads."

There was. The staff was so busy they hardly noticed us. It took a lot of food to feed two hundred of Ulster's best, and the place was stocked with it. Several cooks were preparing racks of lamb, trimming the bones and seasoning the meat. Vegetables were being chopped, potatoes peeled and boiled, cases of wine opened, and trays of appetizers laid out. Not a BAR in sight, and everyone looked like they knew what they were doing.

We kept walking around the building. No one stopped us or asked who we were. Maybe Carrick's men knew us by now but the building sentries should have been on their toes. Yet how could they cope with this many guests flooding the place?

"I don't know what to do next," I said as we returned to our starting point. Carrick met us just as I saw Bob Masters park his jeep and head over. The two men nodded in greeting as they approached.

"All my men are accounted for," Carrick said, in a quick, clipped tone. He tried to hide his relief.

"I ran into Sergeant Farrell," Masters said. "They found a nest of four IRA men, right at the bend in the road. Two sets of BARs pointed in each direction. He's got three of them tied up and guarded."

"The fourth?" Carrick said.

"Farrell said three of them gave up easy, one went for his weapon. He had to use his knife."

"Where are your men now?" Uncle Dan asked.

"I've got two groups making a sweep of the perimeter, just inside the tree line. The rest are close, in case something happens here." He nodded his head slightly, indicating the trees nearest the house.

"Unfortunately, we don't know where O'Brick and the rest of them may be," Carrick said. "We've searched the house thoroughly, and your men are taking care of the grounds. Where could they hide?"

"Cold feet?" Uncle Dan said, without much enthusiasm.

"They wouldn't have left the rear guard behind," I said.

"We'll search the house again, but forty men armed with Browning Automatic Rifles can't be easily hidden," Carrick said.

"Did you check the tunnel?" Masters said.

"What tunnel?"

"You know, the one I told you about. Lord Brownlow's tunnel, the one he had built so he could sneak out on his wife. Supposedly it leads into the town somewhere."

"Good lord, I'd forgotten about that completely," Carrick said. "It's been sealed up for years."

"So it hasn't been checked?" I said.

"No, I doubt any of my men even know of it. How did you learn of it, Lieutenant Masters?"

"A chaplain told me. He'd been studying the history of the building."

"Very well," Carrick said, with an edge of suspicion in his voice. He didn't care for a Yank showing him up on the details of Brownlow House. "I think I remember where it is."

DI Carrick led us to a set of double wooden doors at the far side of the building, away from the main entrance and stone veranda. It was built for everyday use, not show. He pointed to tire tracks in the grass, where a vehicle had pulled close to the doors. They opened into a short hallway, with rubber boots and tools lining the sandstone walls. Cans of oil were stacked next to a large red can marked PETROL. Another set of doors led down thick wooden steps into the dank and musty smell of a basement. Carrick pulled a string hanging over the steps and a single lightbulb cast a yellow, feeble illumination into the low-ceilinged room. Masters had a flashlight and searched the far corners of the cellar with its beam. Sagging shelves choked with cobwebs, dust-encrusted barrels, three-legged chairs, and the debris of decades crowded each wall. Carrick pointed and Masters followed with his beam. It found a door less than five feet high, thick oak secured by cast-iron bands and heavy nails. It looked hundreds of years old, as did the sliding bolt lock, left open. Masters pointed the flashlight in front of the door. Prints and scuff marks of many feet were visible on the hard-packed dirt floor. Carrick put his finger to his lips, and we all backed out into the first room.

"We have them," he said in barely a whisper.

"The trick is, to get them out. Where does the tunnel lead?" Uncle Dan said.

"In the old days, it ran to Castle Street, but it's been caved in for years. I can send some men over there, just in case. But it's likely we have them boxed in. If I were that evil fellow in Mr. Poe's 'Cask of Amontillado,' then I'd say seal up the door and be done with it."

"A creative approach, Hugh, but Billy needs his BARs back. Why not let me talk to them?"

"It is my responsibility, Daniel, but thank you all the same."

"Now listen, Hugh," Uncle Dan said, turning away from Masters and me to face Carrick dead on. "You're an excellent police officer. But I nearly fell down laughing when you ordered Taggart to give up in the name of the Crown. Not that he had any notion of giving up at all, but if he had, any mention of the Crown would have driven it out of his Red Republican head. Give me a chance to talk to these lads for only a minute. If I don't have them out as meek as lambs in short order,

then you go ahead and tell them the king orders them to surrender."
He ended with a laugh, to show it was all a matter of tactics, nothing
personal.

"All right. I'll send a squad over to Castle Street. Lieutenant
Masters, bring up that squad you have close by; we'll need them if
Daniel gets lucky."

"Yes, sir," Masters said, running off. Carrick left at a more sedate
pace. I drew my .45, realizing we were the last line of defense.

"Luck will have nothing to do with it, Hugh, my friend," Uncle
Dan said to himself as he picked up the can of petrol and gave it a
shake, a good healthy slosh showing it was more than half full. I followed him down the steps but not too closely.

"If any of you boys are smoking in there, which I doubt, you'd best
put them out," he said loudly as he poured out the contents of the can
at the bottom of the door. The gasoline went *glug glug glug* and disappeared beneath the door frame. He slid the bolt shut, locking them in.
"And don't even think of firing a shot or you'll set off the fumes and be
roasted alive." Shouts and pounding echoed from inside the tunnel, the
words barely understandable through the heavy door.

"What if the other end is open?" I asked.

"Then Hugh better hurry. I couldn't wait. He'd never let me do this.
Worth a chance, Billy, don't you think?" He had to holler over the noise,
now more frantic.

"Quiet down and listen," he said, his face up against the door. "One
man talk to me. Now."

"Jesus, let us out of here, we can't breathe," came a faint voice. The
sound of panic rose behind it.

"I'll be happy to, one at a time, hands on your head. First man to come
out any different gets a bullet, and that will be the end of you all. OK?"

"Yes, yes, let us out!"

"Everyone in there agrees?"

"Yes, please, we agree!"

I heard the sound of boots behind me and saw Masters and a
couple of men behind him. Uncle Dan nodded and I readied myself,
automatic raised, dreading what might happen if I pulled the trigger.
He opened the door, and one man came out, reeking of gasoline, gasping for air, his hands gripping his hair. They all followed, leaving their
BARs behind, clambering over each other, retching, falling, all the

while clasping their heads in their hands. I watched them, looking for Grady, wondering if he'd been overcome in the tunnel. As Sergeant Farrell got the last of them out of the cellar and up to the lawn, I took the flashlight from Bob Masters and aimed it inside the tunnel. It was small, no more than four feet wide and five high. Ancient timbers supported the walls and ceiling, and about twenty yards back, a collapse had totally blocked the tunnel. No wonder they'd emerged so quickly, they'd been crammed in like sardines. The fumes were thick and I gagged. But Grady wasn't there, just piles of BARs on the ground and bandoliers of ammo strewn about.

I went out for some relatively fresh air, then ducked back for a minute to count BARs. I came up with thirty-six. Six had been taken at the bridge, and four here in the woods. That left Grady O'Brick and four Browning Automatic Rifles unaccounted for.

I couldn't wait to get out into the open. Taking in a lungful of air, I saw Masters's men standing guard over the recent residents of the tunnel, now sprawled on the ground. Gas fumes seemed to rise off them, and some rubbed at their eyes while others retched and spit.

"You could have gotten yourself blown up, not to mention burning down Brownlow House, and I haven't even begun to think about what laws you may have broken. What if they'd come out shooting, did you ever think of that?" DI Carrick stood with his hands on his hips, bawling out Uncle Dan. Then I saw him glance at the prisoners, and I knew his heart wasn't really in it.

"Hugh, you know it's one thing to fight for a cause when your blood's up. It's quite another thing to think about dying while underground in the dark, waiting for the gas to take you. It puts things in perspective, and can make the bravest fighting man weep for his home, and one more chance to see it. That's something I know, Hugh, and I'd say you do too. And whatever happens to these lads, it's something they've learned today as well, God help them."

"I won't argue that," Carrick said. "Or with the results."

"We're not out of the woods yet," I said. "Grady O'Brick and four BARs are missing."

CHAPTER · THIRTY SIX

"THEY'VE GOT TO be the diversion," I said as we got out of the RUC police car at the church. "The signal for the main group to come out of the tunnel and start the attack. That's the key to the whole operation, and Grady would see to that himself."

"Well, I'm game if it will help," Masters said, following Carrick into the church by a side door. He held it for Uncle Dan and me, and I hesitated for just a moment as I shivered at the memory of what I had been taught in catechism class. It was drummed into us that every Catholic must fulfill his obligation by attending Mass where Jesus Christ himself is physically present in the Eucharist, where prayers are offered for the living and the dead, and where reparation is made for sin. I can still remember that litany. Not to mention the fact that it was forbidden to worship in a Protestant church or, for good measure, to enter one, since they made a mockery of Holy Communion by insisting it was nothing but crackers and grape juice.

"Come on, lad, crossing that threshold is nothing compared to what we have to do next," Uncle Dan said. So I stepped inside, making the sign of the cross as subtly as I could, to ward off the sin I was committing, comforting myself that Saint Patrick himself must be watching over us and explaining to the Big Guy that it was all in a good cause.

I had started everything by saying Grady was likely to get close with his diversion, figuring he'd want to see the enactment of his vengeance after so many years. We still had no idea where he and the final members of his team were, and questioning the prisoners had revealed nothing. In the bright light aboveground, the threat of immediate immolation gone, they'd found fortitude and told us all to go to hell.

I volunteered to keep close to the marchers but I didn't want Grady to spot me either. That's when Carrick came up with his grand idea, and even Uncle Dan had to admit it was a good one.

Bob Masters had the look of a Unitarian about him, so he didn't care one way or the other. But Uncle Dan and I were about to become the first two Irish Catholics ever to march in an Orangemen's parade. Any others who ever got this close likely hadn't lived to speak of it. We'd be in the front row, fitted out in full lodge regalia, beneath the Union Jack and the rest of the heathen Ulster banners the men carried. It was the best camouflage we could ask for, and it would give us a vantage point from which to scout out Grady and his gang.

Carrick led us into a hall off the church itself. It was dominated at one end by a portrait of King William of Orange at the Battle of the Boyne, that terrible event of 1690 that spelled the end of Irish sovereignty for hundreds of years. Here it was celebrated with as much fervor as it was mourned elsewhere. The present-day king smiled from the opposite wall, and between the two English monarchs were hung banners with blood red crosses, skull and crossbones, and the fearsome Red Hand of Ulster. If someone had grabbed me and slit my throat it wouldn't have come as a surprise.

Everyone was dressed the same: dark suit, bowler hat, satin aprons like the Masons wore, and colorful sashes around their chests, black with red and gold trim, jaunty fringe along with strange symbols and more medals than George Patton ever wore. They eyed us warily, and we stuck close to Carrick, unsure of our welcome.

Carrick called the men around him and gave a little speech. He spoke plainly, telling them there was danger of attack during or after the parade; that most of the IRA conspirators had been caught but that if anyone wanted to bow out, they should feel free to do so. No one wanted to, it was clear. They weren't a cowardly bunch, I had to give them that. Then Carrick pointed to three men, and asked if they'd be willing to make a sacrifice to help us find the last of the conspirators. Each said he'd give his life for king and Ulster, and there were cheers all around. Carrick said that wouldn't be necessary, all he wanted was their clothes and regalia. Hoots and hollers followed. Having offered to surrender their lives, they could hardly decline to turn over their trousers.

Carrick introduced us as his American guests and asked the lodge men to grant us every courtesy, and made sure to say it was through our efforts that the plot had largely been foiled. Meaning that even though two of us were papists, they should tolerate us since we'd saved their Royal Black behinds. There was a bit of grumbling but soon we were each being dressed by our counterparts, who stood in their skivvies adjusting our ties, sashes, ribbons, and medals.

"There, you look like a proper Orangeman," my guy said as he popped the bowler on my head. "No offense intended, of course." He gave a sly smile and stepped back, viewing his handiwork. I stuffed my .45 in my waistband and put a full clip in each pocket.

"None taken, pal. I'll try to return the suit with no holes." We shook hands, and the three Royal Black Knights in their underwear went off for a cup of tea in the church kitchen.

Carrick signaled us to form up outside. In the road by the church a kilted bagpipe band had formed up, along with a contingent of British and American officers. Behind them were other Royal Knights in the same general garb but with their own banners. Some sported pictures of old King William, others displayed biblical scenes. Flags with the red cross stuck through a crown, the symbol of the Knights, fluttered in the afternoon breeze.

"These are our overseas guests from other lodges," Carrick said, pointing to the officers. "Actually we call them encampments but not everyone grasps what that means."

Some of the officers joined our group and, with the Union Jack snapping briskly above us, the pipes swirling their tunes, drums pounding, and the flag of Ulster unfurled with great ceremony, we set off under the Cross of Saint George with the Red Hand smack in the middle of it.

"I think we should keep this to ourselves when we get back home," Uncle Dan said.

"With the pipes and all, it's a bit like Saint Patrick's Day," I said.

"Sure it is, only without the saint himself. If I get killed, my only joy will be never to be reminded of this again."

"Don't say that. Besides, if you get killed, you'll go to hell for not going to Mass after being in that church. So keep your eyes peeled." He laughed, and we marched in step. It might have been my imagination but it seemed like the other marchers kept their distance from us. I was in the middle of the front line, with Uncle Dan and Masters on my right. Carrick had been to my left but an Army Air Force bird colonel worked his way between us.

"You're a Yank," he said. "Did you bring all your regalia with you?"

"Listen, Colonel, we have sort of an undercover operation going on here. You might want to step back."

"I heard there was some trouble up at Brownlow House," he said.

"There was. Colonel, you're bound to get shot at enough in this war as it is. You might want to drop back a few rows so you don't start too soon."

"Hell, boy, I've been flying B-17s over France and Germany for a year now. I made it back from the raid on Schweinfurt, so don't tell me to drop back. They've got me over here now flying a desk for bit of rest. You're not a Royal Black Knight?"

"This is my first parade as one, sir. Probably my last."

He fell back one row. The wind gusted up and blew leaves across the road as we entered the grounds of Brownlow House. I tried to work out where Grady would be. I looked into the woods but I was sure Masters's men had checked them out. I scanned the trees, wondering if they'd checked for sniper positions, but a BAR is damn heavy to carry up a tree. We marched straight toward the curve where the rear guard had been, and I tightened my gut as we drew closer, imagining BARs opening up at close range.

We turned, and a small crowd of onlookers in front of Brownlow House cheered. It looked like off-duty GIs, wives, and locals, a few MPs and RUC constables mixed in. On the stone veranda, some chairs and a lectern stood at the edge closest to the lawn. I could make out a few elderly Black Knights, resting their hands on canes, plus some British and American brass and a little girl in a red dress, holding a bouquet of flowers. I caught Carrick's eye and he shrugged, as if to say he hadn't known about the girl but it was too late now.

"Where, Billy, where?" Uncle Dan muttered, his head swiveling from side to side. We had about one hundred yards to go to the veranda, where I guessed we would end the march and face the speaker. Carrick held up his left hand, halting the parade. The pipe band moved around us, and we stayed put long enough for them to pass by on the right. Then we started again, making our way to where the viewers had gathered, near the speaker's stand. The band took up position on our right, in front of the line of vehicles where we'd left the ambulance. The pipes and drums have always stirred me, an otherworldly, ancient sound that served as backdrop to battles through the centuries, from broadswords to bayonets. If ever there was music to keep a man in the line of battle, this was it. I wondered what it was doing for Grady and his men, hidden somewhere nearby, hands clenching their weapons.

One of the Knights on the veranda stood, then the others did too, as the banners came closer. One of them held the little girl's hand. The veranda was open, no low wall to separate it from the lawn. No cover for the little girl in the red dress. Fifty yards to go. It could happen any second now. I felt sweat drip down the small of my back and a gnawing fear eat at my gut. I had to stop it. I didn't want to face the bloodshed and the guilt if I failed. It's what I was supposed to do, what Dad had drummed into my head: Protect the innocent, punish the guilty. Thoughts of carnage filled my mind, and I imagined dozens of bodies, the sharp breeze flapping bits of bloody clothing against lifeless limbs. No, no. no. I didn't want that, didn't want to witness that, didn't want to remember it for the rest of my life.

"Where, goddamn it?!" Uncle Dan said it again louder, and I knew his cop's sense of duty was at work, desperate to stop the shooters before they inflicted harm.

Where, where, where? The Jenkins truck had seemed perfect, especially if they didn't think we were onto them. Twenty yards, only that many paces to go. I could see the faces waiting, smiling, hands clapping, pointing out the banners, waving to their husbands and sweethearts. More officers strolled out onto the veranda, admiring the procession. Now, now is when I'd do it. Or wait, wait until we'd halted. Carrick looked at me. I was at a loss.

The truck. Why hadn't they used it? Because somebody might question why a Jenkins truck was still here. It was a delivery truck, and delivery trucks deliver—and leave. What about a truck that doesn't leave? We'd driven in without anyone checking us out, and our ambulance was still there. Right next to a U.S. Army deuce-and-a-half, parked head in instead of being backed in, which was standard procedure.

I turned to look again, and I was right—all the other vehicles were backed in. The pipe band was right in front of the truck, between the tailgate and the veranda. I broke ranks, pulling my automatic out, screaming for everyone to get down, get down, *get down!* I raced at the truck, pistol held out in front with a two-handed grip, waiting for everyone to move out of the way, waiting for movement in the truck. Pipers dove out of my way, one drummer at the end of the line standing and drumming in spite of the madness around him. The dying wails of the pipes sounded like so many death rattles. I jumped over a drummer hugging the ground and felt my finger tighten, just a little, wanting that extra split second that could mean another day in the Irish sun.

The tailgate dropped. I fired two quick shots then sidestepped, saw a muzzle blast, fired at it twice, then ran to the side of the truck and fired the last four shots through the canvas, dropped the clip, loaded another as I ducked and ran around the front, popping up on the other side, squeezing off four more shots through the canvas, angling them downward, thinking they'd be flat on their bellies, aiming prone. There was more shooting, and I fired my last three rounds and ran my last clip in as I realized it wasn't the sound of a BAR I was hearing, thank God, but the sound of police revolvers. I stepped back, automatic aimed at the truck, and worked my way left. Uncle Dan was kneeling, his arm extended, searching for a target. Carrick held his revolver steady as well, Masters at his side, bowler still on his head. After the sound of gunfire, silence filled the air, the marchers and onlookers on the ground, holding their breath, waiting for the next volley. I don't think I've ever experienced such a complete absence of sound.

Then a man in the truck began to cry. Choked sobs at first, then a torrent of anguish, the kind of agony that comes not from bullets on bone but from deep within a fearful heart. I edged around, watching Carrick and the others closing in with one eye and the interior of the truck with the other. The canvas flap was tied off above the tailgate, so I had to stoop for a clear view.

There had been four of them in the prone position, BARs set up on their bipods. One was crying great gobs of tears and wailing like a child with a skinned knee. He was curled up, unharmed, at the rear of the truck, staring at the two dead men still at their weapons, one with the top of his skull blown off, the other in a great pool of blood.

Grady O'Brick lay on his side, grasping a BAR, trying to pull himself upright. His eyes were unfocused, and blood oozed from his mouth. He'd been shot in the shoulder and once in each leg, those last probably by me. I hoisted myself up into the truck bed as Masters pulled out the abandoned BARs. Kneeling by Grady, I holstered my weapon. I didn't know what to say. I was glad we'd stopped them, glad that the killing wouldn't spread any farther in Ireland, north or south. But this was a genuine hero of the War of Independence, a man tortured and maimed by the British, whose purposes I had served today. I felt sick.

"No," he said, falling back and clutching the last BAR to his chest. His hand fumbled at the trigger, and I reached for the gear change lever and set the safety. But he wasn't going for the trigger, he was holding onto the weapon, cradling it, his mouth set in grim defiance. "No! You'll not have the Lewis gun, never!"

His eyes, wide open, glowed with determination as he stared beyond me, past years of struggles and plots, back to the turning point in his life, when everything hinged on a secret that broke him and began his quest for revenge.

"No, they'll never get it, Grady Ó Bruic," I told him. "*Agus bás in Eirinn.*" Death in Ireland.

His eyes flickered for a moment, tried to focus, and his mouth curled in an attempted grin. "Never . . ." His last word came out hot and harsh, smelling of blood, a faint rattle sounding in his throat. Then he was gone.

The man had tried to kill me, and I'd killed him. Still, I knelt and wept. Death in Ireland—that toast would never sound the same again.

CHAPTER ▪ THIRTY SEVEN

BESIDES GRADY AND two of his men, no one else had been killed. Bob Masters hadn't noticed he'd been shot until blood squished in his boot. A slug had hit his calf but it was a clean shot; he'd be running up Slieve Donard in a couple of weeks.

The Army Air Force bird colonel, a guy named Dawson, had caught it for real, a .30 round in the shoulder. He'd had a .38 Special in a shoulder holster, and charged the truck, blazing away, as soon as he figured out what was going on. The ambulance we'd stolen came in handy; he and Masters were bundled off in it to the hospital immediately. I stayed with Carrick and Uncle Dan, seeing to the prisoners and helping Masters's men load the BARs and ammo into the truck after the bodies were removed

I lingered, watching the crowds disappear, feeling the darkness creep in as the sun set, the blood red colors of dusk filtering in through the trees. I think I couldn't believe it was over. It was hard to leave the scene, because once I did, I would have to leave Ireland behind.

"Come, lad," Uncle Dan said, draping his arm around my shoulder. "Let's give these costumes back to the boys in their skivvies." We walked to the church, enjoying each other's company, silent, letting the feeling of peacefulness seep back into our bones. As we came to the church door, we opened it without a thought. Entering the Church of Ireland had lost its forbidden quality. It was just a building.

Back in our own clothes, Carrick drove us to the hospital. I wanted to see Sláine and tell her the case was closed. Maybe it would cheer her up. Maybe it would cheer me up. Carrick dropped us off and I felt tired, achingly tired, as we tramped up the steps to the hospital entrance. Major Cosgrove stood at the top, looming large above us.

"I must say, Boyle, splendid job today. Well done."

"Yeah, splendid. How is Sláine?"

"She was awake but the doctors appear to be concerned. She doesn't look well."

"She was shot, for Christ's sake. How do you want her to look?"

"There's no need for that tone, Lieutenant Boyle. Need I remind you, I am your superior officer?"

"What's going to happen to Subaltern O'Brien?" Uncle Dan broke in, trying to short-circuit my temper before I blew. "After she recovers?"

"Well, there's no question of her returning to MI-5, after her questionable conduct. I will leave it to District Inspector Carrick if charges should be laid against her."

"You didn't question her conduct when she got things done for you," I said, stepping up into his face. "But now you're ready to throw her to the wolves. What is it, an Irishwoman doesn't deserve your loyalty?"

"There are larger questions at hand, young man."

"Next time, get somebody else to do your dirty work. You aren't worth it," I said, brushing by him, fighting to keep my fists at my sides, a haymaker begging to be let loose.

"And you, Mr. Boyle, you're supposed to be in police custody!"

"Go to hell," Uncle Dan said, and followed me down the hall, patting me on the back.

We found Colonel Dawson first. He was awake, stretched out in a hospital bed, a cast enclosing his shoulder and arm. Bob Masters sat with him, his bandaged leg up on a chair.

"Well, if it isn't the walking wounded of Brownlow House!" Uncle Dan said. "How are you both?"

"Glad to be alive, thanks to you boys," Colonel Dawson said. "Bob here has been telling me the whole story. You put a stop to something that could have snowballed into a real problem. Nice work."

"Thanks for lending a hand. Sorry you were shot. Doesn't that hurt?"

"It will when the morphine wears off, you can count on that. Listen, you boys ever need anything from the Army Air Force, you look me up. Bull Dawson, at your service. OK?"

"We may need your assistance sooner than later," Carrick said from behind us. "I just ran into Major Cosgrove, and he's demanding that I arrest you, Daniel."

"What?" Dawson said.

"It's a long story, Colonel," I said. "This is my uncle, Dan Boyle. He's a police detective from Boston, and it will be a whole lot easier if you don't ask what he's doing here. But he needs to get out of the country, pronto. He's a little lacking in the paperwork department."

"I've been to Schweinfurt and back, Lieutenant. I don't give a damn about paperwork. You get a telephone in here and I'll have your uncle on the next C-47 flying home. And if he needs to hide out until it takes off, leave that to me."

"See, Daniel, this is how the Royal Black Knights look out for each other," Carrick said, a grin lighting up his usually dour face. I'd seen that look before, the strain and tension vanishing from a policeman's face after a case was successfully solved. Relief for a brief moment, perhaps long enough to get drunk or spend time with your family, depending on your inclination, until the next corpse turned up.

"Saints preserve us," Uncle Dan said.

I left them to plot Uncle Dan's escape and went in search of Sláine. I found her room and waited by the door as a doctor checked her with a stethoscope and felt her pulse. He wrote notes on her chart and left, brushing by me without a word. I pulled up a chair and sat by her bed, watching as her eyes focused and found me.

"Billy! What happened? Tell me, please." There was energy in her voice but she looked weak and withered against the white sheets. A thick dressing covered her chest, and tiny drops of sweat beaded her forehead. Her hair was damp and flattened against the pillow, the curls faded and limp. I tried not to show my surprise.

"I'll tell you everything, don't worry. You look pretty good for having been shot and left for dead."

"I guess not all Irishmen have a way with words but thank you. I feel horrible, though. Tell me, what's happened?"

"It's all over. Guns recovered, Taggart dead." I told her the whole story, starting from when she was shot and finishing up at the truck with Grady hugging the last BAR to his chest.

"It was last night that I was shot? I'm so confused." She tried to raise a hand to her head but let it drop halfway.

"This morning, actually."

"And you, you were shot too, weren't you?"

"Yeah, right through the arm. Hurts like hell, but I'm fine."

"Major Cosgrove came to see me," Sláine said. Her lips pressed together, and she blinked her eyes, determined not to shed a tear.

"He have anything useful to say?"

"That I should take all the time I need to recover, and that he'd find an easy posting for me when I was ready. Out of the way, I suppose."

"Maybe I can help. I do have friends in high places. When you're better, we can arrange a transfer."

"I don't know, Billy. All I know is Ireland. I wouldn't be much use elsewhere. But never mind that, I think it'll be a long time before I'm out of this bed, if only to judge by the look on your face."

"It's just a shock seeing you all bandaged up."

"You're very diplomatic," she said, forcing a weak smile.

"I may have to leave soon," I said. "We need to get Uncle Dan out one step ahead of Cosgrove, and once that's done I should report back to General Eisenhower."

"Yes, of course." There wasn't any way around it but I could see the sadness in Sláine's eyes. She'd be left alone, disgraced, without a job of any consequence, and maybe facing charges. I doubted that DI Carrick would open up that can of worms but it was a worry nonetheless. I tried to think of something else to talk about, other than Cosgrove or MI-5.

"Remember back in Jerusalem, you told me there was one Irish-American you thought highly of? Who is that?"

"Oh, I'm sorry, Billy. I can be rude sometimes, I know. I think the world of you, and what you accomplished here. You saved many lives."

I knew she was right because I'd come to learn the arithmetic of war. Some deaths now equaled fewer deaths later. It all made sense but when it was you pulling the trigger, you only focused on the deaths now, not the lives saved later.

"Thanks. But who is this other guy anyway? I think I'm jealous," I said, making a joke of it.

"My father read a lot of history, and he left quite a collection of books. He enjoyed reading about your American Civil War, and I picked up his interest when I was older. Did you know that the Irish fought on both sides?"

"Yes, the Fighting 69th, right?"

"On the Union side, yes, they were called the Irish Brigade. There were Confederate Irish regiments too. A boy named Michael Sullivan fought with the 24th Georgia, mostly Irish. At Fredericksburg, commanded by General Meagher, the 69th charged the heights against the 24th, both sides knowing they were fighting and killing fellow Irishmen. It didn't say in the history books but I can imagine that they wept as they fired and reloaded."

I looked at the floor, unable to meet her eyes, having done all those things myself. "What happened to Michael Sullivan?"

"The Irish Brigade retreated back across the Rappahannock River, leaving behind their regimental banner. It was the green flag of Ireland with the golden harp upon it. Michael Sullivan, who had killed his share of Irish brethren that day, came upon the flag. He wrapped it around his chest, hiding it under his shirt, and swam the Rappahannock to return it to the Union Irish. His own men, thinking he was deserting, fired on him, wounding him in the leg. When he was taken prisoner, he asked to be brought before General Meagher. Once there, he removed the regimental banner and presented it to the general. Meagher was so overcome he had Sullivan's wounds treated, and offered to release him anywhere within Union territory. Sullivan declined, asking only to be taken to the river, so he could swim back to his own lines, which he did. He was an Irishman to admire. Loyal to all, even when divided by war. And always faithful to his duty."

The story had drained her, I could see. She was pale, and her face bathed in sweat. I took a washcloth from the bed stand and gently ran it across her cheeks and forehead. I struggled to speak, the sadness of the slaughter fresh in my mind. Today's and yesterday's as well.

"Hell of an Irishman" was all I could say.

"My father wrote much the same thing in the margin of his book. That's why I always remembered the story," she said, a glow of excitement showing in her eyes before they nearly closed. A minute passed, and she struggled to keep them open. "I'm sorry, I have to sleep now, Billy. Will you come back to see me before you go?"

"I'll stay right here for now. Sleep. I'll be here when you wake."

She smiled, a faint, childlike smile, as she closed her eyes. I pushed the chair against the wall, leaned my head back, closed my eyes, and let sleep find me as well.

■ ■ ■

"BILLY, WAKE UP, lad." I sat up, not knowing where I was
or who was speaking to me. It was Uncle Dan, his hand on my
shoulder. "I've got to go now, Billy. Dawson has an aircraft leaving
tonight."

"Quiet," I said, motioning him out into the hall. "She's sleeping."

"Wait a minute, Billy," Uncle Dan said, his hand still on my shoulder as he watched Sláine. "I don't think so."

I went to her side as Uncle Dan called for a doctor. It wasn't necessary. No pulse, no breath, her lips pale. I held her hand and there was
no warmth, no life, no movement or response. She was dead, whether
from Taggart's bullet and the damage it had done, or the wounds, lone-
liness, and guilt of a lifetime. It didn't matter which had killed her. *Agus
bás in Eirinn.*

It was time to leave. I placed her hand on her breast and turned
away as the doctor and nurses rushed in, knowing it was too late, hoping that Sláine had had time for one last dream, of peaceful green fields
perhaps, or maybe Michael Sullivan himself, waiting for her, and all the
other Wild Geese who had served every cause but their own.

CHAPTER ▪ THIRTY EIGHT

HUGH CARRICK DROVE us to Langford Lodge. I sat in the back as he and Uncle Dan chatted, comparing notes, talking shop, probably each thinking the other was not a bad sort, considering. I wished death could roll like water off my back, letting me join in on the cop talk and sly jokes. But instead it clung to me, as dreary as the darkening sky and the too familiar gray landscape of Lurgan drifting past the window. Our route to Lough Neagh took us through the city but bypassed Brownlow House, which was fine with me.

The air had turned cold, winter showing its bite on a fading autumn day. Smoke drifted from rows of chimneys, and I wondered who would take the peat from Grady's croft.

It wasn't fair, any of it. We were in a war, and there was plenty of killing to go around. That Grady and Taggart had planned to trigger warfare in all of Ireland, for revenge as much as for the Cause, didn't bear thinking about. But I couldn't stop. The waste of innocent lives, the suffering, all for a blood debt that could never be repaid, always demanding a new reprisal, a repayment of pain again and again through the generations. It made me wish I was a common soldier fighting the Germans, man to man. It had been the last thing I wanted when I started working for General Eisenhower, the thing I avoided with all the wit and lies I could muster. But now, recalling the combat I had seen, it seemed cleaner—somehow purer in its intent—than the furtive murders and planned slaughter I'd seen here. Combat had been horrifying, and I'd never been so scared, but it was straightforward. Live or die. No gray areas, no wondering about each pull of the trigger. In combat, you knew who the enemy was; they had different uniforms, and they wanted to kill you. It was simple.

I dug out Pig and ran my fingers over his belly. I understood why Pete Brennan had wanted to leave all the black market intrigue, investigations, and suspicions behind. Put a rifle in his hands and he'd know where to shoot. It was appealing in a way. It would burn away any guilt he felt about his role in the black market, leaving him pure and clean, or dead. It took an honorable man to choose either of those over a rear-area job and plentiful graft.

I rubbed Pig again and understood something else. Diana. It was the same with her. She hadn't yet burned away the guilt she felt, the memories of the wounded soldiers drowning when that destroyer went down in the channel, and the death of her sister, Daphne. Diana was still alive, and that would never be anything but a burden until she did everything she could to prove she deserved to live.

It might kill her. It might free her. Either way, I finally understood.

"We're here, Billy boy," Uncle Dan said. I looked up and saw the sign for Langford Lodge, USAAF Base Air Depot. The MP at the gate consulted a clipboard, gave a snappy salute, and we drove down a road running alongside the main landing strip. Dark shapes of B-17s and B-24s, bristling with machine guns, stood out against the stars. Beyond the runways was Lough Neagh, the huge lake that I'd flown over on the way in, black water as far as the eye could see in either direction. The base was operating under blackout conditions, and the darkness combined with the large, silent aircraft to produce an eerie feeling of barely restrained lethality.

A jeep met us near the main building, and the driver signaled for us to follow. He took us to a hangar, its massive doors open to reveal a C-47 being readied for takeoff. He told us Colonel Dawson had said this was as good as it was going to get, leaving in twenty minutes for Bradley Field in Connecticut—with refueling stops in Iceland, Greenland, Newfoundland—and that he never saw us and never wanted to see us again. He waited, watching us as we said our goodbyes.

"Uncle Dan, I'm sorry you got pulled into all this," I said.

"Ah, Billy, I jumped in feet first, and I was glad to give you a hand. It was good to be by your side. We all miss you back home, you know? You've become quite a man out here. But are you all right? I know this hasn't been the Ireland of our dreams, has it?"

"I don't know what to make of it. Every time I think I understand something, it changes. I can't find any solid ground."

"Or maybe you see another side of things. Remember, these fellows Taggart and O'Brick, they're the sort who outlived their time. It would have been better for them to have died heroes twenty years ago. Instead, they lived on, nursing their hatred into madness. Don't feel bad about putting a stop to that. I don't. I was sent to do a job, and I did it. So did you. So stand tall, boy. It doesn't mean the cause is a bad one, just that standing close to its center for too long can burn any man out."

"Thanks, Uncle Dan. Really," I said. I put out my hand and he grabbed me in a hug, slapping me on the back, rubbing his hand on my head.

"Give my love to Mom and Dad and little Danny, OK?" I said, burying my face against his neck. He took me by the shoulders and put on a stern look.

"I will give your love to all of them, and Danny's not so little anymore! But if you don't write your mother right away, and more often, I'm going to tell her you're drinking and smoking and whoring all over England. Now go on, don't waste any more time here."

We hugged again, and he shook hands with DI Carrick before boarding the plane through the rear cargo door. Our escort, an Army Air Force lieutenant, gave Uncle Dan a sheepskin leather flight jacket, cap, and gloves.

"Compliments of Bull Dawson," he said. And with that, Uncle Dan was gone. We watched the crew close up the plane, and it taxied out into the darkness, the drone of the engines deafening, until it rose into the night and vanished among the stars.

"You look to come from a good family, Lieutenant Boyle," Carrick said. I knew that was a major compliment from an Ulsterman when it concerned an Irish Catholic. Maybe there was hope after all.

"I try to live up to them," I said, "every day." We stood, watching the darkness in the empty hangar. "Thanks for all your help," I finally got out.

"Don't mention it; it was my duty. Where can I take you now? You deserve some rest."

"I think I'll stay here, to wait for the next flight."

"Don't you have a report to make?"

"Only to Major Cosgrove, and he can come get it if he wants. The army has its BARs back, the German agents are in custody or dead, and the IRA plot has been stopped. What else is there?"

"Indeed. You've done well, Lieutenant. Good luck." We shook hands, and he clasped my arm before he let go, and drove off into the night.

"So, Mac, what's your story?" the air force lieutenant asked me.

I thought about all the places I could go. A side trip to London, drop in on Kaz, spend a few nights of luxury with him at the Dorchester. It would be easy, and I could talk things over with him. Maybe even have a few laughs.

"I'm headed for Algiers," I said. It wasn't Kaz I needed to see.

"Well, Bull said, whatever you guys want. I can have you in Gibraltar by tomorrow night, Algiers the next day. We got a B-24 outbound in the morning, ferrying VIPs to Gib for when the president and General Marshall stop there on the way back from meeting Stalin. Room for one more if you don't mind being squeezed in with admirals, generals, and journalists."

"That's fine, I like newspapermen."

CHAPTER · THIRTY NINE

IT TOOK FOUR days, two of them grounded in Gibraltar due to a storm in the Atlantic. The generals and admirals complained, the reporters played cards. I stuck with them, and ended up with a fistful of pound notes, a sign that my luck was improving. We landed at Maison Blanche airfield, east of Algiers, and I hitched a ride into the city as far as the docks, then trudged up Rue Marguerite, sweating in my woolen uniform, hoping somebody I knew at headquarters would be on duty. Halfway up, I stopped to catch my breath and turned to see how far I'd walked. It was a dizzying view, so intense it almost didn't seem real, palm trees and blazing sunshine reflecting off whitewashed stone. Minarets pointing the way to heaven, and church bells echoing against the drab, brown hills. Turquoise blue water, sparkling in the distance. A long way from Ireland.

The rest of the walk was cooler, in the shade of the giant palm trees in the Hotel St. George gardens. I walked along the drive, dodging jeeps and staff cars as they went about their important rear-area business. Allied Forces HQ had grown from a few hundred officers and enlisted men after the invasion to thousands, a bloated, bureaucratic beast that had taken over seven other buildings at last count. I was nothing but a drop in that bucket, and the sentry at the main entrance didn't recognize me and didn't want to risk his PFC's stripe by letting me stink up the lobby.

"Call Ike's office, see if Kay Summersby or Mattie Pinette are in," I told him. "They know me."

"Why are you wearing that uniform, sir?" he asked, taking in the sweat-stained, dirty wool. Four days in the same clothes hadn't helped my appearance, and I sensed his suspicion that I was a Kraut spy dumb enough to wear a winter uniform in the North African sun.

"Because it's cold in Northern Ireland. Now telephone the office, that's an order."

Five minutes later Kay had me by the arm, pulling me along to Ike's office, filling me in on what had happened since I left, her words coming out in a breathless jumble.

"The president and his party are returning from Tehran. The general is going to meet them in Tunis, and everyone says Roosevelt is going to appoint General Marshall to command the invasion of Europe, and that Ike is going to go back to Washington. What's going to happen to all of us, Billy?"

She sat at her desk while I collapsed in a chair, waving to Mattie and the other familiar faces in the office. Kay took out a handkerchief and dabbed at her eyes, glancing at the other WACs. I wondered what they knew about her and Uncle Ike. I wondered if I could forget it.

"I don't know, Kay, maybe we'll all go home with the general." As soon as I said it, I realized that wasn't what Kay wanted to hear. Home meant Mamie Eisenhower.

"I'm not an American citizen, Billy. They'll split us all up, after everything we've been through. I can't bear the thought of it."

"Don't jump to conclusions, Kay. From what I hear, the president thinks General Marshall is too important to let him leave Washington. And the boss is already over here. You never know."

"I'm sorry, Billy, I suppose I'm overreacting. There's a new rumor every day, and it's gotten to me, that's all. Tell me, how was your assignment in Ireland? You look dreadful, if you don't mind me saying." She dabbed her eyes one more time and put away the handkerchief.

"It was resolved," I said. "But I've been traveling for four days, and I need clothes, chow, a bath, and a bed, not necessarily in that order. Can you fix me up?"

"Sure, Billy. I think we can get you into a room here, at least for a couple of nights. We've got VIPs and VGDIPs coming in every day but I can take care of it. I'll get someone to get your gear together too."

"Thanks. What's a VGDIP?"

"Very Goddamn Important Person," she whispered. "At least in their own eyes." She laughed, and her face lit up with that mischievous look that made a beautiful woman even more attractive.

"Have you heard anything from Kaz? When's he coming back?"

"No, nothing," she said. "And the Poles in London aren't talking. The general had me contact them but all they said was that Lieutenant Kazimierz had been recalled indefinitely. Something is damned odd there."

"It's a damned odd war. Is the general around?"

"Yes, but he's leaving shortly. Do you want to see him now? The way you look?"

"I'll be dead asleep on my feet in ten minutes. Now or never."

"Is there anyone else you want to see?" Kay said, with a coy smile.

"Is Diana here?"

"Yes, she came back from her briefing yesterday; she's on a forty-eight-hour leave."

"You mean her SOE briefing," I said in a low voice.

"Yes. You should see her, Billy." She stared at me, her expression hardening. She couldn't fully have the man she loved, and here I was, throwing away a good chance at love through stubbornness and pride. I didn't blame her for the dagger look.

"I want to," I said, and she led me to Uncle Ike's office and knocked.

"William," he said, getting up from his desk and shaking my hand. "I hadn't heard you were back. Just got in, by the looks of you. How are you? How was Ireland?"

"I'm fine, sir. That situation in Northern Ireland was resolved, nothing to worry about."

"Excellent! Here, have a seat," Uncle Ike said, gesturing to a pair of chairs opposite his desk. "Was Major Cosgrove pleased with the outcome? And what was her name, Miss O'Brien?"

"Subaltern Sláine O'Brien. She's dead, sir."

"My God, that's terrible. As a result of this business?"

"Yes, sir. Several others too. British, Irish, Americans. More than I'd like but we put a stop to it, so I guess it was worth it."

Uncle Ike nodded as he lit a cigarette. Less than a year ago, I wouldn't ever have said such a thing. Now I could, and I saw the strain on Uncle Ike's face, as he dealt in numbers that would dwarf mine, the deaths I could count on my fingers with a few to spare.

"You did well, William, and I'm sorry about the losses. Tell me, did you enjoy seeing Ireland?"

Perhaps someday I'd look back and remember what I'd seen and recall some of it fondly. The smell of the peat burning, the green fields after a rain, the sound of Irish voices everywhere. Not yet, though. And it was part of Great Britain I'd seen, not the free Republic. But Uncle Ike was a man with enough worries of his own, and I never felt like saying anything that might burden him.

"It was grand," I said, feeling that was not quite a lie. Grand, magnificent, terrible. "Can I ask about the rumors? Are you going to get General Marshall's job?"

"That's up to the president, William. Looks like one of us will command the invasion of Europe and the other will be chief of staff."

"Which do you want, Uncle Ike?" I spoke softly, taking advantage of the permission he gave me, when we were alone, to call him that.

"I'll happily do whatever the president orders," he said. Leaning close, he spoke in a whisper. "I've always accepted whatever orders came my way, William. But I'm a changed man now. No one could have experienced what I have and not be different from the man he was in the beginning. I want to command the invasion, and see this war to the end." He leaned back and ground out his cigarette. He had dark circles under his eyes, and his forehead seemed permanently creased.

"My money's on you, General."

"Thank you, William. Now get some rest. Kay will get you squared away."

SHE DID. A room, a bath, a tray of food, a full set of tropic khakis, and all the gear I might need. One thing about working in a headquarters, there was never a shortage of supplies. After I ate, washed, and shaved, I decided to close my eyes, just for ten minutes, before I went in search of Diana. I opened the doors to the balcony to let in the cool breeze from the Mediterranean and stretched out on the bed. It was four o'clock, 1600 hours. Maybe half an hour, a catnap. I closed my eyes.

I dreamed of a city with white gleaming buildings and narrow streets. I was looking for someone but never could find her. I'd get lost in dark passageways, until I was back at the hotel, and then a bomb hit, and there was fire and smoke.

I woke up instantly, my heart beating fast and fear in my gut. I knew

the city was Algiers, and the bomb was from another time when Diana
and I had been here. Close to death, the companion that haunted us both.
I blinked my eyes, thinking I was still asleep. I wasn't, and it was dark. I
looked at my watch, rubbing my eyes awake. Nine o'clock, damn.

I dressed and headed for the general's office, hoping Kay would still
be there. She was, the place still a beehive of junior officers and WACs.
She'd told Diana I was here, but Diana was headed out with someone, and
said she'd see me in the morning. It sounded like the cold shoulder to me,
and I pressed Kay as to where she'd gone. She told me after a little coaxing:
the Café Continental in the Casbah. She didn't want to tell me who
Diana's companion was but I got it out of her bit by bit. Yes, it was a man.
Yes, a young man; no, not an American. He was British, an army captain,
and yes, he was quite good-looking; actually, all the girls thought so.

A little voice at the back of my head told me to go back to my room
and get a good night's sleep. I didn't listen; I was surprised that voice
kept giving me advice after all the years I'd ignored it. It wasn't always
bad advice; it just came when I didn't want to hear it. I jumped in a taxi
and asked the driver to get me to the Café Continental fast, tossing a
bunch of British pounds on the front seat, probably enough to buy the
cab and a couple of donkeys to boot. He floored it with abandon, weaving around a colonel who almost lost his service cap in the slipstream.
My kind of cabbie.

He came to a stop that sent me slamming into the front seat, in
front of the Cathedral of Saint Phillipe, its twin minarets, graceful
curving arches, and decorated tiles revealing it had been a mosque
before the French took over. Or so Diana had told me, last time we
were here, walking to the Café Continental. The cathedral was lit up,
the blackout long gone since we'd chased the Luftwaffe all the way back
to Italy. I legged it along the side of the limestone building, the stones
looking as old as the ruined temples I'd seen in Sicily. The side street
brought me into the Casbah proper, a maze of narrow streets and wind-
ing alleyways. It was easy to get lost but all you had to do was walk
down the hill and you'd end up at the harbor, where you could turn
around and try again. But I knew my way around. I knew where you
could buy hashish, sell your sister, hire an out-of-work spy, or arrange
for a smuggling route into the desert, to Spanish Morocco or the Río
de Oro. What I didn't know was how to talk to Diana when I found
her, or whether she'd listen.

I dodged Arab women, their robes covering every inch of them, embroidered head scarves and veils drawing the eye though I thought the idea was to discourage male glances. Boys pulled donkeys weighed down with dates, jugs of water, blankets, firewood, and wooden crates stamped U.S. ARMY. The alleys were dark, the only light coming from overhanging balconies built out over the street so far they almost touched their neighbors across the way. I'd left my pistol back at the hotel, figuring that it would go better if I didn't arrive armed, and I cast a few glances over my shoulder before I hit Rue Marengo, a wider street where, during the day, open markets sold everything from fruit and vegetables to trinkets for GI tourists, brass baubles, Arab daggers, and German Lugers.

I slowed my pace, collecting myself, trying to calm down so I wouldn't punch out the Brit officer before we were introduced. The evening was cool but I wiped sweat from my temples as I adjusted my fore-and-aft cap, loosened my field scarf, then tightened it again, before rubbing each shoe on the back of my pants to get rid of the dust. I stuffed my hands in my pockets and sauntered off, just another bored soldier looking for a new bar or brothel. The Café Continental was around the next curve in the street, and I wanted to scout the position from a safe distance.

I knew the layout: a gleaming white building with sky blue doors and shutters, the sign in the same blue and white over the door, the main entrance on the street. Off to the side, there was a courtyard shaded by trees, where Diana and I had eaten a couple of times. Strings of lightbulbs hung low in the tree branches, casting a leafy glow over the tables, each flooded by candlelight.

I saw Diana—no, I heard Diana—that laugh, like glass chimes in a low wind, quiet but insistent, with the promise of more to come. Then I saw her profile in the candlelight, the yellow glow reflecting off her honey brown hair. Her FANY uniform fit her well and she looked even better than the last time I had seen her. More at ease and confident. There was no hesitation in her gestures as she raised a glass of wine to her lips, patted her companion on the arm and leaned closer to whisper to him. I turned away. I had hurt her, waited too long to stand by her side, and now she was out with one of her own, a British captain. He even outranked me.

I walked back the way I had come, waiting for the downward incline to propel me out of the Casbah. Maybe Diana had thought about the same things I had, the difference in who we were, where we came from, and found it easier to imagine her future with a country-man. I'd glimpsed that with Sláine, the comfort of thinking how easy it would be. No hard road there.

No, I told myself. No, I needed to talk to Diana. Things had gone this far because I hadn't said the things that needed saying. I turned again, rehearsing my lines.

I walked through the restaurant before the maître d' could intercept me, and before I could regain my senses. I watched Diana nodding at her date enthusiastically, smiling up at him. He looked like a recruiting poster, his brass and leather gleaming, khaki dress uniform unwrinkled, his face tanned and his hair burnished blond by the desert sun. And he wore medals. I was definitely outclassed but he'd seen me already, and raised an eyebrow, signaling Diana.

"Billy!"

"I'm sorry to intrude, Diana, I was just passing by and saw you. I wanted to say hello, and wish you well, with whatever you're doing next." I avoided looking at the other guy's face and resisted the urge to vault the wrought-iron fence and run screaming down the road.

"Billy, I didn't expect to see you tonight," Diana said, standing to face me.

"That's obvious," I said. "Look, I know we didn't part on the best of terms. I just wanted to say I'm sorry. And that you should do what-ever you think is right, not that you need my two cents' worth."

"Billy, I—"

"Never mind, you don't need to make excuses. I was a bum, I know it, and you deserve someone better. Now enjoy your dinner, sorry I interrupted." I watched her eyes for some signal, some evidence in them of desire or longing. All I saw was blue.

"Diana, I thought you said he was terribly smart," the Brit said, his long legs crossed and one hand idly resting on a knee.

"Listen, bub, you butt out or—captain or not—I'll bust you wide open," I said in a low growl. This was hard enough without some aris-tocratic twit chiming in.

"Champagne, monsieur and mademoiselle," announced a waiter carrying an ice bucket. This was too much.

"Champagne, what the hell are you celebrating, Diana? Couldn't you have waited until I was out of town? It's not like we have any claim on each other, but—"

"Would you like a chair, sir?" the oblivious waiter asked as he set down the champagne on ice.

Diana stood, put her arms around my neck, and kissed me. Not a glad-to-see-you kiss and not a goodbye kiss. A real kiss, a hungry kiss, a kiss full of passion, a lingering, come-on-upstairs kind of kiss. She finally let me go and a table of French officers applauded.

"I think I'd like that chair now," I said to the waiter.

"Billy," Diana said, taking me by the arm, her eyes twinkling. "I think it's time the two of you met. Lieutenant Billy Boyle, this is Captain Peter Seaton." I watched both of them suppressing grins. Of course. Diana's brother, Peter. She and Daphne had both spoken of him; he was serving with the British 8th Army, now fighting in Italy. We shook hands.

"Glad to meet you," I said. "And sorry for the scene."

A chair and a third glass appeared. We sat as the waiter poured. I watched Diana, transfixed by her beauty, her presence, her scent, the taste of her still on my lips.

"What are we drinking to?"

"My engagement," Peter said. "To a wonderful American girl on the embassy staff in Cairo. We met at a party, one of those incredibly boring duty events. We both fell head over heels. Audrey's from New York City, somewhere in Manhattan. She's been to Harlem, all the jazz clubs, can you believe it?"

"Congratulations," I said. We clinked glasses and drank.

"Well, I promised some chaps I'd meet them at the hotel bar. Now that Billy's here, I'll leave you in his care."

"Oh, Peter," Diana said. "You don't have to go."

I didn't say a thing.

"Catch up with me at the bar. You two finish the champers and . . . well, whatever."

We watched him leave, a bit nervous at being left alone. I took another drink.

"Listen," I said. At the same time she started to speak.

"No, you go first," we both said at the same time. That was good for a laugh.

"Let me get this out, Billy. Kay told me about how exhausted you looked, and your long trip back here. Peter is only here for two days, then he goes to Tunis as part of the conference with the president and the prime minister. So I thought it best to let you sleep and see you in the morning. Or maybe later tonight." That was promising.

"I don't blame you for wanting to spend time with your brother, and I'm sorry I made a fool of myself. But when I thought he was your date, I wanted you to know how I felt."

It occurred to me that Kay had set me up, withholding that final bit of information about who Diana was with. She was one smart cookie.

"I liked hearing it," Diana said, reaching for my hand.

"I had no right to stand in your way about the SOE," I said, lowering my voice instinctively. "If it's important to you, I'm all for it."

"What changed, Billy?"

"In Ireland, I began to understand. Then this afternoon, General Eisenhower said something to me. He said he was a changed man, that no one could go through what he had and not be. It's as simple as that. I've changed. I've discovered what's important, and that it's more than simply living. It's how you live. A long life filled with regrets and guilt is worse than a short life without them."

"I've missed you, Billy. Terribly. I've wanted nothing more than for you to be here. For us to be together. Not forever, if that's not in the cards, but for now. For each other. I want to be happy with you, to drink champagne, introduce you to my brother, talk to you, and listen to you. To wander the Casbah. To see you come safely back to me."

"It took Ireland to show me I was almost throwing all that away."

"What happened there, Billy?" Diana grasped my hand in both of hers.

I leaned in and kissed her softly, her full lips tender against mine.

"I love you," I whispered, and heard the echo as it settled into my mind, the sight of her by candlelight, the smells of the Casbah, the taste of champagne all mingling and forming a memory I knew I'd carry with me always.

"What happened?" she said again.

I took Pig out of my pocket, rubbed his belly, placed him in the palm of her hand, and started to tell the story.

AUTHOR'S NOTE

THE HISTORY OF contacts between the Irish Republican Army and the German intelligence service go back to the First World War, when the Irish revolutionary Roger Casement attempted to recruit Irish prisoners of war from German camps to fight against the English. He did secure the promise of twenty thousand German rifles and ammunition for the planned Easter Rising in 1916. As with efforts that would follow, his plan fired the imagination but resulted in disaster, his capture, and execution.

During the late 1930s, German-Irish contacts began again, the IRA looking for aid and arms in their fight against the British and the Irish state. The IRA took advantage of England's predicament in 1939 and let loose a bombing campaign in major cities, hitting utilities and transportation centers. The killing of a number of civilians later that year in Coventry led to widespread revulsion in Great Britain and Ireland, and the bombing campaign effectively ended after three hundred explosions and seven deaths with little impact on the war effort. The briefing on that situation given by Major Cosgrove and Subaltern O'Brien in Chapter Three is factual, including how funds were raised in America and channeled to the IRA.

The German Abwehr sent a number of agents into neutral Ireland during the war, initially impressed by the Christmas Raid described in this book. The successful theft of the Irish Army's ammunition caused the Germans to think the IRA was larger and better organized than it

actually was. The implications of most of the ammunition being quickly recovered escaped them, and their subsequent attempts to work with
the IRA were comical. One agent, still partially dressed in a German
uniform, stopped at a police station to ask directions to the nearest IRA
unit. None spoke English without a marked German accent.

The IRA Northern Command did engage in actions against the
English in Northern Ireland, mounting what was known as the Northern
Campaign in 1942. Down to about fifty active members, this so-called
campaign accomplished little, and dwindled down to nothing more
than escape attempts by captured IRA men.

This novel imagines a more robust Northern Campaign, one ably
aided by the Germans and supported by an arms theft similar to the
Dublin Christmas Raid of 1939. All the pieces were in place for this
to happen, all the players were on the stage that was Ireland during the
Second World War. Northern Ireland was a great way station for
American troops heading first for the invasion beaches of North Africa
and later Normandy. If the IRA and the Germans had managed to
work together and strike at the Anglo-American forces, who knows
what the repercussions might have been?

The little wooden pig is not my invention but an actual good luck
charm as described in Rick Atkinson's *The Day of Battle: The War in
Sicily and Italy, 1943-1944*. Brought ashore at Salerno, it represented to
me the mystical attachment to good luck charms that soldiers have
always had, their faith invested in all sorts of strange objects.

An Irish-American like Billy, I began working on this story with
much the same attitude he began with. The IRA, certainly in its early
stages, seemed to me heroic in its fight against British dominion over
Ireland. In conducting research for this book, I learned of the distinction between famine and blight, and of the oppressive laws used to keep
the population of Ireland in subjection. But I also learned of the bitter
infighting among the Irish rebels, how they would turn on each other,
causing more of the same agonies as were visited upon the island by the
English. The story of the lone policeman at Dublin Castle on the day
of the Easter Rising is, sadly, true. Sad for him, for the loss of that great
prize, and for the heedless sacrifice of life and opportunity.

The story of Michael Sullivan, Sláine O'Brien's hero of the
American Civil War, is taken from *The Irish Brigade* by Paul Jones.
There were Irish on both sides of that conflict, and on several occasions

they did fight each other. Michael Sullivan found himself in a complex web of competing and contradictory loyalties, much as Billy Boyle does in this story. How he stayed true to his cause and countrymen proves once again that if truth is not stranger than fiction, it is at least more revealing of the depth of courage in human nature.